T0162638

HEARTSTAR

HEARTSTAR

THE GATES TO PANDEMONIA

ELVA THOMPSON

HeartStar
The Gates to Pandemonia

iUniverse books may be ordered through booksellers or by contacting:

iUniverse
1663 Liberty Drive
Bloomington, IN 47403
www.iuniverse.com
1-800-Authors (1-800-288-4677)

ISBN: 978-1-4917-8957-5 (sc)
ISBN: 978-1-4917-8956-8 (e)

Library of Congress Control Number: 2016903521

Print information available on the last page.

iUniverse rev. date: 4/22/2016

Contents

ACKNOWLEDGEMENTS

Thank you to my husband, Harold; my reader, Randy Hutchinson; and Michael Salchert for their support.

Man, tread softly on the Earth
What looks like dust
Is also stuff of which galaxies are made.
　　　　　　　—Evelyn Nolt, *The Glory Which is Earth*

CHAPTER 1

OMEN

Kilfannan of the House of Air stood in the dawning, gazing out over the stonewalled meadows and mist-ridden valleys of his beloved Eiru. A poignant sense of loss welled up within his spirit as he listened to the singing of the birds in their joyful chorus to the sun. Of late, something had changed in his world of Faerie; a veiled menace had cast a shadow upon his mind – a lingering shade for which he could find no images or words.

As light splashed aslant the rolling hills and the sun rose in its glory, Kilfannan's spirit soared in the glow of a young morning, and the shadow that was haunting him withdrew, bested by the brilliance of the sun.

Every morn since the Separation of the Breath, he had made salutations to the sun, powering his essence with the dazzling light bringer to the Green. He was the rising breath of the HeartStar, the Breath of Life in five dimensions, and the spinner of the Green Ray to the heart of the mortal world – the vital unseen force that energised leaf and blade of grass, growing trees and plants.

In the War of Separation, the third world had been ripped away into the doom of mortality, and the House of Air had become divided into High Faerie and Faerie. One breath became two, giving rise to the creation of Kilfannan of the up-breath and Kilcannan of the down-breath, the sylphs of the House of Kilfenoran in the fourth dimension. They were opposites yet also complementary. The down-breath dipped into fire and the up-breath into the vacuous realm of space. Kilfannan was the seer of air; and Kilcannan, the warrior.

Putting forth his long, slender fingers, Kilfannan gathered birdsong to his heart and spun green-song to the sedge grass and dark-leaved lilies in the bog.

Hearing hoof beats behind him, he turned around and saw his brother Kilcannan astride Finifar, his racehorse, trotting along the grassy sward towards him.

"Well met!" Kilcannan cried, pulling up his steed. "The day is fair, and once again the heart of the living earth is greening. And" – he raised his eyebrows conspiratorially – "'tis the races at Boolyduff this very afternoon. We have a chance to race our charges and take the goblin bookie's gold. Saddle thine horse, Red Moon, and let's be off!"

Kilfannan smiled dreamily. "'Tis market day in Kilfenora; I have a rendezvous with my Mary. When the sun is overhead, 'tis time for musicians in the mortal world to make merry music in the Black Orchid Inn, and" – he waved his fingers in the air – "I will spin their songs into the green of oak and new leaves unfurling in the hedge."

Kilcannan patted his horse's neck. "Well, sir! I will see thee later."

Kilfannan watched his brother canter away along the rutted track leading to the mortal road, and hoped his hot-headedness wouldn't involve him in a fight with goblin knock jocks and scheming bookies at the racecourse. At the last meet at Boolyduff, a goblin bookie had tried to sneak out of the betting enclosure without paying the winning wagers. When Kilcannan caught up with him and demanded his winnings, the scum had pulled a knife, and the steward had to intervene. Kilfannan despised goblins, but he had never known them to be so forward and aggressive.

Turning away, he went through the golden archway of his sheen and down the grassy steps into his hall. The chamber was spacious, with a springy turf ceiling, and softly lit by the shimmering green of delicate faerie fern that carpeted the walls. Over the hearth was a portrait of a woman with long cascades of copper ringlets and gentle emerald eyes. Kilfannan paused reverently for a moment before the radiant face of Niamh, his creator.

Turning his thoughts to Mary, his mortal friend, Kilfannan wondered what he should wear to their rendezvous. He loved lace and frockcoats, pantaloons and buckled shoes, tricorn hats and his long, copper-coloured hair queued with emerald ribbon. He had clothed his airy formlessness after the fashionable attire of the Regency period in the mortal world, delighting in its grace, manners, and exquisite chivalry.

He decided on a frilly cream shirt with an emerald cravat and waistcoat, a magenta velvet frockcoat and pantaloons, green stockings, and stacked heels with glittering emerald buckles. When he was dressed, he poured himself a glass of blackberry brandy. Holding the glass towards the East, he said softly, "En astralar-la. Praise to the HeartStar."

A deep, sweet silence fell around him, and his spirit flew into the mystic heart of the Green World, his senses revelling in the perfumes of enchanted woods and meadows.

Draining his glass, Kilfannan made ready to depart. Taking his tricorn hat and silver walking stick, he left his sheen and took the short walk across the flower-studded hillside and along the tree-lined lane to Mary's cottage.

He had met Mary in the time of falling leaves. One night, as he was walking home under the starlight to his sheen, he had passed a well-lit cottage. The front door was open, and strains of a lament could be heard floating on the air; the plaintive music spoke of a passing in the mortal world. Wishing to spin the haunting melody to the Green of dark fir, he had entered the cottage. Inside the front door was a small table holding shot glasses full of whisky, and helping himself to a drink, he looked around. All the clocks in the room had been stopped at four o' clock – the time the mortal had passed on. There was sadness and yet an air of merriment amongst the people gathered in the room. Many were laughing as they told hilarious tales of their friend now lying peacefully at rest. *Sing a song at a wake and shed a tear at a birth*, Kilfannan thought. He had often heard that sentiment in the mortal world.

A young woman with freckles and long, curly auburn hair was sitting on a stool next to the coffin, playing a harp. Unseen in the mortal world, he had walked over to her, and settling at her feet, he began to spin the music into Green. When the lament ended, she looked down and smiled at him with kind brown eyes. For a moment Kilfannan was taken aback; the beautiful lady's heart was resonating upon his frequency in Faerie. Few were the mortals that had faerie sight, and he was eager to make her acquaintance. He smiled shyly and, holding out his hand, said, "My name is Kilfannan of the House of Air. I am pleased to meet thee, ma'am."

From that day forth, Mary was his faerie friend, and they would oft and merry meet at the taverns in the town. Their friendship gave Kilfannan great joy, a spiritual reconnection with the mortal world that harkened back to elder days before the Separation.

When he arrived at Mary's cottage, she was putting a small harp into the back of her estate car. Kilfannan doffed his hat with a flourish. "Good morning to thee, Mary."

"It's good to see you, Kilfannan. Yourself looks like a grand painting, so you do," she said, admiring his attire.

He grinned. "One hath to do justice to so beautiful a lady."

"Hush now!" she laughed. "It's time we were leaving for the pub."

"What have you been doing with yourself in the week," Mary asked him as they drove off along the hedge bank lane towards Kilfenora.

Kilfannan grinned, and his emerald eyes sparkled with mirth. "I have been spinning the Green at the music festival in Crusheen, and merry were the nights of sweet music in the Flying Pig Inn."

Mary laughed. "You have a grand life, to be sure."

Kilfannan gazed dreamily out of the window at the sun-washed hills and violet valleys. The trees were putting forth their leaves, and the rock-strewn fields bordering the road were tinged with the fresh promise of springtime. Feeling his heart swell with ultimate love, he murmured, "'Tis a grand life, to be sure!"

It was market day in Kilfenora. In the mortal world, the high street was noisy, echoing with the shrill cries of stockmen and the bleating of sheep and goats. Burnt sugar from the tinkers' rock candy filled the air, blending with the smell of freshly baked bread, and the hoppy aroma of beer flooded from the open doors of taverns around the market square.

The market in the faerie world was also all abustle. Trooping elves and fear deargs were clustered round the horse sale rings, and Kilfannan could tell by their gestures and their strident voices they were in fierce competition with each other. Fear deargs were elementals of the House of Fire. They were sunny personalities and were inclined to be short and portly with red faces, yellow eyes, and lustrous blue-black hair. Being horse racing enthusiasts, they kept many fine mounts in their stables, and were in constant rivalry with the trooping elves who bought the fastest horses for their moonlit games of hurling.

Mary pulled in to a side street by the back entrance to the pub. "Time to spin!" Kilfannan cried joyfully, twitching his fingers. She took her harp from the back of her estate car and, with Kilfannan by her side, went into the pub.

The mortal bar in the Black Orchid was warm, and the firelight glittered red upon the horse brass nailed to the old black beams that stretched across the ceiling and the walls. The long bar was crowded with chattering tourists drinking beer while eagerly awaiting the musicians, and waitresses scurrying to and fro with plates of food for customers sitting at the tables.

Kilfannan switched his gaze into Faerie. The bar was full of elves celebrating a game of hurling they had won the hour before dawn. Groups of fear deargs sat together, laughing raucously at one another's silly jokes, and a cluricaun was drinking at the counter. He waved when he saw Kilfannan and beckoned him over.

"Kilfannan!" he cried, looking at him with a rheumy eye. Grabbing the glass before him, he took a big gulp of wine and then handed it to Kilfannan for a refill.

"Greetings, Rickoreen. What hast thou been doing with thyself?" Kilfannan asked, signalling to the landlord.

"Drinking!" Rickoreen gave a high-pitched giggle, and his purple wine-soaked nose bobbled up and down. The landlord put a bottle of red wine upon the bar and popped the cork. Rickoreen's eyes lit up at the sound. He didn't bother with a glass and, grabbing the bottle, took a long pull. Some of the wine dribbled down his chin onto his stained cravat.

"Very generous of you, sir," he slurred, pulling out a dirty lace handkerchief and dabbing at his chin.

Kilfannan smiled to himself. Cluricauns were chronic alcoholics, but there was no vice in them. They were happy drunks who lived only for the wine.

Saying farewell to Rickoreen, Kilfannan wandered over to Mary and stood beside her. The musicians were setting up on stage, and Mary sat down between a bodhrán player and a violinist, with Kilfannan at her feet. The group began to play a jig, and the customers joyfully clapped their hands in time with the beat.

In a dream, Kilfannan spun the lively music into meadow grass, moss upon damp rocks, fragrant fern, and sweet green weeping willow. The mortal hours sped away in the ticking of a clock.

"Last orders, gentlemen," the landlord called. After packing up their instruments, the musicians hurried to the bar for the final round of drinks. "I go to the market," Kilfannan whispered in Mary's ear. "To see if they hath any emerald ribbon."

He saw her furtively glance around to see who might be looking. There were already rumours floating around the town that she had a habit of talking to herself whenever she played music. "Now don't you be stealing cream from the buttery," she whispered back.

"Stealing is stealing, and the dairyman doesn't stand a chance with you being invisible and all."

Kilfannan grinned and held his hands up in mock affront. "Faith, ma'am. What are a few spoonfuls of cream to a gallon? 'Tis hardly enough to miss, I'll warrant."

He was leaving for the market when he heard the landlord ask, "Four Irish coffees and a whisky for Mary, did you say?" Kilfannan stopped in his tracks. There would be fresh cream floating on the top of an Irish coffee. Whipping out his spoon, he went back to the bar and waited for the landlord to put the order on the counter.

Mary had her back to him as the landlord put the glasses on the bar. As quick as a flash, Kilfannan scooped the cream from one coffee and then the other three.

"You forgot to put the cream on the coffee," the bodhrán player said, staring at the glasses. The landlord slowly shook his head and turned away for more.

Kilfannan saw Mary look over her shoulder and stare at him disapprovingly as he licked the last few drops of cream. Blushing emerald green, he put the spoon back in his pocket. He'd been caught in the act again!

Leaving the Black Orchid, he crossed the road to the market. There he sidled over to the dairy stand, whipped out his spoon, and dipped it in the cream container. *Mary wouldn't approve*, he thought, a trifle contritely, but cream from the human world was a delight he could not resist, and he dipped his spoon a second, third, and fourth time.

"That there cream really starts to evaporate this time of the day," Kilfannan heard the stallkeeper say to his wife. "Are you sure, woman, that no one stole any while I was in the pub and you had your back turned?"

"'Tis the faeries that's taking it," his wife answered. "God bless you, gentlemen," she added under her breath.

Guiltily putting his spoon away, Kilfannan left the stand and went to a haberdashery stall for green ribbon to queue his long, copper-coloured hair. After finding a suitable width, he took a length and left a gold coin in its place for payment. Cream was one thing, but stealing anything else was another!

He sauntered through the walkways between the rows of stalls looking at the different merchandise. Finding nothing of interest, he decided to go back to the faerie bar at the Black Orchid for a tot of brandy. Making his way between the aisles, he smelt a touch of fetor on the air. He sniffed and immediately recoiled. It was the rank, putrid, greasy stink of goblins. Speeding up, he made his way past the stalls, but the further he went, the stronger the stench grew. "Damnation!" he gasped, and he swiftly took a perfumed handkerchief from his pocket and held it to his nose.

As Kilfannan rounded a corner, he saw a band of goblins approaching and quivered with disgust. He despised the treacherous minds of the foul folk of the mines, for they knew not the ethics of honour or virtue. Trying to avoid them, he turned on his heel and retraced his steps. He stopped by the last stand in the walkway and peered uneasily round the corner. The way was clear, and after hurrying through another aisle, he stepped out on the square. Before he could cross, he was confronted by a swaggering, evil-looking goblin with his magg strung out behind him. Kilfannan stared in dismay at the hideous shape. The goblin was of a dark caste, taller and broader than the rest, sprouting a crown of malformed horns from his scaly, neckless head.

"Where you be a-goin', gentry scab?" The goblin snarled, pointing at him with a filthy claw.

Surprised at being accosted in such a manner, Kilfannan answered, "'Tis none of thy business! Now make way!" Glancing swiftly over his shoulder, he saw more goblins behind him, blocking his retreat. He was confounded by the goblin chief's aggression; apart from a few fisticuffs at the races over bets, it was unknown in Faerie for a sylph to be accosted by goblins, and he wondered what the deuce was going on. Bewildered and angered, he stepped back a few paces and, raising his cane, shouted, "Faith! I have no quarrel with thee; now let me pass!"

The goblin chief leered at him. "Me name is Grad, and all those around these parts trembles when they hears me name." He gave a throaty, rasping laugh. "Is you trembling yet, gentry scum?"

"Indeed I am not!" Kilfannan answered. "Clear the way and give me passage."

"Ee wants to pass!" Grad jeered. "Think you own the place, do you?" Lunging forward, he snatched Kilfannan's hat and threw it to his magg. "Heh!" Grad shouted. "I asked ye a question. Forgot your own name, have ye?" The magg began jeering and crowing. "Give me your stinking name, and I'll let 'e pass." The goblin fingered his knife and then picked his nose and flicked a large brown booger at Kilfannan.

Feeling something hit his sleeve, Kilfannan looked down and saw the ball of snot splattered on his frockcoat. Realising Grad was trying to provoke him to fight, he glanced in alarm around the market to see if there were any faeries that could aid him, but he saw none. Realising he would have to try to bluff his way out of the confrontation, he tightened his grip on his cane and, drawing himself up, said with authority, "I am Kilfannan of the House of Kilfenoran. I have caused thee no offence. Let me be on my way."

"Ha!" Grad yelled to his magg. "The fop has caused us no offence! Did you hear that, boys?" He spat a glob of tobacco on the ground. "You gentry scum are rich, and us folk poor. I know you have gold. Hand it over. I wants it."

Seeing Grad pull out his knife, Kilfannan knew robbery was at hand. It would be best to give the scum what he wanted, he thought, and as soon as chance offered an escape, make a dash for the Black Orchid across the road. The alehouse was owned by his friend, a fear dearg, and he would find refuge from the goblins there. He took out his money bag and emptied the contents into Grad's thick and calloused palm.

"Doubloons," Grad crooned. He sniffed the gold, rubbed the coins across his lips, and then bit them to see if they were real. "What else you got, eh! Say!" His beady eyes fell upon the emerald buckles on Kilfannan's shoes. Flicking his thick blue tongue greedily over his yellow fangs, he hissed. "I wants your pretty buckles. Give them to me, or I'll cut your feet off at the ankles."

The air was vibrating with murderous hate, and the change from threats to the actuality of violence came as a profound shock to Kilfannan. Grad's boldness baffled him; robbery was one thing, but murder of a sylph was without precedent in Faerie. His intuition was screaming that his essence was in peril, and swiftly summoning a wind, he surrounded himself in a roaring vortex of swirling air that ripped the plastic roofs from nearby stalls and sent merchandise sailing through the market. In the turmoil, he tried to dodge around Grad and make a run for the pub, but he suddenly found himself arrested by an invisible field of force. His escape route had been blocked. *Goblins do not have the power of containment*, he thought desperately, and letting his intent rise from the air field into space, he probed the ether. An icy tremor of fear shocked throughout his being as he realised he had been entrapped by an evil spell.

"Did I tell 'e you could pass?" he heard Grad snigger.

The space beside the goblin chief began to shimmer with the tainted yellow light of Lower Faerie, and Kilfannan saw the outline of a thin shape appear beside Grad, swaddled in a hooded cloak of shadow. Lowering his cane, he stared in horror at the malignant husk-like face and averted his gaze from the incandescence eye slits burning with triumphant malice. Kilfannan recognised the apparition as a knocker. The fiends from the mines had not been seen in Faerie since the War of Separation, and for a reason he could not fathom, he was suddenly aware that the knocker had a mind to murder him.

"Me name is Aeguz," the knocker hissed, regarding him with spiteful eyes. "So thou art Kilfannan of the House of Kilfenoran."

"I am indeed!" Kilfannan raised his cane in bravado. Desperately trying to control his shaking voice, he said, "Make way and let me pass."

"Let thee pass. I think not." Aeguz flicked his forked tongue over his needle-like teeth and hissed, "After I have collected the reward upon thine head, I've a mind to dine on thy tender parts."

A chill gripped his heart as he wrestled with the monstrous thought of his annihilation and the fall of the House of Air. His only defence against the knocker's dark and murderous spirit was a sylph bolt, but he knew it was perilous to use the splitting wind without the down-breath of his brother. Without both polarities meeting at the centre of the HeartStar, he himself could be blown apart and scattered to the winds. But he had no choice; there was no other way. He must play for time and keep the knocker talking while he gathered the air from six directions to him. He slowly took an up-breath and sent it spiralling into space.

"A reward for my head, thou sayest!" Kilfannan snapped back, securing the power of the winds within him. "Who accuseth me of iniquity? I demand an answer."

"Thy fancy words art as naught! Thou art surrounded by me servants, and without thine accursed twin, thou art powerless against me," Aeguz jeered, sliding back his hood, exposing his pricked ears and flaking domed head. "Thy green blood will feed a brood of monsters far wickeder than me servant Grad. That is, after I have supped. And the bounty on thine head will pay for many a little treat for me allies on the Burren."

Air swirled around Kilfannan, and as the knocker's robes fluttered in the rising wind, Kilfannan saw a star emerald hanging from a leaden chain around the fiend's neck. The shock of seeing a token of his house adorning the devil legate's shrivelled throat gave way to fury, and Kilfannan gathered the wind into a ball and hurled the spinning vortex at the knocker.

The whirlwind hit Aeguz in the chest, and he fell over with a piercing cry, landing on his back several feet away. Seeing his image shimmer, Kilfannan knew he was trying to escape and sink through the road into Lower Faerie. Thrusting his cane under the emerald necklace, Kilfannan hauled the knocker upward and then, using the point of his cane, pinned him by the throat to the side of a stall.

"Filth! Vile scum!" Kilfannan screamed, snatching the star emerald. The knocker writhed, and his dry robes fell away, revealing his desiccated body. Aeguz struggled to escape, but Kilfannan caught the sun in the emerald again and trained the brilliant, burning light into his eyes.

"How comest thou by a token of my house?" Kilfannan shouted. He saw a sudden movement from the corner of his eye. Grad was raising his knife and moving towards him. "One step further," he shouted, "and I will burn thy master's soul to ash."

"Stay!" the knocker shrieked as Kilfannan brought the emerald closer to his eyes. Grad stepped back, and the magg, now bereft of their knocker's will, started quarrelling with each other, while others stood around blankly watching the confrontation.

"How comest thou by the star stone?" Kilfannan thundered again.

"A mortal named O'Shallihan," the knocker shrieked, thrusting its bony fingers across its hooded eyes.

"And where canst O'Shallihan be found?" Kilfannan asked, bringing the emerald laser even closer.

The knocker's cyanic flesh began to pit and blister, and with a venomous hiss, he moaned, "The mortal is at Lake Carn in the Crystal Mountains."

"Is it truth thou tellest me, or a lie?"

"'Tis the truth! I swear! Now stay thy demon light."

The market was suddenly plunged into shadow, and as dark clouds raced across the sun, the light in the star stone faded. Kilfannan felt dizzy, and his head began to swim.

"Gentry scum," the knocker hissed, trying to force the cane from his throat. "Thine accursed house will soon lie in ruin, and the Green will be no more."

Without his brother's down-breath, the power of the elf bolt was splitting Kilfannan's energy, sapping his will. Desperately gathering the remnants of his scattered energy, he jabbed the end of his cane deeper into Aeguz's throat. With a piercing screech, the knocker slowly sunk down into the Under-Earth of Lower Faerie.

Re-energised by the knocker's will, Kilfannan saw Grad charging at him with a knife. He tried to dodge but felt a blow to the face that sent him staggering backwards as a searing pain shot through his jaw. As he steadied himself, a troop of elves surged past him, armed with whips and swords. In a daze, he heard Grad shouting for the magg.

Feeling a restraining hand on his arm, Kilfannan turned round and saw a tall elf in golden armour. "I am Taeron, fire lord of Taera," the elf said. "Go quickly! Let the House of Fire Descending protect the House of Air."

"Many thanks," Kilfannan gasped, wiping away the ichor from the corner of his mouth with his handkerchief. Seeing a clear path across the square to the inn, he stumbled through the market. Oaths and curses broke out behind him. Glancing over his shoulder, he saw Grad with a smaller goblin in hot pursuit. "Stinking fop," Grad shrieked. "I's going to rip your cowardly heart out!"

Kilfannan felt Grad try to tackle him from behind and wrenched himself free. He used his cane as a brace and somersaulted forward to the entrance. His eyes were darkening as his hand closed upon the doorknob, and with a last effort of will, he pushed open the door and fell down in the hallway.

* * *

Kilcannan was parading Finifar in the paddock at the races in Boolyduff when he felt a shortness of breath. He could not complete the down-breath and knew his brother was in trouble. Leaving the racecourse, he rode like the wind to Kilfenora.

Dismounting in the stable yard at the back of the Black Orchid, he saw an elf lord approaching. Kilcannan eyed him in shock. There was a livid gash upon his brow, his face was streaked with ichor, and his golden mail was covered in the black ooze of goblins.

"Hail to the House of Kilfenoran," the elf lord said. "I am Taeron of the High House of Taera. Your brother was attacked by goblins at the market, and me troop came to his aid. In the fray, I deem he lost a jewel of your fair house." He handed the star emerald to Kilcannan. "Now that meself hath returned the jewel, I must leave forthwith. Many of me troopers are inflamed with ale and will recklessly pursue the goblins back to their filthy holes. I must gather them together, for in close ranks there is safety."

Kilcannan's peridot eyes blazed with fire. "My brother Kilfannan – is he safe?"

"The captain of me troopers saw him fall through the entrance to the inn." Taeron gestured towards the side door. "'Tis best to enquire inside."

"Thank you, Taeron, lord of the House of Fire Falling," Kilcannan said with gratitude, embracing the elf.

"May the stars protect the House of Air," Taeron said, and with a wave of his hand, he left the stables.

Arkle the landlord was filling a shot glass at the brandy measure when Kilcannan rushed into the bar. "Dost thou know the whereabouts of my brother Kilfannan?"

"He is in a swoon, sir. Meself hath laid him on a daybed in the parlour. Please come this way."

Kilcannan followed Arkle and saw Kilfannan lying on a day bed with his shoes beside him on the floor.

"By the stars!" he cried in concern, seeing a livid bruise on his brother's pale cheek and a jagged rip at the corner of his mouth.

"Meself will get a sun-ice pack for the gash upon his mouth," Arkle said, going through the door.

Aghast and alarmed, Kilcannan gently shook his brother's arm. "Brother! 'Tis I. Wake up!" There was no response, and taking Kilfannan in his arms, he held him to his heart and tried to harmonise the air field at the centre of the charge.

Agonising moments passed, and then Kilfannan's eyelids fluttered, and he looked at Kilcannan in confusion. "Faith! How did I get here?" He started to sit up. "Agh!" He gingerly touched his lip, staring at the green ichor on his fingers.

"I brought you a pad to clean your wound," Arkle said softly, handing the aromatic swab to Kilfannan. "'Tis treated with marigold oil to cleanse away the poisonous filth of goblins."

Kilfannan put the healing pack on the side of his mouth and felt a soothing chill dispel the stinging heat. "Thank thee, Arkle. Praise to the House of Fire Rising," he said with gratitude and love. "Tellest where thou found me."

"Yourself came in through the front door and collapsed," Arkle responded, "A goblin tried to follow you inside, but I threatened to burn the hide off his back and he retreated." His yellow cheeks glowed hotly from his red, smooth face. "I brought you in here so no one would see you. You gave me a scare." He passed a hand over his sleek hair. "Now your brother is here and you have awoken, I had better tend to me business." He turned to Kilcannan. "I will take your horse to the stables and give him sweet hay and water."

"Brother! I felt thy distress and came hither," Kilcannan said once they were alone. "While I was dismounting in the stable yard, Taeron of the House of Taera told me thou wast involved in a fight with goblins at the market. Faith! Thou scarce go near the filth, they disgust thee so. What provoked them to assail thee, for such a gratuitous attack on the House of Air is unknown within our realm?"

"Grad the goblin chief was full of spite when he eyed me at the market, and had a mind to rob me, plain enough," Kilfannan replied. "And methinks robbery and insults were all he had in mind. 'Twas when in bravado I told him my name that I saw the malicious gleam of his knocker Aeguz burning from his eyes."

"A knocker!" Kilcannan exclaimed in horrified disbelief. "The sorcerers from the mines hath not been seen in Faerie since the War of Separation. How can this be?"

"I know not what to think," Kilfannan replied. He looked at Kilcannan with anguish in his eyes. "A nightmare hath entered our realm and walks abroad under the sun, and the knocker had a star emerald – a token of our house – around his stinking neck. Smiting the fiend with the sylph bolt, I took the star stone from his possession." He searched through his pockets for the star stone. Failing to find the emerald on his person, Kilfannan cried in panic, "Faith! In the fray, I lost the emerald. I must return to the marketplace and find it."

"Stay!" Kilcannan ordered, putting a restraining hand on Kilfannan's arm as he struggled up from the daybed. "The elf who came to thine aid is Taeron of the High House of Taera. He found the emerald on the ground and returned it to me when I arrived here." He took the star stone from his pocket and handed it to Kilfannan.

"Thank the stars 'tis safe," Kilfannan said, putting the jewel in the inside pocket of his frock coat for safekeeping. "Brother!" he said fretfully, "The knocker told me he got the emerald from a mortal. How can it be that a man from the third world hath possession of a token from our High House? And he gloated there was a bounty upon my head, and no doubt there is a price upon thine head as well."

Kilcannan's eyes glowed peridot, and flame was in his eye. "This is the evillest of news. If 'tis true that there is a bounty on our heads, we will be hunted for reward." He sniffed in disdain. "Brave will be he who tries to take our heads."

A down-wind swirled around him, blowing the landlord's race cards off the table. "Brother! 'Twas a terrible risk to call the splitting wind without my presence as a balance," he said, looking anxiously at Kilfannan. "'Twould seem Taeron arrived in the nick of time to save thee."

"'Tis true, but desperate times beget desperate acts, and we are fortunate the elves were there to aid our house," Kilfannan replied. "But now thou art with me to steady my breath, my strength returneth, and there is great virtue in Arkle's healing oil to cool and soothe my wounds."

Arkle came bustling into the parlour with a pair of riding boots, a jacket, and breeches. "Meself thought a change of clothes is in order," he said to Kilfannan. "'Tis the best I can do at such short notice. I'll be away to get you some refreshment."

Kilfannan smiled appreciatively. "Many thanks."

"Let me help thou rid thyself of the foulness of goblins," Kilcannan said in disgust, looking at his brother's snot-streaked frock coat. "'Tis alright, brother," Kilfannan said. Taking the star emerald from his pocket, he slipped off his frock coat and threw it on the floor.

While Kilfannan changed his clothes, Kilcannan pried the emerald buckles from his brother's shoes, put the gems in his pocket, went to the parlour door, and peered into the snug. The bar was closed, and their refreshments were sitting on a table.

Returning to Kilfannan, he asked tenderly, "Hast thy strength returned?"

Kilfannan nodded.

"Come to the snug, brother. There is blackberry brandy, cream, and cheese waiting for us on a table."

Kilfannan's eyes lit up. "Cream!" he whispered to himself, and he whipped out his spoon.

Taking their refreshments, they sat down in chairs by the fireside. Kilfannan leaned back. "There are many pressing questions to be answered," said he. "We must go forthwith to Black Head and consult with the wizard Ke-enaan. He is wise in the lore of all three worlds and may be able to tell us why a mortal had an emerald from Gorias, and why a knocker can walk freely in daylight."

Kilcannan shifted restlessly in the chair. "For the breath of me, I cannot fathom why there is a bounty on our heads! Let us hope Ke-enaan will have an answer."

Kilfannan nodded, and his emerald eyes darkened into fir light. "In truth, Kilcannan, a shadow hath been on me for a while — a foreboding, a threat to the nature of our house. Evil, it seems, is rising against our house, and 'tis my sense that there is a change in the quality of the Green … a lessening." He paused for a moment. "We will take our questions to Ke-enaan for'with; we can brook no delay."

Arkle came through the door carrying Kilfannan's soiled clothes and shoes. "With your permission, sir, I will burn these for you. Is there any other way meself can be of service?"

Kilfannan smiled and nodded. "I am in need of a steed. Dost thou have a horse I can borrow? 'Twill not be for long, and I will be returning shortly."

"Yes, sir. I will go and saddle her." He disappeared hurriedly through the door to the backyard.

In a few minutes, Arkle was back. "Good sirs! All is ready."

They finished their refreshments and followed Arkle to the stables. When they got to the horse boxes, Arkle introduced Kilfannan to his mount, a grey mare called Ellafey.

"'Tis a beautiful horse and no mistake," he trilled, whispering words of greeting in the mare's ear.

"'Tis indeed, sir, and fast to speed you on your way. And, if 'tis not an impertinence to ask, are you going far?"

"To Ke-enaan at Black Head," Kilfannan answered. He took a doubloon from his purse and handed the gold piece to Arkle. "This is for saving me from the goblin," he said. "And in the meantime, speak to no one of my tussle with the goblins, unless 'tis Trevelyan of Wessex that comes asking."

"Very generous of you, sir," Arkle said, putting the coin in his pocket. "Trevelyan is a fine gentleman indeed, and have no worry; meself will keep your confidence." He smoothed Finifar's neck. "Your steed is as fine as any horse I have yet to see," he said to Kilcannan. "'Tis a goblin bane, to be sure!"

Kilcannan grinned. "My charge is the finest horse in Ireland. I have been in many a fight to get my winnings from the goblin bookies at the racecourse."

"I have won a fair bit on him meself." Arkle laughed, and turning away, he opened the back gate onto a green road.

"Farewell, and may the stars bless you," Arkle said softly as they mounted and rode through the gate and into the lane behind the pub.

CHAPTER 2

REVELATION

The sky was stormy and heavy with the threat of rain as the Kilfenorans left the Black Orchid and started along the hedged boreen leading to the green way.

"Gulls are flying inland, and there is warning in their cries," Kilfannan said, breaking Ellafey into a canter. "We must make haste! Let us take the road north to Lisdoonvarna, and then on to the sand dunes of Fanore."

Doubt continued to plague Kilfannan as Ellafey plunged forward through the damp air and sluggish water meadows to the rocky heath beyond. Seeing a token of his house around a knocker's neck had been shock enough; but to know the fiend had got the jewel from a mortal filled him with even greater apprehension – for an emerald from the fifth dimension could not manifest within the death world unless corrupted and entrained to evil. He found himself suddenly creating fearful scenarios around the emerald and had to still his mind lest he create a malign fulfilment of his morbid speculation.

They thundered on past undulating pastures and gorse-strewn bogs towards the coast. When they reached the village of Fanore, Kilfannan pulled up by a grey stone sea wall that bordered the road.

As he looked along the lonely beach and sinister, shadowy hump-backed dunes, an ugly chill tingled through his body. Mary had told him that the sands were quick with sinkholes and many a mortal had been trapped in churning sand and sucked below by a denizen of darkness. "The dunes hath an evil feel and are not a place to linger," he said to Kilcannan. "See! Fog banks are moving in across the steely sea and will soon make fall upon the land. Let us ride on afore shadow overtake us."

The two of them rode north, and soon the beach was left behind and the dunes gave way to a wild and rocky shoreline. Kilcannan pulled up by the side of a wall. "Brother! If 'tis true there is a price upon our heads, bounty hunters from Lower Faerie may well be on our trail. We must be cautious," he said grimly. "The road from Fanore to Black Head is twisty and narrow, and there are rock overhangs on one side and the sea wall on t'other. 'Tis ripe for ambush."

"Aye, and every mile is a caution."

A mile farther along the road, Kilfannan stood up in his stirrups and looked ahead to an outcrop in the limestone rock, now hardly visible in the thickening fog. "Black Head is yonder," he cried. "'Twill be good to leave the peril of the road, for my heart tells me a shadow stalks us – a hate wanting to be fulfilled."

The fog thickened as they stopped on a grassy verge outside the wizard's halls.

Kilfannan shivered. The atmosphere was tense with energetic threat, and in the fume above, he fancied he could discern a horde of malignant bat-like phantoms flying southward towards the Giant's Cliffs. His heart quailed at the sense of seething hate incarnate, and he wanted to turn back and run away – but there was nowhere to run. His world had been plunged into horror, and he knew that worse awaited.

Slipping from Ellafey's back, he stood gazing at the wizard's image in the rock face. Two dark eyeholes looked west across the sea, and below a craggy nose, water flowed into a small lily-padded pool.

Taking the up-breath, he cried with the power of the wind, "'Tis I, Kilfannan of the House of Kilfenoran. Kilcannan and I have come to seek thy counsel."

There was a moment of profound stillness, and then Kilfannan saw the outline of an arched entrance appearing in the dark, mossy limestone wall. In the centre of the door, the protective rune Sraibh, the blackthorn tree, blazed with a gamut of colours, splashing him with the tints of realms unknown. He swallowed hard and tried to overcome his trepidation. He had only been in the presence of the wizard in Trevelyan's company and was in awe of Ke-enaan of Black Head. He was the Old One who had stayed behind in Faerie after the War of Separation, and had made an oath at the splitting of the worlds to be ever watchful of the Cathac and the western marches of the sea.

The door opened, and standing in the frame was a tall blue-cloaked figure with a long and noble face. "Greetings to the House of Kilfenoran," Ke-enaan said, stepping out onto the verge. The diamond ring upon the wizard's finger flickered eerily in the gloom, and for a moment Kilfannan was at a loss for words. Gathering himself, he bowed and then responded with humble tone, "Salutations from the House of Air."

"Thou must make haste off the road, for I deem evil is abroad," the wizard said, glancing at the smothering, eerie fog. He made a pass with his hand, and Kilfannan saw a passageway appear in the rock beside the entrance.

"Take the horses through the passage to the forge of Uall Mac Carn of Slieve Elva," Ke-enaan said to Kilcannan. "'Tis not far to the forge, and they will be safe from evil there. When thou returneth, look for a lighted door. 'Twill give thee entry to my halls."

Kilfannan followed Ke-enaan through the arched doorway and into a long chamber that was bathed in the fluting candlelight of ages. The cold fire of dragons was burning in the hearth, and the air was fragrant with the perfume of fresh rushes from the floor. On both sides of the fireplace were natural limestone shelves filled with flagons of flowers, herbs, mandrigora roots, jars of unction, and bottles of depth-dark liquid.

In the centre of the room sat a table stacked with ancient grimoires, runic texts, and a half-written scroll with inkpot and feather quill beside it.

"Sit thee down by the fireside," Ke-enaan said kindly. There were seats on each side of the wide fireplace, and Kilfannan sat down on the nearest rest and stretched out his legs before the blue glow of the hearth. Even though he was consumed with questions, he thought it best to wait until Kilcannan returned before he broached their fears.

There was the sound of footfalls in an outside passage. Ke-enaan crossed the room and, opening a side door, bid Kilcannan enter. "Come!" he said courteously. "Sit thou by Kilfannan at the dragon fire, and take a goblet of cowslip elixir as refreshment. I have no cream or cheese to offer!"

"Brother!" Kilcannan said excitedly, sitting in the chair opposite. "A wondrous thing hath happened. After a few steps along the passageway, I found myself in a long pasture of soft grass, heady with the sweet perfume of wild chamomile and daisy. At the bottom of the meadow, glimmering under a star-specked sky, was a long, low forge ablaze with the cold blue fire of dragons. Seeing no sign of the blacksmith, I left the horses beside a pool of sparkling water." He smiled wistfully and said, "For myself to see the blue-lit forge in starlight and take the fragrant meadow's breath – 'tis a beautiful world of dreaming, so it is."

Kilfannan smiled. "In truth, brother! What is life without a dream?" Glancing at Ke-enaan, he saw for a moment soul sadness in the wizard's eyes, a yearning for a time long past, a haunting memory that could never be assuaged.

"My realm of Black Head and Slieve Elva are one in heart," Ke-enaan said, "until Faerie fails and all comes to naught in the heartbreak of desolation." He poured out a goblet of elixir and handed it to Kilcannan. "A toast to the House of Air! Drink deeply, for 'tis a magic potion of yellow fire to bring courage to your hearts, a liquid gift wise with understanding."

Sipping the elixir, Kilfannan felt the chilling shade of dark destiny awaiting; and glancing at Kilcannan, he saw the same fateful spectre mirrored in his brother's eyes. Deciding to face his fear head on, and wanting resolution to his nagging doubt, Kilfannan turned to Ke-enaan. "This very afternoon, I went to the market in Kilfenora and was attacked by goblins," he said. "'Twas their intent to rob me, but when I told the goblin chief my name, thoughts of theft turned to murder. Their knocker arrived and told me he was going to collect a bounty on my head." He put his hand in his pocket and brought out the emerald. "Faith!" he cried, looking anxiously at the wizard. "I took this star emerald, the symbol of our high house, from the fiend's stinking neck." A turbulent up-wind blew around him, fluttering the woven tapestries on the walls.

Ke-enaan's face grew grave. "Peace, Kilfannan," he commanded, taking the emerald from his shaking fingers. "Come now! We will place the star stone in the cunning mirror, and all will be revealed of its journey into darkness."

Ke-enaan rose and led them to a large oval mirror of shimmering quicksilver set into the grey rock wall at the far end of his hall. As he placed the star stone in the mirror, the quicksilver quivered, and as the jewel disappeared, Kilfannan saw an emerald sheen appear within the pearly light. The radiance increased until the glass was swallowed up and a gleaming four-pointed star blazed from the mirror.

Kilfannan stared at the star emerald with rising panic. Plagued with dread, he peered into the glass. In a swirl of misting stars, he saw the Coach of Air – drawn by Brea, the graceful silver mare of Gorias – appear. The mirror shivered with waves of shifting silver, the veil of misting stars cleared away, and he saw two tall, elegant figures cloaked in an oval of pulsing emerald light descending from the coach.

For a moment his fear was forgotten, his heart swelled at the sight of his creators, and he revelled in the ecstasy of the one love that only mystic dreamers feel.

Yet in the midst of his joy, Kilfannan felt the ugly shade of doubt that throttled his spirit and will. Why were Niamh and Caiomhin in a carpenter's workshop in the mortal world? The question resonated in every fibre of his being. And why would they need to reveal themselves within the doomed, dark world of men?

The sound of Niamh's sweet voice cut short his thought. "News of thy exquisite craftsmanship in the building of fine coaches hath reached the world of High Faerie," she said to a small, sandy-haired man standing before her. "We are to set forth on a mission to thy world, and we request thee to build us a coach, for such is thy skill, surpassing that of any other we have seen in the mortal world. The coach thou art to fashion is to be an exact copy of the one thou seest before thee, and 'twill need a silver-grey horse to draw it. What sayest thou?"

The carpenter looked with wonder upon the star-misted coach and the radiant couple floating in the air before him. "It is a long-held secret desire of my heart and a cherished dream come true to behold the world of the Faerie Sidhe," he said shyly, "for I know now the old stories told to me by my grandmother were true. There is more to life than most will ever know." He nodded vigorously. "I will build your coach even if it means working day and night. To be sure I will." Taking a tape measure from his pocket, he measured the faeric coach from top to bottom and jotted down the dimensions in his notebook.

Niamh handed the carpenter a bulging purse of coin. "The gold will buy thee a wee silver mare and all the supplies thou needest, and it shall provide payment for thy service. Our errand to the mortal world is pressing, and we need the coach in twenty days, when the new moon in thy world comes again."

"It will be my sacred obligation to have the coach ready when you arrive," the carpenter replied.

Niamh smiled. "We will return with the new moon. Until then, farewell."

The mirror rippled with quicksilver, and when it cleared, Kilfannan once again beheld Niamh and Caiomhin in the carpenter's workshop. Before them was a beautiful wooden coach, hand painted in alternating glorious green and brightest crimson, with gold accessories and rack.

Kilfannan saw Caiomhin stiffen and point at two beautiful manikins sitting on a shelf. "'Tis forbidden to make a likeness of our face and form," he cried out. "Thou hast made replicas of us, and now our images exist within the mortal world. Thou must put them to the fire without delay."

"Forgive me, sir and ma'am, but so beautiful you are that I thought it only right that your similes should be crafted into beauteous form; I meant no harm," the carpenter answered apologetically.

With a nod of forgiveness, Caiomhin said, "In thy dimension we have no grounding root and cannot stay for long within thy presence. I bid thee in trust! Destroy our images for'with."

The emerald light around Niamh and Caiomhin shivered and began to fade, and Kilfannan heard an echo in the sighing air. "We will return this eve, and as the new moon rises, we will meld with the coach that thou hast made and begin our journey into the world of men."

The mirror clouded over, and when it cleared again, Kilfannan saw visions of a magenta dawn flood the glass. In the distance, he could see the jagged peak of Ngarjto, the mountain of the wind; and above, in a soft violet sky, floated the emerald city of Gorias, born in cloud and glimmering in the radiance of the HeartStar. The vision faded, and small, green octahedral polyhedrons appeared within the mirror, swarming on a flowing silver tide. As the waves retreated, Kilfannan saw an emerald light take shape. In the darkness of mortal night, the Faerie sheen waxed strong, casting a glow upon the shadowy workshop.

The air suddenly tingled with malign expectancy, and the hateful tints of Lower Faerie swelled within the glass. In a hideous glow, Kilfannan saw the monstrous pockmarked face of Grad appear with a tall, dark-faced mortal in the workshop. The man was shining a torch around the floor. "Ah! Now you're talkin'," Kilfannan heard him snigger to the goblin. "This miniature coach will bring a pretty penny. It's all hand painted, and the rack is made of gold." The beam of the torch rested on a pair of beautiful porcelain dolls dressed in the finest silks and satins, sitting on a shelf. The mortal took them down and put them side by side on the coach seat. Kilfannan felt an icy finger of fear stab at his heart. The dolls were the lifelike images of Niamh and Caiomhin. The carpenter had not destroyed them, and as beautiful as they were, there was now the taint of mortality upon them. It was with great fear that he looked again into the mirror.

"Have you found anything else of value?" the mortal hissed to Grad.

"A box of gold and silver nails," he growled, and he put the boxes in the coach.

The mortal searched a small compartment by the coach boot, took out a delicate golden key, and turned it over in the torchlight. "This is made of gold, and it's got strange markings on it," Kilfannan heard him say, and a shiver ran down his spine as he watched the mortal lock the coach and put the key into his pocket.

He saw the emerald glow coalesce into a four-pointed star stone blazing with the outer-spectrum colours of the Heart Ray. Within the glorious light, he saw the Coach of Air appear and hover over the mortal coach.

A pale, hungry knocker light was burning in Grad's eyes, and in deepening horror Kilfannan watched the grey-robed form of Aeguz appear beside the goblin. The knocker glided upward like a foul grey snake and, with a sweep of his withered fingers, snatched the star stone from the air above the coach. Screaming with rage and pain, the fiend threw the jewel down onto the floor and hawked spittle on his fingers. The mortal picked up the star stone and was about to put it in his pocket when Kilfannan saw Grad stop him. "Me master saw the pretty through me eyes, and he tried to take it, but the radiations were so foul they burnt him," Grad said as he picked the snot from his nose ring and flicked it on the floor. "But now the vibrations of the gentry filth are gone, and me master can use the star stone to cast spells against the hated House of Air." Kilfannan shivered as Grad looked slyly at the mortal, and obscenely licking his fangs, he tittered, "He will give you gifts – the soft, squirming little girl bodies that you likes to play with."

The man leered. "All right then."

The mirror shivered and swelled with a rushing miasma of foul light, and Kilfannan heard the terrified whinnying of a horse; his senses were flung headlong into screaming chaos. A kaleidoscope of images rushed him, so grotesque in implication that it was easier for him to doubt his confused senses than accept them. A mortal with a golden key, and two porcelain similes of their creators, rose and fell before him in the mirror, mingling with terrifying screams; there was a click of key in lock, and a feeling of smothering suffocation. The coach quivered and shook, the horse reared, and in a churning vortex, a clawing evil swept the Coach of Air through the uttermost gates of space and into the outer darkness.

Kilfannan joined his mind with Kilcannan as the mental cataclysm swept their beings. The HeartStar and their souls were in peril. In a rushing nightmare of cosmic horror, they prayed for sanity and strength to endure whatever evil deeds awaited. A vortex of tortured air swirled around the brothers and down the hall, blowing books and grimoires off the table to the floor. Bottles and jars were falling from the shelves, and rushes and tattered parchments were flying in the air, caught up within the whirling chaos.

"Peace!" Ke-enaan commanded, and with a glance, the jars and bottles returned to their places on the shelves and the rushes once more lay flat upon the floor.

The brothers struggled to make sense of what they'd seen and heard. The feeling of loss that had haunted them now swept through their psyches in full magnitude, and they wept long and bitter tears. They realised that in the transition from one coach to the other, the knocker had snatched the star stone – the portal through which the Coach of Air had entered the mortal world. In that fateful moment, the connection between dimensions was broken, and Niamh and Caiomhin became imprisoned within the porcelain replicas of themselves.

"By my arts," Ke-enaan said, "I will bring the Coach of Air through the angles of darkness into the realm of Faerie, but Niamh and Caiomhin I cannot free, for their essence remains trapped in the outer darkness."

The Kilfenorans gazed hopelessly at the wizard with stark fear in their eyes – eyes that hitherto had looked only upon the beauty of the Green but now bore the stain of innocence destroyed.

"Where is the coach?" Kilfannan gulped.

"Trevelyan hath it at his home in England for safekeeping. The door of the Faerie Coach is locked, and the key made of air is missing, so we will assume that the thief hath it on his person. Now our hunt is on for the key and mortal coach."

Ke-enaan refilled their goblets with elixir, and when they were settled, he said, "'Tis best if thou stayest within my hall until the sun is born again, for I have news to tell thee, and much that hath been hidden since the time of the Separation will be revealed."

"'Tis a relief to stay the dark hours in the safety of thine hall," they answered as one, "for a great shadow lieth in our hearts, and fell things are hunting in the fog."

"What hath brought this great evil upon our house?" Kilfannan asked miserably. "For aeons we have lived in joy, and now we are beset with soulless horror."

Ke-enaan's face seemed to grow old; his image weakened and his eyes burned with the mysteries of Elder days. Kilfannan sensed a deep melancholic sea pervade every space within the hall.

"The tale is long and dark, so drink deeply of the draught I have given thee, for it will give thee courage in the face of revelation," Ke-enaan said.

"In the War of Separation," he began, "the Cathac ripped the realm of men from the Faerie worlds and made it mortal. As a result of the split between the realms, the HeartStar, the Breath of All, divided into two parts. This separation gave rise to your creators: Niamh of Air Rising into Space, and her consort, Caiomhin of Air Falling into Fire in the fifth dimension of High Faerie. Their divided essence gave birth to your House of Kilfenoran and the sheens of air in the fourth dimension."

Kilfannan caught Kilcannan's eye. The brothers had never questioned how or why they had come into being. Their first memories were of floating in a gentle breeze of silver sound and seeing, with eyes of the heart, the jagged peak of Ngarjto. The twins of air had come into awareness in the citadel of the eternal city and together had woven the harmony of the spheres into the fourth dimension, establishing the House of Kilfenoran. They were autonomous eternal spinners of the Green, and it was only of late, Kilfannan recalled, that the shade of death had encroached upon the Faerie realm.

Ke-enaan rose, gathered their goblets, and refilled them with elixir. "After the war ended," he continued, sitting back down, "and the Cathac was bound in rock, Niamh and Caiomhin called the elemental lords of earth, water, fire, and space to a council in the city of Gorias. Niamh knew the division of the HeartStar had created the curse of duality upon the Faerie worlds and that it was only a matter of time before the Cathac would find a way to break the spells laid upon him and attack the fourth and fifth dimensions. For clarification of the enemy's return, it was decided by the council that the oracle of Ophire be consulted."

The sphere of Ophire, Kilfannan recalled, was a cunning mirror carved from an enormous ruby by the dwarf lord Ophirius, king under the Wicklow Mountains. Circles and squares the dwarf had cast around the mirror, summoning the dark vampiric spirits from the inner earth to show him visions of the future and snare and destroy those who would usurp his wealth or try to use the cunning glass.

"The oracle of Ophire is a legend to us," Kilfannan said to

Ke-enaan, "and 'tis dangerous to approach." He heard his voice falter. "'Twould seem in these fell times that legend walks alive."

Ke-enaan nodded. "Indeed! The mirror of Ophirius is fraught with peril. Only those skilled in high magic can gain mastery over the geometry of the crystal sphere and force the cunning mirror to show its visions of the future. Becuille, the seer of Gorias, was one who had this ancient knowledge and was able to gain access to the oracle of Ophire, at great peril to herself. Having lost her mortal form at the time of Separation, she could not ground herself in earth and ran the risk of being sucked through the mirror by demonic forces and cast into oblivion. However, her love for the HeartStar spurred her on to take the risk.

"After four days of purification," Ke-enaan went on, "Becuille was ready to approach the mirror. As Narannan, the crucible of stars, reached his zenith in the light-specked sky, Niamh placed the winged emerald heart upon Becuille's brow to protect her. The elemental lords began to sing the sounds of their elements to support her trial, and upon entering the room of oracle, she looked into the great sphere of Ophire. Visions she was shown of the future.

"In the mirror she saw the cataclysmic splitting of the worlds. The realm of man was ripped away, and a sapphire – a stargate to nine dimensions – was caught up within the tumult of the storm wind and swept down into the earth. So dense was the vibration of the mortal world that its glowing blue spectrum of celestial radiance was extinguished, and no trace could be found upon the light waves.

"Becuille warned a time would come when the stars would stand together in alignment and form a gleaming pentagon shape within the heavens – a cosmic mirror of the lost sapphire stargate. By sympathetic resonance, the sky-born jewels would have the power to awaken the stargate from its dark, dense sleep and the portal would reappear upon the ether for love and hate alike. She counselled that a great spiritual conflict would ensue for possession of the sapphire. If evil prevailed, there would be another Separation, and the realm of Faerie would be consumed into the mortal world.

"Dismayed at her news, the council set their plans. Oaths were taken by the elemental lords to protect the Faerie realms. Enchantments were cast; crystals were programmed with special vibrations to block the encroachment of evil. The elemental lords spoke aloud their sacred phonetics, the audible keys to their kingdoms, so all could hear and memorise the sounds. Then, in future times of need, they could call on each other's realities for aid.

"The elemental lords of earth, water, fire, and air decided to appoint one warrior from their house to take on mortal flesh at the time of the prophecy and embark upon a desperate mission to retrieve the sapphire. The lord of space pledged a warrior from beyond the stars to aid the House of Air."

"A warrior of my house in the mortal world! I know naught of this," Kilfannan said, glancing at his brother in bewilderment.

Ke-enaan nodded. "'Tis a secret entrusted only to a few, for 'tis in the mortal world the fate of the sapphire will be decided. Of the four warriors, only one remains. Her name is Emma Cameron, the warrior of air. Trevelyan of Wessex is Emma's protector, for he is the emissary of the space beyond the stars." He refilled their goblets with elixir.

"For aeons we have scanned the star-specked sky for signs of the pentagon appearing," Ke-enaan continued. "But no trace could we find upon the light waves. Word hath come of late from Gorias that the geometric hath appeared in the sky above the city, and Trevelyan and meself knew 'twas time for the warriors of the stargate to descend into mortal flesh. And if 'twere not for Trevelyan's tireless vigilance, the enemy would have already claimed Emma, for dark sorcery has been cast upon her. The moon hath stolen the memory of her High Faerie nature."

Kilfannan shivered, and for a moment black despair swept over him. He caught Ke-enaan's eye and heard soundless words echo through his being. "All is not lost while the Green lives for 'tis love that creates it. Hold strong to the vision of oneness in the HeartStar."

A fiery light smouldered in Kilcannan's eyes. "What hath happened to the other three warriors?"

Ke-enaan sighed. "I know not. After meself and Trevelyan had learned of the fall of Niamh and Caiomhin, we sent a warning on the ether to the warriors in mortal form but found no resonant response apart from the warrior of air. I too wonder what hath happened to the other three, for I can find no energetic trace of them. My heart tells me we have been betrayed, and the hate that snatched the human world hath now turned its hunger for conquest towards Faerie. Love is fading fast within the mortal world, and violence prevails, and 'twill not be long before one of Zugalfar's mortal minions will find the sapphire and open the gates to Pandemonia." He drained his goblet and leant towards them. "The Cathac's eye hath turned to Faerie, for he hateth the House of Air and conspireth in both the mortal world and Faerie to destroy thee."

An ugly, dragging pain snaked down Kilfannan's neck, and once again his mind fell into the utter blackness of despair. It seemed to him that the depth and magnitude of the evil arraigned against his House of Air was undefeatable, and his spirit quailed in the face of such adversity. Yet he could not allow himself to dip into the heart hurt, he thought, for it would consume him with misery, fear, and failure.

Taking the up-breath, he said, "If Gorias falls to Zugalfar, our sacred articles will be lost. We will need them to succour what little hope we may have." A gusting upwind blew around him, ruffling the leaves of an ancient grimoire on the table and shaking the bottles on the shelf.

Ke-enaan raised his hand, and the wind diminished. "Fear not, Kilfannan. Trevelyan hath gone forth at great peril to himself on an urgent mission to Gorias and collected the sacred articles of thine House. He hath taken Naka, the sacred dagger of air, to aid Emma, and I trust he will return with Ennuiol, the staff of growing tree, and Delphuaan, the silver flute that calls the wind, before thou settest forth upon thy journey. If there is no meet between thee, I will take them for safekeeping – if indeed in these dark times safekeeping is possible, for we are in double jeopardy." He fell silent for a moment and then said, "Even as we speak, sorcerers are searching for the sapphire in the mortal world; and in Faerie, the key made of air is missing. Engraved upon it are the geometrics and symbols to the Faerie worlds, which, if found by the denizens of Under-Earth, will be used to gain entry to thy realm." He sighed deeply. "This is our dark hour, for the love of life is about to be overtaken by the Hating. I have no solace to offer thee."

Kilfannan stirred, and a fey light glowed around him. "My brother and I will search for the key. I forced the knocker to tell me the name of the mortal thief, and now I have seen his likeness in the glass; 'tis stamped upon my mind. He hath gone north to Lake Carn at the foot of Binn Breac in the Crystal Mountains."

"We must go at once and apprehend the thief, for every moment that passes is a hazard. I will kill him and take both coach and key!" Kilcannan cried angrily.

"Friends!" Ke-enaan cautioned gently. "Do not be hasty in action, for many a slip is made in ill-thought speed. The knocker hath lost the star stone, and it hath warned us of the peril ranged against us. We should take heart that evil in its error hath shown its hand." He took the emerald from the mirror and, holding it in the palm of his hand, said, "Kilfannan! Tone the sound of air rising into space, and I will burn away the jewel dross with dragon's breath from the fire."

As Kilfannan toned upon the sacred interval of five, he saw a spiralling blue flame shoot from the fire and engulf the star stone in Ke-enaan's hand. The jewel crackled with dazzling sparks of red and blue, and as his sound and colours blended, the fire faded and an emerald light shined through.

"The star emerald is purified," Ke-enaan said, putting the jewel in a pocket of his robe. "The sacred stone of air hath shown us the machinations of our enemy, and forewarned is forearmed. 'Tis clear we have been betrayed and are the target of a dark spell, a hateful design long charted upon the drawing board of time. The quest for the coach and key will be fraught with incalculable evil, and 'twill chill your very souls." He gazed solemnly at Kilfannan. "With the loss of the HeartStar, thou art now the leader of thine house." He took the star stone from his robe and pressed the jewel into Kilfannan's brow. "Use thy intuition, and may the Green guide thee wisely."

Kilfannan put his hand upon his heart and gazed into Ke-enaan's eyes; in the look was love – the love that needs no words to blind it.

After taking the diamond ring from his finger, Ke-enaan handed it to Kilcannan. "Behold! The ring of resolution, fashioned by Sharn, dwarf lord of the Wicklow Mountains. 'Twas brought through the fire of the Separation and now will ride to war for the living Green. May it serve thee well."

Peridot fire gleamed in Kilcannan's eyes as he took the ring. "I will not fail it while the Green lives," he murmured in thanks.

"Come," Ke-enaan said, refilling their goblets, "let us put our hearts together and see what manner of hope we can devise, for there is yet much to talk of. But first let us make a toast to our endeavour." He raised his goblet to theirs. "Slainte!"

Reaching into his pocket, Kilcannan brought out a piece of rolled yellow parchment and handed it to Ke-enaan. "Forgive me," he said. "The last hours have blinded me and driven the letter from my mind. This morning I was on my way to the races when a mortal stopped me on the road. He gave me a parchment and told me it carried a warning to the House of Kilfenoran from the Faerie prince Donne of the Dunes. I opened the seal, but the parchment was blank."

Ke-enaan gazed intently at the little scroll. "It hath the four-leaved clover seal of Prince Donne of the Dunes," he said, opening the letter and holding it to the firelight. As the light played upon the parchment, runes appeared. "These are the runes of Nuadan, he of the star brow and sunlit face." He peered at the writing. "An age hast passed since I last saw this ancient cypher. 'Tis a caveat – a warning to the House of Air that evil awaits them in the element of water. And there is more," he said, holding the parchment closer to the fire. "'Over land and across the sea'," he read, "'I bid thee hasten to find the key. Hasten in this vital quest or Eiru will meet her final rest.' But tell me, how knowest thou this mortal that gave thee the missive from Prince Donne? For oft those of the third world are steeped in treachery."

"His name is Ronan, and he is a faerie friend of Prince Donne," Kilcannan answered. "'Twas himself gave me the letter."

Ke-enaan nodded. "Some mortals are still true to the faerie dream, and others spy for the adversary. One rode past my halls this very morn. He was evil with goblin sight and scanned my cliff, looking for an entrance. I distracted his thoughts, and he rode off southwards towards the Giant's Cliffs. He is a thief and consorts with goblins. Their knocker will give him gold if he can lead them to thee." He looked at an hourglass on the table. "Dawn is upon us, and 'tis time to collect the horses from the forge and set out for your green hills, for the sand of time is flowing and destiny awaits." Holding up his hand in caution, he said grimly, "Heed the warning of Prince Donne. Be watchful of lakes, rivers, and the sea."

He passed a long, gaunt hand through his grizzled hair and, leaning towards them, said, "In anticipation of possessing the sapphire, the Cathac hath sent his thought to the denizens hiding in the dark labyrinths of Under-Earth and Under-Sea. I have watched the rushing nets of clouds in which devils travel and the sinuous waveforms in the sea moving south towards the Giant's Cliffs. When you leave my hall, let vigilance be your guide, for every knocker in Ireland and their maggs will be out to collect the reward the Cathac hath placed upon thine heads."

Kilfannan frowned. "In truth! The odds are stacked against us. I deem we are no longer safe in Clare … or anywhere."

"'Tis true, and every mile north will be a hazard," Ke-enaan answered. "But while the Green lives and sings in the soul of every heath, glen, and vale, there is hope. Pass by my halls on your way north. Meself will have prepared helpmeets for thy journey. Farewell for the present, Kilfannan and Kilcannan of the House of Kilfenoran. May the stars shine upon your faces and light thy way with favour."

Kilfannan followed Kilcannan into the passageway and walked in wonder upon the stone that, in a fleeting moment of no time, became the soft green turf of a meadow dreaming under the violet sky of evening. The magic of soul light brought joy to his heart, and the perfume of wild chamomile enveloped his senses like the liquid loveliness of a fragrant draught.

At the far end of the pasture a forge glowed with blue fire against the swelling stars, and dark green peace lay upon the land.

There was the sound of hoof beats, and Kilfannan heard the snickering greeting of their horses. Kilfannan smoothed Ellafey's neck and whispered, "I am taking thee back to thy master. Thou art a grand lady, to be sure."

Leading the horses through the passage, they stepped out into a cold light and stood on the verge. The fog had lifted, and a watery sun was shining, but Kilfannan saw storm clouds looming on the sea horizon. Sensing a touch of malignity in their blackness, he slipped into his saddle. "Storm will soon be upon us. Let us make haste to the Black Orchid and return Ellafey to her stable. If we meet no delay, we should be on the road north before the shadows of evening fall. 'Tis all clear," he said, looking along the road. "Let us ride!"

The brothers rode for a mile or two along the road and then galloped across the rugged hillsides and through meadows harbouring swelling streams to the greenway leading to the stables at the Black Orchid.

When they trotted into the stable yard, Arkle came out of the side door to greet them. "Well met!" he cried, taking Ellafey's bridle.

Kilfannan slipped from the saddle and, smoothing the mare's face, whispered soft words of thanks in her ear. "She is a fine mare, make no mistake. Tell me, Arkle, hath anyone come here asking questions?"

Arkle nodded and, staring at the emerald on Kilfannan's brow, said, "Trevelyan arrived just after yourselves had left. I told him you were attacked by goblins at the market and had taken refuge here. He was much relieved when he learned you had gone forth to Black Head to seek the wizard's counsel. He left this for you, sir." He handed him a small phial of colourless oil. "'Tis a bottle of orange blossom oil, and Trevelyan thought it may be a helpmeet on the road."

After taking the cork out, Kilfannan breathed in the fragrant flower scent and for an instant forgot the peril they were in. "Thanks be to thee," he said, corking the bottle and putting it in his pocket. He pressed a doubloon into Arkle's hand. "I insist."

"And many thanks to you, sir." Arkle's yellow eyes sparkled as he looked at the gold piece. "'Tis a while since meself hath seen a piece of sunken Spanish treasure from the mortal world. Good day to you."

"Mount up behind me, brother," Kilcannan cried. "Good afternoon to thee, Arkle."

CHAPTER 3

THE SPRIGGAN

At the end of the greenway Kilcannan slowed Finifar to a walk. "Brother," he said, looking east to their twin hillocks, "methinks we should each take a purse of gold doubloons, for we know not what expense may lie ahead."

Kilfannan nodded in agreement. "When words fail, gold has the power to open many a closed doorway."

When they got to the foot of his hill, Kilfannan slipped from Finifar's back. "Hurry to thy sheen, brother. We will take the tokens of our house and then lay a sleep of concealment upon our hills."

Kilfannan walked swiftly back up the humpbacked hill and down the steps into his sheen. The sight of his beloved Niamh's portrait hanging over the mantel filled his heart with grief. Imprisoned in the outer darkness the HeartStar, Niamh and Caiomhin could be discovered by demons at any time. He tried not to think about the plight of his creators. Sighing deeply, he smoothed back his hair. He was a spinner of the Green – a dreamer, not a warrior – but he was the head of his house, and the Green depended on him and Kilcannan for survival.

There was a dark wooden box on one of the shelves, and Kilfannan took it down. He opened the lid and took out a bulging bag of doubloons and a long, thin blade in a sheath. He fastened the blade and money bag to his belt, and then, filling his flask from the decanter of blackberry brandy on the sideboard, he took one final look around his hall. With a last glance at Niamh's portrait, he went back upstairs to the outside world.

Above the golden arched doorway was the winged emerald, the herald of the House of Air in the fourth dimension. Taking down the jewel, he turned to face east, the direction of air, and drawing in the power of the wind, he cast a spell of forgetfulness about his green hill so all who climbed it would remember only an elusive reverie of grass and wind.

His eyes roved over the flower-fragrant hillsides and beyond to heath and naked rocks. The meadows were alive with yellow cowslips and orchids pale against the vibrant green, and he wondered if he would ever gaze again upon their beauty in a future springtime. Turning away, he put a final blessing on his hill, causing a deep and heavy silence to fall over all.

Kilfannan put the winged emerald carefully in the inside pocket of his jerkin. He then mounted his horse and rode the short distance to Kilcannan's sheen.

Kilcannan took the low road across the meadow to his sheen. The afternoon was waning into evening, and a violet haze lay upon the land. He left Finifar to graze at the entrance and took the stairway to his halls. He went to an old oak chest at the back of his chamber, opened the lid, and looked inside. There were purses of gold, glittering buckles, jewelled stock pins, racing silks, and bridles. Digging deeper, he took out a short sword in an emerald-encrusted scabbard and strapped it round his waist. Then, after taking a purse, he crossed his hall and stood for a moment, gazing sadly at a portrait of Caiomhin that hung above the mantel. His creator's eyes had darkened, and there was a hint of terror in his lean and noble face.

Putting one hand on his heart and the other on his scabbard, Kilcannan swore a silent oath to free the HeartStar – or perish in the trying. After filling his flask with blackberry brandy, he put it in his pocket and went upstairs to the outside world. It saddened him to leave his beloved home, but he was impatient to follow the thief north and get on with the business at hand. Raising his hands, he cast a spell of sleep upon his sheen and a deep green mist to conceal the entrance to his hall. Hearing the sound of hoof beats, he turned and saw Kilfannan riding towards him on Red Moon.

"We'd best be getting on the road while daylight lasts," Kilfannan said as he rode up alongside.

"Aye," Kilcannan answered, taking down his winged emerald from above the entrance. When all was stowed away, they donned dark cloaks with hoods and took the greenway north to Lisdoonvarna. At the junction with the road, they pulled up.

The sense of impending doom had put Kilfannan in a fey mood, and he felt instructed or coerced, he did not know which, to look upon the Cathac, the serpent encased in stone in the Giant's Cliffs. "Brother," he said, "we have been driven from our sheens by the evil that encroacheth upon the Green, and with the entombment of our creators, the power of Under-Earth grows every day. I wish to look upon the Cathac, the enemy of love and destroyer of the Green, and his seat of evil in the Giant's Cliffs."

"The stone gates to Pandemonia! 'Tis an evil view!" Kilcannan answered, the colour draining from his face. "I have always avoided the cliffs, for I know what lies beneath in Under-Earth and have no will to look upon the hideous enemy of life that hungrily gazes at the sea. Nay, brother, we are all that remains of our house, and 'tis not wise to go that way."

Wrapping himself in fey-light, Kilfannan said in the language of the wind, "Brother! The Cathac is caught in time and space and encased in rock. He is blind to our realm, and the gates to Pandemonia are shut. I will look upon the image of the enemy and his kingdom, for 'twill harden my resolve for the task ahead."

"As thou wilt," Kilcannan answered, shaking his head.

41

The brothers jumped off and galloped westwards across the fields, breaks, and stone-clad banks towards the sea. Stopping on a high headland, they listened for a moment to the noisy, chattering sea birds on the stone ledges, and the ebb and flow of waves. Gulls were riding the air, and a dark purple sheen lay on the placid ocean. Kilfannan looked out across the sea and fancied he could see a golden haze and hear the faint rippling of harps from the blessed elven realm of Tir Na Nog. Yet the salt air held a threat and the breeze a brooding malice that cast a shadow of great fear upon his heart.

Movement beneath caught his eye, and staring at the foaming sea, he saw meresna sitting on the rocks, smoothing their long green hair with combs made of mortal finger bones. The sight of the sirens gave him an uncanny feeling, and an icy finger of portentous fear trembled down his back.

"Brother!" Kilcannan said as they looked out to sea. "I am braced by the wind and the quarrel of birds, and even though I am half paralysed with terror, what thou sayest is true. The Cathac is blind to our realm, so I will join thee and look upon the hidden menace in the haunted cliffs."

Joining their minds to fortify each other in the face of evil, the brothers rode on to Serpent Head and the tower of the guard, a lonely stone sentinel that stared with empty split-eyed windows at the sea. In ancient days, after the chaining of the Cathac, the giant Finn McCoul had built the tower to stand guard over the hideous features of the Cathac's image in the cliffs. Age after age, the vigil was maintained, until the threat of the horned serpent faded; the gates to Pandemonia became a myth, and the tower was slowly abandoned.

Let us take refuge in the tower and climb the stairs to a window that overlooks the cliffs, they thought, slipping from the saddle. *We can spy upon the image of the Cathac from there.*

Leaving the horses in the shadow of the tower, the brothers climbed the stone steps and found a long slit window that gave a view along the cliffs. On each towering headland were the sinister serpentine outline of the gates to Pandemonia and the hideous visages of the Cathac's allies, imprisoned in stone. Hardening their resolve and centring themselves in the HeartStar, they glanced at the titanic stone features of the Cathac staring out from the cliff face across the Western Sea. The dying sun glowed red upon the questing head and hateful hooded eyes.

In an instant, the shocking sculpture seemed to come alive. The eyes of the Cathac swivelled in their sockets and turned balefully upon them. A black tide of hate and loathing swamped their hearts, blasting their psyche with waves of desolate cosmic horror. For a moment reason lost its hold upon their minds and they shrank back against the wall of the tower, away from the horror that had caught them by the throat, choking them with hatred and revulsion. Violence battered at their very being, demanding entry, carrying with it thoughts of bloody conquest, cowled figures, pale knives, and hideous sacrifice – a brown world where only terror reigned.

They were suddenly seized by a diabolical summons and transfixed with atavistic fascination to gaze upon the Cathac once again. In panicked fright, they felt their feet automatically shuffle forward and their eyes rise upwards to the slit window.

In the turmoil of their being, they saw a faint green spark shine for a moment in the coiling miasma of the Cathac's hate, and with a supreme effort of will, they wrestled their minds away from the serpent's drawing spell. Catching one another's hands, they bolted in terror down the stairs and onto the turf outside.

Keeping their backs to the cliffs, they looked around for the horses.

Our charges have fled in terror, they thought. Despair swept over them, and a dark thought invaded their mind. They felt a compelling mental command to go to the edge of the cliffs and jump, shredding themselves on the jagged rocks below. For an instant they entertained the prompting and started forward to the cliff edge. The whinnying of horses broke the killing spell as Finifar and Red Moon galloped alongside them. The brothers leaped into their saddles, thundered

43

down the hillside to the road, and did not pause for rest until they reached the sand dunes at Fanore. Separating their minds, they looked out over the sea wall at the dark and lonely sea.

"The Cathac hath awoken in our realm of Faerie," Kilfannan said shakily. "'Twas indeed folly, brother, that I gainsaid thine advice to stay clear of the cliffs. For in my arrogance, I vastly underestimated the depth of evil that hath come upon us." He shuddered and then resumed. "We have felt the sting of the enemy, and even in his containment he casteth spells, images, and suggestions within our minds. When we fled, he cast a spell of death wish upon us, and if it had not been for the intervention of our horses, we both would have perished. Folly, thou sayest, brother. In truth thou art correct."

"I do not doubt thine intuition," Kilcannan answered. "We have been delivered, and 'tis my mind that we have received an understanding that will aid us. The Cathac's mind spell is strong and hath shown us to be ever watchful of our thinking. So chidest not thyself, dear brother, for forewarned is forearmed."

"Yet 'twas a desperate risk for the foolhardy to undertake," Kilfannan answered. "We must thank the stars that the binding spell the Old Ones put in place still holds." He sighed. "But for how much longer will the light endure against the darkness?"

Trotting along the coast road, Kilfannan began to feel more relaxed within the moment, and gazing at the sea, he noticed a strange asymmetry in the waves breaking on the shore. He sent his mind into space trying to sense what was creating the irregularity in the breakers, but whatever the cause, it was hidden from his awareness. Feeling no threat, he watched the waves and observed one was higher and stronger than the others in a sequence. Counting the waves, he found it was the ninth breaker that was different from the rest. Sensing portent, he commented to Kilcannan, "The ninth wave breaketh to beach much higher than the others."

Kilcannan watched the waves. "Sink me!" he cried in astonishment. "So'tis."

Noticing black gulls circling overhead, Kilfannan said urgently,

"Methinks we are being watched. Spies fly above us in the air. I sense they are marking our passage and will alert our enemies of our position on the road. I will take the up-breath into space and see what manner of spiritual evil rides the airwaves."

Kilcannan nodded. "I will take the down-breath into fire and see if hate is present."

Kilfannan had an eerie, apprehensive feeling as he sensed the ether. "Brother! We must hasten to Black Head. There is hidden menace on the airwaves, and 'tis not wise for us to tarry. See! The gulls are flying like black smoke inland to the Burren."

"Aye, and there is the distortion of malice in the fire field."

They were about to set off again when a sudden thrill of ineffable rapture rippled through Kilfannan, and his eyes were compelled back to the sea. "Wait!" he cried. "Hazard there may be, but I deem there is virtue on the ninth breaker. My intuition telleth me we should go and stand before the waves."

After dismounting, they climbed over a low stone wall that bordered the road and ran across the beach to the water's edge. As the ninth wave raced up the sand to greet them, a jenny wren flew up and landed on a small rock in front of them. The bird fluttered up and hovered for a moment in front of their faces before turning and flying out to sea.

The feeling of rapture surged over Kilfannan once again, and he saw an enthralling vision of a slender woman clothed in tapestries of shifting light floating on the foaming crest of the incoming ninth wave.

The brothers looked in awe upon the nebulous figure as it glided closer.

"I am Cliodna, queen of the sea," the waves said in the melodious language of ebb and flow. "I bid you warning. Take heed! An evil shadow stalks you on the road. I will leave you a gift to aid you on your way."

A cold wind blew in their faces, and they were suddenly aware of frothy water swirling round their ankles. Spellbound by the splendour of their vision, they looked along the beach and out to sea, but the dream had disappeared and there was nothing but the ebb and flow of water.

Seeing a fiery light blazing from the sand, Kilfannan bent down and saw a small oval mirror in a beryl frame. "See! 'Tis a looking glass," he said in wonder, picking it up. "And blessed with the power of sea and sand. A wondrous gift indeed!" Turning to the sea, he held up his hands and trilled a blessing to the kelp growing in the depths.

"Methinks 'tis a gift of protection," Kilcannan said.

Kilfannan nodded. "And meself thinks it will show its virtue soon enough. I thank thee, my lady; it does my heart good to know that we have the blessing of High Faerie to aid us." He put the mirror in the pocket of his jerkin and then followed Kilcannan back to the road.

Mounting their horses, they started along the narrow road beside the sea and soon saw the rocky karsts of the Burren looming before them. The road was twisty, and their view ahead was obscured by high rocky outcrops that sloped steeply to the ground. Rounding a bend, they saw rocks and small stones tumbling from the cliff onto the road.

"There is a rockslide up ahead," Kilcannan said in a low voice, bringing Finifar to a halt. "Even though 'twill not hinder our way forth, I do not like it."

"Nor I," Kilfannan answered, remembering Cliodna's warning. "Let us wait until the fall subsides."

A few long minutes passed, and then all seemed peaceful on the road. Still Kilfannan hesitated. The road was quiet – too quiet. "Where are the birds?" he asked in a hoarse whisper.

"They are hidden, brother. Feel ye not the veil of malice and oppression all around us?"

Kilfannan nodded in agreement. "We must heed Cliodna's warning. Ke-enaan's halls are not far along the road. Let us ride, for I feel ill things will happen if we tarry here."

As they rounded the outcrop, a shower of grit and small boulders fell into their path, and an enormous spriggan jumped down from a rocky ledge, blocking the road.

Kilfannan gasped at the sight of the red devil. The creature was troll shaped with long arms; thick, muscular legs; and tendons of appalling strength. His scaly hide was covered in patches of stiff yellow hairs, and an exulting hate shined from his red, baleful eyes. "I, Zarg, have been waiting for you," the spriggan roared. "News of your passage has been broadcast far and wide, and a princely sum has been placed upon your heads. I have a mind to collect the bounty for your heads and hearts and then dine upon your tender parts. It's been too long since I tasted gentry flesh." He hungrily licked his long brown fangs and, without warning, lunged forward, grasping for them with bloodstained talons of horrifying length and sharpness.

"Take Finifar!" Kilcannan shouted. Flinging the reins to Kilfannan and leaping from his horse's back, he drew his sword and charged, slashing and thrusting at the spriggan. "Clear the way, devil!" he shouted. "Away with thee!"

Giving a hollow, throaty laugh, the spriggan raised his spiked cudgel and, with a mighty sweep, swung it at Kilcannan's head. The blow missed him, but the energetic force around it knocked him off his feet.

Whinnying in fear, Red Moon baulked and shied away. Finifar pulled away from Kilfannan's grasp and, rearing up, struck at the spriggan with his front hooves, forcing the demon to retreat. Grabbing his fallen sword, Kilcannan got to his feet. Charging forward, he leapt over the spriggan's bulky frame and stabbed it from behind. With a howl, the demon whirled round and grasped him in his talons.

Having regained control of his horse, Kilfannan drew his knife, slipped from his horse's back, and went to aid his brother. The sun sailed from behind the clouds, and a thought wave washed over him – a command in the language of the sea to take out the mirror. Sunlight flashed upon the glass as he took it from his pocket, and sensing a hidden command to entrain the spriggan with the glass, he trained the sunlight into the monster's eyes. The glass lit up with radiant fire. Blinded by the blazing light, the spriggan dropped Kilcannan on the road and lurched forward, grasping for the mirror.

Kilfannan held the mirror steady as the spriggan crouched down in front of him and stared into the glass. Again he heard a command in the music of the sea. "Cast the mirror around the demon's neck and bind him in the spell of his reflection." Obeying the instruction, Kilfannan threw the chain over the demon's head, but the spriggan made no move. Holding the mirror in his claw, he gazed at his image.

Realising that Zarg was spellbound and hypnotised by his own reflection, Kilfannan shouted, "Zarg! Thou wilt obey me."

"Let me kill the vile creature!" Kilcannan said, struggling to his feet.

"No!" Kilfannan held up his hands in a gesture of denial. "He is docile; a spell is upon him. We will take his evil heart to Ke-enaan. He may use him as he wishes, and that will be punishment enough," he said with a grim laugh.

Kilcannan went over to Finifar and mussed his mane. "Thou art my friend indeed, to come to my aid," he whispered in his horse's ear. Finifar nuzzled his face and gave a quiet whinny.

"We can linger no longer. Other evil creatures may yet lurk amongst the rocks. We must hasten to Black Head," Kilfannan said, looking uneasily up at the craggy rocks. "I will lead the spriggan, and thou canst follow with the horses."

They started off along the road, and just as they rounded a bend, Kilcannan stopped. "Brother! Finifar hath an unsteady gait. Methinks he is lame." Swiftly bending down, Kilcannan examined his horse's hooves. "Faith!" cried he, glaring murderously at Zarg. "Finifar hath lost a shoe. I must go back and find it."

Seeing storm clouds gathering on the horizon, Kilfannan responded, "There is no time. The light is waning, and soon 'twill be gone, and there is a storm brewing out to sea. We must go on."

"Brother!" Kilcannan countered. "The shoe belongeth to our

house, and if found by one with evil in his heart, it could be used to lay a curse upon us."

Kilfannan nodded. "Return, then, but be swift. I will take the horses and the spriggan to the wizard's door."

Holding the spriggan by the chain and commanding the horses to follow, Kilfannan walked along the darkling, twisty, narrow road to Black Head.

* * *

The door in the rock face swung open as Kilfannan stopped before the wizard's door, and Ke-enaan stepped out onto the verge. Staring in horrified astonishment at the spriggan, he said, "Faith! How came thee by this brute?"

Kilfannan noted the shocked alarm in the wizard's voice and felt a subtle stirring of doubt around him in the air. "The spriggan knew of the bounty on our heads and ambushed us on the road. In the fight, Finifar lost a shoe, and now my brother looketh for it."

Ke-enaan's mouth set in a hard line. "'Tis fell news indeed! Any measure of energy from thine house left upon the road could bring thee ill. How far from my halls wert thou when the spriggan attacked?"

"'Twas a mile back, where the way is narrow."

"A mile," Ke-enaan muttered, shaking his head. "My power waneth, for there was a time when no fell thing could pass within five miles of my door." He stared at the mirror around the spriggan's neck. "I see 'tis the mirror of Cliodna that hath tamed him." Putting his hand in his robe, Ke-enaan brought out a phial of orange powder and blew the dust into the spriggan's eyes. "Zarg! I am your master now. At the back of my hall is a flight of steps leading to a pool," he said, taking the mirror from the spriggan's neck. "Go forth and cleanse thyself." Zarg hurried off.

"But come!" the wizard said, handing the mirror to Kilfannan. He took a violet-gold coin from his robe. "This is an offering for the faerie blacksmith Uall Mac Carn of Slieve Elva. Take the horses to the forge and leave them there. Place the charm in the wall of the furnace with a prayer of gratitude, and then return to my hall. At first light, your horses will be shod with enchanted shoes, and the virtue of violet and gold will be your shield from any evil spells cast with the missing shoe." He waved his hand and said, "Go now; the passageway to the forge is open."

Kilfannan stepped outside onto the verge and took the horses through the passage to the starstruck meadow. A blue light was glowing from the forge and leaving the horses to graze, he took the violet-gold piece Ke-enaan had given him and placed it into the wall at the side of the furnace. The horses had followed him to the forge, and as he turned to leave, he heard an electric crackle in the air and watched in wonder as a great swirling spiral of flame shot up from the cold fire of the forge and flowed around their hooves. The perfume of chamomile caught him, and before he could behold the magic of the shoeing, he found himself walking along the passageway to Ke-enaan's halls.

"Sit thee by the fireside" the wizard said as he entered. Seeing that Kilcannan had not yet returned, Kilfannan wondered what was keeping him, but feeling no stress upon his breath, he sat down at the fireside.

"We will take a little elixir while we wait for Kilcannan to return," Ke-enaan said, bringing the drinks and joining Kilfannan by the hearth. "Tell me of thy journey, for I sense a shade upon thine heart."

"After we left our sheens, we took the road to the Giant's Cliffs, and a fey mood came upon me. I desired to look upon the image of the enemy of old in the Giant's Cliffs. Even though my brother tried to persuade me otherwise, I would not be gainsaid." As Kilfannan told Ke-enaan what had transpired at the cliffs, he saw the wizard's face grow grave.

"What madness took thee," Ke-enaan said when he had finished. "Thou canst not withstand the evil of ages. The alignment of the stargate in the heavens hath empowered the serpent's will and awoken him in Faerie." He stared at Kilfannan. "And thou chosest to reveal thyself to him. The Cathac's arm hath grown long indeed if he can seduce thy mind and draw thee to him."

Kilfannan blushed emerald, and a hot glow came to his cheeks.

"Oft there is gold in darkness," he replied. "And though I do not excuse myself for folly, yet there is also wisdom to be found."

"If one survives," Ke-enaan said grimly. "Tell on."

"We fled in terror and did not rest until we reached the dunes at Fanore, and there we were loath to linger, for we felt evil was tracking us. I felt drawn by some inexplicable force to the singing of the waves, and forgetting all peril, we stood upon the beach and gazed out to sea," Kilfannan said, taking a goblet of elixir from the wizard. "Cliodna appeared to us on the ninth wave and left us a gift in the sand."

"Cliodna saw the peril you were in from afar, and risked her own essence to gift thee with the magic mirror," Ke-enaan responded. "In Faerie, her form doth not exist, as it once did, and the rising dark could easily have snatched her."

Sending a prayer of loving thanks to Cliodna on the airwaves, Kilfannan asked, "What dost thou know of her?"

"Cliodna was the daughter of Poseid, ruler of the sea. Beautiful beyond hope she was, surpassing the fairest of flowers in the meadow. Manannan Mac Lir, the Son of the Sea, desired her, but Cliodna scorned him, choosing instead Prince Donne of the Dunes to be her consort. Consumed with rage and jealousy, Manannan set a trap for her as she walked upon the waves. Rising from the deep in serpent form, he tried to snatch her and take her to his city in Under-Sea. Great was the battle between them, lasting many hours, and when Cliodna could fight him off no longer, she turned the blade upon herself." He sighed deeply. "She was a grievous loss to us. For during the War of Separation, she would send her birds to warn us whenever the Cathac left the cliffs."

At the mention of Manannan, the Son of the Sea, Kilfannan felt a sense of foreboding. Manannan was a mighty sorcerer, master of wind and wave – a lusting serpent that fed on human flesh and could take the likeness of a man.

"'Tis said in Faerie lore that as the darkness rises, Manannan will come forth from the red bog of Magh Cuilen," he said. "And take up his abode in his deserted city in Under-Sea."

Ke-enaan's face grew grave. "Indeed! 'Tis my thought that Manannan will come forth, and as yet we do not have the power to stop him." He put his hand supportively on Kilfannan's shoulder. "'Tis easy to despair in what might or might not be, but thou must keep thy mind centred in the Green, lest fear render thee useless for the task thou must embark on."

"I am in fear," Kilfannan admitted. "For the Cathac hath awakened, and the sight of his hateful visage is stamped with terror upon my mind."

"Thou must bridle thy fear, for 'tis the weapon and servant of the enemy."

Silence fell upon the hall; the shadows grew long, and Ke-enaan lit the candelabra. After refilling their goblets with elixir, he handed one to Kilfannan.

Sipping on his drink, Kilfannan wondered where his brother was, and he grew anxious in the waiting. He was suddenly aware of a sense of suffocation. Rising in alarm, he cried, "Evil hath befallen Kilcannan, for my breath is laboured. I must go and find him." Putting his goblet on the table, he moved swiftly towards the door.

"Wait! I will come with thee!" Picking up his staff, the wizard followed Kilfannan through the door and into the darkness. A shrilling wind blew along the rainswept road as they stepped onto the verge, and a pelt of stinging raindrops hit them in the face. Kilfannan felt Ke-enaan take his hand, and breaking into a run above the surface of the road, they raced into the darkness.

CHAPTER 4

TREACHERY AND FLIGHT

The light was failing fast, and a cold, wet wind was blowing from the sea as Kilcannan walked back around the bend to seek the missing shoe. In the gloom ahead, he saw a mortal cycling towards him. The man stopped, and Kilcannan saw him pick something from the road and put it in the pocket of his raincoat. The man then got back on his bicycle and started pedalling towards him. As he approached, Kilcannan saw the mortal's sunken eyes were sneeringly fixed upon him as he deliberately rode through his faerie form.

Kilcannan shuddered as the hateful, chilling energy of Lower Faeric swept through him, and he closed his inner eye against the bestial visions that it brought. Realising the mortal was evil with goblin sight, he anxiously ran forward to where the spriggan had attacked them, desperately searching the road and verges for the horseshoe. An ugly chill ran down his neck as he realised the man had found the shoe. The fearful revelation paralysed him for a moment, and in a panic, he hastened back along the road towards the wizard's hall.

Rounding a bend, an appalling stench of carrion and corruption flooded his nostrils, and he heard the sound of scrabbling claws and the hiss of stones falling on the road. The way ahead was still hidden from his view, and drawing his sword, he stealthily moved forward and turned the corner.

Crouching in the road was a brocshee, a devil badger, flexing its huge, white-ridged, spiny body, its flat black head thrust forward, and its lidless, glowing eyes shining with rage and malice.

Kilcannan stared in horrified amazement at the loathsome creature. The brocshee was a fearsome denizen of Under-Earth and had not been seen in Faerie since the War of Separation. He wondered how the demon had gained access to his world, and he desperately tried to recall what legend told about the demon badger. They were fast, with unnatural speed for such bulk, he remembered, and their horn and long spines were tipped with a slow-acting numbing poison which immobilised their prey. Only the underbelly was spine free and the weak point in their armour.

"Kilfenoran sylph spawn," the brocshee growled, whipping its long, spiny tail towards him. "There is a prize upon your foul head and heart, and I wants it."

The brocshee had blocked the road. Looking wildly around for a means of escape, Kilcannan saw he was hemmed in by cliffs on one side and the sea wall on the other.

Drawing his sword in bravado, he shouted. "Clear the way, devil's spawn."

"Your head and heart are mine!" the brocshee roared, and lowering the horn atop its scaly head, it charged towards him.

Caught by the swiftness of the attack, Kilcannan tried to leap aside, but he wasn't quick enough, and the brocshee's horn stabbed him in the knee, ripping through the tissue in his thigh. A throbbing pain shot through his body, but anger was uppermost. Holding his sword with both hands, he turned to face his charging foe. Using his sword's point as a pivot, Kilcannan spun around, and as the brocshee rushed towards him, he threw himself up and over its body. His injured leg gave way as he landed on the road, and he fell backwards. Hearing the brocshee snorting and scuffing the ground for the final charge, he knew this was his last chance to escape, and he tried to struggle to his feet. His legs were like jelly, and he found he couldn't stand. In desperation, he took the down-breath and created a roaring air current on the road. He took the horizontal wind and shot underneath the brocshee's body. Holding his sword with both hands, he stabbed upwards through the slimy, crepitating flesh.

With a venomous hiss, the brocshee dropped its weight upon him, trying to crush him. Gasping for air, Kilcannan twisted the hilt of his sword, and as the blade cut through the brocshee's heart, the hideous body contracted in a spasm and then lay still.

Suffocating from the stench and crushing weight, Kilcannan crawled out from the brocshee's foulness. His breath was weak, and the wind beneath his feet slowly petered out. After staggering up, he stumbled along the road towards Black Head.

The wind had picked up, and the driving rain battered at his face as he struggled forward. The pain in his leg was growing, and a numbing sensation crept throughout his body. His vision clouded, and giddying nausea swept through him. His head spun, and his good leg felt like rubber as he staggered forward against the howling wind. Limestone cliffs loomed ahead of him, and the blear grey rocks seemed to pile themselves up into ghostly, monstrous shapes shuffling forward to the road. Shadowy monsters reached for him with groping claws, threatening to snatch him away into Lower Faerie and through the forbidden gateway into the dark labyrinths of Under-Earth. Sweat poured from his brow, and with a gasp, he fell forward.

* * *

Ke-enaan and Kilfannan left Black Head and started along the road to Fanore. The rain came down in torrents, and waves whipped up by the frenzy of the wind crashed against the beach in torment, throwing blinding sheets of sea foam into their faces.

"'Tis a spell storm," Ke-enaan muttered, holding up his staff, and Kilfannan saw a jet of light pierce the gloom. Up ahead in the road was a dark shape, and as he made way against the wind, he saw the shape was a body. Settling on the road, he ran forward. "'Tis Kilcannan!" he cried in anguish, smoothing his brother's cheek. "He is injured. There is blood upon his leg; his skin is cold and stained with purple."

Ke-enaan put his hand on Kilcannan's heart and traced the outline of an octahedron on his forehead. "A spell of poison is upon him, and 'tis working to his heart." Gathering the wounded sylph into his arms, he said to Kilfannan, "Let us take the wind back to my hall, for Kilcannan's strength wanes and the poison grows. I have sent mental instruction to Zarg to be ready at the door."

Strengthened with Ke-enaan's power, Kilfannan took the up-breath and, weaving the wind into rotation, took them in a spiralling vortex to Black Head.

* * *

Zarg was waiting at the door when they settled on the verge. "Bring water, cloth, the phial of red liquid, and a jar of brown unguent from the shelf," Ke-enaan ordered while carrying Kilcannan inside. "Make haste!"

Ke-enaan lay Kilcannan gently down on the rush floor beside the fire, took off the sylph's breeches, and examined the wound. There was a deep and livid gash on his leg that stretched from his thigh down to his knee.

"'Tis a poison indeed," Kilfannan said. "I can feel the taint of Under-Earth in my veins." Laying his hand on his brother's heart, he sang soft words, calling him with the fragrant breath of flowers, but to no avail. Kilcannan made no move and lay still and sweat-drenched.

Zarg came forward to the hearth with a tray, gave it to the wizard, and then stepped back into the shadows.

Making passes with his hands over Kilcannan's heart and throat, the wizard said, "Slowly tip the phial of liquid into thy brother's mouth while I cleanse the wound."

Kilcannan offered no resistance as he administered the liquid, and when he was finished, he watched Ke-enaan pack the injury with brown unction from the jar. Picking up Kilcannan's soiled breeches, the wizard instructed Zarg to wash and mend his garments.

"What doth the red potion do?" Kilfannan asked, putting the empty phial on the tray.

"'The bloodroot will ease his pain, for it is potent with the red power of the earth, the opposite of Green, and the contrary forces will neutralise the poison in his blood."

A few anxious moments passed, and then Kilfannan saw the sickly violet taint begin to fade from Kilcannan's face, and an emerald blush returned. Kilcannan opened his eyes and looked at them with dazed confusion.

"Brother!" he gasped. "A brocshee from Under-Earth attacked me."

"A brocshee!" Kilfannan repeated in horror. "'Tis an evil myth in Faerie and hath not walked our reality since the time of the Separation. How can this be?" Glancing at Ke-enaan, he saw the wizard was grey and great age was upon him.

"Only with a sabbat, a mortal blood rite, can the portal be opened between Lower Faerie and Under-Earth," Ke-enaan responded. "I deem wicked men have conspired with Zugalfar to breach the spell of holding cast at the time of Separation. He is releasing monsters to hunt down the House of Air."

Kilfannan glanced uneasily at his brother as a heavy silence fell upon the hall, and in the flickering candlelight, Kilfannan felt the hand of dread upon him.

"The spriggan had prior knowledge of thy passage on the road," Ke-enaan said. "Let us plumb his memory and read its past, and in the finding we will see what we may."

The wizard went to a shelf and took down a bottle of blue liquid. He pulled out the stopper and poured a little of the viscous liquid into two small silver goblets. "The elixir will lower our frequency and give us access to the spriggan's memory," he said, handing the potion to Kilfannan. "I will cast a protective field around us so we will not be harmed by the foul visions we will see," he said, drawing four circles in the air with his hand. "Zarg! Come stand before us." The spriggan shuffled from the shadows and stood before Ke-enaan with his head bowed.

The four circles spiralled around Kilfannan as he drank the bitter draught, enveloping him in an eight-sided geometric that swirled with bands of outer-spectrum colours. Ke-enaan tilted up the spriggan's chin, and as Kilfannan looked into the spriggan's vacant eyes, he felt a chill wind course through his body and shivered with disgust as the vibrations of Under-Earth became visible. Tainted colours and a rotting stench flowed around him, and he saw a filthy, dripping cave in the honeycombs underneath the Burren. Slimy stalactites hung like jagged teeth from the porous ceiling, the walls were covered in gore, and the floor was littered with bones and the remains of elves, cluricauns, and horses. A round rotting lump with human hair lay in the muck against the wall.

The cavern began to glow with a pale acid-yellow glare, and in the devil light, he saw a thin, grey-cloaked figure riding a brocshee emerging from a tunnel into the cave. Throwing back its hood, the knocker glared around the cavern with triumphant eyes.

Kilfannan stiffened, and a wind blew up around him. 'Twas the knocker Aeguz – the one he had bested at the market. From under his mildewed cloak, Aeguz pulled forth a screaming mortal child. Holding it by the scruff, he waved it in the air.

"In a while, gentry scum will be riding on the road from Fanore to Black Head," he heard Aeguz croak. "Me spies in the sky have been tracking them." The knocker glided from the brocshee's back and threw the terrified, whimpering child into the muck upon the floor. "An hors d'oeuvre!" he crooned. "A sample of the gifts I will bring thee for thy service."

The words reverberated through Kilfannan's being, and he watched in abject horror as the spriggan greedily seized the screaming, squirming child and bit off a leg and then a hand.

"Bring me the heads and hearts of the foul House of Air, and I will bring thee many squirming, tender morsels for thou to dine on," he heard the knocker hiss above the screams.

Kilfannan's mind shuddered and shrank back as he confronted the unspeakable and appalling truth – the reward for the heads and hearts of the House of Air was the flesh and blood of mortal children. He heard Ke-enaan's voice telling Zarg to leave. The visions ceased, and slowly the geometric faded.

Ke-enaan brought a jug and three goblets to the table. "The knocker knoweth that as the darkness rises, the power within me fades. And with sorcery and the blood of innocent mortals, he hath summoned the denizens of Under-Earth into Lower Faerie." He passed his long fingers across his brow. "These are the darkest of days, to be sure." He poured the elixir, and Kilfannan took a goblet to his brother. "How fare thee?"

"The pain hath gone, and there is naught to see but a thin green line," Kilcannan answered, flexing his injured leg. He got to his feet and sipped his drink. "Thanks to thee," he said to Ke-enaan with a respectful nod of his head. "When I returned to look for Finifar's missing shoe, a mortal on a bicycle rode through me. His eye was evil with goblin sight, and methinks he found the horseshoe."

"In truth! Kilfannan told me of the lost shoe, and I have taken steps to mediate the evil," Ke-enaan said. "Zarg!" he called. There was the sound of padding footsteps, and the spriggan shuffled into the room. "Bring more elixir."

Kilcannan quivered with hostility when he spied the spriggan, but so absurd and pitiful did he look that his anger swiftly faded into laughter. "Brother! Think not that himself looks pretty in that long brown robe?"

Kilfannan flashed his eyes. "Ugly though he is, his docility and his garb are charming, and quite tolerable; now the monstrous stench hath gone, and I can breathe a little deeper."

Zarg put the elixir upon the table and then disappeared into the shadows, awaiting further orders.

Ke-enaan handed round the drinks and then sat beside the brothers in the flickering candlelight. "You must rest here tonight, for evil will stalk you in the darkness. On the morrow, with the rising of the sun, you can take the road north to Binn Breac."

Kilfannan was restless. The horror of the last few hours had drained his energy. Already weakened by the elf bolt, and needing to re-energise for the dangerous journey north, he felt an overwhelming desire to find music in the mortal world. Turning to Kilcannan, he said, "'Tis Saturday in the mortal world, and tonight there will be merry music in the inn at the Harbour of the Bell. I have great need of the sustenance of the Green."

"I too am in need of song to spin into the magic of the Green," Kilcannan answered. "What sayest thou, Kilfannan – shall we go?"

"The road and meadows are not safe," Ke-enaan cautioned. "Remember, all the knockers in Ireland, their maggs, denizens of Under-Earth, Lower Faerie, and mortal spies will be searching for ye. 'Twould be prudent to stay here."

'Twill be safe enough, Kilfannan thought, *if we are chary and stay off the road.* He rubbed his hands together wearily. His life force was low, and he needed to replenish it. "The inn is just a couple of miles across the meadow, and I feel 'twill be safe enough – safer than the leagues that lie before us," Kilfannan argued. He knew it wasn't safe, but he longed for music, cream, and the merriment of his old life, and he would not be gainsaid.

Ke-enaan stared at the brothers in dismay. "'Tis not safe for you to be abroad in the shadow of night. The land swarms with evil, and foul creatures will be tracking you."

"We will take care and move with caution," they said in one voice, "but we need energy for the long road ahead of us, and this may be our only chance. For us, 'tis a trip of spiritual necessity."

"The Green can be spun by night sounds and the ebb and flow of waves upon the shingle," Ke-enaan countered.

Knowing he was being reprimanded, and rightfully so, Kilfannan blushed emerald, and his face grew hot.

"Seeing as you cannot be swayed," the wizard said, "as you will then. Take the footpath path across the rock-bound hills to the fields below. Come! Stand before me."

Ke-enaan sang a pure bell-like tone and, with a sweeping motion of his hands, cast a shimmering light about them. "No spy of the enemy can see you leave my hall, for I have bent light around thee, but once you leave the Burren and descend to the fields below, the light shield will diminish."

Ke-enaan opened the door. "May the stars protect you," he said as they stepped outside into the darkness.

Kilfannan turned to face the ocean and listened to the waves breaking on the shore. The tide was turning, and he could hear the hiss of gravel under drag. A yellow moon, glaring fitfully down upon the sea, gave him a feeling of foreboding, and for a moment he had second thoughts about going to the inn.

"What ails thee, brother?" Kilcannan asked.

"'Twas a fit of melancholy, but 'tis gone," Kilfannan said. "I am in the mood for fun and frolic."

They climbed the limestone escarpment to the Burren and, taking the sleeping breath of flowers, gazed up at the star-specked sky.

Above them, Kilfannan saw the brilliant starlit outline of a pentagon glowing with supernal radiance, blazing free above the vapours of the worlds. "The prophecy hath come to pass," he said to Kilcannan. "Behold the stargate blazing from the sky; 'tis the harbinger of doom and the herald of sorrows."

They crossed the shadowed pavements, and a fitful moon marked their passage across the rocky hillside to the stonewalled fields beyond. Knowing they were no longer under Ke-enaan's protection, they stopped and listened for any noises on the night air.

An owl hooted, and they heard the sound of whirring wings in the darkness. "Night birds are flying," Kilfannan said uneasily. "We must make haste, for they may mark our presence and whisper evil to the wind."

There was a stone wall opposite the inn, and here they halted.

Kilcannan peered over the wall and looked both ways along the empty road. "'Tis all clear, brother," he said, waving his fingers in anticipation of the merry night to come. After slipping like shadows over the wall, they crossed the road to the pub.

The Four-Leafed Clover was a long, low two-storeyed building. The walls were painted yellow, and warm light was streaming from the windows. Inside they could hear the sounds of laughter, sweet music, and voices raised in song. "Come, brother!" Kilfannan said, eagerly twitching his fingers. "Let us look for some cream and cheese in the mortal world, and then spin the Green and lift our spirits in the leaf of bramble and the sleeping summer grasses in the meadows."

The singers and musicians took a break as the pair entered the pub, and in the interlude, Kilfannan looked around the faerie version of the inn. The room had a low ceiling of great dark beams ornamented with horse brass and hanging antique lanterns that shed a soft green light upon the old oak chairs and tables. From the beams hung bundles of fresh hops, and on the shelves behind the counter were mugs, goblets, and tankards of all sizes. The bar was full of trooping elves in their silver liveries and gold brocade, laughing, talking, and reliving the goblin fight.

Kilfannan saw the captain sitting by the fire with a mug of ale in his hand. "Kilcannan!" he said excitedly. "There is the elf captain of the troop that saved me at the market. Come, brother! Let us visit him."

They pushed their way through the jubilant troopers to the hearth where the captain was sitting. "Well met! I am Kilfannan of the House of Kilfenoran and am in thy debt."

"'Tis good to see you well!" the elf captain replied. "'Twas me wish indeed that we should meet again in more convivial times. I am Taeron, of the House of Taera, at your service." He smiled, and his copper-coloured eyes glittered red in the firelight.

"I say to thee, many thanks for coming to my brother's aid," Kilcannan said, nodding his head in gratitude. "Things would have gone ill, hadst thou not intervened."

"I was buying a filly at the horse sales for the hurley when me sergeant told me the filth from the mines was attacking a member of the gentry. 'Twas good fortune we arrived in time to thwart their murderous plan."

"Good sir, let us wrestle our way through thy troopers to the bar, and I will buy thee a tankard of beer and dish of cream," Kilfannan offered.

The three of them pushed their way through the noisy crowd to the counter.

"Landlord! A refill for my friend," Kilfannan said, putting the tankard on the counter. "Two blackberry brandies, two saucers of cream, and a slice of cheese for my brother."

The landlord put their order on the counter. "Would you like to try an invention from the mortal world?" he asked, and with a flourish he offered them plastic straws. "For the cream, sir."

"Faith!" Kilfannan grinned. Feigning horror, he waved the straw away and whipped out his spoon. "'Twill be a sorry day in Faerie when I resort to the likes of that!" He dipped his spoon into the cream. "This is good! Very fresh indeed," he trilled.

The innkeeper laughed. "The landlord in the otherworld has a cow, so I help meself," he said impishly. "That's the grand thing about having mortals about the place; there's always a plentiful supply of cream and cheese for us faerie folk to sup on!"

"Tell me, Kilfannan," Taeron said, sipping on his tankard of beer. "If I may be so bold, what caused the fracas with the goblins at the market?"

Looking round the bar for a place they could talk and not be overheard, Kilfannan spotted an empty table in an alcove. "Let us go yonder, where 'tis more private," he said, leading the way to the table.

"Grad had robbery on his mind when he waylaid me at the market," Kilfannan said once they were seated. "But his mind changed to murder when his knocker heard my name. The knocker was out to kill me and gloated there was a price upon my head. The foul creature was wearing an emerald from our House of Air as a badge of office around his scrawny neck. I hit him with a sylph bolt and ripped it from his throat. 'Twas the emerald that thou foundest and had the grace to return to my brother."

Taeron's mouth hardened. "A knocker with an emerald! What infernal sorcery is this?"

"'Tis a conspiracy of hate – an evil plan long in the making to destroy the House of Air," Kilfannan replied. "Niamh and Caiomhin have been imprisoned in the outer darkness, and we have left our fair green hills. We lodge this night at the halls of Ke-enaan of Black Head, and on the morrow we travel north to the village of Lake Carn on a quest to free them."

"Faith! This is ill news indeed!" Taeron responded, and Kilfannan sensed an aura of terror around the elf. "If the House of Air fails, 'twill not be long before the House of Fire will succumb to darkness, and then our fair isle in the sea will wither, and the music fade, for 'tis true our fates are interwoven in the Green."

Kilcannan stirred in his chair. "Be vigilant of the road and dark spaces," he said. "Darkness creeps into Lower Faerie from Under-Earth, and fell creatures not seen since the War of Separation roam free upon the land. We were attacked by a spriggan, and later a brocshee attacked me upon the road."

"By the stars!" The elf's eyes took on a fiery hue.

"Take warning, my friend," Kilfannan said grimly. "Through Ke-enaan's magic we plumbed the spriggan's memory and saw the remains of thine eleven kin in his filthy hole."

Taeron stared in horrified shock at Kilfannan. "Faith!" he cried out, the light of vengeance flaring from his eyes. "Members of me troop have disappeared in days of late. They will be avenged a hundred times their measure." He leant closer and said in a whisper, "'Tis rumoured in the living Earth that the enemy of old is waking in the Giant's Cliffs."

Kilfannan met Taeron's eyes, and a heavy silence fell, for in the glance was stark confirmation that the rumour he had heard was true.

"My brother and myself have looked upon the face of the Cathac in the cliffs," Kilfannan said after a while. "'Tis true what the earth rumours. The enemy came alive under our gaze and turned its hateful eyes upon us."

Taeron paled and drained his mug. Holding out his hand, he grasped Kilfannan's fingers. "The way to Lake Carn is long, lonely, and fraught with danger," he said earnestly. "Me troop will scout the road and byways north and destroy any beast that walks in evil."

"There is hope while the Green lives," Kilfannan answered. "And every hand and heart is succour to our quest."

Hearing the musicians strike up a merry jig, Kilfannan said, "Forgive me! I must away to spin the Green and rejuvenate myself for the journey north."

Taeron nodded, smiling. "Perchance we will meet upon the road."

Kilfannan nodded. "'Twould indeed be a merry meet."

"Hail! Kilfannan," a voice said. Looking round, he saw his nephew Cor-cannan of the down-breath from the House of An Carn.

"Well met!"

"Hast thou come to spin the Green?" Cor-cannan asked.

"Indeed! May I buy thee a drink?"

"Nay! I am with my mortal friend," Cor-cannan said, getting onto a stool beside an old man. "He hath been keeping me in cheese and brandy since I arrived. He is a fine musician and can play the coins on the bar with one hand and the spoons on his knees in t'other."

The mortal turned his head and smiled at Kilfannan. "My name is Martin," he said. "Pleased to meet you."

"I am Kilfannan of the House of Kilfenoran. Well met, faerie friend."

"I live next door and have very good cream," he said, and winking his eye, he turned back to the counter.

The Kilfenorans took their drinks to where the musicians were playing. Kilfannan sat at the feet of a young girl playing a violin. The night was merry, and they spun the Green to the wild flowers and grasses growing on the Burren. His heart dissolved into joy, and time and space were swept away in rapture.

Halfway through the evening, the musicians took another break and went up to the bar for drinks. Kilfannan looked around the faerie bar. Seeing Rickoreen sitting at the counter, he went over to him. "Greetings, Rickoreen," he said, getting on a stool beside him.

"Kilfannan. Well met!" he cried, swaying forward and spilling wine on his faded pantaloons. Looking at the cut on Kilfannan's mouth, he said, "Meself overheard a conversation amongst the elves that yourself was attacked by goblins after you left the inn this afternoon."

Kilfannan nodded. "'Tis true! I was assailed by the rabble from the mines, and 'twas the elves that aided me."

"The troopers said 'twas Grad that attacked you. 'Tis ill when carrion eaters from the mines attack the House of Air." Kilfannan saw a flame flicker in the cluricaun's rheumy eye. Rickoreen straightened his back, and his demeanour took on an air of unwonted dignity. In his tone Kilfannan felt presage, and a chill thrill of expectation raced through him.

"What can I be getting for you, sir?" the landlord asked.

"A blackberry brandy and a glass of wine for my friend," Kilfannan answered, putting a guinea on the counter.

"This afternoon," Rickoreen said, "meself went back to me master's house to turn the wine barrels in the cellar." He drained his glass and wobbled precariously forward on his stool. Reaching out, Kilfannan gently supported him until he found his balance. "There was a shoot on the estate, and the master's hoity-toity friends were killing birds." Here he belched, giving Kilfannan his empty glass.

The landlord put fresh drinks on the counter. "Anyways, as I was saying," Rickoreen said, grabbing a fresh glass of wine and taking a swig. "After turning the barrels, I came upstairs from the wine cellar, and seeing a carafe of red wine on the sideboard, I decided to help meself. The master was sitting at the table with the English magistrate and a guarda. They were drinking brandy and smoking cigars, talking about a ceremony that was taking place in England at Bealltainn. I don't, as a rule, bother much with mortal talk, but earlier I had frightened one of the maids, and the master threatened to curse me with dark taking. Wanting to keep informed of his intentions towards meself, I stopped by the table and listened to their conversation. The master was tittering about how they had sacrificed a man, slit his throat, and hung him on a hook to drain his blood." Rickoreen gulped down the rest of the wine. "The master said the man was a human sacrifice and that now everything was in place for the conjuring."

Kilfannan shuddered. "Human sacrifice! What dost thou know of this?"

"Meself doesn't know." Rickoreen shook his head, and his purple nose shook with him. "The master is a cruel man – to be sure he is." He swayed in his seat. "The guarda told the master that there was a theft. The cleaning woman who found the man said a wee coach and a silver mare were taken from his premises." He sniffed. "And that's what meself is getting round to."

Kilfannan gulped his brandy down in one. He realised Rickoreen was talking about the craftsman who had fashioned the mortal coach. He had to ply the cluricaun with enough wine to keep him talking but not enough to render him senseless. "Go on with thy news," he said, signalling the landlord for another drink.

"A few days past, meself was sitting in the Black Orchid, and I happened to gaze out of the window at the street," Rickoreen said. "I saw Grad the goblin chief with a mortal, and wondering what the scum was up to, I watched them take a wee coach into the antique shop across the road. Meself is wondering if 'twas the same coach that was stolen from the mortal's workshop."

Kilfannan's heart skipped a beat. "A few days past, thou sayest?"

Rickoreen rubbed his brow with a dirty lace handkerchief. "Meself don't rightly remember one day from t'other most of the time," he said foggily.

Using the musicians as an excuse to leave the counter, Kilfannan said, "Thank thou, Rickoreen. The band in the mortal world is making ready to play again, and I am anxious to spin the Green."

"Good day to you." He scratched his head. "Or is it good night!"

Kilfannan looked around the bar for Kilcannan and saw him talking to elves by the fireside. Catching his eye, he beckoned him over.

"Brother!" Kilfannan said, "Rickoreen hath told me much. The craftsman that made the coach for our high House hath been murdered. He was a human sacrifice. And there is more. The coach was sold to the antique shop across the road from the Black Orchid. It might still be there." He thought for a moment. "'Tis Sunday on the morrow, and the shop will be closed. Let us hasten to Black Head and take the wizard's counsel."

Sensing a hostile frequency on the airwaves, Kilfannan glanced around the mortal bar and saw a seedy-looking man with bloodshot eyes and thinning, straggly hair standing by the door. "Brother! Standing yonder by the door is a mortal," he said in a low voice. "He watcheth us, and his eye is evil with goblin sight. A rotter he is, to be sure."

Kilcannan shuffled round and glanced across the room at the ruffian and stiffened. "'Tis the oaf that rode his bicycle through me on the road; I can feel his evil taint," he said angrily, putting his hand on his sword sheath. Kilfannan saw his brother's eyes flash with fire and knew his rage was growing stronger for the want of vent. Feeling an overwhelming compulsion to get clear of the pub, he said, "We must leave. I fear we will be in danger if we tarry here."

"Brother! Let us attack the mortal and take back Finifar's shoe."

Kilfannan shook his head, and after draining his drink, he put the glass on the counter. "Nay! Ke-enaan hath assured us that the shoe can do us little harm. Drink up, and let us leave. The man is spying for the enemy," he said, glancing in the mortal's direction. An ugly thrill ran down his neck. The man had disappeared. "The spy hath gone! We must leave now," he said to Kilcannan. "Perhaps 'twould be better not to return to Black Head the way we came, for evil night birds may have tracked our passage across the meadows to the inn."

Looking round for Cor-cannan, Kilfannan saw him sitting with a party of fear deargs. "Brother," he whispered. "Bring Cor-cannan hither. 'Tis not safe for him to take the road back to his hall alone."

Kilfannan was waiting at the entrance when Kilcannan returned with Cor-cannan by his side. "Nephew," Kilfannan said, "we are in trouble. Our House of Air is under siege." Seeing the dumbfounded look in Cor-cannan's eyes, he added, "There is no time for explanations. A mortal was spying on us in the bar, and he hath slipped away. Misfortune will soon find us if we tarry here. We must stay together, for there is strength in number, and hasten to Ke-enaan's halls."

Opening the door, he peered into the shadows and sniffed the air. "There is the taint of goblin foulness on the airwaves. 'Tis as I feared; we have been betrayed."

"We cannot take the road to Ballyvaughan. It will be watched," Kilcannan said, looking up and down the road. "Say, rather take the lane that leads past the abbey and cut across the fields further on."

The treacherous moon sailed out from behind a cloud, casting a fitful glare upon the road as they stepped out into the night. Kilfannan stiffened. A ghastly grey knocker light was flowing onto the road from the lane leading to the abbey. A cold tingle of fear ran down his back as he watched the evil light grow stronger.

"Evil stalks us," he hissed. "There is a foul issue from the lane. We cannot go that way; we have to take the meadows to the Burren."

Shadows were moving in the darkness by the wall, and suddenly the air came alive with the foul voices of goblins. More harsh cries and oaths sounded, and looking up and down the road, Kilfannan saw they were cut off in each direction. "We are surrounded!" he said grimly.

Drawing their weapons, the sylphs stood back to back. The leering goblin horde closed in around them, fingering their daggers and licking their fangs in gleeful anticipation.

CHAPTER 5

THE GIFTING

A snaking vapour glided towards Kilfannan, and out of the gloom a long, grey hooded shape flew towards him. The knocker's eyes gleamed with pent-up viciousness as he fluttered his mouldering robes and stood before him. "We could kill thee now," he hissed malevolently, glaring into Kilfannan's eyes. "But" – he passed his split tongue caressingly over his needle-like teeth – "that would be too quick and too easy an end for filth like you." He shook with hollow laughter.

Kilfannan's hand was on his knife, and he slowly drew it out.

"Aeguz is waiting for thee in his cavern," the knocker crooned. "He will slowly slice and dice thy tender flesh until only thy filthy hearts and heads are left. Meself will dine upon thine eyes, and thy blood will feed a brood of little monsters to hunt down thy filthy kin." He lunged at Kilfannan with his long, sharp claws. Quickly sidestepping, Kilfannan avoided the knocker's charge. Spinning round, he saw the fiend had taken to the air and was hurtling towards him. As he thrust upward with his knife, he saw his brother wield his sword and chop off the knocker's head. The mouldy robes and bony body hit Kilfannan in the face, and he retched at the dry rot of corruption.

Cursing and snarling, the goblins grew closer, and another knocker sailed over their heads, weaving the airwaves into a web with his skeletal fingers. "He is casting a spell-net about us," Kilcannan cried, slashing at the filmy strands.

We are lost, Kilfannan thought, and for a moment he realised that it was his own wilfulness that had led him to flout Ke-enaan's warning. Taking the up-breath, he threw his knife at the knocker, felling him to the ground.

"Take this!" Cor-cannan hissed, giving Kilfannan a boot blade.

The ground shook with thundering hooves and the angry neighing of horses. Shining knights with tall plumes upon their helmets and wild eyes came jumping over the wall and into the road, thrusting at the goblins with long lances. More knights appeared, and the shrieking goblins ran in every direction, looking for escape, but the ghostly riders hemmed them in.

Seeing a chance for escape, Kilfannan shouted, "Let us fly!"

In the confusion, the sylphs made their escape over the wall and across the meadows to the rocky pavements of the Burren. Here they stopped and rested, still shaken by their terrible ordeal. A twig cracked in the darkness, and fearing the worst, they drew their weapons. They heard the rustling of robes, and a tall, dark shape appeared in the gloom. Dodging behind a rock, Kilfannan closed his fingers around the handle of his knife, and then, signalling to Kilcannan, he poised himself ready to strike.

"Kilfannan!" A voice said softly in the darkness. "'Tis I, Ke-enaan. I have been waiting for you. Come, make haste, for the goblins will soon realise the warriors are phantoms and will be hard upon your trail."

The sylphs followed Ke-enaan across the pavements and through some scrubby thorn trees to a low outcropping of boulders. Standing in front of the rocks, Ke-enaan made a circular pass with his hand and said commandingly, "Tash-Ka!"

Kilfannan felt a slight tremor beneath his feet, and the rocks began to shimmer. A round, dark doorway appeared in the outcrop.

"Quick!" Ke-enaan ushered them into the passageway. Once they were all inside, he made another pass with his hand, and the opening behind them disappeared. "Long hath the door remained a secret for dark days such as these," he said. "'Twill take us to my hall."

They followed Ke-enaan along a passage. The walls gleamed with a faint phosphorence, and the path led slowly downward to a silver curtain of falling water. There was a narrow trail leading around the waterfall, and Ke-enaan beckoned them forward into a cave and up a flight of steps into his hall.

"Sit down by the flame and let the power of dragon fire burn away the viciousness that hath assailed you. Methinks a draught of elixir is in order," he said, pouring the yellow liquid into goblets and bringing them to the table. Drawing up a chair, Ke-enaan joined them at the hearth. "Fearing for your safety," he said to the Kilfenorans, "I kept watch on the inn through the cunning glass. I saw a mortal leave the inn wreathed in the blasphemous colours of Lower Faerie, and recognising him as the spy that had stopped outside me halls, I marked his passage along the lane to the ruined abbey. There was a knocker hiding in the shadows of the ruin, and after a brief conversation, the man carried on along the footpath. Leaving the mirror, I went forth in haste to the forge at Slieve Elva. There Uall and meself conjured a fearsome warrior upon a horse from the cold fire of the forge. Multiplying his image into a glowing host, we sent the ghost riders forth to aid thee." He stared at Kilfannan. "Without my aid, you would have most certainly been lost. Perhaps now you will understand the peril you are in. War hath been declared upon your House, and 'twas folly that led you to the inn and into the arms of waiting evil."

Hearing Ke-enaan's words of rebuke, Kilfannan flushed emerald. He knew the wizard's words were true. He had led the life of an elemental of the Ruling House of Air, charged with spinning the laughter, music, poetry, and song of the mortal world into the glowing Green of nature. He liked to drink and gamble at the races, enjoying everything his world had to offer, and harming none in the doing. On the contrary, he was charged with the happiness of the world, and it was his own wilfulness, his desire for the carefree life, that had almost led to their destruction. He looked into Ke-enaan's eyes and saw them soften.

"Too well I understand the joy that has been your life, and the naivety that goes hand in hand with innocence," Ke-enaan said. "Think not that my words are a chastisement; they are not. 'Tis concern for the Green, the House of the Heart, that charges me to nourish and protect your well-being."

Kilfannan rose and bowed to the wizard. Wrapping himself in fey light, he said, "Folly maybe, but yet much understanding hath been revealed by our visit to the inn. We have news of the whereabouts of the stolen coach, and 'twould seem that after the theft, the carpenter was murdered and the blood drained from his body."

"How came you by this information?"

"A cluricaun by the name of Rickoreen," Kilfannan answered, and he went on to tell Ke-enaan what he had heard.

The wizard's face grew grave. "Bealltainn in the mortal world is a few days hence, and Trevelyan brought ill news while you were at the inn. While waiting for Emma in a pub, Trevelyan overheard a conversation. A mortal had an evil vision of a sylph running for his life from the Coiste Bodhar."

Kilfannan gulped, and his eyes widened in terror. Crom Dubh was the headless driver of a coach filled with coffins who hunted souls in the mortal world.

"What is the meaning of this riddle?" Kilfannan asked. "Crom Dubh has never troubled Faerie, for he hunts only mortal souls." He glanced anxiously at his brother.

"'Tis said in the mortal world that gold dispels Crom Dubh," Kilcannan responded. "Think thee that gold would deter him in our realm?"

"'Tis true, gold hath the power to dispel him," Ke-enaan replied. "But it may no longer serve as protection in either world, for Crom

Dubh's power is waxing. In the last hours of the Separation, the lords of Earth and Fire bound Crom Dubh's black heart to the water fields of Ireland, but with the Cathac's will, he hath found a way to free himself from the spell the Old Ones put in place and hath come forth into Faerie. You must take extra caution and be off the road by twilight. Only in darkness can he ride out." He paused for a moment. "And there is more. A sorcerer hath found the sapphire and at Bealltainn will summon Zugalfar in the blood rite, and together they will open the gates to Pandemonia. Only Emma and her friends stand against them. Methinks the sacrifice of the carpenter is connected to the sabbat."

A heavy silence descended on the room, and once again Kilfannan was confronted by the depth of hate arrayed against his House. "'Twould seem the imprisonment of Niamh and Caiomhin and the sacrifice of the carpenter is not by chance," he said grimly. "And 'tis imperative that I get word to Mary to go the antique shop and buy the coach if 'tis still there. In the Faerie world, 'tis only myself, my brother, and Trevelyan that Mary trusts; therefore, in spite of the peril we are in, we will ride back and tell her."

Ke-enaan nodded in agreement. "The knockers will not expect you to return south; instead they will be marking the road north. Your steeds will be fey-shod, and your hope lies in speed."

Cor-cannan turned to the wizard. "What in the stars is going on?" he asked in bewilderment. "Meself hath asked my cousins to explain, but they are reticent to answer."

"Cor-cannan hath no knowledge of the evil that hath befallen our House of Air," Kilfannan responded. "Yet he was forced to flee, along with my brother and myself."

Laying his hands on Cor-cannan's head, Ke-enaan told him of the imprisonment of Niamh and Caiomhin, the theft of the coach, and the Kilfenoran's quest to find the key made of air.

Cor-cannan was dumbstruck and wept long. "The death of the Green," he uttered, his eyes flashing a fiery peridot light. "No! Never! I pledge to fight alongside the House of Kilfenoran until the down-breath is no more." He got up and walked swiftly to the door. "I must away to An Carn. The fell news of the fall of the Radiance hath frightened me. Cor-garran must be warned of the goblin threat to the House of Kilfenoran and all the sylphid houses of Ireland … and the world."

"Wait!" Ke-enaan said sharply. "'Tis not safe! Let the rabble clear away, and let the sun rise in her glory, before you cross the Burren."

Ke-enaan went to the back of his hall and returned with two long bundles, the top one swathed in emerald cloth and the other in silver. Sitting down, he laid the bundles on his knees, and as he unwrapped the first one, Kilfannan saw Ennuiol, the growing tree, and Delphuaan, the silver flute, shimmering with light. His face lit up with joy. "Trevelyan hath triumphed and brought forth the sacred power objects of our house," he cried.

Stepping forward, Kilfannan took Delphuaan and held it to his heart, and thence to his lips; and with a melody of ravishing sweetness, he called Ennuiol, the growing tree, to life. The vine around the wood blazed with fire as the wizard placed the staff in Kilcannan's hands. For an enchanted instant, as the harmony of flute and living tree poured liquid loveliness into their souls, they were free from doubt and the clawing horror that had overtaken them.

"These sacred articles we will leave within these walls for safekeeping until we are ready to take the road," they said as one. Ke-enaan bowed, and taking the flute and staff, he reverently wrapped them in the emerald cloth.

"Within the silver coverlet are four bows of black-stained yew, and four black quivers, each with thirteen arrows," Ke-enaan said, undoing the cover. "These have not been used since the time of the Separation," he said to the Kilfenorans. "One set is for thee, Kilfannan, and the other for Kilcannan."

The Kilfenorans bowed low, and taking the bows and quivers from Ke-enaan, they said, "We are pledged to the Green, and the bows of those who fought for love and life will ride with us once more."

Kilfannan looked closely at the ancient bow that glowed in his hands as if it were newly made, and running his fingers along the polished wood, he marvelled at its smoothness. Turning it over, he saw the inside of the bow was backed with iridescent inlay that glittered with a pearly sheen. The quivers were made of heavy black cloth and were decorated along the edges with golden-threaded cross knots that glittered in the candlelight.

"Cor-cannan, come forth," Ke-enaan commanded. "Thou hast pledged thyself to aid the House of Kilfenoran, and I charge not only thee but also Cor-garran to go north and protect the Kilfenorans in their search for the key."

Cor-cannan paled and hesitated for a moment, and Kilfannan sensed a duelling of dread versus fiery excitement within him. Recovering his composure, Cor-cannan stepped forward and stood before the wizard.

"These two sets of bow and quiver are for your House to carry in the service of the HeartStar," Ke-enaan said, handing him the bows in their coverlets and the two quivers full of arrows.

Cor-cannan looked at them in wonder. "'Tis a mighty gift thou hast given our house, and I can only trust I will be worthy of it," he said, kneeling before the tall Danaan.

A cock crowed in the mortal world, and Ke-enaan looked eastward. "The sun is rising, and the horses await you. Cor-cannan! Go forth with the House of Kilfenoran. I will await thy return."

The sylphs went through the side door and along the passageway and stepped out onto the flower-dotted pasture. They felt they had stepped into a dream, a time remote when only starlight reigned. A tall figure appeared – or was it a light in the heavens? A voice of no sound, yet all sound, vibrated through his being. "Welcome to my realm, Kilfannan and Kilcannan of the House of Kilfenoran, and Cor-cannan of An Carn. Take the darkling door before you, and I will await you in the forge."

A shimmering arched gate of starlight appeared before the sylphs, and stepping through, they found themselves in a warm brick smithy with a roaring bed of coals. Standing beside the anvil was a red-haired giant with a long face and bright blue eyes.

Putting down his hammer, he said, "Greetings! 'Tis long since members of the gentry graced me forge. I am Uall Mac Carn of Slieve Elva, brother to Finn Mc Coul."

Kilfannan stared at the giant in wonder. Even though he was as tall as a tree, he somehow seemed to fit under the low roof of his forge.

Uall motioned to a wooden seat. "Sit down on the settle and take refreshment. I know what hath befallen your House and the evil that hath come against you." He poured wine from a flagon into three stone cups and handed them around. "And I have news of the missing shoe," he said. "'Twas found by a mortal with evil for a heart. He took it to a goblin, who in turn gave it to his knocker. The fiend and his magg followed you across the Burren, but when you reached the borders of my land, he could not pass. The Cathac knows well that the way to Binn Breac is long, and he hath sent news of you and your errand far and wide. 'Tis hammered through the mines that there is a hefty price of gold upon your heads, so every low-grade spirit both mortal and faerie will be after you."

Uall went to a small recess in the wall beside the forge and returned with a velvet bag covered in golden spider designs. "This pouch holds four sets of web mail made by the spider queen Dinhcara," he said, giving the pouch to Kilfannan. "They were worn by the Danaan wizards that fell before the gates of Cnoc Na Dala, the great city on the Gaillimh Plain in the War of Separation. The dwarf lords of the stone kingdom retrieved the bodies of the dead Danaans before they could be defiled by the enemy of life, and the web mail was saved. The web of Dinhcara hath no weight or size, can fit any form at will, and can turn any shaft or poisoned bolt that comes against it."

Uall uttered a sweet, bell-like note that echoed in silver waves upon the shore of timeless space, and Kilcannan saw a tiny star fall through the roof into the giant's outstretched hand. "This is the

Brax. 'Tis a wee magic horseshoe forged in the dwarf halls of Duir, and 'tis a gift for you," he said, handing the small gold-coloured horseshoe to Kilcannan. "The road north will be a peril; dark things will track you. When shadow comes upon you, the Brax will serve you well. 'Tis time the Duirshoe rode forth in service of the Green. 'Tis the singer of the storm, and when you are in danger, 'twill sound a warning." He held up his hand. "But remember, the fate of all life is in your hands. Trust in secrecy rather than conflict."

Kilcannan bowed. "A grand gift indeed, and I am honoured to receive it."

"The violet-gold piece you left within the forge hath been transformed into horseshoes of the Wind," Uall said to Kilfannan. "Meself shod Finifar and Red Moon with the winged shoes of Mercury; in dire need, they can fly into the sky. The word of rising skyward is 'A-num'. 'A-num'." He repeated the word, imprinting it upon their minds. "Now 'tis time for you to go forth upon the road of your destiny, and that of the living Green," he said. "Fear not the shadow. The gifts that I have given you will help protect you on your journey north. Farewell, Kilfannan and Kilcannan of the House of Kilfenoran, and Cor-cannan of An Carn. May the stars smile upon your errand and shine upon your road to the Crystal Mountains."

Picking up the web mail, Kilfannan bowed. "I thank thee. The House of Air is in thy debt."

Taking their leave, the sylphs stepped out of the forge and into the meadow. Looking west, Kilfannan saw the shadow of a spying moon and felt in the midst of tranquillity a threat from the orb's reflection. Casting off the spell of doubt from those sinister rays, he looked back along the meadow. The forge was gone, and a pale light was glowing in the east.

The door to the outside world was open. After making sure all was clear, they left the horses to graze upon the grass beside the wizard's hall.

Ke-enaan opened the arched doorway and beckoned them inside the warm fragrance of his hall. "Uall hath given us wondrous gifts,"

Kilfannan said, looking at the pouch. It was made of a heavy black weave with gold spiders embroidered around the edges. Opening it, he gasped. Inside were layers of shimmering spiderwebs.

"'Tis the spider armour of Dinhcara," Ke-enaan said as Kilfannan took one set out and held it in the air. The mail glinted in the firelight, and Kilfannan marvelled at its lightness and the delicate intertwining lines of gold, bronze, and a metal unknown to him that shimmered with sunlight of its own. The mail seemed to enthral his eyes and sing to his soul, and for an instant he had visions of tall warriors in battle for the Green in the long years of yesterday.

"In the final hours before the Separation, the gossamer weave saved many of my people on their flight north to the pyramid at Brugh," Ke-enaan said. His face clouded, and Kilfannan saw the wizard's image consumed in the darkness of the blood field, only to reappear a trifle weaker in power than before.

Ke-enaan caught his eye. "'Tis not wise to study the dark magic of the enemy too deeply," he said softly. "At the time of the Separation, myself and my brother Criedne were desperate to find a weakness in the enemy's advance. We delved into the darkness of his magic looking for fault in his strategies, and in the process we became tainted by evil ourselves. This will be my last war in this world – in any world – for I am tired and wish to go to my long home on the Green star of dawn and eve."

Kilfannan saw the wizard's shoulders bow under the weight of his portentous words and felt the weariness and resignation in his voice.

"I too have a gift," Kilcannan said, taking the horseshoe from his pocket and showing it to Ke-enaan.

"The Brax! The Duirshoe, as it was once called," Ke-enaan said, gazing at the tiny shoe. "'Twas forged by my brother Criedne and Uall as a protection for the Faerie realms in the War of Separation. 'Tis a charm of great strength, and their hearts will be glad to know it rides to battle for the Green." He looked at the sand running in his hourglass. "Now, my friends, the sands of time are running, and you must run with them or get lost and lose the path. Let us make a toast. To the HeartStar! Slainte!"

After they had drained their glasses, Ke-enaan opened the door and saw them outside. "All ways will be watched," he cautioned. "Take not the road much travelled to the Crystal Mountains, for it, too, will be spied upon. Travel only by day on secret tracks across the moors." Raising his hand, he turned his sea-born eyes upon them. "May the sun shine upon your faces and the stars light your road with safety."

Taking their leave of Ke-enaan, the sylphs assembled on the verge outside his hall. Fog banks were moving inland, and a cold, damp wind was blowing.

Kilfannan looked over the grey stone wall at the sea. The water had a leaden cast, and fingers of misty rain seemed to be crawling towards him up the beach. "A grey, dripping day hath dawned," he said gloomily. "'Twould be welcome to see the sun."

"'Twould indeed, but there is little chance," Kilcannan said, looking at the cloud-ridden sky.

Taking the web armour from the pouch, Kilfannan handed one set to Kilcannan and the other two to Cor-cannan. "Let us don the mail and be prepared to meet evil on the road." He pulled his mail over his jerkin, and the webs shined with pale light.

"'It hath an airy feel," Kilfannan said. "In truth! It hath no weight at all."

Cor-cannan slipped both sets of mail over his head and put the quivers of arrows on his back. "I will go back to An Carn, and Cor-garran and I will see you before the sun sinks into the west. We have Orcan and Red Leaf, our beloved horses, to speed us north. Where shall we meet?"

"Dost thou know of the Horse and Jockey pub in Kinvara?" Kilcannan asked.

Cor-cannan nodded. "I know it well. The landlord is a friend of my brother."

"We shall await you this night at the inn," Kilfannan said.

"Fare ye well upon the road," Cor-cannan cried, and with a wave of his hand, he disappeared onto the Burren.

"We will take the road to Fanore and then cut across the hillside and go south to my Mary's. 'Tis a fair distance," Kilfannan said, mounting Red Moon. "We must make haste and be in Kinvara by nightfall to meet the House of An Carn." Urging their horses forward, they took the road to Fanore.

They saw no one on the misty road and heard only the drip of water from the rocks and the hissing of breaking waves upon the shingle. When they got to the dunes, they stopped. "We will ride south across the hillside towards Kilfenora. A few miles on, there is a sunken boreen that will take us to Mary's back gate," Kilfannan said, looking ahead at the ghostly, rock-strewn land. He led the way across the hills and into a dark valley beset by gloomy thickets of thorn trees and brambles. Rain began to fall as they found the sunken lane leading to Mary's cottage. The path was narrow and hemmed in by trees with their great roots creeping through the earthbound banks like giant spiders.

"'Tis hardly more than a deep, muddy ditch," Kilcannan said, peering into the gloom.

"'Tis true! But the knocker's spies are everywhere, and the trees will give us cover," he said, urging Red Moon forward.

The path was twisty, and the going was slow in the heavy mud. Kilfannan thought he heard a restless rustling in the trees, and pulling up Red Moon, he said to Kilcannan, "List!" They listened for a moment to the murmuring trees. "The trees take counsel together," he said uneasily. "They too are aware of the dimming of the Green."

The lane widened into a greenway that wound around the side of Mary's cottage. Kilfannan pulled up at her back gate. Leaving his horse with Kilcannan, he climbed over the wall and ran nimbly along the path, through the wall, and into her bedroom. Seeing she was sleeping, he gently smoothed her cheek with his fingers, bathing her in a green glow from the emerald on his brow. "Mary! 'Tis I, Kilfannan," he whispered as she opened her eyes.

"Kilfannan," she said in surprise, staring at him in wonder. "What are you doing here?"

"Mary," he said. "I bring evil tidings. Darkness hath fallen upon the House of Air."

Mary gasped and looked at him in bewilderment. "What has happened?"

"Meself and Kilcannan are fleeing north to the Crystal Mountains, and we need thine help to find something that hath been stolen from our high house."

Mary gasped again, and her eyes widened. "What!"

Knowing she would be devastated by the truth, for a moment he couldn't find the heart to tell her. But he had no choice.

In a halting voice, Kilfannan told her the history of the sapphire stargate, the imprisonment of Niamh and Caiomhin, and the quest to find the key made of air.

Mary's eyes widened with shock, and horror overtook her face. Clutching Kilfannan's hand, she burst into tears. He reached for a handkerchief – a habit of his old life – but remembering he had none, he jerked his hand back down as the spectre of the reality of Now engulfed him. Everything had changed, and his carefree existence had been enveloped in fear and doubt. A sad wind blew around him at the thought of their parting, and he tried to comfort her as best he could. But he knew, and so did she, that there was a chance he would perish in his quest for the key, and that the Green of field and meadow would fade away. He looked into her tear-stained face, taking a mind-picture that he would carry with him – for the misery in her eyes would be the fate of the mortal world if he should fail in his task. Her face would be a constant reminder to go on when his spirit failed, for he knew the darkness and despair that awaited. A sad wind moaned around him once again.

Mary trembled. "The wind … what is it?"

"Air only turns in torment because the heart is troubled."

"What is it you want me to do?" she asked with brave eyes.

"A miniature coach was sold by a mortal to the antique shop

along the high street. I want thee to go and see if 'tis still there. If so, I want thee to buy it," he said, handing her a few gold coins.

"Will the owner take these?" Mary asked, looking doubtfully at the burnished gold.

Kilfannan smiled. "Do not worry; he'll be willing to do a trade when he sees them – mark my words."

She nodded. "Well, if not, I have a charge card. The antique shop is closed today, it being Sunday and all, but I'll go first thing in the morning. I'll keep the coach here for you when you return."

Kilfannan put his hand upon hers. "Mary, my heart tells me that it is not safe for thee to keep the coach. Dost thou know Black Head on the road from Fanore to Ballyvaughan?"

"I do." She looked at him uneasily.

"Take the coach to Black Head and stand before the likeness of the wizard in the rock face and ask for entry. Ke-enaan is a Danaan, a son of Danu, and is one of those who came in a silver mist long ago and fought against the evil that caused the Separation of our realms." He saw Mary tremble and knew she was afraid, for mortals had not stood before the wizard's door and asked for entry for many generations. "Few now are the mortals with the gift of sight – and even fewer those who seek to engage it. For the love of life and joy, I bid thee do not be afraid, for the peril that faces the living Green can only be trumped by those who have the courage."

"Kilfannan! Why is it not safe to leave the coach in my cottage?" She fiddled nervously with her hair.

"There are satanists living nearby, and they are in league with a sorcerer in England," he answered grimly. "The sorcerer is in league with Zugalfar, and with the blood rite of human sacrifice, he will conjure the archdemon." His mind flitted to Emma for an instant as he felt the icy touch of portent. Shaking off the ugly feeling, he continued. "Together they will use the sapphire to open the gates to Pandemonia." Seeing Mary shaking, he put his hand upon her arm. "There is another matter I have to tell thee. 'Tis not my intent to strike fear into thine heart, but if a fat, scruffy man with a bald head tries to accost thee, have no dealing with him. He is spying for the goblins, and 'tis likely he hath knowledge of our friendship."

Mary burst into tears. "'Tis all too much for me," she cried out, and leaning forward, she clasped both hands upon her knees. "Everything I love is in danger, and now a low-life man is following me."

"I will get thee a stiffener," Kilfannan said, not knowing what else to do. He went to the kitchen cupboard, where she kept her whiskey. After finding a glass, he poured her a drink.

"I'll call the guarda and have him arrested for stalking me," Mary said, having followed him into the kitchen. "That's what I'll do …"

Kilfannan handed her the drink. "'Tis all bad news I have brought to thy door, and I ask thee to forgive me."

Mary shook her head. "There is nothing to forgive, Kilfannan. I have seen the slow dying of the Green. The seabirds and seals are dying, and many a spring has come, yet no thrush sings. I try not to think about it, for it's upsetting to me." She looked at him, and he saw the warrior in her eyes. "I'll do my part to save the Green. Is there any other way I can help you?"

Kilfannan took her hand and looked into her tear-stained face. "Indeed there is. In the hours and days ahead, put a little cream into my saucer and think of me and my brother on the long road to the Crystal Mountains. And say a prayer for the mortal warrior of air, Emma Cameron, for the sorcerer is planning her destruction. For 'tis true that the power of prayer is strong in mortals of the heart. Farewell, beautiful Mary." Seeing the tears well in her eyes again, and feeling her pain, he turned away and, disappearing through the wall, rejoined his brother.

"How farest thou with Mary?" Kilcannan asked as they started along the track to the greenway.

"She will go to the antique shop and buy the coach. I told her to take it to Ke-enaan for safe keeping. Let us pray 'tis still there." He sighed. "'Twas a sad parting, for we both knew that we may never meet again in either world."

A misty rain began to fall as they reached the greenway. "Which way shall we go?" Kilcannan asked, looking up and down the road. "'Tis not wise to go back the way we came, for who knows, the enemy may have tracked us here."

"We will ride across country to the Harbour of the Bell and then take the road to Kinvara, for we have to meet the House of An Carn at the inn when the shadows fall."

Kilfannan cast a fleeting glance at his hill. "Kilcannan!" he cried, taking an up-breath. "There are dark, sooty smudges on our hills. I can see darkness moving in the green spell." A wind blew up around him. "Goblins! They are searching for our sheens."

They heard an eerie croak behind them, and turning, they saw a crow flying from the shadows of the sunken lane. As it flew over their heads in the direction of their hills, it gave another eerie croak.

"'Tis a spy!" Kilcannan cried. "We must ride!"

The rain grew stronger as they rode across the meadows and flooding brooks. The land grew wilder. Reaching a high point on a ridge of hills, they pulled up and looked out across the stone-walled fields towards the Burren, now hardly visible in the pouring rain.

"We must ride across the pasture to Black Head and pick up the tokens of our house," Kilfannan said, peering into the gloom for enemies. At first he saw nothing but shades of grey and green, and then he became aware of dark smudges moving about in the fields below. "Goblins," he hissed, turning Red Moon away from the top of the ridge. "We must get out of sight. The filth are searching for us. Damnation take them! They stand between us and Black Head."

"Our sacred articles will be safe within Ke-enaan's halls," Kilcannan answered as they trotted away from the ridge and down the other side into a meadow. "We cannot tarry; the filth will find us, and we can brook no delay. There is a track yonder that will take us to the Harbour of the Bell."

They rode on to the bottom of a long pasture. "Here is the path," Kilcannan said, pointing to a track leading into a patch of woodland.

Pausing for a moment before riding through the trees, Kilfannan listened for any disturbance on the airwaves, but there was naught save the sound of raindrops thudding on the turf. "We should make our way forward," he said, urging Red Moon into the trees.

CHAPTER 6

THE ROAD TO KINVARA

The track met the road not far from the Four-Leafed Clover Inn, and seeing the road was clear, they took the right fork at the crossroads and started forward along it. Turning a corner by the harbour, Kilfannan stiffened in dismay. A shabby mortal was lounging by the sea wall, and a shudder ran through him as he felt the man's sneering eyes upon him, hateful with the tainted hues of Lower Faerie. As he turned his eyes away, he thought he saw the stain of a darker sorcery gleaming from the mortal's eyes. "Brother!" he said urgently. "'Tis the mortal spy from the inn, and 'tis he that betrayed us to the knocker. We should pass quickly and give him wide berth."

"I recognise him. He is the one that stole Finifar's shoe," Kilcannan responded angrily. "He hath tried to harm us, and 'tis my wish to show him the error of his ways."

Feeling Kilcannan's breath dip into the fire field, Kilfannan cautioned, "Tether thy temper! 'Tis true the mortal hath evil on his mind and will report news of our passing to the goblins, but there is a poison about him that repels me, and the less we have to do with him, the better."

Steering their horses away from the wall and into the middle of the road, they rode by. Kilfannan watched the mortal from the corner of his eye and shivered with disgust at his loathsome, swart face. "Where do you think you're going, copper knobs?" he heard him snarl. Ignoring the mortal's insolent question, Kilfannan looked straight ahead.

"Lost your tongues, have you?" The man laughed viciously. "You'll soon be losing them; that's for sure. Next time you won't have any sorcerer's fake army to help you get away."

"Damnation! I will smite the filthy spy." Kilcannan fumed, turning Finifar in the man's direction.

Before Kilfannan could gainsay him, he saw his brother charge away and blow a jet of scalding air into the mortal's face.

The man shrieked and recoiled against the wall. He raised his hand and threw something at Kilcannan. "You'll pay for this, you witches," he screamed, pawing at his face.

Knowing the mortal would report news of their passing to the goblins, Kilfannan sent air rising into space, formed a pentagon, and hurled it at the mortal. It would confuse his mind; although he would remember seeing them, he would not know where they passed him by.

"'Twill make the spy think twice before he insults the House of Air again," Kilcannan said, riding up alongside.

Kilfannan responded, "Brother, I have cast confusion o'er his mind. 'Twill give us time to get clear. The mortal threw something at thee, and I can see no trace of it upon the road."

Looking quickly around at the ground for any object that was amiss, and seeing nothing, they rode on. They had not gone far along the lane when Kilcannan pulled up. "Brother," he said, sniffing the air. "There is a stink of corruption in my nostrils." He looked around and then down at the ground. "There is a lump of black rot upon my boot," he said with disgust, flicking it onto the road with his fingers.

Fear gripped Kilfannan's heart as he saw the inky black cap on the road. The grotesque fungus was rerg, the ghost toadstool grown by knockers in caves deep within the mines, and fed on blood and carrion. The toadstools turned inky black when they found prey, tormenting their victims with terrible visions until their minds fled into madness; their bodies were then sucked down as nourishment into a nighted fungoid world.

"'Tis rerg!" Kilcannan responded in panic, looking wildly at Kilfannan. "And I have touched it. We have to find scabious the pincushion before the evil visions appear," he cried desperately, "for 'tis the only power that can neutralise rerg's poison."

"The pincushion will not be found here; 'tis too stony," Kilfannan said, looking at the verge. "We have to ride on past the ruined church to the grassy banks beyond."

The rain eased, and a cold drizzle began to fall as they rode along the verge. Rounding a corner, they saw not far from the road a tall, thin grey pillar of stone looming before them in the misty rain. Kilfannan shivered. The stone needle and the ruined church beside it were of ill repute in Faerie and the mortal world, being the haunt of wraiths and demons. The stone pillar had been raised by dark druids at the time of the Separation and was drenched in the blood of human sacrifice. Knowing the evil influence that lingered in the pillar would add to rerg's power over his brother, he looked anxiously around for another path they could take. The pillar was surrounded by a mouldering churchyard with blackened cenotaphs and crumbling stone crosses, and on the other side was a dark wood.

"We must make haste past the stone needle," Kilfannan said urgently.

As they started off, Kilfannan noticed his brother was trembling and swaying in the saddle. Seeing he was succumbing to the spell of the toadstool, he cried out, "What ails thee?"

"'Tis the round tower yonder. See! The shades of men, they battle in the shadow of the stone. Look! Monks from the church are running to the tower. They are screaming. Agh!" He put his hand across his eyes and turned away.

Kilfannan felt a knot of fear tighten in his chest. "Quick! Let us ride to the banks and meadows beyond and find the antidote for the poison."

Seeing Kilcannan shake his head as if to clear it, and pass his hand across his eyes, he asked anxiously, "Brother! Canst thou ride?"

Kilcannan nodded slowly. "The evil hath passed away for the present," he said, "but there is a dark cloud over my eyes. All is grey and cold around me."

They trotted on along the road, and the stony verge gave way to grassy banks and fields. "Stay with Finifar," Kilfannan said, slipping from his horse. "I will look for the pincushion." He swiftly searched along the verges on both sides of the road but saw no sign of the silver leaves. Suddenly he heard the Brax in Kilcannan's pocket ding a muted warning. "Goblins are near!" he cried in alarm, and he raced to his horse and leapt into the saddle. Glancing anxiously at Kilcannan, he saw his brother grimacing and mumbling to himself. The Brax chimed out again, louder this time, and Kilfannan knew the goblins were closing in.

The narrow road ahead of them was hidden by a bend, as was the road behind, and seeing a gap in the hedgerow and the beginnings of a path, he grabbed Finifar's reins and urged Red Moon forward through the gap and up the hillside. The Brax chimed incessantly as they reached the top of the hill, and Kilfannan could hear shouts, jabbering, and cries of pursuit. Glancing back, he saw Aeguz meeting up with another knocker that had come from the opposite direction. He had been right; if they had stayed on the road, they would have been caught in a trap. The knocker accompanying Aeguz was a smaller breed from the Northern Hills. *Two knockers means two maggs*, he thought. He knew the knockers would be able to follow the vibration of the fungus and would know which way they went. Their only hope was to abandon the search for the antidote and ride as fast as they could to Kinvara. Once there, he would have to find a fear dearg, a master of herbs, to help his brother and neutralise the rerg's poison.

At the bottom of the hill he saw a greenway – a twisty path that would take them to the town. As they reached the greenway, the Brax chimed a muted warning.

"Let us wait for the knockers … they mean us no harm," Kilcannan crooned, straightening in the saddle.

Kilfannan glanced at him in rising panic. Kilcannan's face was twisted and unrecognisable. For a moment Kilfannan was overcome by a wave of sickness and repulsion. The figure beside him was no longer his brother but a cursed focus of rerg's hallucinations. Ordering Finifar to follow, Kilfannan rode to the track at the bottom of the hill. The Brax chimed again with the sound of imminent danger, and as the horses jumped off along the greenway, an arrow glanced off his boot.

Three goblin scouts riding shaggy ponies came charging after them along the greenway. In a flurry of flying hooves, the Kilfenorans made their escape along the rutted track into a narrow hedged boreen that led to a junction with the road to Kinvara.

Kilfannan pulled up at the junction and, with an anxious glance at his brother, slipped out of his saddle and walked into the road. Knowing the knockers were following the trail of their toadstool and would be swift upon their track, he took out the phial of oil Trevelyan had left for him with Arkle. The perfume of orange blossom was fast in frequency, and it would mask rerg's vibration and confuse the knockers long enough for them to get away. He took out the cork and blew a few drops of the perfume onto the road, and then, mounting his horse, he ordered Finifar to follow and trotted out onto the verge.

Riding past the racecourse, Kilfannan heard the Brax chime and swiftly looked around. From the urgent tone of the chime, he knew the goblins would soon be at the road, and he prayed the perfumed oil would confuse the filth long enough for them to escape to the town. The road ahead was hidden by a bend with grey stone walls on either side, but there was a gateway on their left leading to the stables. "Come, brother!" Kilfannan said. "Let us take the track leading to the stables; 'tis the only way off the road."

Kilcannan did not move but looked back. "'Tis the House of An Carn that cometh after us," he said. "We should wait for them to catch up." He started to babble inanely and leered at Kilfannan in the most frightful way.

Realising the toadstool was trying to delay them by altering his brother's perception, Kilfannan grabbed Finifar's reins and raced forward up the hill towards the racecourse. There was a hedge around the stable yard, and riding round the back, he pulled up behind the bushes. The stench of goblins was in the air, and he could hear oaths and curses on the road below. He was in a quandary. His brother was a gibbering caricature, and he knew it would not be long before the hallucinations took him over completely. A thought crossed his mind that Kilcannan might, in the throes of madness, try to attack him. He took a tense breath. He had to find the pincushion before it was too late – but they could not go forth in safety; nor could they go back.

The Brax chimed again, and Kilfannan heard the sound of harsh cries and tramping feet on the road below. Peering through the bushes, he saw knockers and their maggs milling around the junction where they had left the road. The fiends were pawing at the air, weaving dark sounds with their claws, looking for any trace rerg may have left of their presence upon the ether. Gliding low, they crossed and recrossed the road, circling, tasting the air with their flickering forked tongues.

Suddenly he heard Kilcannan shriek, "Go back! Keep away!" Drawing his sword, he saw his brother jump from Finifar's back and start running down the hillside towards the goblins. Leaping from his horse, Kilfannan ran after him and, tackling him from behind, brought him to the ground.

"Kilfannan!" Kilcannan screamed, struggling to get away. "Our nephews from An Carn have been wounded. See! They writhe in agony on the hillside, and crows peck at their eyes. We must aid them!"

Knowing his brother was hallucinating, Kilfannan hastily looked towards the road to see if his piercing scream had reached the knockers' ears. Seeing one look up the hill towards them, he dragged his brother back behind the bushes.

Suddenly he heard uproar and commotion coming from the racecourse. Parting the bushes to get a better view, he saw trooping elves and goblins spilling from the grandstand onto the grass outside. The elves were drunk and in a fist fight with the goblins, punching and kicking them to the ground. Some of the goblins had escaped and were running down the hill towards the road, shouting to their knockers for help. Thanking the stars for the respite, Kilfannan helped his brother into the saddle, but Kilcannan slumped forward across his horse's neck. Seeing he was unable to ride, Kilfannan ordered Finifar to follow Red Moon.

They rode around the back of the racecourse. There they found a track, and they followed it through a patch of scrubland to a junction with a greenway. Kilfannan heard the beep of the Brax in his brother's pocket. The sound was muted, and knowing he had a little time, he looked along the verge for the pincushion. Spying the yellow flowers of dandelions, the protector of High Faerie shining from the grass, he slipped from his saddle. The virtue of the dandelion would hold the effects of the rerg at bay until he could find the pincushion. Gathering the leaves and flowers, he rolled them into two balls. He returned swiftly to his brother and put one in Kilcannan's cold, damp hand and the other in his pocket.

Kilcannan made no movement, and Kilfannan saw that his eyes stared into nothingness and his mouth worked in a soundless spasm of a scream. Realising Kilcannan was succumbing to the rerg's poison, Kilfannan leapt onto Finifar's neck and forced the ball of dandelion into his brother's mouth. "Hold fast unto the Green," he cried out. "We must get to Kinvara and find a fire elemental. He will have the precious leaves to heal thee."

Seeing Kilcannan rally a little, he asked, "Brother, canst thou ride? Goblins are close."

Kilcannan nodded weakly, swaying slightly in the saddle.

"Aye. We must go forth in search of healing while the virtue of the dandelion is upon me."

Urging their horses onwards, they started on their way. The Brax was now insistent in its warning, and Kilfannan looked swiftly around. The view ahead was hidden by a bend, and there was naught but stonewalled fields on either side. Black shafts whined through the air towards them, and he heard hoarse shouts and yells. An arrow thumped into his back but was repulsed by his mail, and another stuck in the pommel of his saddle as he raced away. Hearing Red Moon scream in pain, he glanced over his shoulder and saw an arrow in his horse's rump. Fearing to go further along the track in case goblins were waiting to ambush them, he took a glance at Kilcannan. His brother was once again slumped forward. Commanding Finifar to follow, Kilfannan raced over the fields and up a hillside to a patch of woodland.

Once they were in the cover of the trees, he slipped out of the saddle, examined the injury to his horse, and pulled out the arrow. He then packed the wound with the other ball of dandelion from his pocket.

Slipping into the saddle, he was about to ride off when he saw two horsemen appear at the bottom of the hill. The riders were looking at the tracks in the turf as they came galloping up the rise towards them.

"Hail to the House of An Carn," Kilfannan shouted with relief as they rode up to him.

"Hail to the House of Kilfenoran!" Cor-garran shouted, reining in Red Leaf. "My brother and I have been following your tracks. We found spent shafts upon the path, and fearing for your safety, we made haste to find you." He held up a grotesque goblin head. "The filth that ambushed you was a scouting party, and they have been dealt with. There is a furious fight between elves and goblins on the road." He grinned. "The goblins were too busy to notice us as we slipped past them." Cor-garran dismounted, found a sturdy upright sapling, and jammed the hideous head on top of it. "Let this serve as a warning to the others!"

Hearing Kilcannan groan and mumble, Kilfannan looked at him in panic. His eyes were glazed with terror, and he was trying to push something away from his body with his hands.

"What ails Kilcannan?" Cor-garran asked, staring at him in horror.

"He hath been touched by rerg, and terrible visions are assailing him," Kilfannan replied grimly. "We did not have time to seek out the pincushion, for goblins attacked us. We must make haste to Kinvara, for not only is my brother in peril, but my horse as well. Red Moon hath a wound in his rump, and goblin arrows are oft poisoned." He thought for a moment. "'Twould be best," he said to Cor-cannan, "if thyself ride with Kilcannan and make sure he doth not fall." Giving his reins to his brother, Cor-cannan sprang up behind Kilcannan.

"Dost thou know of another way into the town?" Kilfannan asked. "One that is less travelled and on which, if fortune aids us, we will not be watched?"

"There is a boggy trail that leads towards the sea," Cor-garran said, looking around the woodland. "There 'tis." He pointed to the beginnings of a path in the trees. "Follow me."

Twilight was settling in as they trotted through a stand of trees overlooking the town. Kilfannan looked uncomfortably over the tangled rooftops and tall houses that lined the narrow, dreary streets, which appeared unfriendly in the failing light. The high street led to a small harbour – a good place for the goblins to lay ambush, he thought. They had to find shelter, and if they were attacked at an inn, at least there would be elves and fear deargs to aid them.

"The high street is steep," Cor-garran said, slipping from his horse's back. "The inn is halfway down, so 'tis best if we dismount and walk from here. The landlord is a friend of mine, and there are stables for our horses in the courtyard at the back. He is a fear dearg and a doctor; he will have herbs to aid Kilcannan and Red Moon."

Leaving Kilcannan in the saddle, they walked the horses down the road, through an alleyway, and into the stables. Kilcannan screamed and violently struggled as Cor-cannan tried to help him from the saddle. "Brother! Help me with Kilcannan. He is in the throes of rigour, and I am afraid he may break free."

A fat fear dearg came out of a side door as they entered the yard. "Faith!" he cried out, staring at Kilcannan. "What ails the House of Air?"

"We are in need of healing help," Kilfannan said, desperately looking at his brother's twisted face. "My brother hath been assailed by rerg, and evil visions are upon him."

"Me name is Gercle," the fear dearg said to Kilfannan. "We have little time to save your brother, for as night deepens, he will not be able to withstand the rerg's summons and will become a prisoner of nightmare in the toadstool's fungoid realm. Take off his clothes and boots, and bring water. There is a tap and bucket over there." He pointed to a wall. "I will get me bag," he said, going swiftly through the door into the inn.

"Cor-garran, go and fill the bucket with water and bring it hither," Kilfannan said. "I and thy brother will disrobe Kilcannan and make sure he doth not get away." As Cor-garran brought the water, Gercle came hurrying up to Kilfannan with a battered doctor's bag. He rummaged through the contents and took out a bundle of dried silver leaves with faded mauve flowers. He dropped the bundle into the water and stirred it with his hand. Kilcannan was moaning and thrashing violently as Kilfannan and the sylphs of An Carn dragged him forward to the bucket.

"I cannot touch devil water," he shouted in a hollow voice.

"Hold him," Kilfannan cried desperately, seeing a mind-shattering fear in his brother's distorted features. He grabbed Kilcannan's hands and forced them into the water.

The surface heaved and frothed, and he heard Kilcannan give an unearthly shriek as spinning octahedrons swarmed over his hands and body. A tremor ran through him, and then he grew limp and still. Feeling the pressure ease in his chest, Kilfannan took a gulping up-breath.

"Stand aside," Gercle ordered. Spinning like a top, he burst into flame. He breathed out a jet of fire that consumed Kilcannan's contaminated clothes. "The best way to deal with the physical residue of rerg is to burn it," he said grimly. "Bring Kilcannan into me parlour. He is lost and wandering in the fetid twilight world of the toadstool. He will need me help to break the rerg's spell upon him."

Steadying himself, Kilfannan picked up his brother's body and, holding him to his heart, followed Gercle into the parlour. After Kilfannan laid Kilcannan on a daybed, the fear dearg covered him with a sheet. Gercle produced a knobbly root from his bag and breathed fire upon the end. When it was smouldering, he held it under Kilcannan's nose. "Breathe," he commanded.

Kilfannan looked into his brother's staring eyes. The spasm of fear was fading from his face, and his dull eyes were brightening. "Kilcannan," he said softly, taking his hand, "'Tis I, Kilfannan."

Kilcannan stirred and opened his eyes. "I thought I was lost," he said, sitting up. "I was drowning in a shadow world of madness, and a terror of unrequited hate was seeking to possess me." He suddenly realised he was naked. "What hath happened to my clothes?"

"Meself burnt your attire to get rid of the stain of the rerg, and I have purified your armour with me fire. 'Tis in your brother's care. Worry not, Kilcannan; meself will find you clothing," Gercle said, hurrying off.

"Brother! We cannot tarry here," Kilfannan said. "As soon as you are able, we will have to leave. The knockers will track the vibrations of rerg to the stable."

"A new pair of boots and riding attire for your brother," Gercle said, handing them to Kilfannan. "Stay with Kilcannan until he has recovered, and then, when you are ready, come into the bar and have a stiffener."

"A drink will have to wait. My horse hath been injured in a fight with goblins on the greenway and is in need of healing."

"Meself will tend the wound," Gercle said, digging in his bag and disappearing into the stables.

Kilfannan helped his brother to get dressed. Kilcannan was shaky, but an emerald blush was upon his cheek, and Kilfannan saw a fiery light gleam from his eyes.

"Brother," Kilcannan said. "Thou didst tell me to stay clear of the mortal spy, and my hot-headedness hath brought the evil of rerg upon us. I listened not and put us all in jeopardy."

"Fret not, brother. Thou art safe from rerg, and it hath no power over thee. If thou art well enough, accompany meself to the stables. I wish to check on Red Moon."

"Aye," Kilcannan said, getting to his feet. "Gercle is a grand doctor, to be sure."

"Kilfannan! 'Twould be prudent to hide our web mail," Corgarran said urgently. "'Tis so fabulous and rare that if seen by faeries in the bar, 'twill be the talk of these parts for many a song to come ... and others will talk! And if I may be so bold, the House of An Carn, not wishing to draw attention to themselves in your respected service, wear their mail underneath their jerkins and not over them!"

"Well said, nephew," the Kilfenorans agreed as one, slipping their web mail under their jerkins.

"In truth, 'twould be prudent to hide the web." Kilfannan remarked. "Our bows and quivers will draw attention, but as we are the gentry, the weapons could well be taken for tokens of our House."

The Kilfenorans followed the sylphs of An Carn outside into the stables. Kilfannan went to Gercle's side. "How fares Red Moon?" he asked, seeing the fear dearg blow a yellow powder into the arrow hole.

"'Tis a nasty wound, but 'tis not poisoned. Meself will dress it again before you take your leave." Gercle produced a needle and thin twine from his bag. "A stitch is all that is needed to help close the wound."

Kilfannan was uneasy. Even though the Brax was quiet, he knew the knockers would not be far behind. He led the way into the faerie bar and looked around. The only other occupant was a cluricaun slouching at the counter. "Good health to you, sirs," Gercle said affably, putting four blackberry brandies on a table.

Knowing they would have to leave immediately, Kilfannan took a guinea from his pocket and handed it to the landlord. "For thy service."

Gercle shook his head and waved the coin away. "Meself is glad to be of service to the House of Air."

"But I insist," Kilfannan said, putting the coin in his hand.

"Thank you, sir," Gercle replied, and he hurried off behind the bar.

"Aeguz will be able to track rerg's vibration," Kilfannan said to the others. "'Twill draw him here, and even though all is washed and burnt, the vibrational residue of the toadstool will linger in the stable yard. Methinks 'tis best to drain our drinks and go." He turned to the sylphs of An Carn. "Check the road outside and make sure it is clear. Kilcannan and I will bring the horses."

"In truth, we could be discovered at any moment," Cor-garran said anxiously, draining his glass. "Come, brother!"

Finishing their drinks, the Kilfenorans bade Gercle goodnight.

"Meself thought you would be staying this night," he said. "There is still more doctoring for your horse."

Seeing the surprised and disappointed look on the landlord's face, Kilfannan responded, "We are being pursued by goblins. They are following the trail of rerg, and it will lead them here. Naught will happen to thee if we are gone."

Gercle nodded. "'Tis very considerate of you, Kilfannan, but meself will burn the hides off their backs if they dare to barge in here."

"The maggs hath knockers with them, and such is thy service to our House, we will leave thy fine abode."

"Knockers!" He saw the fear dearg's red face pale. "Well, sir, if that be the case, I appreciate your candour. May the stars protect you," he said, bowing, and he then went behind the bar.

"'Twould be prudent to get clear of the town," Kilfannan said as they assembled in the yard. "But I fear the goblins are close behind, and will have blocked all exits. If we leave, methinks we will walk into ambush. So 'tis best if we pay heed to Ke-enaan's warning and take shelter from the dark."

The sylphs led the horses from the stable and along the alleyway to the road. Cor-garran peered around the corner of the wall into the road. "'Tis clear," he said, waving them forward. "There is a quaint little inn on the quayside. It too hath stabling and is out of view of the street."

The night was clear, and the sight of the glittering stars nestling in an indigo sky lifted Kilfannan's heart, and for a nostalgic moment, he was transported to his old life. His anxiety returned as he led Red Moon down the road towards the quayside. The sea was dead calm, and a stealthy mist was creeping in towards the harbour wall. He fancied it stopped when he turned his attention to it. The harbour seemed to take on a sinister quality of unreality, and he shivered at the silent grey boats at their moorings, and ghostly lobster pots. Glancing back along the road towards the pub they had just left, he thought he saw a grey shadow flit into the alleyway leading to the stables. "A knocker," he hissed in alarm. "He is searching for us at the inn. We must find shelter and get off the quayside."

"The tavern is yonder," Cor-cannan responded, pointing ahead. "'Tis called The Shipwreck Pub."

The quayside narrowed into a strip of road bordered by the sea wall, and Kilfannan saw both road and wall ended a little ways past the inn at the foot of a steep, rock-strewn hill. He looked at the dark and narrow space with great unease. *No more than a carriage width betwixt stone and stone*, he thought. *A good place for an ambush.* But there was no time for indecision; they could not go back.

The inn was a bleak stone house overlooking the harbour. Above the door was a painting of a shipwreck wracked in storm, and the sign hung motionless on its hinges in the clammy, windless air. Candlelight was filtering through the small windows, casting flickering shadows on the salt-stained walls and rough, damp slabs below.

"There is an alley leading to stables round the back," Cor-garran said. "Follow me!"

A quintessence of fear ran icily down Kilfannan's neck as he led Red Moon around the back of the inn to the stables. The only way of escape was across the narrow forecourt and onto the quayside. They were boxed into a dead end. Looking around the stables, he saw a large, empty stall.

"The magg is close," he said to the others. "'Twould be best to stable the horses together and draw the bolt across the door."

"I see no reason why the horses should not be left in the yard," Kilcannan said. "We may have need of a quick escape, and a locked door could cost us precious time."

"If we are found and a battle doth ensue, the goblin scum will kill and eat our horses while we are busy in the fight. Or our mounts may take fright and run blindly along the quayside and cast themselves into the sea. For no matter how we fare, 'tis unlikely the goblins would dare attack a fire elemental's horses, as they are one in heart. The filth know that a fear dearg's wrath is strong, his vengeance swift, and his memory of transgression unforgiving."

Kilcannan nodded. "As thou wilt."

They led their horses into the stable and instructed them to stay quiet in the face of noise. Kilfannan shut the stable door behind them, and after sliding the bolt into place, he stood indecisively for a moment in the yard. "Let us check the quayside for any sign of a knocker," he said to the others.

Peering round the corner of the inn at the waterfront, Kilfannan saw the sea mist had reached the harbour wall, and groping fingers of mist were crawling on the quayside. There was no sign of a knocker, and sniffing the air, he could find no stench of rot upon the airwaves. He breathed a sigh of relief. The Brax was at rest, and the knocker had not yet discovered their whereabouts. "Let's have a drink," he said to his companions. "'Twill help harden our resolve."

"There is a private bar in the cellar," Cor-cannan said. "'Tis used by racing folk and may offer some concealment. And if elves and fear deargs are in the bar, 'twill be added protection for us."

Cor-cannan opened a side door to the inn, and Kilfannan followed the others down a flight of stairs to the bar.

CHAPTER 7

AINE

The cellar room was warm and dimly lit, with tiny lights twinkling upon the walls. A cluricaun was lying in a stupor under a table, and in a corner nook, a group of fear deargs were happily bragging about their horses and scribbling bets between themselves. The sylphs went to the counter to order drinks, and sitting on a stool at the bar Kilfannan saw Mistress Aine of Ahascragh. Her flaxen hair was plaited in a long braid, and her soft white wool leggings and tight green silk shirt revealed the sensuous outline of her body. "Well met, the House of Kilfenoran and the House of An Carn," the succubus purred.

"'Tis good to see thee, my lady," Kilcannan greeted her, sitting on a stool beside her. "What can I be getting thee to drink?"

Stretching her sensuous body like a cat, Aine purred, "'Twould be me pleasure to accept a glass of the green faerie."

"Thy wish, as always, is my command! A glass of absinthe for the lady Aine, and four blackberry brandies," he said to the landlord.

"'Twill not be a moment," the innkeeper said, putting a cube of sugar into the silver strainer on the glass. He put the brandies on the counter.

Seeing an empty stool on the other side of Aine, Kilfannan sat down beside her.

"Well met, Kilfannan of the star brow," she said smoothly, looking quizzically at the emerald on his forehead.

"'Tis a pleasure, ma'am," he replied lightly, gazing in fascination at the small sprays of orange roses that were budding and blooming in her pale blue face. She was an exquisite faerie. *Damnably beautiful,* he thought as the heady perfume of wood hyacinth engulfed him.

"Forgive meself for staring, but I have never seen a jewel grace thy countenance before."

At the mention of the emerald, Kilfannan felt a shadow touch his heart, and for a moment his grief returned. He could feel Aine's eyes upon him, and calming his breath, he picked up his glass and said, "A toast to a beautiful lady! Slainte!"

She stared at him for a moment, and the roses faded from her cheeks. "Kilfannan, you are the sweetest of hearts," she purred, gently kissing him on the cheek; but mirrored in her eyes, he saw questions.

Turning to Kilcannan, she said, "Meself missed thee at the races today." She nudged him with her riding boot. "'Tis not like thyself to miss a meeting."

Knowing she was looking for answers, and fearing Kilcannan would inadvertently reveal their mission, Kilfannan answered quickly, "No, my lady, 'tis not. Our House hath business at the village of Lake Carn, and we journey there."

"So you are on an errand to the Crystal Mountains?" Meeting Kilfannan's eyes, she held them for a moment; and then, with a half-smile, she eyed their weapons curiously. "The bows and quivers that you carry were worn by the Tuatha De Danaan ... long ago. I see there is a mystery here," she purred. Her slender fingers rested lightly on Kilfannan's arm, and there was the liveliest curiosity in the dark turquoise eyes that looked at him from under long, fringed lashes. "Tell me, Kilfannan, what brings thee and thy brother, and I deem the House of An Carn, from your green hills to seek the northern road?"

For a moment, her question caught him by surprise and he was at a loss for an answer. He couldn't take the chance of telling her the truth – or anybody – for fear of a betrayal. *'Tis true*, he thought. *Aine hates goblins and all despoilers of the Green, but she is also wayward and capricious.* She was the changeling child of a satanic rape, and her sire's reptile seed had cursed her High Faerie nature. Before Kilfannan could think of an answer to her question, he heard the Brax chime a warning in his brother's pocket.

"Enemies are outside," Kilcannan shouted, leaping out of his chair and running to the stairs. "We must fly!"

Bounding out of his seat, Kilfannan followed his brother up the stairwell, out of the front door, and onto the quayside. Once out into the stenchful air, he stopped in his tracks, and every fibre in his body froze. The grey shape of a knocker and his magg were racing along the quayside towards the tavern.

"Goblins!" he shrieked. Glancing round, Kilfannan saw the sylphs of An Carn behind him. "Cor-garran! Let us climb onto the roof and fire upon the filth from there." He looked for his brother and saw him standing by the entrance to the stables with his sword drawn, ready to fight.

"Cor-cannan! Stay with my brother! I go to the roof of the inn."

Shinnying up the drainpipe, behind Cor-garran, Kilfannan took up a position on the peak of the roof beside him. The two knelt down, drew their bows, and fired into the goblin horde running towards them in the street below. The sea wall narrowed in front of the inn, and packed into a narrow space between the sea wall and the pub, the goblins made easy targets.

Kilfannan saw the thin, cold form of Aeguz push his way to the front line of his magg. The knocker made passes with his bony hands, and looking skyward to the roof, he began to keen a droning, discordant incantation. Dark shadows wove themselves around his thin shape as it shifted and expanded.

"Nephew!" Kilfannan cried. "The knocker is casting a spell against us. Let us kill him."

As their arrows streaked towards Aeguz, several of his magg jumped in front, shielding the knocker's body with their own. As they fell dead, more ran up, forming a wall around him. Kilfannan saw Grad come running around the corner, yelling orders. More goblins joined the ranks, and jumping over the bodies of their fallen comrades, they made a semicircle around his brother and Cor-cannan. He saw them draw their swords and charge into the goblins that had got to the alleyway. Using their superior speed and lightness, the sylphs thrust and parried, evading the thrusts of the goblins' knives and hammers.

"Nephew! Thy back!" he heard Kilcannan scream as a goblin made a run from the stables. Cor-cannan spun upon his heel and drop-kicked the demon in the throat, sending him sprawling to the cobbles.

Arrow after arrow Kilfannan let fly into the goblin ranks as they closed in around his kin, and he watched in horror as a goblin forced his brother's head back and a jagged blade reached for his throat. Before he could loose an arrow, he saw the goblin's head fall with a greasy slap upon the street and heard his evil blade clatter as it landed on the road. Standing behind Kilcannan was the succubus, black blood dripping from her blade.

The goblins backed away, and Kilfannan saw Aine step forward. Her flaxen hair faded into green scales and puffed up around her elongating face like a cobra's hood. The black slits of her eyes glowed orange, and clothed only in scales, her sword pointed before her, she darted forward to the fight. Venom sprayed from her mouth onto the knocker, and as his thin, cold voice reached a crescendo, he morphed into a vampire bat and took flight towards the rooftop. Kilfannan saw Aine jump into the air and catch him in her hands as he took flight. She then staggered back as a grey pulsing fume tried to force her fingers open. A sweat broke out on Kilfannan's brow as he strung an arrow in his bow, and for an agonising moment, he watched her struggle to contain the lurid light. Taking aim, he made ready to shoot the knocker if he should escape. He saw Aine's arms ripple with undulating waves of energy, and with a hiss she forced her hands together. A thrill ran through him as she dropped a pile of ash onto the road. She had destroyed the knocker scum.

"Kilfannan!" Cor-garran cried out excitedly. "Aine hath vanquished the knocker."

"Indeed! She hath triumphed." He peered into the road. With the loss of their knocker, he thought the goblins would back away and run, but instead they were surging forward, jumping over the bodies of the slain, and attacking his brother and Cor-cannan with renewed hate. "Damnation!" he cried out. "The goblins are attacking our houses again."

Firing arrows as fast as he could into the squirming, cursing filth, Kilfannan heard Grad scream. "Kill the scum! Meself is your leader now. Get on the roof and take the scumbags' heads."

Looking for Aine in the goblin scrum, he saw her in the road wielding her blade with both hands. Arms and heads rolled onto the cobbles, and black blood stained the ground. Covering their eyes with their claws, the goblins bellowed and cursed as venom splattered on their hides.

He felt Cor-garran nudge his arm. "Look, Kilfannan," he hissed. "Fercle, the steward from the racecourse, hath arrived in his rig. The goblins are attacking him."

Fercle was the up-breath of the House of Fire. The lord of Gort and Kilfannan knew him well. The fire elemental was a great healer of shadows and one with the fiery heart of the dragon Trax. Peering into the seething mass of goblins, he saw Fercle grab his whip and dash headlong into his attackers. From his mouth issued a stream of fire, and a gold dragoneen appeared. Taking flight, the dragon sent blast after blast of cold fire into the seething, cursing goblins. Seeing Grad desperately trying to shield his face from the fiery breath, and screaming to his magg to retreat, Kilfannan cried, "The filth is in rout; they are scuttling off into the darkness."

Making sure all was clear, they shinnied down the drainpipe and over to Kilfannan's brother and Cor-cannan, who were leaning against a wall. Kilcannan had an ugly slash across his cheek, and green blood was congealing in his hair.

"Art thou all right, brother?" Kilfannan asked in concern.

Kilcannan's eyes were sparkling with the yellow light of fire. "I am alive!" He grinned. "Thank the stars for the web mail. It hath turned a hundred thrusts but left meself a little sore."

Putting his arm gently around his brother's shoulders, Kilfannan murmured, "'Tis a strange and wondrous thing. The quiver that Ke-enaan gifted us is indeed a charm. The black arrows are quickly replenished as we use them. Methinks they fly back to the quiver."

"Few in numbers we may be," Kilcannan answered with the fey light of battle in his eyes, "but in truth, in the battle, brother, we are many."

Kilfannan turned his attention to Cor-cannan, who was nursing his hand. "How fare thee, nephew?"

"I have a badly bitten hand," he replied, wincing with pain. "'Tis a miracle I did not lose my fingers."

"Come!" Kilfannan ordered. "Let us take healing and refreshment at the inn. Methinks Grad will need time to regroup. The loss of Aeguz and the arrival of Aine in defence of our house will have given him plenty to think about, and I am sure he will not bother us again tonight. He is in no hurry, for he knoweth the leagues that lie before us. He will wait and ambush us on the road." He looked around for Fercle. The steward was breathing in his dragoneen. Grabbing a black bag from his rig, he came forward to join them.

"Well met!" he cried. "What the deuce is going on? Meself came for a drink and saw a battle raging." He smoothed back his blue-black hair and stared at the sylphs. "'Tis a dark day indeed when the filth from the mines attack the House of Air," he said, following them to the entrance of the inn.

The front door to the inn was locked, and the shutters drawn. Fercle hammered on the door. "'Tis meself, Fercle. Open up!" There was no reply, and Fercle hammered on the door again.

After a brief wait, the door slowly opened, and Kilfannan saw a cluricaun peer out.

"Let us in!" Fercle demanded. "Me friends are injured and need healing."

The landlord opened the door and let them in before closing it and bolting it behind them. "What was going on outside?" he asked, staring at the bloodstained sylphs.

"Goblins attacked the House of Air. Damnation take them," Fercle responded angrily.

"First I knew there was trouble brewing," the cluricaun said, "was when my brother came running up the stairs from the cellar bar and into the public bar shouting 'Goblins!' Trying to find out what was happening, we opened the front door and looked into the street. Seeing a knocker and goblins running down the hill towards us, we bolted the door and closed up the windows. Goblins is one thing, but a knocker … they're bad," the landlord said. "We went downstairs and locked ourselves in the wine cellar." He belched loudly, and swaying slightly, he went behind the bar.

Fercle nodded a touch impatiently. "Do not worry; the goblins will not trouble you, for they have fled back to their holes. Now, may I come behind the bar and get water and a cloth to clean the wounds of me friends here?"

"Right you are, sir," the landlord replied.

"Kilfannan!" Cor-cannan said, joining them in the bar. "I counted twenty-nine dead goblins." He put his hand in his jerkin pocket. "And there are these." He emptied the contents of a greasy bag into Kilfannan's hand.

"Faith!" Kilfannan frowned, looking at the glittering rubies in his palm. "Arms in need are one thing, but 'tis a sorry day in Faerie when a sylph of the House of Air rifles through the grimy pockets of slain goblins. 'Tis not wise to steal from the foul folk of the mines for gain's sake." He handed the rubies back to Cor-cannan.

"And 'tis not wise, Kilfannan, to leave jewels for their filthy kin to find. Who knows – we may have need of barter."

Fercle joined them carrying a bowl of water and cloths in one hand and a doctor's bag in the other. "All is ready," Fercle said.

"Come, Kilcannan! Sit yourself down, and meself will tend your wounds. There is a nasty deep gash on your face and three gouges on your scalp. Was it blade or claw?"

"Blade *and* claw," Kilcannan replied, wincing as Fercle cauterised the wounds with his fiery breath.

"Remember the time yourself and Doon-vannan were attacked by a score of goblins at me racecourse and had to take refuge in the weighing room? Both of you were a mass of cuts and bruises."

"'Twas a fight, all right!" Kilcannan grinned. "And we kept the gold!"

"There, 'tis done," Fercle said, putting puffball unguent on the wounds.

"Blessings, Fercle, for thine healing. I am fortunate indeed that thou art here to help me."

"And thank thee, Fercle, for coming to our aid," Kilfannan said, beaming. "And blessings to Trax, thy fire dragoneen."

"'Tis a pleasure to be of service to the House of Air," he replied. "Now, Cor-cannan, let me take a look at the goblin bite upon your hand."

"Cor-cannan!" Kilfannan said. "Give the rubies to Fercle for his healing. The stones may carry goblin stain, and he will cleanse them with his dragon's breath. We have no need of barter, for our House carries purses of gold."

Fercle bowed, taking the stones from Cor-cannan, and sent a flickering blue flame around the rubies. The fire blazed with the taint of Lower Faerie and then glowed red. "Blue fire has cleansed the jewels and consumed the foul vibration clinging to them," he said. He wrapped the rubies in a handkerchief and put them in his pocket. Then he took a root from his bag and blew on it until the end began to smoke and smoulder. "'Tis a deep and ugly wound. Inhale the smoke treatment," he commanded, waving the smouldering root under Cor-cannan's nose. "'Twill ease your pain and cleanse your energy from the corruption of the goblin's poison."

When Fercle had finished with his treatments, the company gathered at the counter.

* * *

Aine stood in the shadow of the inn and morphed back into faerie form. The shape-shift had drained her energy, and the destruction of the knocker had sapped her last reserves. She sighed with fatigue. The gnawing, shrieking hunger to hunt and devour mortal sperm was upon her again, and she feverishly prayed to her mother's essence to help her overcome the evil, lust-filled need of her father's reptile seed.

Her mother was Erin, the queen of water from High Faerie, who lived in a crystal waterfall on Vanala, an enchanted isle beyond the ninth wave of Earth's dreamland. One day as she swam in the clear, warm waters of the sea, she was snatched by Manannan Mac Lir, the reptilian lord of the underworld, and taken to his underwater city. There he brutally raped her and impregnated her, and Erin gave birth to two sets of twin girls and boys, succubi and incubi, part demon and part divine. Aine's sister Graine had a sacred wood in Limerick, and she would oft join her in the soirees held by the sisters of the wood and their wanton daughters. Her thoughts lingered on Nala, her brother. He was an incubus, and she saw him only once in every age, at the time of the mating, when she would flood him with mortal sperm to fertilise the eggs he had stolen from mortal women.

Warmth and a need for release coursed through Aine, and she knew it would not be long before the coupling. She wondered if the sylphs were in the bar, and as she walked towards the door, she felt a hot spasm of desire run down her back.

Recoiling against the wall, Aine tried to fight the carnal desire that slithered like a snake through her body. Suddenly all vestiges of Faerie left her and she was consumed with the lust of the hunt and the ecstasy of the feed. Ravening with hunger, she entered the inn and, stepping into the faerie bar, looked into the mortal version of the pub. Her body shivered with excited expectation as she looked around the bar. She needed the sperm of three mortals to assuage her hunger and rejuvenate her being.

The bar was lively and full of people. Musicians were playing traditional music, and instantly her attention was drawn to a tall man sitting on a stool while playing a violin. Aine eyed him predatorily. His gonads were full and heavy, and she determined to take him first. Glancing along the counter for her second feed, she saw the gleam of a peridot, a stone of fire and air. Focussing her attention, she saw the glow was emanating from an older man who was watching the band, and from his aura she could see he had faerie sight. She tensed in anger. The foul vibrations of the peridot could put her to flight, and to avoid a possible interference, she decided to give the mortal a wide berth. Looking away, she scanned the tables in the bar. A paunchy man was sitting on his own, tapping his foot in time with the song. She looked between his legs. His gonads were ripe for plucking, and she determined to take him as well. Being in Faerie, Aine was invisible to the mortals, and it would be easy to approach them unnoticed and get her pheromones upon them.

The song came to an end, and Aine glided across the room to the violin player and stood beside him. As he got off the stool, she cast the hypnotic spell of a snake around him. Pressing up against his body, she breathed out the perfume of the wood into his face. Her smell would sink through his pores, inflaming his blood and erasing his memory of any women other than her. Unable to contain her compulsion to ensnare him, Aine put her hand between his legs and gently squeezed his scrotum. It excited her to feel the mortal squirm under her touch and hear him groan with pleasure.

To her irritation, he was suddenly joined by a pretty, heavily pregnant young woman. "Oh, Dirc, that was grand music, to be sure," the girl said, linking her arm in his. Aine watched him shake the girl off. Going to the hearth, he picked up a poker and thrust it into the fire. Following him to the fireplace, she fondled him again.

The mortal's eyes were smouldering with lust as he groped the space around him. His breath was fast and heavy, and Aine knew she had conquered him. She was just about to move to the table to claim her second victim when she heard the girl say, "Dirc! What's the matter? Why are you groaning?" She put her hand on his arm, but he sloughed it off again and moved away.

"Have I done something to upset you?" she cried out.

Dirc said nothing. Aine heard the hiss as he thrust the poker deep into his glass to mull the ale, and the action inflamed her passion even further. She pressed up against him once more as he stood by the fire and sensuously licked his neck.

Leaving Dirc for a moment, Aine went to the table where the paunchy man was sitting, and breathing out her perfume, she sensually caressed him.

* * *

Jack the gravedigger was sitting on a stool at the bar watching the band when he noticed an orange glow forming around his friend Dirc. Having the gift of faerie sight, Jack knew the red-orange fume was the vibration of a succubus. She was hidden in the Faerie realms, and he suspected he was the only one in the bar that knew she was there. After she had marked her prey, she would materialise in alluring form and take the men away. He shuddered as he thought of the dead bodies of the young men that had been found lately in the area on riverbanks and rock-strewn hillsides. He had dug their graves, and even though the coroner's report said they had died from natural causes, he knew better. The men had desiccated testicles in common, and that was the work of a succubus.

The tainted orange light was growing stronger, and he could smell a sweet and sickly perfume in the bar. He thought about joining Dirc and intervening before the deadly liaison between him and the succubus took place. He could put her to flight with the peridot ring he was wearing, but he knew the demon would not forgive his intrusion and would find a way to kill him. But he thought that if Dirc's wife could get him over to the counter, the succubus would not draw near and would instead go in search of other prey. Glancing at Yvonne, he saw her pulling on Dirc's arm.

"What's going on?" he heard her say.

The stink of the succubus was growing stronger, and Jack saw an orange flame strike Yvonne in the ribs. With a gasp, she staggered backwards.

"Yvonne!" He beckoned her over.

"There's something wrong with Dirc," she said in distress. "He jabbed his elbow into me ribs, and it hurts." She started to cry. "And he's groaning like he's having sex."

"Having sex!" Steve, one of Dirc's friends guffawed, making a vulgar gesture with the middle finger of his hand. "I'd like some of what he's having!" Suddenly, he dropped his glass of beer on the floor and, with his arms outstretched, started writhing in his chair.

* * *

The orange glow glided to a table, and thinking there might still be a chance to save his friend, Jack said, "Yvonne! Try to get Dirc to come over to the counter next to me." Seeing her dithering, he added sharply, "For the love of God, get your man out of here."

Aine could wait no longer. She was hungry and excited, and she had three men upon which to feed. Imaging an orange silk shirt to cover her sumptuous breasts, she undid the first four buttons to expose her cleavage. Adding a tight black skirt and a pair of stiletto heels, she glided across the room to Dirc. Shivering with desire, she lowered her frequency to resonate with the mortal world, and she appeared beside him at the hearth.

"Where did you come from, bitch?" Yvonne said angrily. "That's my husband you're with. Leave him alone and go back where you came from." To Aine's fury, his girlfriend tried to pull him away from her.

Aine gave her a wicked grin and lashed out at Yvonne with her nails. The woman screamed and clutched at her face. Blood ran down her fingers, and with a shriek she fell down on the floor.

* * *

Jack fingered his peridot ring. He felt compelled to act. Standing beside Dirc was Steve and another man, and all three were amorously groping the voluptuous body of the succubus. He had to use the peridot against her. Lowering his gaze to avoid eye contact, he got off his stool and moved towards Dirc. His eyes suddenly felt dry, and he tried to blink but found them stuck wide open. The succubus had cast a spell on him, and slowly he was forced to raise his head and meet her eyes. For an instant, he was consumed by a hot orange-and-turquoise sea of blazing, lethal warning, and in that dreadful moment, he knew that if he interfered with her prey, she would exact a terrible revenge and call forth evil things buried in the churchyard to haunt him into suicide or madness.

Jack saw Yvonne struggle up and grab at Dirc's arm again. "What about the baby?" she wailed.

Jack looked away as the succubus swung round in a fury and body-slammed Yvonne to the floor. The bar was in uproar; customers were rushing by him and running for the door, and he heard the landlord calling the police.

Chancing a look across the room, Jack saw the succubus going through the side door. Her victims were following behind her like dogs after a bitch in heat. "I'd better get ready with me shovel," he murmured resignedly to himself.

* * *

Aine crawled off the last of her feeds and, opening the door of a van belonging to one of her victims, stepped outside into the carpark at the back of the inn. Her hunger had been satiated, and she could feel the mortals' life force coursing through her, replenishing and invigorating her faerie form. Raising her hands in tribute to the leering moon, she imaged her attire as riding clothes. She was curious about the House of Air and decided to return to the Shipwreck Inn and visit with them, believing that their errand to the Crystal Mountains must be of great import. She had noticed the spasm of pain that had crossed Kilfannan's face when she had asked him about the star emerald on his brow. He had quickly masked his grief, but she knew he was concealing an awful secret. She decided that whatever fell mission the House of Air was embarking on, she would offer them her blade and join them on the northern road.

CHAPTER 8

SMUGGLERS' COVE

Switching his gaze to the mortal bar, Kilfannan saw the landlady trying to help a sobbing pregnant woman that had fallen on the floor. There was the orange stain of a succubus around the woman's body and four livid scratches on her cheek. Glancing around the bar, he saw half-filled glasses left on the tables and unattended cigarettes burning in the ashtrays, and he gleaned that many of the customers had fled.

He knew Aine had left with mortal men, but he did not judge her actions. She was a succubus, and the curse of Manannan was upon her, and even though she was a bane of mortal men, in Faerie she was a champion of the Green. Without Aine, the HeartStar would have surely fallen. A shadow clouded his mind, and he was suddenly full of dread and doubt. They had barely survived the ordeal at the inn, and there were many miles to travel.

"Brother," Kilcannan said. "I read thy thoughts and have also been wondering where Aine is. She saved my life, and 'tis true that without her valour and prowess we would have surely been defeated."

Shaking fear loose from his mind, Kilfannan answered. "Destroying Aeguz would have drained her, for he was strong with dark magic. I trust she will return, for I too would like to thank her."

"Good sirs," the landlord said. "Meself is going to close the common room. You may take your drinks downstairs to the cellar bar."

The company followed Kilfannan down the stairs into the bar. "Let's take our drinks to the table by the fire," he said to the others. "There we can talk."

"A toast with me friends," Fercle said, pulling up a chair. "To our victory over the goblins! Slainte! Tell me how you found yourselves in a battle with the scum from the mines, for 'twas a killin' party that came against you, it would seem."

Kilfannan took a drink and leant back in his chair. "I went to the market in Kilfenora, and goblins tried to rob me."

"Tried to rob you!" Fercle exclaimed. "Meself hath never heard of such a thing."

Out of the corner of his eye, Kilfannan saw Aine walk into the bar and go to the counter. "Excuse me for a moment," he said to Fercle. "But Mistress Aine hath arrived, and I will invite her to our table." He went over to Aine, who was sitting at the counter. "Well met!" he said, gazing at the Venus flytraps blooming in her heart-shaped face.

"Well met yourself," she said lightly. "Meself is waiting for me green faerie. Wouldst thou like a drink?"

"No! 'Tis I that should be treating thee," Kilfannan answered, taking a gold coin from his pocket and putting it on the counter. "We are sitting at the table by the fireside and pray that thou wilt join us." He took her delicate hand in his. "In truth, I looked for thee after the fight, and for a moment I thought thou hadst come to harm, but thank the stars thou art safe."

The landlord put a tray on the counter. "For you, ma'am," he said. "The sugar cubes, silver strainer, and fancy glass meself stole from the mortal world. The wormwood liqueur is me own."

Aine flashed him a smile, picked up the tray, and followed Kilfannan to the table, where she sat down next to Kilcannan. "Aine! I owe thee my life," he said with gratitude. "Without thine help the Green would have fallen and all that we hold dear would have perished."

"How can that be?" she asked, pouring her drink. "The Radiance gives thee life! You cannot be destroyed while the Green lives."

"'Twas true for many turnings of the stars," Kilfannan answered. "But a tragedy hath befallen our creators."

"A tragedy!" she cried in astonishment. "To the High House of Air. I know naught of this! Those of us who love the Green are normally aware of any disturbance in the Green-spun. Tellest me what hath happened."

Kilfannan caught his brother's eye, and much was carried within the glance. Kilcannan gave a slight nod of his head. "May the truth be told," he said.

"Niamh and Caiomhin are trapped in the outer darkness," Kilfannan said, and he went on to tell Aine and Fercle the story of the coach. "And if we cannot find the key made of air, we are all doomed. 'Tis said the thief is at Lake Carn in the Crystal Mountains, and we travel north to find him." He saw a mixture of emotions pass across Aine's face: disbelief followed by a fearful understanding and then sadness.

"'Tis a terrible and deadly portent for the Green, and no mistake," she muttered.

"Aye," Fercle agreed. "And now 'tis clear to meself why a killin' party came against you."

The air grew close and heavy, charged with doubt and sorrow. Kilfannan glanced nervously at his brother. "I think it best we leave," Kilcannan said. "Aeguz is dead, and the magg is in disarray. In the respite, we might be able to leave the town unhindered and strike north, for others will find us if we tarry."

"You dare not leave in darkness," Aine declared. "You have barely made it this far, and now the goblins have more slain comrades to avenge. 'Tis folly! Thou wilt never make it through the mountains. Word of Aeguz's death will have travelled through the mines like wildfire on a windy day. Knockers and their maggs will be combing heath and bog, searching for thee, and all roads will be watched. There will be many a demon abroad in the dark that knoweth of the reward upon your heads and covets gold."

"'Tis indeed folly for the House of Air to go forth on their journey alone," Fercle exclaimed worriedly. "The chances of you reaching the Crystal Mountains without being harried and attacked are slim indeed."

"We have to try," Kilfannan responded. "For if we fail in our mission to free our creators, Ireland will become an empty, barren, brown wasteland, and all waters great and small will lie in stagnant pools, as will the entire world, for the House of Air will have vanished from the earth."

For a moment, Kilfannan's youthful countenance grew old, and his eyes misted over into sea foam. "With the loss of Niamh and Caiomhin, our slow death hath begun. As the Green fades, I will die, and so will Kilcannan. For us, the House of Kilfenoran, 'twill be a long, slow death of suffocation. As we diminish, then too our kin will fade, and their sheens across the land will stand empty and forlorn."

The sylphs of An Carn hung their heads in despair at Kilfannan's words.

"If the Green is lost in our world, then it is lost in the mortal world as well," Kilfannan went on. "There will no longer be any laughter or songs of happiness in the realm of man. Indeed, 'tis the harps, the flutes, the drumming of the bodhrans, the ringing of the trumpets, and the tinkling of the silver spoons that give us sylphs life. We are the music of air rising and air falling, the Breath of Life, and the heart centre of the Green. The lonely piper on the heath, the fen man playing on his whistle, and the singing of the birds – this is our food and our delight. In turn, it is our sacred obligation to spin the vibrating patterns of sound into the harmonies of leaf, grasses, moss, and sparkling woods, for both our realms. That is our purpose. For 'tis true that the colour of happiness and joy is green."

"Where would the water be without the wind?" Aine said, rising, and about her Kilfannan saw the mystical, shimmering radiance of High Faerie. "If the green of leaf and meadow is no more, me heart will break, and I will pine away and die. 'Twould be me honour to serve the House of Kilfenoran in this desperate quest, for now the fate of all the living Green hangeth in the balance. I will accompany thee on thy journey north, if thou wilt have me. I pledge to help thee save the Green." She offered her blade to the Kilfenorans.

The room was hushed, as if the very air were listening. Fercle rose from his chair and stood beside Aine. "Without the lords of Air, the House of Fire cannot last," he cried. "For who will fan the flame? I too pledge to protect the House of Air and travel northward. Me warmth will take away the chill of fear, and when the shadow strikes, me brightness will dispel it."

The emerald upon Kilfannan's brow blazed forth with the brilliance of the Green. "This is beyond good fortune!" the Kilfenorans replied in one voice. "May the blessing of the HeartStar be upon thee."

Kilfannan was overjoyed and relieved. He knew the goblins would come after his House with a vengeance, but the six of them together were worth a full magg of the stinking rabble. For the first time since he left Kilfenora, he felt relieved, even exhilarated, by the dangerous energy of the fight with the goblins. "A toast!" he shouted, raising his glass. "To Niamh and Caiomhin. May the stars protect them and the company of the key deliver them."

Fercle got up. "Meself will get more drinks," he said, and Kilfannan watched him go behind the counter and pour five blackberry brandies and a green faerie. After putting a guinea on the counter, Fercle brought the drinks and a bottle of brandy over to the table. "Let's fill our flasks," he suggested, opening the bottle. "'Twill lift our spirits on the journey north. Meself is going to saddle Sunbeam and stow me carriage in the pub yard."

They filled their flasks and chattered about the fight. After a while, the talk died down and the room was wreathed in silence, save the crackling of the fire in the hearth. Kilfannan leant his head back on the seat, dwelling on the monstrous chain of events he had been forced to confront. The fate of beauty in all worlds hung in the balance, and he wished he could wake up and find it all an evil dream.

He felt Aine's soft hand upon his arm. "Kilfannan," she purred, "once in every age there comes a time for meself to mate. The time cometh soon, for I feel the heat of replication pulsing through me. I will have to leave thy side, but me time of absence will be brief."

Kilfannan smiled and nodded. "My lady, thou hast succoured our House, and 'tis a boon to have thee with us. Thou mayst take thy leave at will."

"Which way were you a-thinking of going to the Crystal Mountains?" she asked, sipping on her drink.

"'Tis my mind," Kilfannan answered, "to take the road around the bay to Galway, and thence on to Oughterard by the Lough of Corrib."

She looked at him and frowned. "The goblins will be watching the Galway road, and they will expect to find us hurrying upon it. If we go that way, we will be outnumbered and outmatched, for the knockers will cast enchantments to ensnare us."

"'Tis the only road to Lake Carn," Kilfannan answered. "I know not another way."

"The knockers and their maggs will track us," Aine responded. "They know the nooks, crannies and places ripe for ambush on the northern road. We will have to outwit the filth and do the opposite of what they expect. Let us take the road to Clarinbridge and along the old east road to Cnoc Na Dala, the hill of the Great Assemblies, and on to me cottage in the enchanted woods of Ahascragh. The road is overgrown and forgotten, and with luck 'twill not be watched."

Kilfannan gazed at Aine across the table. Delicate forget-me-nots were blooming in her skin, and her shiny turquoise eyes flickered with orange fire. She was a changeling, and both sides of her nature had to have expression. In Faerie she was a champion of the Green and a friend to wild things living in the woods and meadows. His only concern was that her desire might unwittingly betray them.

"Aine," he said softly, leaning towards her. "Methinks 'twould be best for thee to feed again in the mortal world so thou wilt not have desire on our journey north."

She glanced at him, and he saw a shadow in her eyes. "Of late, me need hath grown sixfold. I should be energised with the feeding, but it does not last as it once did. With thy leave, meself will go and hunt again."

Kilfannan nodded. Aine's frank admission had unnerved him. He sensed her father's power was waxing, and he felt afraid for her High Faerie self.

"The mortal bar is still open, so meself will see thee in a little while," she purred.

Kilfannan leaned back in his chair and sipped his drink. *A lull before the storm*, he thought to himself. His relaxation came to an abrupt end as the Brax beeped a warning, and Aine came rushing through the door, followed by Fercle. "Knockers!" she hissed. "Meself saw them gliding along the quayside towards the inn."

"What can we do?" Cor-garran asked anxiously. "This is a cellar, and the only way of escape is up the stairs." He turned to Kilfannan in a panic. "We are entrapped!"

"Trapped, brother?" Cor-cannan tittered. "Why sayest thee this lie? 'Tis only knockers ... and they will not trouble us."

Kilfannan looked at him in shocked surprise. Cor-cannan's eyes were glassy, and a fell light dwelt within them. In his nephew's ears were diamond stud, and the stones were livid with the yellow taint of Lower Faerie. Before he could act, Aine grabbed his arm. "Kilfannan!" she said anxiously. "The knockers will soon enter the inn and, finding no one in the common room, will venture down here to search for thee. Me father's power over me is increasing, and even though meself hath fed, 'tis not enough, it seems, to power me reptile form. The only defence I have to offer is me sword – and the perfume of the wood, for 'tis like poison to a knocker. But 'twill only be a temporary respite. Make ready for battle as best thou canst." Her eyes filled with tears. "For the Green," she said, blowing the perfume of hyacinth up the stairs.

Kilfannan knew there was no way of escape but up the stairs from whence they had come. They had to get past the knockers, for there was no concealment in the room. He thought of Trax. Fercle could summon his dragoneen, and with his fiery breath, he would drive the knockers back and allow them to escape to the stables. He was about to ask Fercle when he saw fear and disappointment in the fear dearg's eyes, and knew his request, before even spoken, was in vain. "Meself called upon Trax," Fercle said grimly. "But there is no response upon the fire waves."

The Brax sounded a loud chime and then another. Kilfannan looked wildly around the bar. There were plenty of chairs and tables they could use to build a barricade. He was just about to call Aine when he was confronted by Cor-cannan's distorted, wrathful face. Before he could act, he felt a tremendous blow to his stomach that sent him crashing into a wall. He saw Cor-cannan pull out his knife and run towards him. In a blur, he saw Cor-garran and Kilcannan wrestle his assailant to the ground. "'Tis the fell stones thou art wearing that have caused this madness," Cor-garran cried out, ripping the diamond studs from his brother's ears and throwing them on the floor.

Cor-cannan was shaking in every limb as he stared at Kilfannan. "Forgive me," he said sorrowfully. He put his hand across his eyes and shrank back against his brother's body. "I know not what fell spell laid hold upon my mind."

There was a sudden hissing on the stairs. "'Tis forbidden to pass," Kilfannan heard Aine say commandingly. He glanced at the door and saw her standing on the bottom step with her sword drawn. "Ladies of the nightshade are gathering in the private cellar bar. Yourselves are not invited or welcome here."

The perfume of the wood grew stronger, and with it came a warning. Kilfannan leapt to his feet. He knew that Aine would not be able to deter the knockers for long, and they had to be ready to defend themselves. He looked around for the best place to give them a fighting chance and decided they should gather behind the bar.

"Fercle! Join Aine at the bottom of the stairs. If fortune favours us, the knockers will fear the summoning of a dragoneen and be loth to take the stairs. We will make our stand behind the counter and fire upon the filth from there. Come! Let us make ready."

The polished wooden counter curved outwards from the wall with shelves full of glasses and bottles behind it. "'Tis a cramped space," Kilfannan said to the others. "We have to find something to build a barricade to act as a shield against the arrows and missiles of the goblins."

The perfume of the wood flooded him with warning, and once more he heard a scuffle on the stairs and the hoarse shouts of goblins echoing above.

"Thy ploy is useless," he heard the thin voice of a knocker jeer. "Since when does a lady of the nightshade hold a soiree dressed in riding clothes?"

As Kilfannan glanced desperately around the shelves and cubbyholes for wooden serving trays that could serve as shields, he saw a long, low bench on the floor below the bottles. "Kilcannan! Helpest me with the bench; 'tis heavy and thick and will afford us some protection."

There was the sound of curses on the stairs, and the foul stench of the mines flooded Kilfannan's senses. He glanced over the counter at the door. Aine and Fercle were retreating into the bar, and he knew that at any moment the goblins would come pouring down the stairs.

Grabbing both ends of the bench, the Kilfenorans pulled it forward, away from the wall. Kilfannan heard a click and then a sliding sound. "By the stars!" he exclaimed, peering into the yawning black space in the floor. Seizing a lamp from the counter, he lowered the light and saw a flight of worn steps leading down into darkness.

"Quick! Down the stairs," he hissed, giving Cor-garran the light.

Following them down, he stood on the second step. He had to find a way to close the hidden door or the goblins would find it – and they would be trapped in a dead end with their backs against a wall.

He ran his hand around the edges of the door to see if he could find anything that could be pushed or turned, but there was nothing, and he stood there in despair. "I know not how to close the door," he said resignedly to Kilcannan.

"Brother, if the door was sprung open by pushing the bench forward, let us try to pull it back aways."

The bar exploded with shouts and curses, and Kilfannan heard the knocker venomously hiss, "Where art thou hiding the filth?"

In desperation, he and his brother leant out of the aperture. They grabbed the bench and heaved it backwards towards the wall. Kilfannan heard a click, and the door to the steps began to close.

They ran swiftly down the steps to the sylphs of An Carn, who were waiting at the bottom. Kilfannan took the light from Corgarran and stepped into a small room lined with glass flagons of wine. In a corner stood a vat of wormwood leaves.

At the far end of the room, Kilfannan saw a dark shade in the wall. Going forward with the light, he saw it was a passageway big enough for two to walk through abreast.

"An old smuggler's passage," he said in glee.

The sylphs stood in front of the passageway and smiled at each other. Kilfannan could hardly believe their good fortune. He felt they now at least stood a fair chance of escape. "If we follow it a ways, it should bring us to the sea."

Acting on intuition, Kilfannan viewed the room from a third-dimensional perspective and shivered in disgust at the old, stained mattresses, empty cans, and food bags that littered the filthy floor. Stepping over the debris, he noticed a pair of child's glasses with a smashed lens, and in the flickering light, he saw a red symbol smeared on one of the brick walls. It took him a moment before he realised the meaning. It was a reverse pentacle. *Satanists*, he thought grimly.

Drawing their weapons, they walked forward. The passageway and dripping gloom never seemed to end as they climbed over bits of wood and broken casks. Kilfannan noticed a cool, damp draught upon his face. The lamp went out, and they were left in darkness.

"The passage will probably bring us to the other side of the headland," Kilfannan said. "The air is growing clammy and heavy with the scent of brine."

After a while they came to the end of the tunnel and found the exit partially blocked by fallen rocks. "I will go first and make sure all is clear in both worlds," Kilcannan said, climbing over the boulders. Kilfannan followed and stepped out into a cave leading to a small cove with a shingle beach. "Smuggler's tunnel, to be sure," Kilcannan said, looking round in the darkness. "'Twill not be long before dawn, and 'tis best to stay here until light gives us a view."

"Brother! Dost thou think our friends have come to harm?" Kilfannan said.

"Nay," Kilcannan answered. "'Tis thee and me the knockers are after. When they found no trace of us at the inn, they would have left straight forth to get back on our trail."

"Faith!" Cor-garran cried out. "The tainted diamond studs I took from my brother still lie on the floor in the cellar bar. If a knocker finds them, he can bewitch my brother again."

"Let us pray the filth have overlooked them," Kilfannan answered. "But 'tis a worry indeed, for the goblin stain will draw the knocker's eyes towards them."

"Can the knocker read their memory?" Cor-garran asked. He nervously pulled out his flask, took a drink, and handed it to Kilfannan.

"'Tis me thought he can, and our plans will be revealed," Kilfannan replied. "We have to proceed with caution." Taking Kilcannan aside, he said softly, "Cor-cannan's mind was taken over by an evil frequency, and under its spell he attempted to murder us. 'Tis my thought that, thyself being the warrior of air descending, thou shouldst counsel our nephew. Cor-garran and I will bear witness."

Kilcannan nodded in agreement, and motioning to Cor-cannan to join him, he sat down on the shingle at the cave mouth. "Cor-cannan," he said. "A fell spell overtook thy being, and in its evil enthralment, thou tried to murder my brother."

Cor-cannan paled, and a sorrowful light glowed in his eyes. "'Twas the diamond earrings I took from the dead goblin's pocket. Methought they, being stolen from the mortal world, would be free of goblin taint." He hung his head in shame.

"I am puzzled," Kilcannan said. "Why didst thou not show them to us? Or give them to Fercle to cleanse with dragon breath?"

"For fear of losing them." He glanced regretfully at Kilfannan. "I have never felt such a feeling of desire for a trinket. But 'twas so overwhelming, all I could think about was keeping them for myself." He fell silent for a moment and then said haltingly. "I know now that it was the mortal vices of avarice and vanity that consumed me."

"Thou art not alone in thy travail," Kilcannan responded with candour. "Methinks we are all in danger, for as the darkness hath risen, the Cathac's will hath taken over the realm of men, and such is the strength of his dark dominion that mortal vice hath crept into the Faerie world." He took Cor-cannan's hand and, facing his brother, said, "'Twould seem the energy of the down-breath of air into fire hath been compromised by a taint from the mortal world. My nephew succumbed to vanity and greed, and meself was afflicted by rage and revenge, and brought the wrath of rerg upon us. And is it not so that rage means conflict, and together they weave the mask that terror wears."

Kilfannan shuddered as he pondered his brother's words. He realised that the attack on the HeartStar was not only on the physical level but on the spiritual plane as well. The vices of envy, greed, hate, and revenge had not been present in the psyche of the sylphs of air until of late, and he had noticed a growing penchant for violence in the speech and actions of his brother. He must be vigilant not only of his brother's words and actions but also of his own. His thought was broken by the sound of whistling. "List!" he cautioned to the others.

The whistle came again, long and low, and for a moment he thought he could smell the perfume of hyacinth on the air.

The whistle sounded yet again; more urgent in intensity than before, and the perfume of hyacinth burgeoned all around him. Recognition and joy soared in his heart. "Aine!" he cried out, running onto the beach.

"Fercle and meself are on the cliff above thee," she called down. "We wait with the horses." Looking up, Kilfannan saw the outline of two figures silhouetted in the glimmering dawn.

"Meself is letting a rope down," Fercle said as a thin cord snaked down the cliff and landed at Kilfannan's feet. Catching hold of the line, Kilfannan ran lightly up the cliff, followed by his brother and the sylphs of An Carn.

"Aine! Fercle! How didst thou escape from the knocker and find us?" Kilcannan asked in amazement.

"There is no time for explanations," she answered anxiously.

The Brax beeped in Kilcannan's pocket. "Goblins are close," he cried. "They are scouring the countryside for us."

"We must flee to me woods," Aine said, slipping into the saddle. "Mount up, and let us ride while the light broadens."

They left the clifftop in silence and rode down the hillside to a stand of trees. "The road to Kinvara is yonder," Kilfannan said, cautiously riding forward and peering through the branches. He listened to the airwaves but could hear naught but the sighing of the wood. "We have to cross it and take the chance there are no spying eyes."

Aine rode up alongside him. "I will take the lead. Follow me," she said to the company, breaking Nemia into a run. "With luck we'll reach me wood before noontide."

They left the trees and, crossing the road, galloped up the hillside. The sun was rising, and the sight of its brilliance lifted

Kilfannan's spirits. Cor-cannan's attack had shaken him to the core, and he decided that when they reached Aine's cottage he would talk to the members of his house. Honesty of thought was required to fulfil their quest, and he would urge them to voice any negative emotion that tried to infiltrate their minds.

They rode along an old straight track, and as they neared the hill of Turoc Cnoc Temho, they came to a carved white stone. Here they stopped and let the horses rest.

"This is Lia Fail, the stone of destiny," Aine said. "'Twas here the rulers of Cnoc Na Dala practised human sacrifice to appease their gods. They were shape-shifters and needed human blood to hold their mortal forms."

"The rite of blood hath come again," Kilfannan said grimly, catching Aine's eye. "A cluricaun told me of a conversation he overheard at a big house. There is a sabbat at Bealltainn in England, and evil men from Clare are going to attend. 'Tis me belief that the landlord of the mortal inn that we escaped from is part of the same satanic coven." Aine looked at him quizzically.

"Beneath the cellar bar is a room that leads to the passageway. There were stained mattresses on the floor and a devil sign painted on the wall in blood. Methinks the cluricaun that hath the faerie bar doth not have occasion to look into the mortal world when he is in his storeroom and knows naught of this evil. He should be warned, and counselled to guard his thoughts, for the evil of men is slowly affecting us all." He saw Aine's eyes narrow and the forget-me-nots fade from her face.

"I did not retrieve the diamond studs I took from my brother and cast upon the floor," Cor-garran said worriedly. "I fear that if a knocker finds them, 'twill go ill for my brother."

"Fear not," Fercle said. "Meself picked up the earrings and hath cleansed them with dragon fire." He reached in his pocket, brought out the diamond studs, and offered them to Cor-cannan.

"Nay!" Cor-cannan said, averting his eyes. "I no longer find them attractive. Do what thou wilt with the stones."

"We must make haste to Ahascragh," Aine said, shaking her horse's reins. "'Tis not wise for us to linger in the open, for spies of the enemy ride the wind."

As they approached the junction of the greenway and the mortal road to Doon, Kilfannan pulled up. "Cor-cannan!" he said. "'Tis best if thou ridest to the House of Doon and tellest them the peril that assails our house. Warn them to put a dream sleep upon their sheens so the goblins dost not find them. 'Tis not far to Doon, and thou canst follow on our trail and catch up."

Cor-cannan nodded and urged his horse forward.

"Wait," Aine cried as he rode away. "I hear the beat of horse hooves."

At the end of the greenway, a horseman came in view galloping towards them.

"Hail and well met!" the rider cried out, seeing the company and pulling up his charge.

"Hail and well met, Doon-vannan of the House of Doon," Kilfannan answered. "Cor-cannan was on his way to thy sheen to seek thee out."

"Hail! Kilfannan and Kilcannan of the House of Kilfenoran," he said, bowing his head in respect. "What service can I offer thee?"

Kilfannan noticed Doon-vannan staring uneasily at him.

"With the greatest of respect," Doon-vannan said, "how is it that thou wearest the star emerald of Gorias upon thy brow?"

"I have ill news," Kilfannan replied. "Niamh and Caiomhin are imprisoned in the outer darkness, and the key to the coach of the Green Radiance hath been stolen. We journey north in search of the thief and the key."

"Faith!" Doon-vannan cried out. "The imprisonment of our high house! This monstrous thing cannot be true!"

"Cousin, 'tis Ke-enaan who told me of the tragedy," Kilfannan responded. "I took the emerald from a knocker, and it revealed a conspiracy of evil to destroy our House of Air and the living Green of Heart."

"This is the evilest of tidings," Doon-vannan cried wildly, looking at the sylphs of An Carn.

"Our house hath joined the House of Kilfenoran," Cor-garran said. "We are accompanying our kindred on their errand north."

"My brother and I will join the quest," Doon-vannan said, turning his horse around. "I will tell my brother, and we will join thee straight away."

"Stay!" Kilfannan shouted. "I need thee and Doon-cannan to spread the news to all the sheens in Ireland that the House of Air is under attack. The gate from Under-Earth hath been breached, and all manner of evil monsters are abroad. They wish to destroy us all. I charge thee to go forth and warn our kin across the island."

Doon-vannan nodded. "I will go and enlist the House of Drumkeary. We will alert all the sheens in Clare and send forth riders to all the sheens in Eiru."

"There is more fell news," Kilfannan said. "When the mortal coach was stolen, the thief took a silver mare, the counterpart of Brea, from the stable. We have to find her. Spread the word to the trooping elves and fear deargs, and tellest them that if they should see a miniature silver mare, to steal her and take her to thy stables at Doon. Once thou hast claimed her, send word to the wizard Keenaan at Black Head."

"Indeed! I will scour the markets and the horse sales in Galway and in Clare, and bribe cluricauns with gold to eavesdrop on the talk amongst horse dealers at taverns in every town. I vow to find her," Doon-vannan said, fir-light blazing from his eyes. "But tellest me, Kilfannan, where goest thou from here?"

"To the woods of Ahascragh, and me cottage in the vale," Aine said, and throwing back her hood, she shook out her flaxen hair.

"Mistress Aine!" Doon-vannan cried in joyful recognition. "Greetings! And Fercle!" he said, gazing at the fire lord. "Do you both ride with the House of Kilfenoran?"

"Indeed!" they said as one.

"I now ride back to the House of Doon. May the sun speed thee on thy way and the stars watch over thee," Doon-vannan called, breaking the Tralee Rose into a trot.

"We must press on," Aine said, looking at the clouding sky. "There is still a ways to go."

They rode forward along the greenway, and after a few miles, the fields and hedgerows bordering the path gave way to hill and heath. Aine pointed ahead to a dark wood upon a distant hilltop. "The sacred woods of Ahascragh," she cried. "We will go across country from here and leave the road behind, for meself hath presentiment that evil stalks the road ahead."

The company left the greenway and galloped across the fields and flower-studded meadows, and through peaty bog where rare orchids and gleaming crowfoot peeped out amongst the reeds. They came to a track beside a brook that meandered through meadows to the foot of a tree-clad hill crowned in snowy clouds of hawthorn blossoms. Breathing in the perfumed air, Aine pointed to the trees. "See how the flowers of our sacred tree gleam like a crown of pearls against the glowing sky."

"'Tis a High Faerie place and no mistake," Kilfannan said.

Aine glanced at him with solemn eyes. "'Tis here, to me woods, that I retreat when the hunger of Manannan cometh upon me."

A silver hare ran out of a hazel break to greet them. "Behold!" she cried joyfully. "The talisman of me brother lover Nala hath come to mark our passage to the wood."

They followed the hare up the hill and into the woodland. The sunlight filtered softly through the hawthorn, hazel, beech, and oak, shedding rays of joy upon the flowering ground. "Welcome to the woods of Ahascragh," Aine purred, "where the vine of love and blossoms of enchantment never fade."

The air was cool and windless as they rode through the trees, and bluebells stretched before them like a vivid sapphire carpet. Kilfannan's spirit soared as he noted every nuance of the Green in the leaves of grass, flower, bush, and tree, where sound, scent, and colour were absolute in one. From every thicket and briar, he heard the enchanting harmony of birdsong, and the emerald upon his brow blazed with living light as he revelled in the perfume of the flowers. Letting go of Red Moon's reins, his fingers wove the magic of the Green, and for a fleeting instant he felt the ecstasy of his sylphid life return.

They rode down the hill into a wooded vale and through a shallow ford dark with alder. "Me home is yonder," Aine said, pointing to a low whitewashed cottage. Red clematis sprawled across the walls and golden thatch, and a dark hedge on three sides glowed with delicate white blossoms.

Aine led them along a path and into a grassy sward before the entrance. Slipping from Nemia's back, she picked up the hare and held it to her heart. "I will not cease in the struggle against the enemy of life 'til he is vanquished," she said, "for the innocent lives of the creatures of wood and meadows are caught up in the deadly struggle that is being waged against the Green." She put the hare down and said, "Me heart is thine heart."

Leaving the horses free to roam upon the pasture, they stood together before the entrance to the cottage. And there, in the peace of the Green under a clear blue sky, their souls met as one, and for a moment all thoughts of pursuit were forgotten.

CHAPTER 9

THE WOODS OF AHASCRAGH

The room was warm, dreamlike, and heavy with the scent of hyacinth. In the centre was an oval table and six round-backed chairs, and above the hearth was a painting of Aine's black mare Nemia galloping through flower-studded meadows. Beside the fireplace was a long, dark sideboard with candelabra, a crystal decanter of brandy, and glasses.

Aine poured out the drinks and bade the company sit down. "'Tis time for talk. Meself and Fercle were amazed and much relieved to see that you had vanished. 'Twas fortune herself who smiled upon thee," Aine said, raising her glass. "Slainte!"

"And what of thyselves?" Kilfannan asked. "How did you fare against the knockers?"

"While I was standing guard at the bottom of the stairs, two knockers appeared at the top and demanded access to the dungeon bar," Aine answered. "I tried to prevent, and then delay, their entry to the cellar room. Fercle joined me, and together we blocked their passage. The knockers drew knives against us and, gliding down the stairs, attacked us. Parrying their blows, we retreated into the bar. Finding you had vanished, we were filled with bravado, and standing tall with swords drawn, we watched the knockers glide around the bar and over the counter, to make sure you were not secreted underneath. Yelling goblins came rushing down the stairs and into the bar, but they drew back when they saw meself. One or two of the brutes had venom burns from the fight and bolted up the stairs. 'Twas then that Fercle took a hand," she said, smiling sweetly at the fear dearg.

Fercle chuckled. "I says to the rabble, 'If you don't clear off, meself will summon Trax to scorch your filthy hides.' The knockers hesitated for a moment, but when they saw the summoning fire in me eyes, they retreated to the door and up the stairs, hurling threats and curses at us." He drained his glass and refilled it from the decanter. "We followed the knockers up the stairs and peered through the open doorway into the street. The goblins were milling about, and the knockers were gliding low, tasting the air for any scent of you upon the airwaves. Aine slipped into the alley leading to the stables to reassure the horses, and meself went upstairs and awoke the landlord. He was all affright when I told him what had happened in the cellar room and your disappearance. When he had collected himself, he told me of a hidden door and a secret smuggler's passage to the cove beyond the headland."

Fercle paused and took another drink. "All this talking is making me thirsty," he jested, and he then continued on. "Taking leave of the landlord, I joined Aine in the stables. The road was clear of goblins, and mounting our charges, with the other horses following, we rode along the quayside. At the far end of the breakwater, we saw a hill, and after we had gained the turf, we galloped round the outskirts of the town and across the cliffs to Smugglers' Cove."

Aine topped up the glasses. "Our deliverance calls for another toast." She laughed. "To Smugglers' Cove!"

Fercle chimed in. "And secret passages!"

The sylphs sat quietly sipping on their drinks, discussing the dark spells and murderous pursuit that had overtaken their lives.

"'Tis my belief that we are in spiritual danger as well as physical," Kilfannan said to them. "For evil influence and desires unknown to us are issuing from the mortal world into our energetic realm. Anger, avarice, and murder have stealthily attacked our hearts, and evil, seeking to blind us with its guile, hath sought our undoing," He saw Cor-cannan hang his head. "Any thought that cometh that is foreign to our nature," he resumed, "we should immediately dispel by opening our hearts to one other."

"Aye," Cor-cannan answered. "For the evil feeling came upon me like a thief in the night, and I know not when it will strike again." Cor-garran put his hand on his brother's arm. "Different darkness will try to overcome me, of that I am sure. Fret not, dear brother, for we are all assailed."

"Aye," Kilcannan answered. "Let vigilance of thought be our guiding light."

Kilfannan leaned back in his chair and tried to relax, but he found rest impossible. His world had been turned upside down in such a short time that his thoughts were scattered and confounded with fearful speculation. The roads and country leading to the Crystal Mountains would be fraught with peril. Enemies were at every hand, and he wondered what path to take when they left the sanctuary of the wood. "Aine," he said. "We must think upon our journey."

She nodded. "'Tis not going to be easy to avoid battle, for all roads and greenways north will be watched. We will have to take the road around the bay and then strike north to Oughterard, Maam Cross, and on to the Crystal Mountains."

"I suggest we take the road to Tuam and cross the Loch of Corrib." Fercle said. "The road around the bay will be heavily guarded, and there is no cover for several miles. I fear we will be sitting ducks if we go that way."

Aine's face paled. "'Tis not wise to cross the lake, for I fear what lies beneath. The Loch of Corrib was once called Loch Oirbsen after me father, Manannan Mac Lir. 'Tis foretold that as the shadow rises, he will shake off his sleep and rise again, taking to the sea in the service of the Cathac. Hateful he is of me High Faerie heritage, and he wishes to see me faerie nature dead – as he does yourselves. Nay, 'tis better that we rush the road around the bay in darkness."

"Manannan hath the power to set the Cathac free," Kilfannan said apprehensively. "Hath he been released from the cloying darkness of the bog of Magh Cuilen?"

"'Tis only his mortal body that lies in the sucking hold of Under-Earth. His dark spirit fled into the deep, and he waits, gnawing and hating in the slimy, ruined city that was once his crown upon the earth." Aine pursed her lips and slowly shook her head. "Hath he come forth? To that question meself knows not the answer, but me desire to feed is increasing, and me will to resist the feast of men is weakening. That is a sign of his return."

"Prince Donne of the Dunes sent us warning of evil in the element of water," Kilfannan responded. "And I fear to cross the Lake of Corrib. We should heed his warning."

"His caution is wise," Aine said. "We have to make our way around the coast, and every furlong is a hazard." She thought for a moment. "But 'tis goblins that are our immediate concern, for me father in his reptile form cannot leave deep water. 'Twill be in the crossing of a lake or sea that he will come against us."

She put down her glass. "I have an idea," she said. "Methinks 'tis best if the House of Air dresses as succubi. Goblins are slow-witted creatures, and knockers detest the perfume of the wood. Seeing five ladies on the road with a fire escort wilt not arouse their suspicions straight away. If we are fast, 'twill be a while before they realise their mistake."

"'Tis a grand ploy!" Kilcannan exclaimed. "We may get clear of the coast and be on our way to Oughterard before the goblins realise the deception."

Aine beckoned them. "Come! There is a sea chest in the alcove, and 'tis full of cloaks, wigs, and other alluring trivia worn at the soirees of the sisters of the wood."

The company followed her across the room to the sea chest. Opening the lid, Aine said, "Choose as your fancy takes you, and let us see if you can pass for ladies of the night." She reached inside and brought out a black velvet half mask. "This is for thyself," she said, handing it to Kilfannan. "The emerald on thy brow is a certain giveaway."

Kilfannan looked at the mask in wonder. Around the edges and eyeholes were small rubies, and attached to it was an expandable band for fastening. He tried it on, and in the smoothness of its touch, he felt a little more secure of his deception.

"Tellest me, my lady, how came thee by these fineries?" Cor-cannan asked cheekily, draping a blue cloak around his shoulders.

"Meself was hunting in a fashionable pub not far from Ahascragh," she purred. "I saw a mortal that aroused me passion, but as I went to put me scent upon him, a peridot tie tack he was wearing repelled me advances." She stretched her long, shapely legs. "Meself found another prey, but me passion was not quenched, for I still hungered for the man I had first chosen. He was leaving with a party of others when I returned to the inn, so I followed him to a country house. There was a masked soiree going on in the ballroom, and following him to a bedroom, I watched him put the tie tack on a sideboard." She smiled at them knowingly, and Kilfannan saw little Venus flytraps snapping in her face. "When meself had feasted, as I was going down the stairs, I passed a number of guests dressed in black cowled cloaks, and 'twas then that I realised the true nature of the gathering." She grinned wickedly. "I had a yearning to follow them to their sabbat and feed on their sexual energy, but having already gorged meself, I went instead to their rooms and robbed them of their knicks and knacks."

"Admirable!" Cor-cannan cracked.

Hanging on the wall behind the chest was a collection of bronze-hilted daggers and swords. Aine took down a sheathed blade and handed it to Kilfannan. "This is for thyself to carry into battle."

Kilfannan stared at a curious knotted design on the handle, and pulling the dagger from the scabbard, he noticed the same symbol traced upon the blade. "'Tis the same weave as the cross knots on our web mail," he said in wonder.

"Web mail?" Aine queried.

Kilfannan nodded.

Lifting his jerkin, he showed his web mail. "See, 'tis the same symbol," he said, pointing to the tracings on the dagger.

"'Tis a shielding knot," she murmured, looking closely at the design. "The spider queen Dinhcara spun the mail for the Danaan warriors in the War of Separation and wove in the enchantment to invoke the protective power of the four elemental lords. Tellest me, how came you by this treasure?"

"The mail was a gift from Uall Mac Carn of Slieve Elva to the Houses of Kilfenoran and An Carn," Kilfannan replied. "He gifted Kilcannan with the Brax."

"Uall Mac Carn!" Aine exclaimed. "You have seen him?"

"Indeed! Ke-enaan gave us passage to his timeless world, and the giant gave us gifts of power to aid us in our quest for the key and shod our steeds with the flying wings of Mercury."

"'Tis prescient the mail and dagger hath been reunited and Kilcannan hath the Brax," she said. "For now, as in times of old, the House of the Heart will ride forth in protection of the Green."

"Thank thee, my lady, for the dagger," Kilfannan said with gratitude. "'Tis a great honour thou hast bestowed upon me." Attaching the scabbard to his belt, he put on an elegant curled white wig. Then, draping a dark green hooded cloak around his shoulders, he cried, "Faith!" looking in a mirror. Glancing gleefully at the others, he said, "'Tis a marvellous disguise. I daresay I could pass for a lady of the night."

"Convincing enough to a casual eye," Aine purred, eyeing the sylphs appraisingly. "Meself will ride in front, and the perfume of hyacinth will be all about us. Fercle, take the rear guard." She handed him a cavalier's hat with a plume and a bright red cloak trimmed with ermine to go with it. "Thinkest thou not that the clothing is well suited for a fire lord upon the open road?"

"Indeed! Thank you, me lady." Fercle beamed. "And when we return triumphant from our quest … do I get to keep them? Meself would like to wear the fancy hat and cloak on me steward's podium at the racecourse."

"Of course, sweet one," she purred, extinguishing the candles. "One must not be enslaved by mementos of the mortal world. Gladly do I let them go."

It was time to leave, and doubt crept into Kilfannan's mind. Ke-enaan had instructed them to travel only in the light and to keep away from water, and they were about to do the opposite. But he reasoned evil was abroad both day and night. The goblins expected them to travel only in the light, and the reversal of the pattern would be unexpected, and that might give them an advantage.

The company followed Aine outside into the cool night air and breathed deeply of the perfume of the wood. Hearing his brother give a low whistle, Kilfannan looked across the pasture and saw the horses galloping towards them.

Twilight deepened into starlight, and a hush lay upon the woods of Ahascragh as they mounted their horses. Cloaked, masked, and hooded, the company rode out into the darkness. Aine and the Kilfenorans rode together in the front, the House of An Carn behind them, and Fercle guarded from the rear.

The stars were shining brightly when they reached the greenway leading to Athenry. "'Tis a caution from here," Aine whispered, breathing out the perfume of hyacinth in front of them. "For 'tis a main road north, and there will be goblins hiding in the hedgerows, watching for us."

They passed by Athenry with only stars for company and turned north towards Orenmore and Galway Bay. The greenway ended and joined the coast road that led around the inlet of the bay, and here they stopped.

Fercle took a pull on his flask. "The way around the sea will prove hazardous," he said to Kilfannan. "The goblins will be waiting."

"But not for ladies of the nightshade!" Kilfannan countered. "Succubi travelling on the road with a fire escort – 'twill take a sharp knocker to see through our disguise. Once we are around the estuary, we can take shelter at the House of An Tar."

"Tar-cannan is a good jockey," Aine said, taking a pull of brandy from Fercle's flask.

"I will second that," Fercle agreed. "Meself hath won many a wager on his fine horse at the race meetings in Maam Cross."

"Hide thy weapons, and be ready in case we are attacked," Aine said as they crossed the road and rode on again along the greenway.

Darkness deepened as they rode around the bay, and one by one the stars went out as low clouds rushed inland from the sea. They came to a long stretch of lonely road bordered by overhanging trees, and a hundred yards ahead, Kilfannan saw a grey shape glide out into the road. "A knocker," he hissed to the others.

"Aye. I see him," Aine said, riding forward. "Keep close behind me." She slowed Nemia to a walk, and breathing out hyacinth, she said authoritatively, "Make way for the sisters of water rising and the knight of fire. Make way!"

The knocker regarded them with pale, malignant eyes and, taking to the air, glided around them in a circle. Kilfannan felt the knocker's gaze upon him, and for a terrified moment, he wondered if he could see the emanations of the emerald through his mask. But the shadow passed, and he saw the knocker settle on the road in front of Aine.

"Meself is looking for four horsemen of the House of Air. If thou shouldst see them on the road, and send word to me by hooded crow, I will bring thee the finest man studs from the mortal world."

She looked at him in distain. "The hunt is mine. I need not a devil's legate to provide. Begone!"

Fercle rode up alongside her and raised his sword. "Make way," he shouted, and Kilfannan saw dragon fire shimmer round his body. The air was flooded once again with hyacinth. The knocker coughed as the perfume swirled around him, and holding his bony fingers across his nose hole, he slipped into the shadows.

Fercle came riding back to take up the guard, and the horses jumped off, their hooves ploughing up the soft turf beside the road. As they galloped onward, the wind picked up with a fury, and rain began to fall. Kilfannan felt a shock to his face as a spiteful gust blew his hood off, stinging his chin with salt wind from the sea.

"Duck!" Aine shouted as a tree branch loomed before her.

Hearing her cry, Kilfannan ducked, but the twiggy fingers of a branch tangled in his wig and, pulling him backwards, ripped the periwig from his head. *Damnation*, he thought, pulling up his hood. It would be only a matter of time before his wig would be found by goblins, and the knocker would know he had been deceived and be hard upon their trail.

They thundered on in the rain until they came to a junction with the mortal road leading to Oughterard, where they stopped to rest their horses.

"A tree branch took my periwig," Kilfannan said fretfully. "'Tis not the sort of style a lady of the nightshade would be wearing. I fear this ill stroke of fortune hath given away our passage."

"'Twill not be long before 'tis found," Aine responded. "We must get off the road and find a place to shelter 'til the dawning."

"If we take the greenway north," Kilfannan said, pointing across the road to a trail across the hillside, "It will take us to the air House of An Tar." He rode up alongside Aine. "'Tis hard to get my bearings in the dark, but the hill of An Tar should be a mile yonder."

They plodded on in the driving rain, and in the gloom Kilfannan saw a faint path on the grass at the side of the greenway. They followed the track up the hillock and stopped before the arched entrance to Tar-cannan's sheen. Above the arch was the winged emerald, symbol of the House of Air.

Tar-cannan came bounding up the stairs and stared at the riders. "Mistress Aine," he said, recognising her. "What brings thee to my sheen in the middle of the night?"

"Meself rides with the House of Kilfenoran and An Carn," Aine said, gesturing to the sylphs.

Tar-cannan looked bewildered.

"'Tis I, Kilfannan of the House of Kilfenoran," Kilfannan said, pulling off his mask.

"Hail to the House of Kilfenoran," Tar-cannan said, bowing. "I did not recognise thee for a moment dressed as thou art with an emerald on thy brow. Take thy charges to the stables. There is food in the mangers and fresh water for them to drink. I will summon my brother Tar-fannan."

After the horses were settled, the companions passed through the arched doorway and down the steps to Tar-cannan's sheen.

The hall was bathed in soft green light from faerie fern, and copper lanterns with bottle-glass panes hung from the turf ceiling. An oval table, heavy with patina from ages of use, sat in the centre of the room, surrounded by soft, cushioned round-backed chairs. Taking off their wigs and eye masks, the company sat down.

Tar-fannan came through the door, his emerald eyes flashing with recognition. He bowed before the Kilfenorans. "Well met!"

"Hail, Tar-fannan of the House of An Tar," Kilfannan replied.

Tar-cannan brought a tray with glasses and a brandy decanter to the table, poured out drinks, and handed them around.

The sylphs of An Tar were speechless when they heard of the fate of Niamh and Caiomhin and the quest to recover the key made of air. Kilfannan watched with great pain of heart as the lustre faded from their eyes and the blush of emerald vanished from their cheeks. There was no protestation – just sadness and silence. Tar-fannan was the first to speak.

"There are no words to say," he said miserably. "We are extensions of your house in living form, and as such, we face the same fate as yourselves. Your presence not only graces but also empowers our halls," he said with love in his eyes. "We will dare another deception. Brother, take thine horse and have him foul the path a mile back along the road where a mortal lane meets the greenway. If thou goest now, thou wilt be in front of the knocker and his rabble."

Aine nodded in agreement. "Once the goblins discover we have deceived them, they will be searching for our tracks. The ground is soft, and our way will be plain to see."

"Fear not," Tar-fannan responded. "I will accompany my brother to the road. We will muddy your prints and blow leaves over the fresh turned earth. The goblins will not know you came this way." Bowing to the company, the sylphs of An Tar left the sheen to go about their business of deception.

CHAPTER 10

COISTE BODHAR, THE DEATH COACH

Kilfannan helped himself to another brandy, and leaning back in his chair, he closed his eyes. Ill deeds and murderous pursuit had followed his house every step of the way, and he felt exhausted. Taking an up-breath, he calmed his mind and took refuge in the Green.

Hearing soft footfalls in the room, he opened his eyes and saw Tar-fannan pouring himself a drink.

"Goblins and a knocker are going north again below us on the road," he said to Kilfannan. "My brother is keeping watch. There are goblins behind you and in front, and 'twill not be long before they will be searching for you on the hillside. Stay in my hall until the road is clear. I have put a dream sleep on the hill of An Tar to keep us safe. In the meantime, let us take refreshment."

They passed the hours of waiting by drinking wine and telling and retelling the tale of their battle with the goblins and their escape along the smuggler's passage to the coast.

Kilfannan heard footfalls on the stairs. Tar-cannan appeared and hurried over to the table. "All is quiet, but I deem there is watchful malice in the air. Even though the face of the noon sun is covered by cloud, it will speed you on your way; 'twould not be wise to tarry on the hill. 'Tis best if you go now and strike north across the turf and meet the greenway to Oughterard. There hath been no goblin movement on the road since morn tide, and you will pass unseen from the hill, for the sheens of our house are in a dream sleep. May the stars protect you! Long live the House of Air."

Tar-fannan was waiting with the horses. They mounted, took their leave of the brothers, and started down the hill.

The sky became overcast, and black clouds sped inland as they left the Hill of An Tar. The sight of the churning clouds made Kilfannan uneasy. It seemed to him that a deadly chase was riding within the monstrous thunderheads, with a huntsman of horrible aspect in the lead. What they were chasing he could not make out, but it struck terror to his heart. "I think 'tis best to stay off the road and ride across country," he said to Aine as they reached the bottom of the hill. "No way is safe in these dark days, but the goblins will most likely look for us on the road. And I fear evil rides above us in the clouds, so 'tis best to follow scrub and woodland if we can."

"Aye. We'll follow the hedge a ways; that will give us cover," she answered, wiping a raindrop from her face.

At the end of the hedge, Kilfannan pulled up and looked around. In front of them stretched lonely hilltops and ling-clad heath. The sinister clouds had changed direction and now were speeding north, but still his apprehension lingered. He sniffed to see if there was any trace of foulness in the air, but there was naught, and he could hear no fell voices on the wind.

"The Brax is at rest, and there is no foul stink or harsh voices upon the airwaves," he said to the company. "Let us take the heath."

"We have to turn north along the fens," Aine said to the party. "We must make haste before the storm breaks and turns the path to mire."

The ground became heavy, and mud flew from the horses' hooves as they thundered on under a dark and hostile sky. A wind whipped through the scrubby reeds, and up ahead the shaggy heaths stood bleak and sombre, shrouded in cold mist. A light rain began to fall, and as they pushed on northwards, the rain grew heavier. "Damnation! 'Tis driving down as straight as stair rods," Kilfannan said gloomily.

The trail across the fen disappeared under a swirling tide of water. Ahead on both sides of the way were wide stretches of boggy fen and brackish standing pools.

Aine pulled up Nemia, looking for the road. "'Tis as I feared," she said. "The rain hath swallowed up the path. We must strike a passage north."

In the gathering gloom, Kilfannan noticed the lurid shimmering of a host of tiny flames flitting across the fens and darting amongst the sedgy reeds.

"Aine," he said, "the will-o'-the-wisps have lit their death fires in the bog."

"Evil is abroad," she said, slipping from Nemia's back and testing the ground in front with her boot. "See how the flames flicker and waver. The death lights are beckoning to us. We must be cautious of our movements, for the bog spirits will try to lead us to our doom, fooling us with dissolving views of marsh, and rising ground."

Riding forward through the flooded, sucking earth, Kilfannan could feel his horse quivering with fear. Looking around to see what had frightened him, he saw the evil lights upon the fen gather into a ball and come rushing towards them. Red Moon shied and, rearing up, threw him into the mire.

Kilfannan landed on his back in the bog. He struggled to pull himself free, but the scum pool heaved and gurgled, and he felt the shifting soggy earth begin to suck him down. Fingers clutched at his ankles, pulling him deeper into the suffocating muck. Screaming for help, he tried to keep his head and hands above the stinking slush. He saw Fercle grab a length of rope from his saddlebag. "Catch hold!" he commanded, throwing him the line. He tried desperately to catch hold, but the rope slipped through his muddy fingers.

Fercle pulled the lifeline back and then threw it once again. "Grab the line," he shouted.

The bog was rising fast, and only Kilfannan's head and hands were visible. With a last gasp before he was sucked down, he caught the rope between his fingers.

"Hold on, brother!" Kilcannan shouted as Fercle urged his horse forward.

Slowly, with a sucking sound, they drew him from the grasping, clawing swamp.

Once Kilfannan was on his feet, Aine said urgently, "'Twas a close call for thee, Kilfannan. 'Tis best you dismount and lead your horses through the mire," she said to the others. "We do not want our charges to stumble and throw us into the bog. Follow me."

The party slid off their horses and slowly picked their way across the mire from one grass tussock to the next. Daylight was fading fast, and the rain had stopped when they finally found the road.

"Aine, the light is failing. How far to Oughterard?" Kilfannan asked her with concern, remembering Ke-enaan's warning to be off the road by nightfall.

"We'll be there just after dark if our luck holds. See, 'tis not far," she said, pointing to lights twinkling in the distance.

The banks gave way to dry stone walls, and riding forward in the twilight, Kilfannan noticed a faint smell of rot in the damp air. His surroundings, he fancied, had taken on a sinister quality, which chilled him to his very heart. Behind the walls on either side were stands of fir that crowded like dark and forbidding sentinels spying on the road. As they rode through a deep, dank hollow overgrown with thorn bushes and rank marsh grass, noisome exhalations rose into the air, curling like grey tendrils around the horses' legs.

"We must get clear of the hollow," Kilfannan said as Red Moon became restive. "The reek is spooking the horses, and there is a putrid stink in the air. I will be glad to reach the inn and get off this accursed road."

"As will we all," Fercle agreed.

They rode slowly forward out of the hollow and onto the road. Kilfannan could feel Red Moon quivering beneath him. "Dost thou feel the sudden chill?" he asked Aine.

"Aye. I feel it. We must be cautious, for the smell of death is in the air."

Their sense of foreboding grew as the shadows of night fell around them. Cor-garran rode forward to join Aine. "I do not trust the way," he said uneasily. "The gloom is unwholesome, and there are no birds singing their goodnights, and to my mind that is strange."

Aine nodded. "'Tis too quiet. We must be vigilant." No sooner did the words leave her lips than a deafening chime rang out in the tense and listening air.

"'Tis the Brax!" Kilcannan shouted in alarm.

Before the friends could gather their thoughts, the ground shook beneath them. The sound of galloping horses and the rattling of a coach caused a clamour in the gathering night.

"Hide!" Aine screamed in panic to the company. "'The Coiste Bodhar is coming!"

Hedges had grown up around the stone walls on either side, and Kilfannan looked desperately around for a way of escape. *Our horses could never clear the fence,* he thought anxiously. They couldn't turn back along the road; the death coach was too fast and would overtake them. One soul Crom Dubh would take, but he would breathe the breath of death upon the rest of them and then stalk them one by one until he claimed each of their souls for his dark world. Fear struck at Kilfannan's heart. Desperately scanning the lane, he noticed ahead a low point in the wall upon the right, not fifty yards away. Most of the stones were missing, lying here and there beside the road. Thanking the stars, he shouted, "Follow me!"

Urging Red Moon forward, he jumped through the hole in the wall, disappearing into the darkness of the firs. Aine and Fercle swiftly followed. Cor-garran on Red Leaf took up the run and then jumped clear; Orcan joined him in the air and, landing badly on the stony, uneven ground, tossed Cor-cannan into a thorn bush.

As bolts of red lightning struck around him, the Brax chimed out a warning, and Kilcannan heard the rumbling rattle coming closer. Finifar snorted and pawed the ground in terror, rearing up, and then threw him onto the road and bolted after the others.

Quickly finding his feet, Kilcannan made a desperate run for the gap in the wall, but before he could reach safety, the Coiste Bodhar crested the rise, its tattered, inky blinds flying ragged in the wind.

A blast of withering cold tore at his hair and clothes as the coach came thundering towards him. His surroundings became distorted and then receded into a shadow world of ugly shuffling shapes. Terror struck his heart beyond anything he had ever known. The coach would be upon him before he could gain the wall, leaving him no chance of escape. Spinning on his heels, he fled back along the lane.

The rumbling was deafening as the death coach raced after him, and he heard the crack of a whip. He tried to take the wind, but not a breath stirred in the dank, malodorous air. A pall of decay and desolation swept around him, and he was agonisingly aware of the hollow, stinking breath of the carrion behind him. The Brax was desperately chiming in his pocket, and suddenly a wild hope leapt into his heart as he recalled that the Brax was made of gold. Taking the tiny horseshoe from his pocket, he leapt into the air, and as the coach clattered to a stop, he spun round and threw the Brax at the monstrous hunched shape sitting in the driver's seat.

The road vibrated with a low rumbling sound, and a wave of stench sent his senses reeling. His head swam as a thunderous crash obliterated both sight and sound. With a piercing shriek, he stumbled to the side of the road and collapsed against the wall.

* * *

Hearing a terrible cry and seeing Finifar riderless and running through the trees, Kilfannan was enveloped with dread. His up-breath was laboured, and he knew his brother was in peril. When he heard the thunderous crash overhead, he threw caution to the wind. He urged Red Moon forward and jumped back over the wall into the empty road. Slipping off his charge, he looked anxiously around for Kilcannan. There was no sign of his brother in the dark, silent road.

"Kilcannan!" he cried desperately. The sound echoed horribly in the clammy air, taunting him from a thousand different angles. "Brother! Where art thou?"

Leading his horse, Kilfannan walked slowly along the road, his eyes desperately searching the hedgerows for sign of his brother. "Kilcannan!" he shouted again.

Hearing a whimper in the darkness, Kilfannan ran towards the sound, and on seeing his brother huddled against the wall, he knelt down beside him. His face was a ghastly green, and his eyes stared into nothingness.

"Brother! 'Tis I." Getting no response Kilfannan, chafed Kilcannan's icy fingers.

"My brother is cold and lost in an evil dream," he said anxiously as Fercle rode up with Cor-garran by his side. Getting off his horse, Fercle took a silver flask and a small, round yellow stone from a pouch beneath his saddle, and putting the fire stone in Kilcannan's hand, he bent down and breathed a blue flame into his face. Kilcannan's body quivered, and as his mouth fell open, Fercle slowly trickled the elixir down his throat.

After a couple of anxious moments, Kilcannan stirred. "Do not let Crom Dubh take me," he said faintly, clutching at Kilfannan.

"'Tis all right, dear brother; be not afraid. Crom Dubh hath left," Kilfannan said, trying to reassure Kilcannan that all was well, but he knew in his heart that Crom Dubh would return. The breath of death was upon his brother – and therefore upon himself. Looking away for a moment, he used his cloak to dry the tears that welled up in his eyes. If Kilcannan succumbed to the death breath, the House of Air would fall and the death would take the worlds.

* * *

Kilcannan's world was grey, dead, and lifeless. His brother was just a dark shape in his mind, and a cold dampness was creeping up his legs on its death path to his heart. A vessel was pressed to his lips, and with an effort of will, he opened his mouth; a warm liquid trickled down his throat, invigorating his resolve. Slowly the colours of night returned, as did the concerned faces of Kilfannan and the company.

"Life of my heart," Kilfannan said gently, helping Kilcannan up and smoothing back his brother's tousled hair. "Thank the stars thou art alive."

"We have to thank the Brax for the survival of our house," Kilcannan grimly responded. He suddenly realised Finifar was not amongst the horses. Turning to Cor-cannan, he said, "Finifar and Orcan are not accounted for. Come! We must look for them." He gave a long, low whistle to Finifar but heard no welcoming whinny in return.

Feeling something clenched in his palm, he opened his hand. Seeing a yellow stone, he asked in surprise, "What is this pebble in my hand? Where did it come from?"

"'Tis a heating stone," Fercle replied, gently taking it from him and stowing it with the healing elixir in his saddlebag. "The energy of Crom Dubh is dry and cold, and therefore we had to keep you warm until you found yourself again."

Aine rode out of the darkness on Nemia, leading Finifar and Orcan by the reins. "I have found your horses," she said to Kilcannan and Cor-cannan, "and have calmed away their fear. We cannot linger. Come; mount up. We must ride."

"Wait!" Kilfannan exclaimed. "We must find a hawthorn tree and send word of the Coiste Bodhar's attack on Kilcannan to Black Head. The Brax hath gone, and the demon will return to claim not only my brother but meself as well."

"Aye, and the breath of death will be upon us all," Aine said while dismounting. "I will go on foot and find Thorn-Haw. Stay here, and be on thy guard."

* * *

Aine slipped away and was soon swallowed by the gloom. She searched the banks and looked in all the nooks and crannies but could not find a hawthorn tree or sapling by the roadside. Deciding to leave the lane and explore the hillside, she climbed over a stone wall bordering the road and landed noiselessly on the turf. The wind was in her face, and for a moment she paused; there was the stench of rot upon the air.

Goblins! she thought anxiously. Peering into the darkness, she listened for any sound of movement in front of her, but all was quiet. After she had gone a few steps, she felt a searing pain in her feet. A wire was around both her ankles, and as it was pulled tight, she realised she'd been caught in a loop snare. Shape-shifting into reptile form, she grabbed the snare with her claws and rent the wire asunder.

The night was dark, and for a moment she could see nothing but shadow. Then, from out of the gloom, the grey shape of a knocker came running at her with a dagger, and she heard the foul cries of his magg close behind him. The blade shined with a pale violet light, and she knew it was poisoned with the fell essence of the water dropwort. Drawing her sword, she leapt forward as the knocker closed in upon her, and with a mighty sweep, she severed his head from his shoulders. The skull-like mask fell away, but the spindly, headless body came rushing at her, furiously animated by some infernal sorcery. Aine sidestepped and, grabbing his knife hand, tore his arm from its socket and hurled it at the charging goblins. The knocker was possessed, and she would have to kill all the goblins in his magg to stop the dark advance of whatever devil animated them. Spraying venom on the goblins, she cut and thrust with such vengeance that they retreated back into the darkness. Aine followed, hewing and hacking until the remnant that was left evaded her and fled into the gloom.

She stopped for a moment to get her breath. She knew they would return, but following their trail would take time – time they did not have. Turning her thoughts to the finding of a hawthorn tree, she morphed back to faerie form and continued searching.

A gleaming boulder caught her eye, and yet it was no light of stars or moon that made it shimmer. Realising that the light of Faerie was upon it, she ran over to the rock and saw a small hawthorn sapling growing in a crevice. Standing reverently before the tree, she called on Thorn-Haw.

The air rustled, and Thorn-Haw stood before her, pirouetting on his delicate hooves. "Mistress Aine. I felt thy mind and heard the call within thy soul," he said. "I set a light upon the land to guide thee to me, so tell me, what service can I do for thee?"

"Kilfannan sent me to find thee. We are in dire need," she answered urgently. "Kilcannan hath been attacked by Crom Dubh. The Brax saved him but hath disappeared, and Kilcannan is defenceless. Me heart tells me he will be assailed again before the sun rises. We need thee to take these evil tidings to Ke-enaan without delay and see what aid he can afford us."

Thorn-Haw's hazel eyes took on a darker hue. "Lady Aine, thy wish is my command." He smoothed his silky birch-like skin with long, twiggy fingers. "Wait for a moment; I will return." Thorn-Haw bowed and then vanished. Within an instant, he returned to her side. "My lady," he said. "Ke-enaan hath told me to travel with thee to the Hill of Crann Sidhe. 'Tis four miles as the crow flies," he said, pointing east. "There we will be protected until dawn by the power that dwells in the hill. We must make haste, for 'tis Ke-enaan's thought that the Coiste Bodhar will return to claim Kilcannan within a short time."

"Crann Sidhe!" Aine exclaimed. "'Tis a hill of ill repute."

"There is no other way. We have to reach the portal on Crann Sidhe lest the dark overtake the House of Air. Now," Thorn-Haw said, taking her hand in his knotty fingers. "Visualise the spot where thou parted from the company, and meself will take thee there through the heart of living tree."

As Aine's hand closed around Thorn-Haw's knotted fingers, she felt all things tree-like. In a rush of perfumed sap, she found herself beside a scrubby hawthorn tree not far from where the company were waiting.

* * *

Seeing Aine and Thorn-Haw appear, Kilfannan cried out, "Well met!"

"Well met, the houses of Kilfenoran and An Carn!" Thorn-Haw said to the sylphs. "I bring word from Ke-enaan. We must make for Crann Sidhe. Come! There is not a moment to lose, for the wizard fears Crom Dubh will attack again. Mount up and follow me."

Thorn-Haw sailed on to Nemia's back and settled behind Aine. "We must jump the wall and go east, across the hillside. 'Tis rough with rocks, and the going will be the slower for it, and" – there was a moment of hesitation – "methinks mischief goes before us."

"Mischief! Aye," Aine responded. "There is dark magic abroad this night, for what is slain hath no business with the living."

Shivering with cold, Kilcannan rode up alongside Fercle. "Sir," he said, "I have taken a chill and ask for the service of thy fire stone."

"Cold, you say?" Fercle looked at him anxiously.

Kilcannan nodded. "A chill is seeping through my body to my heart," he said with a down-breath of exhaustion.

"Meself will summon Trax," Fercle said to Kilfannan, "for the chilling breath of Crom Dubh is upon your brother, and only dragon fire can dispel it from his body."

Fire engulfed Fercle, and in the flames, Kilfannan heard him volcano a petition for the dragon's ear.

There was a rumble in the clouds and the sound of beating wings, and the air grew hot with dragon breath. Kilfannan looked up and saw a fiery shape descending, spitting shafts of flame from his arrow-shaped tongue.

"Greetings, Fire Lord of Gort." Trax flared, settling on the ground in front of him. "Thou callest?"

"Hail, Trax!" Fercle said, bowing his head before the dragoneen. "The House of Air is fleeing from Crom Dubh and is in peril. We ask for your protection until we reach the gates of the Ghrian Sidhe."

The dragon's yellow eyes glittered, and small jets of flame issued from his nostrils. "Protector Green dream. Ghrian Sidhe dangerous," he said.

A chill ran through Kilfannan. It seemed to him that all ways were beset with danger. But he was relieved to see Trax diminish in size and circle Kilcannan's head three and one half times and land upon his shoulders.

A funeral shawl of choking darkness crept upon them as they rode onwards through the rock-strewn slopes. Presently, a hill glimmering with fey light became visible in the gloom.

"Crann Sidhe is yonder," Thorn-Haw called softly to the company. "Just a furlong or two and we'll be there."

Galloping onwards to the foot of the hill, Kilfannan felt a sense of impending doom sweep over him, and he looked fearfully up at the dark and menacing sky. Shafts of tainted light were streaming through the clouds, and a faint charnel stink was in his nose. Pulling up at the base of the shadowed hill, he saw two lone hawthorn trees whose intertwined branches formed an archway.

"Me trees hath stood here since the Separation," Thorn-Haw said to him, gracefully slipping from Nemia's back. "They are the entryway to Crann Sidhe and are caught up in the endless spell of nine dimensions. Only me master Pan knows their thoughts. Meself will petition for—"

The faun's words were suddenly drowned by deep rumbling and shaking in the ground. Trax hissed in fury, and with a whir of his wings, he took to the sky. Jets of cold fire rent the clouds, and a stinking grey dust rained down upon them. Kilfannan coughed and retched as the stench of death dust clogged his nostrils. Shielding his eyes from the noisome powder, he glanced up in horror at the boiling clouds and saw Trax in a deadly battle with a monstrous seething shadow darker than the nightshade. Blast after blast of dragon flame was swallowed up by a swirling vortex of age-old charnel dust spiralling like a crushing snake around the dragon's body, pinioning his great wings and snuffing out his fiery breath. Panic seized Kilfannan as he saw Trax plunge onto the rock-strewn hillside in a seething cloud of suffocating dust. Thunder crashed overhead, reverberating like a demonic gong through the shadowy hillsides, and Kilfannan knew it was the herald of a greater terror. The ground trembled beneath his feet, and he heard the sound of thundering hooves and the clatter of a coach.

Hearing Finifar give a screaming neigh of rage, he looked wildly at Kilcannan. A spasm of intense fear swept through him as he saw his brother lying motionless on the ground, his face transfixed with panic-stricken horror. He felt a shortening of his breath and, with a gasp, fell forward.

The indigo sky of Faerie faded into a seething mass of heaving brown and grey, and Kilfannan suddenly felt his essence separate from his form. He was whipped upwards into a stench-fuelled whirl through frigid space and thrown down into foul grey mist that was alive with the stink of aeons of rotting corpses. He looked around and saw he was inside a coach with mildewed, tattered blinds and rotting seats. Forcing himself to concentrate, he centred himself in the HeartStar and joined his mind with his brother's.

With their awareness came an infinitely terrifying realisation of their plight. They were trapped inside Crom Dub's decaying death coach in the lowest chasm of earth's bowels.

They did not scream, but all the nighthawks of the storm wind screamed for them, and they shrank back in a black convulsion of despair. Grief and anguish swept over them as they realised their essence had been snatched from their bodies. Thinking they should escape the coach, Kilfannan tried the rusty handle on the door, but it was locked. He tried to send his mind through the window, but an invisible force blocked his access.

Even though Crom Dubh hath taken our souls, he thought to Kilcannan, *to totally consume our being, he will need our forms as well; and whilst our bodies are free, there is still a chance that we may escape him.*

Peeping through the blind of the glassless window, they saw an ancient graveyard. Desolation and decay hung like a pall over the broken headstones and scabbed antique grey slabs. Rearing up in front of them was an infinitely old and horrible church that rose from the withered grass like a demonic template of unhallowed cosmic horror. Bats flittered in the shadow of the steeple, and its door hung loosely from its hinges, revealing a yawning dark beyond.

Hearing a scrabbling sound outside the window, they peered out into the graveyard and saw a loathsome manlike shape with a wolfish face and long drooping arms climb out from underneath a mildewed slab. The leering ghoul was followed by four more, and squatting on the tombstone, the demons glared hungrily in the direction of the coach. The brothers shuddered, for they knew if Crom Dubh succeeded in snatching their sylphid forms, they would be sport for ghouls and their terror and flight would be replayed throughout eternity.

They heard a loud creak, and looking towards the blackened fane, they saw the hideous outline of Crom Dubh coming through the door of the church towards the coach. A wave of nausea swept over them as they felt a heavy weight climb into the driver's seat. The coach shot into a frigid whirl of fetid space; their vision darkened, and their consciousness fled.

CHAPTER 11

THE GHRIAN SIDHE

"Cor-garran!" Fercle shouted above the tumult. "Quick! Bring the rising wind and blow away the death dust that blankets Trax's body."

Together they rushed to the stricken dragon. Summoning the up-wind, Cor-garran created a vortex of spinning air that moved across the dragon's body, sucking up the loathsome, clogging dust. Once Trax's body was uncovered, he stood aside as Fercle summoned the fire of his being and, filling himself with flame, took Trax to his breast and poured his fiery essence into the dragon's heart.

After a tense moment, Cor-garran saw small jets of flame issuing from Trax's nostrils. The dragon quivered, lifted his noble head, and barked out his thanks to Fercle. After slowly flexing his wings, Trax took to the sky in a burst of blue fire, circled their heads, and landed before them.

With a gasp of horror, Cor-garran saw Kilfannan slump across Red Moon's neck. He desperately ran to him, embraced him heart-to-heart, and took the up-breath for him. His brother had gone to the aid of Kilcannan, and together the twins of An Carn took over breathing for the House of Kilfenoran.

"Trax of the House of Braxach," Fercle said urgently, "wouldst thou take a message to Ke-enaan and tell him of the taking of the spirits of the House of Air by the Coiste Bodhar."

"Yea," he roared in the language of the flame, and with a crackle of fire, he took to the air once more and disappeared into the darkness.

Fercle joined the sylphs, and drawing his sword, he stood guard while Aine and Thorn-Haw lingered by the horses.

* * *

Aine looked anxiously through the arch to the darkling hill beyond. Her mother had told her the Ghrian Sidhe were the ancestors of the Sidhe of Faerie. They were beings who had conquered the blueprint of duality in the nine dimensions and freed themselves from its confines. Crann Sidhe, their sacred mount, was shrouded in the mists of legend and belonged to spheres of different space. The hill was a memory, a living library of their journey and the bloody battles, intrigues, sorceries, and treachery they had cast. It was perilous to approach the memories of the lords of the hill with the stain of Crom Dubh upon them. The lords were arrogant, capricious, and quick to anger, and might well deny them entry – or even kill them on a whim. But they had to try. Nodding to Thorn-Haw, they stepped forward to the archway at the foot of the hill.

"Hail, lords of Crann Sidhe. I am Thorn-Haw, dryad of the hawthorn tree. I have been instructed by Ke-enaan, the wizard of Black Head, to plead for entry to the portal gate upon the summit of thy sacred hill."

Aine saw an aureole of indescribable beauty play like flames around the hilltop, and the air around her became fragrant with the scent of earth that mingled with heady orange blossom and other fragrances unknown to her. Standing under the archway in the still and windless air, she felt the hush of portent fall around her, transporting her to the essence of all beginning. Far off, she heard a low fanfare of silver trumpets echoing through the fibre of her being, and with each note she saw shifting visions – a swift kaleidoscope of moving pictures one after the other.

Crystal headlands rose from a violet sea, and tall ships with sails of cloud glided upon the waves. Tall men stood at the wheel in long cloaks with helms upon their heads, and Aine shivered at the avarice and overweening arrogance in their cold, sardonic faces. She saw gloomy halls of dark magic lit by flaming torches, and altars stained with blood. Cruel priests appeared, crowned with vine leaves, with a throng of cowled, cloaked figures that cast no shadows in the torchlight.

Glancing at Thorn-Haw, she realised that he could not see the scenes appearing before her – for she knew the taint of evil, and he did not.

The vision faded and was replaced with scenes of battle. Warriors with set faces and livid eyes, pale cheeked and bloody browed, hacked and hewed their enemies, and strewn about the battlefield were mangled and bloody bodies with crows picking at their eyes.

Her mind suddenly swept up in vortices of dust and fire that swirled in dark gulfs of space where no time reigned, and her spirit quailed before realms of grandeur and terror that appeared to her startled eyes like a night-haunt beyond all dark dreams.

In the fantasy of chaos, the tall figure of a young man appeared in front of them, clothed in a body of dense starlight. A wreath of blood-red orchids crowned his nighted, lustrous hair, and his regal bearing and dark, compelling eyes held all the glamour and mystique of a daemon. Aine and Thorn-Haw stared at him in awe.

"Messenger of Ke-enaan and Manannan's daughter," he said, "I am known as Alfaan in your world of Faerie. I have knowledge of your quest, for your troubled thoughts and the fears that stalk you in shadow have stirred me from my long sleep in the halls of magic. Many an age has passed since I received a summons to ..." He paused, and a sardonic smile played about his lips. "Succour travellers in distress."

Aine stiffened. She sensed an aura of malice and cruelty around

Alfaan, and recalling the vision of blood-stained altars of sacrifice, she knew they had accessed a time of great evil within the memory of the hill. The timeline of the Ghrian Sidhe they had entered was one of sorcery and sacrifice. And in their caprice, the lords could, on spiteful whim, seize all of them and distort their essence into monstrous form.

"Ke-enaan requests that thou grantest the House of Air access to thy portal," Thorn-Haw said. He gestured to the bodies of Kilfannan and Kilcannan, who were in the embrace of the sylphs of An Carn.

Silence settled over them like a shroud. Waves of power throbbed around the archway and then were suddenly shut off. The figure of Alfaan diffused into starlight, and they were left alone.

"They have barred our access," Thorn-Haw said despondently, turning away. "Crom Dubh will soon return for the House of Air, and we have no weapon to deter him."

Even though she realised she risked death, Aine refused to admit defeat. She had no choice. If they failed to gain access to the portal, Crom Dubh would breathe the breath of death upon them all. Steadying her nerve, she formed an orange glow around herself, and gathering the power of the water field, she cried out, "'Tis the living Green of the HeartStar that is dying, and I would gladly forfeit me own essence to save it. Take me as thy servant, but for the love of life, admit the House of Air and give them permission to ascend to the portal."

After a few moments, an orchid-perfumed wind blew in their faces, and Alfaan reappeared before them. "Mistress Aine, we do not concern ourselves with the affairs of the nine dimensions, and therefore 'tis the decision of the lords of the hill to bar your access to our sacred portal. Leave, and trouble us no more, or face the peril of the memories in Crann Sidhe."

For an instant Aine took refuge in the woods of Ahascragh; and then, rejuvenated by the Green, she said bravely, "With respect, if evil overcomes Faerie, 'twill cast its greedy gaze elsewhere. Greed knows no bounds, and even though thou hast left the nine dimensions, thine essence still lives on within the hill, as thou hast reminded me. If the HeartStar falls, sooner or later, even thy realm may be assailed."

Alfaan's eyes blazed dangerously, and Aine felt the sting of his contempt. There was a moment of terrifying silence tingling with hostility. Alfaan's form flickered and once again faded from their view. In bravado she shouted to the darkness of the hill. "'Tis true the Ghrian Sidhe may have escaped the confines of the nine dimensions, but their hearts have died in the endeavour, and they are shells of nothingness."

Feeling a rumble in the ground, she heard Thorn-Haw cry out in panic. "Crom Dubh is returning for the House of Air!"

Looking anxiously round for shelter, she saw a stand of trees not far from the gate. "Take the Kilfenorans to the trees," she said urgently to the House of An Carn. "We will follow with the horses."

The rumbling and rattling grew louder, and as they turned away from the hill, Aine was engulfed by a wave of ringing sound. Turning back, she saw Alfaan standing before her.

"Mistress Aine, courage is a rare find in the lower worlds, for most are cowards," he said with scorn. "But courage is to be honoured, and as a boon, the Ghrian Sidhe have granted thy petition to ascend to the portal, and thou mayst return if …" Again he paused, and Aine felt an icy tingle stab her heart. "If fate allows. Do not trouble us again, for we will not look upon thee with favour." His eyes gleamed with warning as his image faded, and they saw a path open up before them, leading to the standing stones on the summit.

"I will take the gate to Trevelyan's abode with the sylphs of Kilfenoran and An Carn," Thorn-Haw said to Aine and Fercle.

Aine nodded in agreement. "Fercle and meself will guard the horses and await your return on the greenway below Crann Sidhe."

The ground shook with the thunder of hooves as the sylphs of An Carn carried the limp bodies of the Kilfenorans through the archway.

"Make haste!" Aine screamed.

* * *

Outer-spectrum colours swirled around Thorn-Haw and the sylphs as they passed through the gate and started up the hill. The horror of Crom Dubh was suddenly blotted out, as if a mighty door had been closed upon the Faerie world. The air was fresh and clean, and the House of An Carn took mighty up- and down-breaths to energise themselves as they carried Kilfannan and Kilcannan up the hill to the stone circle.

In the centre of the circle was a standing stone, a single dolmen pointing like a dark finger at the sky. "'Tis the portal that will take us to England," Thorn-Haw said as they walked through the ring of stones.

As Thorn-Haw placed his hands upon the stone, the dolmen tingled with energy, and a dark space formed within. "Come!" he said to the sylphs of An Carn.

* * *

The rumbling of the death coach died away. Aine breathed a sigh of relief. "Tragedy hath been narrowly averted," she said grimly. "All we can do is wait and pray for their return."

"And worry," Fercle answered. "Brave you are, me lady, for having the courage to call again on the Ghrian Sidhe after their rebuttal of the House of Air." He looked at her with admiration. "For is it not true that Alfaan could have crushed yourself with a glance?"

"Indeed ... and may still do so," Aine answered anxiously. "Alfaan's image contains all the Ghrian Sidhe, and the level of their existence we have accessed, is an age long past where arrogance, blade, and sorcery ruled supreme. The lords are cruel and capricious, but we must trust there is honour in them yet." She looked towards the stone circle on the frowning summit. The outer-spectrum lights had disappeared, and she prayed to the stars the sylphs had made it safely to Trevelyan.

"Dread and portent hover over the stone circle on the mount," she said to Fercle. "Even though the Ghrian Sidhe have granted the House of Air access to the portal, meself is fearful for their safety. The shadow of Crom Dubh is upon us and hath called forth an unpredictable force of evil." She sighed and passed her hand over her brow. "There is the stink of treachery in the air."

"Aye, me lady. But let us see their safe return and set a fire in the thought."

An owl hooted from dark scrub as they turned away from the arch. "We must find shelter for ourselves and the horses," Aine said urgently. "The goblin rabble wilts be hot upon our trail, and even though they dare not draw nigh to the hawthorn-gated hill, their spies will be watching from afar. Knowing we will have to leave, they will plot an ambush." Looking around, she spied a stand of dark scrubby trees and bushes in a dell a few yards back along the track. "Let's take the horses to the bushes yonder," she urged. "Low they may be, but they will give us cover and still give us an unhindered view of Crann Sidhe."

They led the horses into the bushes and took shelter behind some scrubby trees. "'Tis a good place to wait," Fercle said, looking at a patch of boggy turf criss-crossed by glistening streams. "There is water and grazing for our horses." He took out his flask. "Let's have a nip to ward away the shadow."

"'Twould seem thy flask is bottomless," Aine said with a grin.

"Ah! The secret of me limitless flask is known only to meself, me lady," he chortled, taking a drink and handing her the flask.

They waited together in the darkness. The leaves on the bushes started rustling, and after a while a stiff breeze began blowing in their faces. "List," Fercle whispered. "There are harsh voices on the wind."

Aine took out her knife. "I will scout the paths leading to the greenway that will take us to Maam Cross. When the House of Air returns, we do not want an ambush on the road."

"Aye, Mistress Aine. Meself will guard the horses."

"In the event that meself doth not return, and the House of Air arrives, take the road without me. Do not wait."

He glanced anxiously at her. "Aye, me lady," he said as she slipped away.

CHAPTER 12

CROM DUBH

Trevelyan left the mortal world and returned to Faerie. His energy had been fragmented by a struggle with an emissary of Zugalfar in the temple underneath Emma's house, and in the battle to protect her, his form had been revealed to the archdemon. The knowledge filled him with anguish, and he feared his image may be used to deceive Emma and destroy her. Feeling an ominous pull from the stars trying to draw his being back beyond the nine dimensions, he swiftly poured a glass of sustaining elixir and drank deeply. The draught helped to cement his form to his will, and after pouring a second glass, he sat down in his chair and tried desperately to bring his scattered thoughts together.

At the council in High Faerie long ago, he had volunteered to protect the warrior of air at the time of prophesy, and when the glittering pentagon reappeared in the sky, he had travelled from beyond the stars and taken up abode in Faerie. Emma was in the throes of a nightmare chase with Zugalfar when he had viewed her in the mortal world, and after thwarting the archdemon, he had hastened to Ke-enaan at Black Head with the news of her discovery. In fear for the other three warriors, they had searched for their energetic mortal signature in the cunning mirror but found no trace of resonance upon the space wave.

Trevelyan remembered Ke-enaan's anguished words: *The warriors of fire, water, and earth have perished; betrayed and moon-cursed, they have fallen prey to stalking evil and were unable to defend themselves against the dark spells of mortal sorcerers. The return of the shining pentagon was a signal for the darkness to raise its crest against us. I fear we are the target of a long-laid spell, a treacherous plan to conquer the nine dimensions, and me heart tells me that the seeds of evil were sown at the time of the Separation. One of the lords of the elements that attended the council in High Faerie long ago betrayed us then – and now! He informs the enemy of our every move and hath revealed the identity of the four faerie warriors to the enemy of life.*

Fear snaked through Trevelyan's being as he thought about the depth and scope of the betrayal. Niamh and Caiomhin had been taken; Emma had been found by Zugalfar. The House of Kilfenoran was fleeing northward with goblins in pursuit.

At the thought of Kilfannan and Kilcannan, an ugly shadow crossed his eyes. He revisited the mortal's vision he had overheard in the pub. The old man had seen a small green-skinned man running for his life from a black coffin-laden coach with a headless driver. Trevelyan knew the vision was a sylph being hunted by Crom Dubh, and he wondered how a predator of the mortal world could gain access to the fourth dimension and cross the sea to England.

Ke-enaan's words echoed in his mind: *Crom Dubh in England! This is ill news indeed. How is this possible? In the last hours of the Separation, the lords of earth and fire bound Crom Dubh's dark heart to the magnetic water fields of Ireland. Evil has found a way to break the spell the Old Ones put in place.*

Only dark empowerment could break the spell of holding the Old Ones had placed upon the Coiste Bodhar, and an icy hand twisted Trevelyan's heart as the truth dawned upon him – the Cathac had empowered Crom Dubh to hunt the House of Air. The sylph running for his life was either Kilfannan or Kilcannan.

The understanding filled him with dark despair, and again he felt the tugging of the stars. Rising from his chair to get more elixir, he saw a flash of gold outside the window. In a whir of dragon wings, he saw Trax morph in size and fly into the room. The dragon settled on the floor, and the firelight glinted on the pointed golden armour running down his spine. Jets of blue fire issued from his nostrils, and in the crackling fire, Trevelyan heard the staccato speech of the language of the flame.

"Greetings, Trevelyan," the dragoneen crackled. "Urgent news: Crom Dubh took Kilcannan's essence; Kilfannan swooned." Fire issued from his nostrils. "Thorn-Haw leads sylphs Crann Sidhe; coming here."

Trevelyan stiffened, and for a moment darkness covered his eyes. It was as he feared. Joe's evil vision had come to pass, and a crisis for the House of Air was supervening. To destroy the sylphs, Crom Dubh would need both their essence and their forms, and he would follow their bodies to his house. Trevelyan had to act swiftly to protect them.

"Zugalfar's legions attack Gorias; Ngpa-tawa, lord of Fire Descending, betray HeartStar; join Zugalfar. Dragon Nag-ta cast fire spell around city; cannot breach spell; battle in sky. Many enemies fall in ruination."

Ngpa-tawa is the lord of fire descending into water, Trevelyan thought. It was he who had betrayed the HeartStar. "Was Ngpa-tawa destroyed in the battle?" he asked anxiously.

"Nay." The jets of fire issuing from Trax's nostrils turned red-orange, and the crackle snapped and hissed like burning timber. "Lord of fire fled; dragon Nag-ta dead. fire spell around Gorias; Braxach cannot breach; travel to eternal fire cavern; find sire Braxa. Undo spell." The fire in the dragon's breast flared with the pumping of his flame-filled heart. "Leaving now; Gorias unprotected. Thou must guard warrior of air. Strong in flame am I; consume darkness." In farewell, Trax breathed a jet of healing blue fire around Trevelyan to bolster his energy for the deadly battle to come, and then, with a snort, he spread his wings and flew out of the window and into the storm-gathering sky.

The dragon fire had strengthened Trevelyan, and knowing the arrival of the House of Air could be imminent, he pulled up the carpet from the floor and focussed his intent upon the grey stone flooring. Imaging a large, four-pointed, glowing emerald star, he surrounded it with a circle of protection, leaving a space on the east side for the sylphs to enter. When he was satisfied the geometric was complete in form, he filled a large shell with cedar needles, lit the smudge, and wafted the purifying smoke around the room to create a sacred space. The pull from the stars came again; his concentration began to waver, and his mind was suddenly assailed with anxiety for Emma. Putting the smudge in a holder on the table, he sank down in his chair and looked into the mortal world.

Emma and Jim were sitting in a bar, talking to an old man. Trevelyan sensed a stain of evil around the old mortal, but seeing no immediate threat to Emma, he returned his mind to Faerie and the task at hand. Gathering his thoughts, he considered what else he needed to thwart Crom Dubh's attack.

He approached a bow-fronted cabinet, opened the top drawer, and took out a velvet bag of gold doubloons and a root for clearing energy. Counting out nine coins, he carefully placed one doubloon at each point of the star, four in the inside bellies, and one in the centre. He put the remaining coins in the pocket of his waistcoat and, steadying his whirling mind, imaged the pattern of the coins in the circle into four dimensions, creating two octahedrons, one inside the other, touching the edges of the circle. Centred within the sphere, the octahedral geometry would serve as his first line of protection for the House of Air once they were inside. He had five elements at his disposal to protect the circle – those of earth, water, fire, air, and the space that surrounded them. All of them had to be present in the pentacle to stand guard in each direction.

Forcing his mind to stay present, he picked up a wicker basket and a small earthenware bowl from a sideboard and went outside to the garden. Stopping before a stand of red and yellow geraniums growing under the window, he picked the yellow blossoms to provide the colour of the fire field, and with a prayer of thanks to the plants, he put the flowers in his basket.

There were molehills in his daisy-studded lawn, and needing soil to ground the earth field, he scooped a little of the dirt into the bowl. Now that the elements of earth and fire were accounted for, he needed perfume to ground the energy of air. The cedar needles in the smudge would suffice, and spring water in crystal bowls would ground the element of water. Noticing a menacing shadow on the lawn, he glanced in alarm at the sky and saw a bank of sinister clouds building above his house. His garden began to shimmer into malign, hazy unreality, and realising the fume was a portent of Crom Dubh, he hastily took the basket back to his study.

He sent his mind into the ether, listening for any sound to herald the arrival of the death coach. Hearing a faint rumbling on the airwaves, he felt his anxiety give way to panicked fear. Crom Dubh was coming, and he had not yet finished with his preparations.

An odour of mildewed rot crept into the room as he went to the west window. Placing a seal of closure upon the glass, he closed the shutters. He then took four green candles in gold holders from a shelf and put one at each point of the star. Swiftly going into the other room, he filled four crystal bowls from a pitcher, and on returning to the study, he put one in front of each candlestick. After refilling the shell with cedar needles, he put the smouldering smudge on the east point of the star, and the bowl of earth in the north.

A sonic boom in his ears made him jump in alarm. It was a warning from Ke-enaan that the arrival of the House of Air was at hand. Crom Dubh's attack and dark dominion would soon follow.

The portal on Crann Sidhe would bring Thorn-Haw and the sylphs into the pink nimbus of the room where he kept the coach, and he prayed for time. All would be lost if he did not get the House of Air into the geometric before Crom Dubh arrived.

He lit the clearing root and blew on the end until it was smouldering, and then, taking the smudge with him, he went swiftly to the room housing the coach. No sooner had he purified the room than Thorn-Haw came through the wall with Cor-garran and Cor-cannan behind him, carrying the limp bodies of the Kilfenorans pressed to their hearts.

"Follow me!' Trevelyan commanded. "Quick! Crom Dubh is coming."

Once they were in the study, Trevelyan closed the door and sealed it with a rune so no goblins or minor demons of Under-Earth could gain entry and attack him.

He saw, to his dismay, a grey and loathsome mist creeping like a fungus over the sill. A darker night shade crept into the room as he lit the candles, and sensing a subtle shift in the air, he said urgently to the House of An Carn, "The east side of the circle is open. Take Kilfannan and Kilcannan into the geometric and lie down with them, heads facing to the east – the direction of the element of air. Whatever happens, stay inside the geometric. Do not break the circle at any time – for all our sakes."

Once the sylphs were inside, Trevelyan closed the east gate and sprinkled the geranium flowers around the outside of the circle. "Thorn-Haw, add fuel to the fire and grab the bellows," he said. "The heat will scorch the death field and help to slow the demon down."

The loathsome mist had turned into a cloud of charnel dust that was pouring into the room and across the floor towards the circle. The west window rattled on its hinges; the shutters burst inward, showering him with glass, and phosphorescent clouds of loathsomeness blew through the room. Trevelyan saw that all traces of his white-washed walls had vanished and were shimmering with a mildew-tainted luminosity that sucked the flame from the candles. He saw Thorn-Haw desperately pumping the bellows and toning fire sonics to keep the fire alight, but the fume of Crom Dubh pervaded all space, devouring the flame from the hearth and chilling the air.

The room throbbed with hate; the geometric quivered, and Trevelyan saw the red fume of Under-Earth slowly begin to stain the emerald radiance of the octahedrons. Knowing the frequency of the geometric was being weakened by Crom Dubh's dense vibration, he desperately joined his voice to Thorn-Haw's and toned fire sonics to energise the circle's failing energetic structure. The emerald light began to swell as they resonated on the air field, only to recede as Crom Dubh's power of Under-Earth waxed again. For many hours Trevelyan struggled for control, and as his energy weakened, he saw the octahedrons change from emerald to a dark and dirty red. The geranium flowers around the outside of the circle turned black, shrivelling into ash, and the gold coins at the tips of the star melted. All his protections were failing. He knew, with a sinking heart, that Crom Dubh was breaking into the circle, and he did not have the strength to stop him. Sensing he was losing his ability to hold his form together, Trevelyan sent a desperate spiralling plea for aid to the ninth dimension – the gateway to the stars. His energetic signal through the ether was weak, and he knew that the chance of deliverance was slim.

Trying to power the failing circle with what little strength he had, Trevelyan saw Cor-cannan roll over on top of Kilcannan and try to hold him down from a sucking force that was pulling him upwards. Clouds of death dust swirled around him, ripe with malevolent, hungry hate. The octahedrons morphed into the blood-red cubes of Under-Earth, and grease bubbled like a fountain from the floor. Gasping for air, he heard the crack of shattering crystal bowls, and as the water streamed athwart, it flowed across the outer circle, breaching the protection. With a thunderous crash and belching blasts of cadaverine, the Coiste Bodhar burst through the wall.

Above the rattling tumult, Trevelyan heard an angry hissing sound and saw Braxach, the emerald dragon of Gorias, fly through the window and hover in the air above the coach. Expanding its form, the dragon fastened his black talons into the mildewed wood and scorched the death coach with his flaming breath. With a crackle, the wormy wood caught fire, the horses screamed, dissolving into piles of ash, and burning coffins fell from the coach, spilling skulls and bones onto the floor.

The octahedrons once again blazed with vigour, and Trevelyan saw a flash of emerald light flee from the inferno and speed into the centre of the circle. He heard a crackling roar as Braxach surrounded the geometric with cold fire, and then he saw the dragon draw back his horned head and engulf the coach in a jet of orange flame. Knowing the souls of the Kilfenorans had escaped the coach into the refuge of the circle, Trevelyan turned to face the mildewing obscenity rising from the flaming wreckage.

The huge bulk of Crom Dubh's headless body loomed up in front of him like dark smoke, accompanied by the twisted faces of a multitude of damned souls young and old, searching for their skulls in an awful pageant amongst the scattered bones.

Pulses of gnawing, hungry hate pervaded Trevelyan's being, in concert with the deep, hollow breathing of the carrion apparition. His senses reeled and his atoms tried to split apart, so great was the grounding denseness of corruption. A paralysing terror struck his heart as he saw Crom Dubh hold up his severed head and a corpse gurgle ululant with triumph issued from the gaping mouth. Crom Dubh would call his name, and even though the demon could not claim his soul, his form would disintegrate and his energy would be dispersed amongst the stars. Staggering back from the evil vibration, he heard a crackling hiss and saw a jet of dragon flame shoot down Crom Dubh's yawning throat.

The air around the dragon exploded in tumult, the walls of the study shook with the battling vibrations of fire and death, and the room was consumed in a whirling, charnel smoke. The battle raged until Trevelyan saw Crom Dubh's great bulk burst into flame and slowly disintegrate into a pile of ash.

* * *

The Kilfenorans were jolted to their senses by a thunderous crash. Crom Dubh's evil universe was suddenly blotted out, and the mildewed, tattered blinds and rotten cushions of the death coach went up in flame. Clinging to the energy of the fire field, the brothers looked through the window of the coach into the fume. They were in a room they recognised as Trevelyan's study, and hope leapt in their hearts. Through the haze, they could make out four figures huddled together at the centre of a glowing octahedral star. Two were Cor-garran and Cor-cannan, and clasped to their hearts they saw their own forms. "The House of An Carn hath succoured our breath," they said as one. "In the gratitude of heart, let us flee to them."

The coach began to sizzle and burn, and seizing their chance to escape, they shot through the smouldering window and sped towards the circle. The air was alive with crackling brands and flaming, winding serpentine sheets that tried to curl around their souls and suffocate their energy. Horror clung to them as they fled into the circle and joined Cor-garran and Cor-cannan at the centre of the star.

* * *

The choking dust that filled the room began to settle on the floor; the cloying stench began to lift as a cool, fresh dawn breeze blew in through the window. The battle with Crom Dubh had been a close call for Trevelyan, and with a sigh of relief he glanced at Braxach. He saw the dragon send a small jet of flame into the hearth and, as the fire roared, suck the flame into his nostrils. There was a deep gash along Braxach's side, and trickles of flame were spurting through the scales. Trevelyan realised in alarm that the dragon had been injured in the battle of Gorias and that his fiery breath was all but spent in the deadly battle for the bodies of the House of Air.

A terrible revelation swept over him, and again he felt the stars tugging at his will. Crom Dubh had been elevated in the dark hierarchy and empowered by the Cathac. His sole mission was to hunt and destroy the House of Air. The understanding rushed in on him with such cumulative force that he felt faint and held onto the table for support. Braxach could not help him; he was alone. The pull from the stars was becoming more insistent with every second, and with a supreme effort of concentration, he tried to keep his form anchored to his will, for he knew that once he disintegrated into the stars, it would take many mortal years to regather the atoms of his form.

He shivered with a sudden chill, the temperature in the room began to drop, and the charnel stench waxed once more. He caught a stirring in the ash pile on the floor and, choking back a cry, watched helplessly as a vaporous corpse light bubbled upwards from unsealed wells of night into the tainted air. Slowly the dreadful light took form, recombining into the hateful, spectral bulk of Crom Dubh.

The room shook with the hollow wheezing of the abominable coachman, and in a moment of black despair, Trevelyan knew that the fate of the HeartStar and the living Green depended on him. If he failed to gain mastery over Crom Dubh and dispel the demon back to Under-Earth, the House of Air would fall and all life would come to naught. The cold, dry fume of Crom Dubh was numbing his will and paralysing his mind, and he desperately strove to keep his mind and the task at hand in focus.

The first rays of the rising sun splashed across the windowsill, sending a feeble ray of light into the seething gloom, and for an instant Trevelyan saw the dreadful image of Crom Dubh waver.

The sight of the sun gave Trevelyan strength, and a wild hope leapt into his heart. Crom Dubh's power had been sapped by dragon fire, and the sun ray had weakened him even further. *Sun ... gold.* He forced his mind to concentrate – and then he remembered; there were still a few gold doubloons in the bag in his pocket. The coins were old gold and were powerful in the resonance of the sun. The power of gold was his last resort to defend himself against Crom Dubh. He brought out the bag and emptied the contents into his palm. Four coins were left. Holding them aloft to catch the frail sunbeam, he watched as they blazed forth the majesty of the sun.

He felt another pull from the stars – stronger now, almost unendurable. He would have to go back to the space of his being.

Summoning what was left of his will, he ordered it to keep his form together for one last try, and lurching forward, he flung the dazzling coins at the hideous head. "By the power of the sun," he said with a dying breath, "begone!"

A terrible hollow scream erupted, echoing through unhallowed pits of stolen souls, and Trevelyan was buffeted by a venomous, seething wind. He felt his senses fractionating, his atoms splitting. In a desperate struggle, he sought to keep his consciousness in the now. He had to hang on to his third-dimensional form; Emma needed him. His head swam as he staggered forward to the table. The elixir would succour him. Putting his hand out for the bottle, he swayed dizzily and, with a convulsive cry, fell backwards.

CHAPTER 13

SORCERY

The Kilfenorans' chests heaved with air; they felt sensation slowly return in their arms and legs, and the ecstasy of wholeness flared within their being.

"Heart of our hearts," the brothers of An Carn cried out, "thank the stars you have returned."

"And 'tis thanks to the House of An Carn that our House of Air still lives," they answered in one voice.

Reunited with their forms, the brothers separated their minds and looked about them in dismay at the shattered glass, blackened flowers, and melted gold.

Looking around Trevelyan's study, a great fear arose in Kilfannan, and the shocking sight of ruination vibrated through his body like an icy string. Death dust covered all the furniture like a shroud; the walls and ceiling were blackened with scorch; and where a current of air from the window had left its tracks across the floor, he saw a pile of charred skulls and bones. "Brother! Mighty and dreadful is the battle that hath taken place," he said miserably, "for 'tis a ruin of scorch and dust … and grief, for I see no sign of Trevelyan." He gulped back a sob as he saw Thorn-Haw standing by the cold hearth with his head down, wringing his knotted hands. Turning to Cor-garran, he saw his nephew's face was drawn and damp with drops of fear. "What hath happened here? Tell me!" he cried with anguish. "Where is Trevelyan?"

Cor-garran swallowed dryly once or twice, and his eyes were dark with sorrow. "Do not ask me to explain as yet, for a great fear and sadness lie upon me."

Kilfannan and Kilcannan rose, left the circle, and went to Thorn-Haw. "What hath happened to Trevelyan, our saviour?" Kilfannan asked.

Thorn-Haw looked up, and the pain in the faun's eyes flew like an icy dart into Kilfannan's heart. "Trevelyan hath fallen into the shadow of the stars," Thorn-Haw said mournfully. "The struggle for your souls was stark with peril, for Crom Dubh hath grown in power. The will of the Cathac is within him, and he hath the might of the abyss for succour."

"Trevelyan! Taken back by the stars," Kilfannan moaned as grief imploded in his being. The airwaves echoed with the Kilfenorans' anguish, and a crying wind of loss blew up around them, sending plumes of evil deposit spiralling in the air.

The wind died away, and mournful silence descended mantle-like upon the room.

A spasm of grief rippled through Kilfannan's face as he said, "Thorn-Haw, tellest of Trevelyan's fall."

Thorn-Haw's voice trembled like an aspen in the wind as he told of their battle against Crom Dubh. "When Trevelyan felt his vigour failing, he beseeched the nine dimensions to aid the House of Air. Braxach answered his plea, and together they battled the fiend from the pit. As Crom Dubh was bested, Trevelyan fell to the ground and did not move, and meself saw Braxach take him to his breast and fly through the window into the dawning. Where he took Trevelyan, I do not know. There may be a chance that he still hath an anchor in our dimension, and we must trust he will return."

Kilfannan thought about Emma and the peril she was in without Trevelyan to protect her. "We have lost an ancient ally, and the struggle for the Green is weakened by his absence," he said. "And without his protection, Emma is in dire jeopardy." He sighed long and hard. "We must return to Aine and Fercle and continue with our quest, for delay, I fear, will cost us dearly, and there hast been cost enough."

The sylphs followed Thorn-Haw into the pink nimbus of the coach room. Entering through the door, Kilfannan sensed an aura of desolation hanging over the coach. The sides were buckling; the bright paint was fading fast and in places was cracked and flaking.

The sight of the lifelike images of Niamh and Caiomhin sitting inside brought great sorrow to his heart. Bridling his thoughts, he tried to keep them in the present. He wondered about the coach in the third dimension and whether Mary had been able to buy it.

"'Tis time!" Thorn-Haw said. A dark, shimmering space appeared, and as the company approached, they were surrounded by the outer-spectrum colours of the Ghrian Sidhe.

Kilfannan felt a vibration run through him as he stepped into the portal, and in an instant, he found himself standing with the others on the summit of Crann Sidhe.

The dolmen they had passed through loomed darkly at their backs, and the ring of stones upon the summit seemed a fortalice of malignancy. Kilfannan fancied there were sorcerous shades concealed within the stones, hidden in a space that only he could see, ready to bear him away into a cloistered sanctuary of evil.

"Brother!" Kilcannan said fearfully, peering into the darkness at the bottom of the hill. "My spirit is troubled. We do not know the fate of Crom Dubh. Though he hath been vanquished in the struggle for our forms, thinkest thou he will return and hunt us once again?"

"I know not the answer," Kilfannan answered, and his heart was once more pierced with sorrow. For if Crom Dubh arose again, then Trevelyan's sacrifice would have been in vain. "'Tis my thought that Crom Dubh was routed but not destroyed. He hath the will of the Cathac with him and may yet return."

As Kilfannan's words sounded in the listening air, a bolt of red of lightning struck the ground before them, bathing the standing stone and hilltop in a bloody glow. A mighty clap of deafening thunder rent the air.

"We must flee," Thorn-Haw cried out, "for sorcery is abroad."

Lightning followed them like a hound upon a deadly chase as they fled from the wizard stones.

Kilfannan was besieged with doubt and panic as they raced down the hill towards the gates, and his thoughts were as bitter as any he had spent. With the loss of Trevelyan, Emma was in danger, and if Crom Dubh rose again, Trevelyan's sacrifice would be in vain and the House of Air would lose his powerful protection. He was suddenly assailed by frightening visions of a malignant, hooded, heavily cloaked shape hovering by the gateway to the hill. A shifting phosphorescent mist swirled around the apparition, spreading an eerie light upon the grass, and Kilfannan's senses reeled in terror, as he saw chewed bones, smashed horse skulls, and ripped saddles scattered on the ground around the gateway. The mist shifted, and peering into the gloom, he saw two bodies bound by chains of flickering lights lying in the archway. A clutching black pit of terror engulfed him as he recognised the bodies of his friends. "Kilcannan!" he cried out in alarm. "See! There is an evil figure waiting for us at the bottom of the hill. Our horses are dead, and Aine and Fercle are lying in the gateway, bound in evil."

"Brother! There is naught as thou describest," Kilcannan answered, taking his arm and pulling him along. "'Tis an evil thought form that hath been cast upon thee."

Realising his mind was under a dark spell that was trying to use his mind to bring the vision into being, Kilfannan tried desperately to shake his thoughts clear of the evil image.

* * *

Darkness gave way to light, and a cold easterly wind began to blow. The morning wore on, and Aine did not return. Fercle became restless, but the horses were quiet, not sensing any danger, and in that he found courage. Not wishing to let his mind indulge in morbid speculation about the safety of the House of Air and Aine's long absence, he took a pouch from his saddlebag and wandered across the boggy turf to see if he could find any herbs of virtue. He was filling his pouch with sticky sundew when he heard a sudden stirring in the bushes. Drawing his sword and gathering his inner fire, he cautiously moved towards the sound. Aine stepped out in front of him in reptile form. Her scaly body was covered in blue welts and the black blood ooze of goblins.

"'Tis as I thought," she said. "The goblins that escaped me earlier marked our passage. They knew we came this way and were waiting in ambush for us on the road north." She secured the knife in her belt and morphed into faerie form. "I harried them for miles across bog and meadow, and followed them to an outcropping of rocks where they disappeared into a dark hole in the ground. Bested they are, but not beaten, and they will return with others."

"Bathe in the stream, me lady, and then let me tend your wounds," Fercle said, eyeing her in concern. He took a jar of unguent from his saddlebag, and when Aine had cleansed herself, he bade her sit down upon the grass.

She fell silent as he applied the unguent, and he saw her looking despondently east, towards the standing stone on the summit of Crann Sidhe.

"While there is life in the Green, the House of Air still lives," he said supportively, applying the last of the ointment to a slash upon her cheek.

"Aye, but 'tis the waiting for news that is hard."

The light began to fail, and still there was no sign of the sylphs. Fercle sat on a tree stump and watched Aine paddling in the rivulets and streams. Feeling sudden warmth in his heart, he knew goodness was approaching. "Aine!" he called. "There is a heart frequency in the fire field."

They listened and could hear the sound of light hoof beats upon the wind. "'Tis a sylph horse," Fercle said.

Leaving the shelter of the trees, they stepped onto the track. In a shimmer of emerald, a rider appeared galloping towards them.

"Hail and well met to the company of the key," the rider hailed, reigning in his horse. He threw back his hood, and his copper-coloured hair streamed behind him in the wind. Slipping from the saddle, he ran forward and embraced them.

"Doon-vannan!" Aine cried joyfully. "'Tis good to see you. The roads and hillsides are alive with knockers and their maggs. What bringeth thee on this dangerous venture?"

"I bring tidings and was looking for you," Doon-vannan answered. He glanced anxiously around. "What news of our high house?"

His expression grew grave and fearful as Aine told him of the taking of the Kilfenorans by Crom Dubh before the gates of Crann Sidhe, and of her struggle to gain access to the portal. "Thorn-Haw and the sylphs of An Carn hath taken Kilfannan and Kilcannan through the portal to Trevelyan in England," she said. "Crom Dubh could not snatch their forms and will follow them. All we can do is wait, watch – and worry."

They sat together on the moss-covered trunk of a fallen tree, and deep was the heart pain that assailed them in that moment. The fate of the House of Air and all they held dear was balanced on a knife edge, and they could do nothing – only wait.

An owl hooted from the darkness, and in its eerie tone the company heard the sounds of unison, as if it too understood the desperation of their hearts.

Fercle took out his flask. "A stiffener is in order," he said, taking a drink before handing it around. "'Twill dispel the shadow that has fallen upon our souls. Tell thy tidings, Doon-vannan, for the wait is long and bitter, and meself is in need of discourse."

"I have some good news in these dark times," Doon-vannan began. "I found the mortal form of Brea of the silver wind and stole her from a dealer at the horse market in Loughrea. She is safe within the stables at my brother's hall in Doon. I rode to Ke-enaan's halls with the news of Brea's liberation, and he gave me urgent counsel. 'Ride north', he said, 'to thy kin in Galway and Connaught, and tell them of the peril that faces the House of Air'. He warned me of the Coiste Bodhar and gave me a gold charm to deter Crom Dubh if he shouldst cross my path."

Doon-vannan took a breath, and a wind blew up around him. "Meself was affright when I left the wizard's door, and mounting the Tralee Rose, we thundered north. Following Ke-enaan's counsel, I avoided the roads and took the north wind across bog, heath, and meadow to the House of An Tar. When I arrived, Tar-fannan told me that the company of the key had but lately left with the noon sun. I galloped on towards the House of Cros-Maam and picked up your tracks along the greenway." He paused for a moment, and a spasm of sadness passed across his face. "A sense of foreboding was upon me as I rode on, and every furlong travelled, I feared for thy safety.

"Reaching the junction of the greenway and a mortal road, I saw a terrible scene of battle. Scattered about the path were the mutilated and headless bodies of a troop of elves; their banner of seven silver stars against a midnight sky lay trampled and blood-soaked on the ground. I dismounted and walked amongst the slain, and picking up their standard, I turned away in horror from the dreadful scene. As I started forward, I caught a movement in the thorn bushes growing by a wall. Looking round to see if all was clear, I ran into the shrubbery. Lying against the wall on his face was the body of an elf. Seeing he was severely injured, I carefully turned him over. 'Twas Taeron of the House of Taera," he said sadly. "And my heart hurt at the sight of one so noble lying rent and broken – a wretched ruin of such high estate.

"Gently picking him up as to afford no further injury, I set him before me on my horse and rode like the wind to the Horsebox Inn at Oughterard and carried him inside. The landlord is a fear dearg, a good doctor, and a friend of mine. When he saw Taeron's terrible injuries, he did not know if he could save him, and meself knows not if he will live." Doon-vannan's eyes glittered darkly in the starlight. "I set the banner of his house at his feet in the hope of his recovery." He gave a great sigh. "I was about to set out to the House of Cros-Maam when a jenny wren brought word from Ke-enaan that the company of the key was pursued by the Coiste Bodhar and had fled to the gates of Crann Sidhe. Meself became alarmed, and as I was nearby, I sought to find thee. On my way to Crann Sidhe, I came upon a score of dead goblins and the body of a headless knocker lying by the road. Much of the filth was scorched by venom burns, and I knew, my lady, thou must be near." He nodded respectfully at Aine.

"I went on a sortie to check for enemies and became ensnared by goblins," Aine said grimly, "And no doubt 'twas the same magg that attacked the elves. Meself gave chase, but a few escaped me. Even though I routed them, they will know of our position, and 'twill not belong before other knockers will take up pursuit."

"I will ride forth to Cros-Maam and warn my kin of what hath befallen our high house," Doon-vannan said as he rose.

"To avoid trouble on the road, 'twould be best to take a detour south and then strike north," Aine counselled as he embraced her. "'Twill be dawn soon. May the sun shine upon thy face and light thy way with safety."

"And may the cold fire of dragons speed you on your way," Fercle said, breathing a blue flame around Doon-vannan and the Tralee Rose.

Doon-vannan mounted and, with a wave of his hand, disappeared into the gloom.

"Let's have another drink to dispel our doubts and fears," Fercle murmured before taking a pull and handing the flask to Aine.

The liquor lifted Aine's spirits, and lying down on the soft turf, she rested her mind in the dreaming woods of Ahascragh.

Fercle sat with his back against a tree and watched the summit of Crann Sidhe. The pale gleam of dawn was in the eastern sky, and as the first glimmering of light touched the hilltop, he saw colours appear on the summit.

"Aine!" He gently shook her arm. "There are outer-spectrum colours on the summit. The House of Air is returning."

His good humour was suddenly shattered and replaced by fear as dark clouds rushed towards the summit, blocking out the dawn, and a bolt of red lighting struck the top of the hill.

"The company is being harried by the Ghrian Sidhe, and we have no aid to succour them," Aine cried out in alarm. "We must take the horses to the gate and, when the House of Air arrives, be ready to take flight. The Ghrian Sidhe may use sorcery against us, and their reach stretches around the hill for many miles."

The jagged flash of lightning was followed by a deafening thunderclap that reverberated in the valley and boomed across the distant hillsides. The horses milled about in fright, and Fercle and Aine ran to them and whispered words of calming. Taking their horses by the reins and commanding the others to follow, they led them out of the bushes. Aine looked up at the hill and saw another bolt of lightning stab the ground behind a swirl of colours that were racing down the hillside.

Swiftly bringing the horses to the hawthorn arch, they waited anxiously in the darkness. The outer-spectrum light was nearer now, and Aine could see five speeding figures with lurid red lightning bolts stabbing at their heels.

The horses snorted and grew restive. "Something evil is afoot," said Fercle, catching Sunbeam's reins. "And there is the smell of corruption in the air."

The speeding figures were nearing the archway, and fear struck at Aine's heart as she saw a faint glow shimmering around the hawthorn trees. As she watched, a menacing purple mist began to form.

"Fercle! Draw thy sword and let the cold fire of dragons be upon it. I fear an apparition formeth in the gateway."

Thunder cracked as the sylphs sped towards the archway, and

lightning stabbed between the trees, barely missing the company as they ran through. Kilfannan felt relief flood through him as he saw Aine and Fercle waiting with the horses. The entrance to the hill blazed with fire, and in the shifting flame Kilfannan saw the outline of a robed figure forming. Terror swept through him as he recognised the hooded figure was the same haunt from his vision.

"Ride!" Aine shouted as he leapt into the saddle. "We are being attacked! The Ghrian Sidhe have summoned an evil wizard from their halls of sorcery to destroy us."

The company swiftly mounted their horses and, casting caution to the wind, galloped across the rocky hillside and down into a vale. Thunder rolled and lightning stabbed the soggy ground around them as they thundered on through bog and misty fen. In front of them, Kilfannan heard the whirring of webbed wings and saw dark, twisting shadows sweeping from mound to mound.

"Sorcerer's bats of the Ghrian Sidhe," Aine screamed in panic.

Madness and menace rode the hell wind, and in the fume, the flapping, sticky cloud came surging towards the company, snapping at their faces with sharp sanguine fangs. Red Leaf stumbled and then shied away in terror from the blood-seeking horde, throwing Cor-garran onto the ground.

Seeing his nephew fall from his horse, and watching the bats close in around him as he tried to rise, Kilfannan sent his will through the emerald on his brow to aid him. The light of the jewel blazed forth, and with shrill, angry squeaks, the bats retreated into the inky patch of shadow.

With heartfelt thanks to Kilfannan, Cor-garran slipped back into his saddle, and the company rode on.

They had not gone far when the inky shadow suddenly moved with terrible rapidity to a tussock a few yards in front of them. The dark miasma grew in length and breadth into a terrible hooded apparition.

An icy wind thick with malignancy blew around them, numbing their fingers and freezing their hearts. Bats issued forth once more from the shadowed form, searching for their prey with sonic squeaking sounds.

In desperation, Kilfannan called upon the wind of his house, and summoning the power of the HeartStar into his being, he channelled the vibration through the emerald on his brow. The jewel blazed with the radiance of the Green, casting an emerald sheen upon the rocks and sleeping hills. As the heart light illuminated the apparition, the hooded figure retreated into inky mist. The bats disappeared into writhing darkness and then faded from their view.

A soft wind blew in their faces, and Kilfannan knew the sorcerer had been thwarted in his effort to destroy them. Seeing a patch of woodland beyond the fen, he urged the company forward.

Light splashed upon the eastern horizon, and a heron screamed in salutation to the rising of the sun as the company followed Kilfannan into a patch of scrubby trees. Here they stopped, and for an instant they rested from their ordeal of persistent peril and enjoyed a momentary peace.

"We are fortunate indeed to have escaped," Aine said. "The Ghrian Sidhe are cruel, and it pleasured them to give us hope before they tried to dash it."

"We must guard our thoughts," Kilfannan said. "For the arm of the enemy hast grown long enough to cast false shadows in our minds."

The sun was climbing in the sky, and as they reached the Oughterard road, the lightning ceased and the rolling, angry thunder died away. Stopping in a patch of scrub beside the road, Kilfannan sniffed the air for goblin taint but could only smell the scent of rain upon the airwaves.

"Safe for the moment we may be, but not without great loss," Kilfannan said sadly to Aine and Fercle. "Trevelyan of Wessex routed Crom Dubh and saved our souls, but he fell in our defence."

"Trevelyan! Fallen!" Fercle said with shock. "This is the evillest of news indeed. Trevelyan hath been me friend for many turnings of the seasons."

Swiftly Kilfannan described their imprisonment and escape from the death coach, and when he had finished, Thorn-Haw added the details of the struggle against Crom Dubh, the arrival of Braxach, and his taking of Trevelyan.

Kilfannan saw white roses flower in Aine's face and then droop their heads in sadness. "And I fear a great evil will be wrought in the mortal world without Trevelyan," she said, "he who walks and dreams beyond the stars. We have to offer our love to him in prayer and succour his return, for without him the darkness will surely close in around us, exhausting us into the nothing that never ends."

"We have to believe Trevelyan of Wessex will return," Corgarran said. "Mighty was his struggle against the gnawing malice that strove to take us one by one into the hell of his reality. Valiantly did Trevelyan fight, and I, for one, believe he will return. Such is his strength and valour."

Cor-cannan nodded his head in agreement. "He hath the help of the dragon of Gorias, and in the cold fire of intent we have to put our love and trust."

"Meself hath to leave and take news of Trevelyan's fall to Keenaan," Thorn-Haw said. "He is strong in magic, and there may yet be time to anchor Trevelyan's essence within our realm." With a nod of his head, he disappeared into a hawthorn tree.

"Let us ride," Kilfannan said, breaking Red Moon into a trot, "for there is still a ways to go before we reach Binn Breac."

Oughterard was now behind them as they journeyed north. A little ways along the road, Kilfannan called a halt and listened. The sounds of tramping feet in the distance were coming nearer. "There is no cover here. Let's go back to the stand of rocks and take refuge there," he said, pointing to a stand of boulders they had passed.

They rode back along the road, slipped from their horses, walked up the hillside, and took refuge behind the rocks.

The sound of tramping feet and harsh voices grew nearer.

"They are looking for us," Aine whispered. "The goblins that escaped me have joined another knocker and his magg."

Kilfannan watched as a grey shape flittered into view. The knocker was ahead of the magg, his bony fingers weaving in the air. "He seeketh our vibrations," Kilfannan whispered in alarm. "He suspects we are close at hand." Remembering the bottle of orange blossom oil in his pocket, Kilfannan pulled out the cork and blew a few droplets down the hill into the roadside.

The knocker coughed as the sweet perfume of the flowers swirled around him, and beckoning the magg forward, he swiftly flitted by them. Swaggering in the front of the pack, picking at his nose ring, was Grad. Kilfannan saw Kilcannan fingering his bowstring, and as his hand went back for an arrow, Kilfannan stopped him. "Stay!" he hissed.

Kilcannan's eyes were burning with the fire field. "Let me kill Grad, and thou canst strike the knocker," he whispered.

"No! Let us lie low. We run from fight to fight, and 'tis not likely we can kill them all. Some will escape and give cry to our position, and more filth will join the hunt. Each mile we cover, the peril grows stronger and our foes more numerous. Let us favour caution's side."

Despair swept through Kilfannan as the sound of tramping feet died away. The goblins and denizens of Under-Earth were in relentless, murderous pursuit, and it would be a miracle if they reached Binn Breac alive. And if they did, there was no guarantee the thief would be there.

He voiced his fears to Kilcannan. "In truth! I am in doubt if O'Shallihan will be at Binn Breac when we get there."

"Thinkest thou the knocker lied?" Kilcannan answered, keeping his eye upon the road.

Kilfannan shook his head. "Nay, the knocker did not lie. The sun emerald was roasting him alive, and so great was his fear that his words had the ring of truth about them."

"Brother! We have no choice but to wait and see."

They mounted their horses and rode cautiously down the hill to the greenway leading to Maam Cross. A short ways further down, a rocky outcrop loomed darkly upon their left, and the ground was strewn with fallen rocks and boulders.

"Take care," Cor-garran hissed. "The ground is treacherous and slippery."

"Something is abroad," Kilfannan said worriedly, looking across the misty pooled water and the bog on either side. "Without the Brax, we will have to trust our senses, and I fear malignity rides the wind."

They were just about to ride on when Kilfannan felt a blow to his back. He slid from his saddle and landed heavily on the ground. Scrambling to his feet, he swiftly turned and looked around to see a black and greasy arrow lying on the turf. "Goblins!" he shrieked, getting back on his horse.

With a thunder of hooves and flying mud, they galloped up a hillock beside the road. When they got to the top of the rise, Kilfannan looked back and saw a knocker with his magg starting after them up the hill. Looking down the other side of the rise, he saw pools of water and a misty fen. "We must make our stand here," he said to the others. "'Twould not be wise to take the road across the bog. The going will be slow and treacherous, and the knocker may call a water sheerie to attack us. Caught in the bog, we will stand little chance of escape."

A hail of arrows whined over their heads, glancing off small rocks that littered the hillside.

"Meself hath an idea," Kilcannan said, testing the wind. "Fercle, create a blaze, and we sylphs will blow it down the hillside. In the fume we will ride forth and trample our assailants under hoof."

Fercle took a deep breath and, exploding into flame, set fire to the damp turf around him. The grass began to smoulder, and a plume of smoke rose. Kilcannan and Cor-cannan fanned the flames, and Kilfannan and Cor-garran blew the fire into space. In a few moments, smoke started billowing into the air.

"The wind is in our favour!" Kilfannan cried. "Let us ride within the burn smoke, and once we reach the road, there will be a smokescreen behind us, but our way forward will be clear."

Mounting their horses, they took advantage of the fume and

galloped down the side of the hill and onto the road. A small band of goblins had got ahead of them and tried to block their escape. Kilfannan urged his horse forward and, with the rest of the company by his side, trampled the goblins under hoof and rode like the wind along the road with the cursing of the knocker ringing in his ears.

CHAPTER 14

AN UNEXPECTED MEETING

As they thundered north, the sky darkened and rain began to fall, turning the road into a soggy path. After a while, Cor-cannan spotted the dark shapes of some stunted trees on the right-hand side. "'Tis no good, us running headlong into danger," he said to Kilfannan. "Stay here, and Cor-garran and I will ride a couple of furlongs up the road and leave some horsy mess upon the way. It fooled them at the hill of An Tar and may deceive them once again. 'Tis worth a try. We can hide in the trees and still have a good view of them as they pass by."

"'Tis a sound idea," Kilfannan replied. "The magg will think we have fled before them and will be hard upon a non-existent trail."

Kilfannan watched the sylphs of An Carn ride off along the road. He then dismounted and followed the others into the scrubland. The fire behind them was smouldering in the rain, and the smoke was thinning out.

A few minutes later, the House of An Carn came galloping into the trees. "Goblins!" they cried as one, slipping off their horses. "The filth are quick upon our trail, but our mounts obliged, and there are piles of horsey stuff up yonder to mislead them."

Kilfannan could soon hear the pounding of running feet and

cries of pursuit, and soon the magg came into sight. Kilfannan shivered as a knocker glided low, scenting the road before them. More goblins appeared further on, shouting and gesticulating to the horse droppings in the road. Without a look to right or left, the knocker glided forward along the road, followed by the magg.

"The ruse worked," Cor-garran said. "But the rabble will not be deceived for long."

"Aye," Kilfannan answered. "We must take to the fen and stay off the road."

Alert for danger, the company set off across the rock fields and grass-strewn pools to Maam Cross.

The deep mists upon the summits of the Crystal Mountains brooded purple in the westering sun and filled Kilfannan with a sense of danger and hidden dread.

They had not gone far along the narrow road when, to their astonishment, they saw a small red-haired dwarf wearing a green tam-o'-shanter standing by a boulder.

"Hail and well met!" Kilfannan cried, and calling a halt, he pulled up by a rocky outcrop in the scree. "I am Kilfannan of the House of Kilfenoran, and this is my brother Kilcannan. The House of An Carn, Mistress Aine of Ahascragh, and Fercle, fire lord of Gort," he said, introducing the company.

"I am Duirmuid, from the House of Duir," the dwarf replied. "Meself hath been on the watch for yees."

"Thou watchest for us? How can that be?" Kilfannan questioned, looking suspiciously at the dwarf, as they were rarely seen in daylight.

"A curious thing has come to me attention," Duirmuid replied. "Messages have been echoing through the mines for days. Knockers from Clare have made an alliance with the knockers from the northern hills to waylay yees and all who travel with ye. Even though the sun is rising, yees will not be safe upon the road, for the goblins are empowered by an evil will that lies hidden in the Giant's Cliffs. They have vowed to destroy the House of Kilfenoran. They are planning to ambush yees at the bridge of Bally Na Hewn. Come in now, if yees will, and take shelter in me halls. If the House of Air is under attack, which I perceive it is, then as lord of Earth, I will give you sanctuary. Come!"

The companions quickly glanced at each other, wondering what sort of trap this might be.

"In truth," Kilfannan said. "Art thou an illusion – an evil spell sent to lead us to the mines and to our deaths?"

The dwarf spread his legs apart and leaned forward on his axe. "I am Duirmuid, last lord of the House of Duir," he stated. "And in answer to thy question, I am true."

Kilfannan sent his mind into space and divined the airwaves around the dwarf for any taint of deception. Finding only goodness, he said, "I thank thee, Duirmuid, son of Duir. Thine offer of shelter we will gladly accept. Forgive me for my sharp remark, but we have been sorely tried upon the road."

"'Tis a sorry time, indeed, when one looks for enemies in every face," Duirmuid replied. Staring at Fercle, he said, "If me old dwarf eyes don't deceive me, thou art the owner of the racecourse at Gort."

"I am indeed!" Fercle replied, warming to his host.

Duirmuid smiled wistfully. "'Tis many years past since meself went to the races. In the old days, when the mortal races were held at Gort, there were lots of lovely ladies wearing the prettiest hats and carrying the fanciest of umbrellas. I liked to look at them. Today there are no mortal races and no sweet ladies!"

Fercle nodded in agreement. "Goblins are a bane to me racecourse. They have become emboldened and cause fights at every meet. These are dark times indeed, when ugliness replaces beauty."

The dwarf went ahead of them up a rocky path. The way was narrow, and the companions led their horses up the scree in single file. They had not gone far, when Duirmuid stopped and looked back at them. "The front door," he announced with a wave of his hand. Facing them was a narrow opening in the rock.

"What of our charges?" Kilcannan asked doubtfully, looking at Finifar and the rest of the horses. "'Tis more like a crack than a door."

Duirmuid laughed. "You'll just have to trust an old dwarf! Follow me now."

"Methinks the door is a charm," Aine said to Kilfannan. "I will go first." Whispering to Nemia, she started forward, disappearing into the gloom. "'Tis a spell," she called to the company. "The way is wide."

Kilfannan was the second to enter, followed by the others. They came to the threshold of a great hall, and there they stopped. Kilfannan caught his breath in astonishment, so marvellous was the splendour that lay before his eyes. The hall was warm and brightly lit. Radiance streamed from bowls of brilliant crystal spheres that had been worked craftily into the stone pillars arching overhead, and precious stones glittered from the granite walls, making the room appear like a living flower garden.

Duirmuid chuckled at their astonished faces. "The cave door is an illusion. Welcome to the dwarf city of Duirglass."

"'Tis a wondrous sight indeed," Kilfannan said as he dismounted.

"Fabulous indeed," Aine purred. "A city of dream and fable."

Duirmuid chuckled. "Leave your horses here; they will be tended by me kin." He led them over to the north surround. "These are the sacred totems of me House of Duir," he said, bowing his head.

Kilfannan marvelled at a great yellow banner edged in red that was fastened to the wall before him. It bore a heraldic fire-breathing green dragon in the likeness of Braxach, and an axe.

Underneath, on a low stone table, was a suit of chain mail, a helmet with dragon wings, a wooden shield bound with bronze, a mighty double-sided axe, and a stone box filled with knives and flints. On the west side was a sparkling fountain sending forth sprays of silver droplets high into the air. The music of the falling water soothed Kilfannan's nerves, and glancing round the hall, he saw dwarfs sitting on stools by a fire, smoking pipes and talking animatedly together.

"Me kinsmen," Duirmuid boomed, "we have guests!"

Soon the company were surrounded by Duirmuid's kin; stocky

they were, with red hair and long beards, dressed in blue-and-yellow tartan kilts, linen shirts, woollen leggings, and brown boots.

The dwarfs were full of excitement and wonder at their guests, and they plied the travellers with questions about the races and other doings in the outer world.

After a while, Duirmuid came to their rescue and shooed his kinsmen off.

"Come sit down," the dwarf said, motioning to high-backed quartzite chairs with soft silver cushions, "before me brethren exhaust yees with their questions and their curiosity."

They sat down at a long, highly polished table of pale blue marble next to the fountain. Flexing his fingers, Kilfannan began to weave the water song into the Green of leaf and grasses, resting his mind in the tinkling of the water as it rose and then fell back to the shallow pool beneath.

"Would yees like a nip of moonshine?" Duirmuid asked, temptingly handing them cups of light blue stone. "I made it meself."

The company's eyes lit up as they took the cups, and the dwarf hastily filled their goblets.

"Slainte!" they all cried together.

"Now, me friends," Duirmuid said, "'tis plain to me that yees are on the run, with all manner of foul creatures in pursuit, seeking your demise. There is a tale to be told here, for certain. But first we will eat and drink." Here he refilled their glasses and pushed the flagon to the centre of the table. "If yees desire more, pour as you like. Ah, our repast arrives. Pray help yeselves. I am sure there is something each of ye will welcome."

A dwarf appeared with a tray and placed the refreshments on the table. "Meself hath one more dish to fetch," he said before disappearing. There were two bowls of cream, each with a small silver spoon, for Kilfannan and Cor-garran, and two plates of cheddar cheese for Kilcannan and Cor-cannan. For Fercle, there was a dish of sun chokes in a lemon butter sauce and a potato in its jacket. Duirmuid had oatcakes and a bowl of gruel. The dwarf reappeared with a silver-domed platter, which he put in front of Aine. "Something special for me lady," he said, opening it with a flourish. Aine purred in delight, for on the dish was a quivering white blancmange surrounded by strawberries.

"Thank thee, master dwarf," she said to him, flashing her startling eyes, "and to think meself believed that dwarfs lived on naught but mutton stew!"

"Our fare is a secret, madam, like our doors," he said light-heartedly.

Another dwarf cleared away the empty dishes and brought a full jug of moonshine to the table. "Now we have feasted," Duirmuid said, "and thou art ready, Kilfannan, tell me why your House of Air is being hunted by knockers and their maggs, for I deem a shadow of fear lies upon your hearts."

Kilfannan sipped his moonshine but gave no answer. The taking of his soul by Crom Dubh and the mind-blasting horror that had followed had confounded his mind, and along with the sorceries cast by the Ghrian Sidhe, his vision was clouded and he was unable to think clearly. Events had come fast and deadly, overwhelming his ability to connect his thoughts; but now, in the safety of the halls of Duir, he had the opportunity to assess their position.

Each step their house had taken had been dogged with peril, and both he and Kilcannan had experienced the gripping terror that gnawed in empty darkness on their soul light. And yet he knew that even though malign pursuit seemed to wield the upper hand, he understood that the House of Air had been delivered by the hidden hand of fortune. Other forces were at work, and he made a mental image to himself that when despair rode waves into his heart, he would trust the love of the Green to deliver him and all who travelled with him.

"Kilfannan!" Duirmuid said sharply.

"Forgive me for my tardiness in reply, but in truth, I had need of clarity before I answered thee," Kilfannan said, and he went on to tell Duirmuid the story of, and reason for, their flight. He saw

Duirmuid's face grow grim as he told of the battle for possession of their faerie forms and the taking by Braxach of Trevelyan's fallen form. "My brother will tell thee more," Kilfannan said, handing the conversation to Kilcannan.

As Kilcannan related the gifting of the Brax, Duirmuid rose to his feet.

"The Brax?" he queried.

"Aye," Kilcannan answered. "The Brax was gifted to me by Uall Mac Carn of Slieve Elva. When Crom Dubh came for my soul and pursued me, I had no option but to use the Brax against him, and when my brother found me, the Brax had vanished." He sighed deeply and, looking at Duirmuid, said, "'Twas like a part of me was taken."

"The Brax! It belongs to ye, then." Duirmuid marvelled. "Brax Invartu!" he shouted, holding up his hands. The Brax appeared and gently floated, like a bubble, to his palm. "May you be reunited," the dwarf said, handing the tiny horseshoe to Kilcannan.

"How didst thou find it?" Kilcannan asked in amazement, putting the Brax in the inside pocket of his jerkin.

"This is its home," Duirmuid replied. "Duirshoe is its name. It was forged deep within the mountain by the giant Uall Mac Carn."

"Uall told me the Brax was made in the Hall of Duir, but he did not say that he had forged it," Kilcannan exclaimed in astonishment.

"'Twas Uall Mac Carn and his friend the Tuatha De Criedne, he of the golden hair, that forged the Duirshoe. Deep within this mountain, they magically blended gold with red iron – sun and earth. Within the shoe they carved the runes of banishment for the demons from the lower worlds. The Duirshoe was forged as a protector of the Faerie realm." He sighed. "But that was before the days of the Undoing." Sadness crossed his worn and craggy face.

Kilfannan was anxious to hear more of his story and urged him to carry on.

Duirmuid sipped his drink and then continued. "In the days when the dark ones took Cnoc Na Dala and raised their mighty palace of Rath Mhil, their magicians made the blood offering at the Turoc stone. Spells were cast, and hordes of creatures flooded through the blood gate into our realm. Slimy monsters swam the underground courses coming from the sea, taking our people to the depths. Long we battled, and many we vanquished; but some escaped, and knockers, draves, and evil giants of living stone still linger, hidden in the secret ways. But only when the sun is dark do they roam through our tunnels. Our magic has kept them away from our city, but in the rising hate, who knows – they may come forth and assail us. We must be forever watchful in these dark days."

Suddenly he smiled, and a red light shined about him. "But as long as there is stone, I will endure, for dwarfs are the shape of rock in living form. With tenderness, and care, we create great roads beneath the mountain, lined with precious gems sparkling in the light of crystal orbs, arched open rooms, and chambers by the lakes. Such are our halls, fashioned with brilliant gemstones shining bright and clear. I am an elemental of the earth."

Kilfannan and Kilcannan rose, cloaked in the light of living green, and bowed their heads respectfully to the dwarf. "The houses of the gentry serve the element of air," they said in one voice. "We are sylphs and spin the thousand shades of green to our island in the sea, for we are the grass that peeps out from the rocky pastures, and the hillsides' mossy slopes; the luminous, throbbing green of leaves unfolding in the spring; the brooding gloom of dark forests filled with fir; the crimpled green of primrose; and the brave dark spears of lilies in the bog. We are elementals of air," they said, and they then sat back down.

Fercle was the next to rise. Yellow light streamed from him like rays from the sun. "I am the fire keeper," he said, "the warmth within the earth. I am the scorching summer sun upon the sand dunes; cool sunlight greening on the meadows and sweet hills; the stab of lightning from a dark and stormy sky; and the dazzling magentas, reds, and oranges of sunset on the bay. I am an elemental of the fire."

Duirmuid glanced at Aine. The succubus stood up from her

chair. Her flaxen hair now shined orange in the light, and proudly she spoke. "I am the changeling, daughter of Manannan Mac Lir, the son of the sea, and Erin of the dream. I am the element of water, the misty rain, the waterfall, the starry tears on leaf and bud. I am one element and at once the other three, forever turning the seasons at the quarters of the year. I am spring, the time of growth and light; summer in its glory; and autumn's slow decay to winter's sleep. I am Aine the half blood." She then settled back down.

"And beautiful you are, sweet Aine, enchantress of the woodland – and so brave!" Duirmuid exclaimed.

Revealing their true natures in such a formal way formed a bond between the elementals, and after the company had introduced themselves, the dwarf turned his stone-grey eyes on the Kilfenorans.

"Your errand is so desperate for us all that you must carefully choose your road to the Crystal Mountain of Binn Breac. I will accompany ye if you will have me. For if the Green Radiance is lost, a storm will follow, and the darkness that it brings will never end." He took his axe from his belt and held it before Kilfannan. "We can shut ourselves away in our halls of stone and live under siege, but when all is brought to naught and love fails, there is no place for us in a world of hate."

The emerald on Kilfannan's brow shined as he rose and stood before the dwarf. "Welcome, Duirmuid, friend of stone, to the company of the key."

A portentous silence fell upon the hall. The dwarfs ceased their chatter, and in that instant, Kilfannan felt strengthened by the stone and powered his intent to win through the darkness. Elementals had gathered around him – whether by chance or by a higher design, he did not know. But earth, water, fire, and air were all represented in the company of the key.

A dwarf appeared at Kilfannan's elbow with a jug of moonshine. "For yees," he said, putting the liquor on the table.

"A toast!" Duirmuid said, topping up their cups again. "To the company of the key. Slainte!"

"Thou saidst thou knowest of secret paths to the Twelve Pins. What are our choices?" Kilfannan asked after they had toasted.

"Meself can take yees on hidden paths to the Crystal Mountains, so you will not have to take the bridge at Bally Na Hewn," Duirmuid answered. "There is a path deep under the mountains of Leckavrea, north to the Loch of Inagh. Another choice is to go northwest, under the mountain, to the tarn of Derryclare. The third option is to take the road west and then turn north, but that way leads us to the bridge, and that is where the goblins are laying ambush. Nay, the safest route is north, to the blue waters of Inagh."

"Methinks 'tis the safest route," Aine said to Kilfannan. "'Tis the last thing the goblins will expect."

Kilfannan nodded. "'Tis decided then. We will take the road under the mountain to Inagh."

The sylphs bid the company goodnight and retired to seats by the fountain to spin the Green. Kilfannan was restless and apprehensive of the journey ahead. Preferring wind and open space, he was not looking forward to the trek underneath the mountain. Sending his mind into the Green, he rested in the magic of flowers and the cool breath that rises from the stream. He was roused from his dream by Duirmuid.

"The sun is rising in the outer world, and 'tis time for us to take the road underneath the mountain," he said. "'Tis better to travel with the sun, for its rays pierce through the stone, keeping the evil demons at bay in their unlighted labyrinths in Under-Earth."

The company made ready to depart, and Duirmuid led them to a passageway. Holding up his arms, he said in a commanding tone, "Ogmana Invartu." Kilfannan saw an orb of light appear at the entrance to the passage.

"This globe will light our way through the darkness of the mountain," Duirmuid said.

Two dwarfs brought the horses, and they started on their way. They walked in silence, the ball of light travelling before them, lighting up the gloom as if it were day. The only sound they heard was that of water dripping from the stony walls and the muffled thudding of the horses' shoes. The corridor ran downwards for a ways, and the air was cool and fresh.

Doubt continued to plague Kilfannan as the company plodded on along the passage. Every step brought them nearer to the Crystal Mountains, and he wondered what would be waiting for them at Binn Breac. Aeguz had informed other knockers about their journey north, and the goblins had planned an ambush at the bridge. Without Duirmuid's intervention, they would have ridden into a trap. He thought disconsolately that it was likely the goblins had warned the thief that they were coming, giving him time to get away.

After a while, they came to a large pool. High above their heads, the sun shining through an opening in the rock sent a great shaft of light into the water, illuminating its crystal depths.

"This is the pool of Duirga," Duirmuid told the company.

The dwarf took off his tam-o'-shanter and bowed his head before a glittering stone pillar. "This is the likeness of Duir, the firstborn of me race," he said, pointing to the statue of a mighty dwarf. "It was here that our tribe began. Long ago the sun sent our seed deep within the pool and the living rock gave birth to the people of the stone. 'Twas here at the pool that our people gathered in the dark days of the sorcerer kings."

They started on their way again, and as they rounded a corner in the rock, the company gasped in wonder. They found themselves in a wide hall. A waterfall cascading down from a fissure in the rock high above their heads formed a foaming pool, and positioned around the falls were four high-backed seats carved out of stone.

"This is the chamber of introspection," Duirmuid said. "It is here that Duir held counsel with the smith Uall Mac Carn and the mighty wizard Creidne; 'twas Braxach who completed the company of four and took the fourth seat by the pool.

"It was in this very chamber that the Brax was made. All the elements were assembled here: the living rock deep within the earth, the water falling to the pool, the dragon's fiery breath, and the air that sent it forth."

"The Brax is a wondrous gift indeed!" Kilcannan said. "'Tis an honour to be its guardian, as it is of us."

Duirmuid whispered to Gwen, his piebald mare, and they started forward down a passage. Soon they came to a junction of four ways, one in each direction. Duirmuid chose the western arch and led them slowly forward. The way became narrower and the passage climbed gently upwards, and Kilfannan felt a stirring in the air. The path broadened, and the party could see a dim light up ahead.

"Ah! The cavern of Anach," Duirmuid cried. "Me friends, we have reached the Loch of Inagh." At a command from Duirmuid, the globe dimmed and disappeared.

They found themselves in a wide and spacious cavern. The cave mouth opening to the world outside the mountain was low and narrow, just high enough for a horse and rider to pass through.

Duirmuid turned to Kilfannan. "'Tis only an hour or two before the sun goes down," he said earnestly. "If you take me advice, we will stay here in the refuge of the mountain until dusk. Then we can venture forth. The darkness will help shield us from the filth of the mines who may be watching for us."

The company stood together at the mouth of the cave with their horses. Kilcannan pulled out his flask of brandy and offered it around. The time passed quickly, and soon the light began to fade.

"Cor-cannan," Duirmuid said quietly. "Come with me on a sortie; we will scout the road ahead."

Kilfannan watched the pair slip away into the gathering gloom and stood quietly with the horses, awaiting their return.

The twilight faded into darkness. Time wore on, yet still Duirmuid and Cor-cannan did not return. Kilfannan became restless. "Aine," he said anxiously, "methinks some ill hath befallen Duirmuid and Cor-cannan. We should search for them. What sayest thou?"

"Meself will go with Fercle and Cor-garran," she replied.

"I would like to join the search party," Kilcannan protested.

"Nay!" Aine said sharply. "Thou art the heads of the House of Air, and 'tis our duty to protect thee. Stay here and guard the horses until we return … and if we do not, ride forth with the sun."

There was a sudden noise outside, and Cor-cannan and Duirmuid appeared.

"Brother!" Cor-garran said with relief. "We were worried that evil had befallen thee, and were ready to make search."

"'Tis wise we made sortie," Cor-cannan answered grimly. "Goblin scum were hiding in the tall reeds by the stream. The ground is marshy there, and we would have made a very easy target for them. Duirmuid and I had to inch our way forward through the rank grass and assail them from behind."

"How many goblins?" Kilfannan asked.

"Four," Cor-cannan answered. "We must leave and make distance before their filthy carcasses are discovered."

"The valley beneath is not safe," Duirmuid said thoughtfully. "There is another way along the foot of the mountain, but 'tis a longer road to Binn Breac and will cost us precious hours. But Cor-cannan is right, 'twill not be long before a spying nightbird haps upon their bodies and sends word to a knocker and his magg. We must leave now, with the night as shield."

Once they were in the saddle, Duirmuid led them from their refuge. The mist thickened into fog as they threaded their way slowly down the rock-strewn ground to the foot of the hill. The air was cold and clammy, and all Kilfannan could hear was the click of shoes on stone and the endless dripping of water. He began to feel dispirited as they plodded on, and he wondered if the drab grey mist would ever dissipate.

When they reached the bottom of the slope, Duirmuid called a halt. "There is a rock field yonder. If me memory serves me right, the way is long and hard, so 'tis best if we dismount, for there is many a cunning crevice in which to break a fetlock."

Feeling in need of warmth, Kilfannan took out his flask. "Let us partake of a stiffener," he said to the others. "'Tis damp, and the liquor will help ward away the cold." The company slipped from their saddles, gathered round Kilfannan, and shared the welcome brandy.

"How far to Binn Breac?" Kilfannan asked Duirmuid.

"'Tis still a goodly way. We will cross the rock field and then strike north across the bog."

The fog cleared away as they started off, and a cold, dying moon cast an eerie light on the seemingly endless rocks before them. Kilfannan kept his eyes on the ground. He was nervous and did not dare look at the grotesque shapes hiding in the shade under the moonlight. The closer they came to Binn Breac, the more his apprehension grew. Aeguz would have hammered a message through the mines to his northern kin as to their destination, and he feared goblins would be waiting. His anxiety was exacerbated by the fact that the town was in a narrow gorge at the mountain's foot. He suspected there was only one road in to Binn Breac, and the same road out, which made it ideal for ambush.

Dawn was breaking in the east as rock gave way to peaty turf and fenland. The Crystal Mountains loomed before them, and for an uncomfortable moment, Kilfannan fancied that in the misty light they looked like the humpbacked, coiling body of a giant sea monster moving through a fogbound ocean.

Duirmuid struck a path leading left into fenland, and they moved slowly forward through the tussocky grass and standing pools of water. Kilfannan was listening to the airwaves for any dissonance of sound that could warn him of ambush, but all he heard was the singing of birds. It comforted him that the Brax was silent, but the closer they came to the mountains, the more his unease built into dread.

The mist cleared with the sun, and by noon the ground became firmer and the going faster. Checking the airwaves for any sound to warn of trouble, Kilfannan heard music on the wind. "List!" cried he. "Harken to the bittersweet music of the mortal realm."

Following the sound of the music, they saw an old man sitting on an upturned crate, playing a whistle.

"The melody is haunting and speaks of one longing for release," Cor-garran said, weaving the harmony with his fingers and spinning the Green to the dark lilies in the bog.

"Time may be pressing upon us," Kilcannan said. "And 'tis true that enemies are at hand, but a moment spinning the Green will renew and refresh us. Brother, what sayest thou?"

Kilfannan nodded in agreement. His old life was one of joyful creation, and spinning the Green would strengthen him to keep the dream alive ere ruin came upon it.

"Binn Breac is not far, and 'tis a small place. There is a chance the mortal knows of O'Shallihan and where he can be found. That will give us an advantage," Kilfannan said as they rode towards the turf cutter.

The company pulled up their horses by a pile of peat and dismounted, forming a circle around the old man. With their long fingers, the sylphs spun the Green of heather, sedge, and reed; sweet asphodel and sundews; and lily flowers in the bog. Fercle flared the sound of fire, Aine sang the song of water, and Duirmuid drummed with his fingers the earth beat on the ground. Together they wove the heart mist around the whistle player, and as his music surged with joy, Kilfannan touched him on the forehead with his finger, bestowing on the mortal the gift of faerie sight.

The old man stared at the company, and after rubbing his eyes, he looked again. "By the saints!" he cried in disbelief, covering his eyes with a calloused hand.

"I am Kilfannan of the House of Kilfenoran," Kilfannan said. "And sir, I am pleased to make thine acquaintance. We are the gentry, the good folk of thy myths and legends. Pray, do not be afraid; we mean no harm."

The old man drew back his hand, and a look of wonder lit up his lined and careworn face. At length he stood up. "Me name is Danny O'Donovan, at your service," he said hesitantly. "Me mother,

Maureen, she was always talking of folk like yourselves, sirs." He then quickly added, "And madam!" while looking at Aine, who smiled sweetly at his weather-beaten face. "Most folks round here, especially the wee ones, don't believe in the old stories anymore. They say it's superstition and old wives' tales. I'm a little overcome that you are here, and a little unnerved to see legend come alive."

"Danny, my friend," Kilfannan began, "I wonder if thou couldst aid us. We are in need of news about a mortal. His name is Patrick O'Shallihan, and he lodges at Lake Carn. He is a thief and hath stolen a thing of great importance to us. Wouldst thou enquire in the inn at Binn Breac for news of this swindler and where he can be found?"

"It would be me pleasure," Danny said. "Meet me at the Currach, the inn beside the water of Lake Carn, this evening. It is the only pub in the village, and you'll find it where the road ends at the foot of the mountain. I will make enquiries and see what I can glean. I'll be seeing you later – to be sure I will."

"May the living light of the Daione Sidhe be with thee," Kilfannan called as they mounted their horses and turned back across the bog.

CHAPTER 15

THE CURRACH

The road to the mountains grew rockbound and uneven, and it was so narrow they had to ride in single file. Their progress was as slow as a snail's pace as they picked their path up the long, steep way. With every furlong travelled, Kilfannan felt threatened and oppressed by the close press of the green and grey granite slopes.

The sky clouded over, banishing the sun, and a chill wind began to blow. Below them in a valley was an inlet, a tidal river that shined like a silver ribbon under the grey-clad sky. "The inlet will take us to Binn Breac and the lake of Carn," Duirmuid said.

They rode down the hillside through the gorse and tall bracken to the riverbank, stopping in a stand of thick green fern.

"'Twould be a good idea for us to travel in the water," Duirmuid said, glancing at the river. "'Tis wide and shallow, and it will throw the goblin trackers off our trail."

They followed the estuary for a ways, but as the tide came in and the water deepened, they assembled on the bank. Before them lay a valley where the inlet wound its way towards the mountain's feet. Kilfannan looked up at the mountains with mounting apprehension. Their steepness and sinister suddenness of size were greater than he had imagined, and he fancied armies of goblins lurking on their shadowed slopes.

The shadows of evening were falling as they trotted along the stony road leading to the village of Lake Carn. Small, narrow streets of cramped, tall houses branched off from the main road, and a few fishing boats were in mooring at the quayside.

The road ended in a dead end with a small paved carpark at the foot of the mountain. "The inn is yonder," Duirmuid said as they rode past a row of grey, grim houses that lined the quayside.

The Currach pub was at the end of the road facing Lake Carn, and the dark water glittered ominously in the dying light. The humped shape of Binn Breac rose before them, and the dark shades of the mountains loomed up on either side.

Dismounting before the entrance, Kilfannan looked without favour on the uninviting, bleak stone walls and the dull light that trickled like a stain through the tiny windows. Tension mounted in his body as he wondered what was in store for them inside. Would they get information on the thief, or had their quest been nothing more than a cruel ruse designed by the knockers to give them hope and then destroy them? He felt strain in his back, and to the question in his mind, he had no answer.

Seeing a passageway leading around the back of the pub, he said, "Let us take the horses through the alley and get them out of sight."

At the back of the inn was a narrow yard stretching the length of the pub, hemmed in by the mountain and tall boulders, fronted by a dark thicket of brambles that disappeared back into the darkness.

"The village is a good place for an ambush," Kilcannan said as they assembled in the yard. "And even if we find the thief and get the key, there is only one road in and out of here, and if 'tis blocked by goblins, we will have no means of escape."

"It cannot be helped," Kilfannan said, cutting him off. "If this is what it will take to retrieve the key, then so be it. We have to do our best."

"There may be another way out of Lake Carn," Duirmuid said, "if meself remembers rightly."

Another way out? Kilfannan thought. "Indeed! Tell on!" he said eagerly.

"In the annals of the House of Duir, there was record of a cave at the foot of Binn Breac, and a tunnel leading into the mountains. The tunnel was bored by monsters in the War of Separation. They slithered through dark passageways into our domain, and many of our people were slain and taken into the dark depths of water. The tunnel the enemy bored in days gone by can be our salvation if I can find it. Meself will look beyond the thorn thickets that hug the mountain's feet and will try to seek out the opening to the passage underground."

"Meself will help you," Fercle said. "The skirt of the mountain is long, and even though me fire eyes can lighten up the darkness and aid us in our search, it may take us hours to find it."

"If indeed it doth still exist and not be blocked by fallen rock," Kilfannan answered. "But 'tis all we have for hope."

"Despair not, Kilfannan. Meself will light a fire in the thought that we will swiftly find it," Fercle said.

Duirmuid looked around and sniffed. "The deep and sombre valleys between the mountains are riddled with caves and goblin vaults. I sense the pub is a den of thieves and liars in the mortal world, and goblins in Faerie. Methinks the horses should not be unattended while you are waiting for Danny to arrive." Pushing their way through the brambles, Fercle and Duirmuid disappeared into the darkness.

"The inn hath an evil feel," Kilfannan said to the others, "but so doth the water."

"Yea, 'tis what lies in the deep of the lake that is our peril," Aine said. "The knockers have had time to plan their attack on us, and as the power of me father waxes, he may take to the water in the hope of our destruction." She glanced at Kilfannan. "Meself will go into the inn and check for goblins. If 'tis not clear of foul folk, we will have to watch for Danny from the alley."

Opening the back door to the inn, Aine disappeared inside. A moment later, she was back and beckoned them forward. "'Tis clear," she hissed.

Kilfannan scanned the narrow space behind the pub, and with a concerned look, he said to the House of An Carn, "Stand guard on the horses while we wait inside for Danny."

"I will follow Duirmuid and Fercle into the thicket and see if I can find cover for the horses," Cor-garran said.

"If danger threatens, I will open the back door and give a crow call as a warning." Cor-cannan added.

Leaving the House of An Carn in the yard, Kilfannan, Kilcannan, and Aine went through the door into the common room of the inn. The faerie bar was empty save for a cluricaun sitting at the counter. "I will get the drinks," Kilcannan said as the others sat down at a table near the door.

Switching his gaze to the mortal world, Kilfannan looked around. The common room was empty, apart from a small crowd of men drinking beer and playing in a darts match. He scanned each face, but O'Shallihan was not amongst them, and he fervently hoped that Danny would soon arrive with news of the whereabouts of the thief. Lake Carn was ripe for ambush, and he felt the goblins were playing a waiting game. "Brother!" he said to Kilcannan. "I see not the thief or Danny in the bar. I will check the snug."

Kilfannan went through the door into the other bar and looked around. It was empty in both worlds, being early in the evening. He was on his way back to the company when the front door opened and a group of elves came bustling past. The sight of them lifted his spirits. If a fight did occur, at least they would have elves to fight alongside them.

"Kilfannan," Aine said as she sat down. "I think 'tis best we make our own inquiries about the whereabouts of the thief, for the longer we linger here, the greater the chance of ambush and attack."

"If Fercle and Duirmuid fail to find the passageway through the mountain, we are trapped," Kilcannan said despondently. "Even if we find O'Shallihan and get the key, the hounds of hell will be soon upon us, and I fear we are stuck in a dead end and shall not get out of here alive. And what shall we do if Danny doth not come?"

Realising the wisdom of his brother's words, Kilfannan looked around, and seeing the cluricaun still drinking at the bar, he wondered if he had any information on the thief. Cluricauns were nosy and oft listened in to mortal conversations. "I will ask the cluricaun if he knoweth of the thief. They like to gossip," he said. Rising and taking a guinea from his pocket, he went to the counter.

"Hail, and well met. I am Kilfannan of the House of Kilfenoran," he said, introducing himself.

"Well met yourself. I am Claggeneen," the little man answered affably, regarding Kilfannan with a rheumy eye.

Claggeneen was very brightly dressed in a red linen shirt under a leather jerkin, turquoise blue britches stained with wine, and black shoes with large buckles and worn-down heels.

"Dost thou know a mortal man by the name of Patrick O'Shallihan?" Kilfannan asked in a low voice.

"Patrick O'Shallihan." Claggeneen scratched his head, and his wine-soaked nose wobbled up and down. "I don't believe I do."

"He is tall and dark, and 'tis likely he hath a goblin with him."

"Ah!" Claggeneen nodded vigorously. "Meself did see such a mortal—"

Before Claggeneen could finish his sentence, Kilfannan heard a soft voice at his elbow say, "O'Shallihan! I know him!" Looking into the mortal world, he saw a dark haired man with a long face and bright blue eyes standing beside him at the bar.

"My name is Dermot Brogan," the man said, introducing himself. "And who be you?"

Kilfannan stepped back in surprise. He had not seen the man amongst the dart players, nor had he seen him enter the bar. Wondering where he had come from, and why a mortal had been listening to his conversation, he felt reluctant to reveal his identity. He was saved from answering by Aine, who joined him at the counter.

"Meself thought I would join you," she said, smiling at Dermot. "I am Aine, daughter of Manannan," she said, watching for his reaction.

Dermot hesitated for a moment, and then he said, "Charmed to meet you."

Kilfannan saw Aine smile, and sprays of orange roses began blooming in her cheeks. "Thou said thou knowest O'Shallihan," Kilfannan said.

"I do indeed," Dermot answered. "A bad lot he is. I don't know why you're looking for the likes of him."

"'Tis a small matter, and as we are here at Lake Carn, we thought we would call upon him," Kilfannan replied cagily.

"He lives along the lake side, just a few minutes' walk from here," Dermot said in his soft brogue.

Kilfannan felt uncomfortable in the man's presence, and testing the ether around him, he discovered Dermot had no mortal energy. The person beside him was a print, a facsimile devoid of self, a counterfeit.

"'Tis a grand idea," he heard Aine say. He caught her eye, and in the meeting of their glances was a warning.

"Aine," Kilfannan said. "A second of thy time." He smiled at Dermot. "We will rejoin thee in a moment."

Together they moved away from the counter. "Aine," Kilfannan whispered, "the man that calls himself Dermot Brogan hath no mortal energy."

Aine nodded. "Handsome he is, but he hath no man balls. Methinks he is a drave."

A chill took Kilfannan as he heard Aine's words. Draves were simulacra created by mortal blood, and he was suddenly affrighted for Danny. He had expected the turf cutter to be waiting for them when they got to the inn, but time was passing and there was no sign of him. "Aine," he whispered. "Do what thou wilt to destroy the drave."

Returning to the bar with Aine beside him, Kilfannan said,

"Dermot, we will accept thine offer, but first Mistress Aine desireth a glass of the green faerie to sustain her," he said, signalling the landlord. "And how about thyself? Wouldst thou like a brandy?"

"I've had enough to drink." Dermot laughed, gently knocking the ashes from his pipe into a tray. "All I do is keep running to the toilet. And talking about running to the toilet, I have to go right now. I won't be a minute, and then I'll give you directions to where O'Shallihan is lodging." He smiled. "Better yet, I'll take you there myself. That way you won't get lost."

Dermot got up and moved towards the door, but Aine intercepted him and blocked his way. "Thou art attractive," she purred, pressing herself against him, and as she thrust her hand between his legs, there was an acrid flash; a stench of rotting flesh and a sharp crackling shockwave rent the air. Dermot Brogan had disappeared.

"A drave requires power far beyond knocker magic," Aine said. "They need mortal blood and human sacrifice to clothe themselves. Pity he was not mortal." For a moment Kilfannan saw Venus flytraps snapping in her face. "But we foiled his plot against us, and 'twill be a while until he can be of use to the enemy again."

Human blood … sacrifice, Kilfannan thought, and once again fear and anguish struck his heart for Danny.

"Kilfannan!" Hearing someone call his name, he looked round and saw Claggeneen waving him over to the counter. "Meself hath remembered the mortal. O'Shallihan." He belched loudly and slid his empty glass along the bar to Kilfannan.

"Landlord! A bottle of wine for Claggeneen," Kilfannan said, putting the guinea on the counter.

"It must have been two nights past," Claggeneen said, grabbing the bottle as soon as the landlord put it on the bar. "O'Shallihan was in the bar with a goblin. Seeing a mortal with a goblin perked up me interest straight away. I don't like goblins, so I was careful not to be seen looking, but I was listening all right." He took a long pull of wine and wiped his mouth on the sleeve of his shirt. "O'Shallihan was drunk and got into a fight. The landlord threw him out. I heard some men talking at the bar the next day; they said O'Shallihan had gone with a party of archaeologists to the island of Inishark to help with the heavy work."

"O'Shallihan hath gone to Inishark," Kilfannan repeated. "Art thou sure of what thou heardest?"

"Indeed!" Claggeneen said, affronted, looking at Kilfannan in surprise. "Meself don't tell lies, and 'tis the truth most definitely." He belched again. "Drunk though meself may be, I knows what I heard. The mortals were discussing payment. Complaining, they was. Said O'Shallihan was being paid more than he was worth, and it wasn't right that an outsider got the job." He swayed precariously on his stool. "I wonder if the goblin went with him to the island."

Kilfannan felt his body tense as he remembered Prince Donne's warning. His stomach churned, and he suddenly felt sick. The mortal had left, and they had no choice but to follow him across the sea to the island. "Claggeneen! I have to take my leave. The House of Air is in thy debt."

"Right you are, sir. Meself is glad to have been of help."

Loud voices erupted from the next table as Kilfannan joined the others. A bunch of drunken fear deargs had arrived and were arguing between themselves about jockeys "pulling horses" at the races.

"Come," Kilfannan said to the others, "let us retire to the snug. The common room hath become rowdy, and we have much to discuss."

As they rose to go, he saw the door open, and a young man rushed into the bar. "May the Lord save us," he heard him cry out. "Why! Danny is lying dead upon the road. I saw him in the headlights of my car. Knocked over, he is. I stopped and called the guarda, and waited for them to arrive. There is blood all over the pavement, and his bike is all buckled up beside him."

The company looked at one another, their faces blank with amazement and horror. Sadness ripped through Kilfannan's being like an icy body slap. He knew in his heart that it was Danny's blood that had called the drave – his blood that had been sacrificed. Aine's words echoed in his mind. *A drave requires power far beyond knocker magic*, he thought. *If not the knockers, who else would have taken Danny's life?* He felt sick with the ugliness and horror his reality had become. And for a moment, he wished for an end to it all – oblivion, where care reigned not – and he wept bitterly, so utterly forsaken and wretched seemed his life.

He felt Kilcannan's hand upon his arm. "Hold up, brother!" he said supportively. "'Twould seem a spy of the enemy must have eavesdropped on our meeting at the bog and sent evil to murder Danny and commit the evillest of deeds. My heart is full of sadness for the mortal, for 'twould seem now that tragedy stalketh us."

"We can do naught for Danny but send our love for him into the ether," Kilfannan responded. He took Kilcannan's hand, and together they visualised Danny's face and surrounded him with the love of the Green Ray, the heart field of the All.

"For the sake of the Green, we have to follow the thief to the island," Kilfannan said, "or all our efforts to save the HeartStar will be in vain."

"But what of Prince Donne's warning?"

Kilfannan shook his head. "Brother! If we cannot regain the key and set our creators free, what hope is there for us? And what option do we have but to follow the thief?"

"None," Kilcannan responded. "Forgive me for my doubt."

"All is in doubt, brother. There is only the quest for the key that need occupy our thoughts."

"'Tis easier said than done when danger threatens," Kilcannan replied.

The three companions left the common room and settled at a table in the private bar. "'Twas Grad that Claggeneen saw with O'Shallihan," Kilfannan said to the others. "That tells me that Grad is near and, for some reason we are not privy to, is keeping out of sight."

"'Tis my thought that Grad waiteth for the drave to lead us into their trap," Kilcannan responded. "They are not yet aware that we have become privy to their trick, and have dispatched their vessel of evil. Forewarned is forearmed, and we must use this time to our advantage. We must seek the dwarf tunnel. 'Tis madness to linger here. 'Tis best to leave and join the company."

Kilfannan nodded in agreement. "I will accompany thee."

"Meself will check the quayside for goblins," Aine said, "for if a path through the mountain cannot be found, we will have to find a way to defend ourselves." She rubbed a delicate hand across her brow. "Kilcannan is right. There is nothing to be gained for thyself by staying here. If the goblins come into the inn, they will see you straight away."

Kilfannan nodded. "Be safe, my lady, for me heart tells me that evil stirreth in the deep."

Switching his gaze to the mortal world as they made their way across the room, Kilfannan saw three young men sitting at a corner table, dressed in anoraks and walking boots. A video camera was lying by their feet, and one was looking at a map.

His curiosity aroused, he whispered to Kilcannan. "The men sitting yonder." He pointed to the table. "My intuition tells me to stay for a moment and listen to what they say. The Brax is quiet, so no immediate danger threatens, and I feel we will learn something of importance to our quest."

Unseen by the mortals, the Kilfenorans sat down beside them on the bench. Two of the men were very blond with strong accents; the third was a brown-haired Englishman who was pontificating about their adventures on the lake the night before.

"Nobody is going to believe us until they see the footage. My, that thing was big!" He bragged in a loud voice so everybody in the bar could hear. "All those nights we spent at Loch Ness when we should have been here. What do you think, Olaf?" he said to the blond man sitting across the table. The Norseman, unsmiling, shook his head and took a big drink of stout.

"Big snake." He burped. "Damn big snake, nearly drowned us. Good thing it wasn't any nearer; otherwise, the boat would have capsized and we all would have been in the water with that thing, whatever it was."

Kilfannan froze, and fear chilled him to the bone. A serpent had been seen in the lake, and he wondered if Manannan had risen in reptile form.

"Roger," the other man said to the Englishman. "Let me see the map, and we will mark the spot."

Roger spread the map upon the table. "The serpent rose about here," Sven said, pointing a stubby finger at a blue spot. Kilfannan craned his neck to see. The mortal's finger was pointing to the Lake of Corrib.

"Find the island of Inishark on the map," Kilcannan whispered urgently, "so we know where we go." Suddenly the Brax beeped in his pocket. "Goblins are near. We should leave."

"Wait!" Kilfannan said, watching Sven tap the map with his finger. Shutting off the sound from the mortal world, he traced a line with his eyes west from the lake to the coastline. Moving closer, he saw an island off Erin's Point which further study showed to be Inishark.

"Time! Gentlemen, please!" the innkeeper shouted in the mortal world. "Drink up now. 'Tis past eleven, and the garda are around."

Roger folded up the map and put it in his pocket. As he turned away from table, Kilfannan deftly stole the map from his pocket, leaving a guinea in its place. The Brax beeped again with urgent tone as he tucked the map under his jerkin, and he heard the sound of harsh voices coming from the common room.

"Goblins!" Kilcannan stiffened and drew his blade.

"Go and warn the House of An Carn," Kilfannan said. "I will join thee in a moment."

"Kilfannan! What madness hath come upon thee?"

"My heart telleth me to wait. Fear not! I say again, I will join thee in a moment."

Kilfannan knew he should flee with his brother, but against all rationality, a force held him to stay in the bar and see if Grad was in evidence.

Peering round the door into the common room, he saw a bunch of elves playing dice with the innkeeper on the counter. At the back of the room was a long table, and he saw Grad sitting with a gang of goblins. He eyed the loathsome creature with disgust that could have bordered on hate if he had allowed it.

There were fifteen of the foul creatures arguing, drinking, and spitting wads of tobacco on the floor. Grad was swigging black rum from a bottle and growling curses at his crew, but they made no sign of leaving for a while. He was just going to join Kilcannan outside when suddenly the front door swung open and three soaked and stinking goblins swaggered into the hallway. For one horrible moment, he thought they were coming into the snug and got ready to take flight to the back door.

"Hoi! Hoi!" he heard Grad scream. "Over here, boys!"

The newcomers had joined their kin. One was whispering to Grad, and the other two had gone to the counter to buy beer. As he turned his attention to the airways, he could hear the rasping of Grad's evil voice. It was obvious from his tone that the goblins waiting at the lakeside had brought fine news.

"Ye have done well," he heard Grad snarl to one of his spies. "The serpent will have a tasty meal tonight, but only after we are done with them. I's going to tear the filthy toffs' heads off and eat them." He drooled in anticipation, and globs of brown saliva ran down his fangs. "I's going to savour the cracking of their skulls and supping on their brains!" He took a swig from his rum bottle. "The drave will lead them into a trap, and two knockers will be waiting to surprise them. After tonight, the House of Kilfenoran will be dead, the master from the cliffs will come forth in glory, and the world will be ours to rule and pillage." He rubbed his greasy hands together. "Get me another bottle," he snarled to one of the magg. "Then we'll be getting off to have some fun."

Kilfannan shuddered at the goblin's callous words. They had

been fortunate. Grad had not yet heard the news that the drave had been defeated, and the thought that Grad had no inkling they were present encouraged him immensely. He was about to go and join his brother when he saw an elf leaving the counter. As he passed the goblins, Kilfannan saw Grad jump up.

"Hoi!" he snarled to the elf. "Give me the gold necklace you got round your stinking neck. I wants it."

The elf made a rude gesture with his finger in reply.

Grad drew his dagger and, with a look of devilish glee, lunged forward, snatching the necklace from the elf's neck. There was a struggle, and Kilfannan saw Grad plunge his knife into the elf's heart, working the blade backward and forward to do a thorough job. After spitting on the body, he turned triumphantly to his leering cohorts and held up the glittering necklace of golden leaves. "See! I's got it."

Having seen the murder of his kin, the captain of the elves drew his sword and, with a cry for revenge, called his troop to battle. A furious fight soon began.

Knowing that he would be discovered if he stayed any longer in the bar, Kilfannan fled back to the rear entrance, opened the door, and ran out into the yard.

Kilcannan was waiting for him. "Duirmuid hath found the path through the mountain, and Cor-garran and Cor-cannan hath taken the horses there. Come, let us follow," he cried out as the Brax chimed in his pocket.

Kilfannan was about to follow when he saw a small lizard climb up onto a stone. Suddenly he was surrounded by the perfume of the wood, and Aine appeared. "We must flee," she said, and taking his hand, she pulled him into a bramble thicket.

The bushes closed behind them like a shield, and they had taken only a few footsteps when they heard a crash and the sound of splintering wood followed by shouts and curses. Scrambling through the thickets, they came to a rocky path leading round the mountain. As they rushed forward, they heard the sound of light footfalls behind them, and a cry. Looking back, Kilfannan saw an elf fall on the path with an arrow in his eye. More elves were running across the rocks, and he could hear the clatter of hobnailed boots in the darkness. "Pursuit is close behind," he said as they ran forward.

More shouts and cries rang out as they clambered over the rocks and tried to keep their footing on the scree. Kilfannan heard a whine as a goblin shaft flew over their heads and bounced off rocks in front of them. The path bent round through a stand of bushes, and as they turned the corner, Kilfannan saw Fercle and Duirmuid at the dark mouth of a cave in the mountainside. Running towards the cave mouth, Kilfannan could hear the rasping voice of Grad cutting through the air, shrieking at his crew to leave the fleeing elves and gather on the quayside.

Once the company had gained the cave, Duirmuid held up his hands and sounded in a low rumbling voice, "Sha-sa-se." Four times he repeated the words, and Kilfannan felt a vibration through the rock bed. The boulders in front of the cave shivered, and as a wall of stone appeared, the shouts and curses were suddenly cut off.

Kilfannan heaved a sigh and embraced his brother and the sylphs of An Carn. "We have come through peril and trial, and even though we have not yet gained the key, we have been delivered from the darkness." He pulled out his flask, and his weary face lit up with a smile. "To the HeartStar," he said before taking a nip and handing the flask around.

After they had toasted, Duirmuid said, "Even though we are in safety for the moment, the goblins will find our tracks, and seeing they end at the mountain's feet, they will summon a knocker. He will see the illusion meself hath created, and he may be able to undo me spell. We must make haste through the mountain. The passage will take us northward, and it will be a ways before we find an entrance to the upper world. 'Tis a detour and will cost us precious time, and once we leave the tunnel, we must be cautious, for we will be in the northern mines – the heart of goblin country."

"'Tis better than the fate that awaited us if we had taken the road along the inlet," Aine said grimly. "When meself went outside to check the quayside, I saw Grad and two knockers sitting on the harbour wall. There was a sinuous shadow moving on the lake towards them, and as I watched, I saw a serpent rise from the churning water. 'Twas an emissary of me father's will. More goblins appeared out of the shadows, and after a brief consultation with the knockers, the serpent disappeared. 'Twas then that I saw Grad and a few of his cronies go into the pub."

"Danny hath been murdered," Kilfannan said to the others. "He was found dead in a pool of blood not far from the inn. He was on his way to see us." His voice faltered. "And he died because of us."

Duirmuid frowned, and his bushy eyebrows met in a straight line across his brow. "'Twas a devilish plan that was laid against the mortal, and in truth, it reeks of more than knocker magic. Some darker power is abroad, and knowing our purpose, it used the mortal's blood to trap us."

"Aye," Aine said, "both maggs of goblins and their knockers were waiting in the darkness further down the inlet to intercept us when we left the inn, while others waited in the shadows at the base of the mountain for Grad's signal to attack us from behind. We would have been surrounded," she said. "And even with your enchanted bows and arrows, methinks we would not have won the day."

"'Tis true," Kilfannan answered. "Without the wisdom of dwarfs, we would have been undone and the HeartStar would have fallen. For truly 'tis said that the House of Earth succoureth the House of Air."

"Praise as ye like," Duirmuid countered. "But we must make haste. Once Grad knows what route we have taken, he will hammer the information of our flight to his northern kin, and their entire foul breed will be on the watch."

Fercle's fiery yellow eyes were lighting up a long, low cave. At the far end, Kilfannan could see a darker shade of shadow – the entrance to the passage underground. The tunnel was narrow and dripping with water, and they were forced to walk in single file.

The air was cold and clammy, and the muffled sounds of foot and hoof echoed through the walls. They toiled on for what seemed an age until at last the air became fresher and they could hear the sound of running water. The way widened, and they came into a cave mouth.

"We have reached the end of the passageway," Duirmuid said. "We must halt by the entrance to the upper world, for we are deep in the heart of goblin country. 'Twill be dawn soon. Meself and Fercle will go forth and make sure the way is safe."

The two slipped off into the darkness, and all that could be heard was the rushing of a river. Cor-garran pulled out his flask. "'Tis cold," he said to the others. "Let us take a nip to ward away the chill of fear that I deem lies upon us."

"Dost thou know where we are?" Kilfannan asked Aine. He pulled the map from under his jerkin and spread it out upon the stone floor.

Aine peered at it. "We are here," she said, pointing to a spot within the mountains. "And 'tis not wise for us to linger, for the twelve mounts are full of mines. We have to take the road south and then westward to the sea." She traced a line with her finger. "If all goes well, we should be at the coast by nightfall."

Kilfannan stared at the map. The thought of the sea voyage dwelt heavily on his mind. "The nearest port to the island is Erin's Point," he said, folding the map and putting it back in his jerkin. "And 'tis a fair journey to the island. Dost thou think thy father will come upon us in the sea?"

Aine shook her head. "Meself knoweth not." As she glanced at him, Kilfannan saw his own fears mirrored in her eyes.

There was the sound of footsteps, and Fercle poked his head into the cave. "'Tis all clear," he said, taking his horse's reins. "A grey dawn is breaking; let's be on our way."

The Brax beeped a soft warning as they led their horses from the cave into a spectral world of mist and running water. "Draw your weapons, and be on guard. Goblins are abroad but are as yet unaware that we are here," Kilfannan hissed, taking his bow and an arrow from his quiver.

CHAPTER 16

THE SKY ROAD

The company mounted their horses and rode off into the mist. Kilfannan joined Duirmuid in the lead. Behind him were Kilcannan and the House of An Carn, with Fercle and Aine as rear guard.

Hearing a scrabbling amongst the rocks, Kilfannan looked nervously around, but all he saw were the dark shapes of boulders in the murk. With each step, Kilfannan expected to hear the whine of arrows, but nothing came against them. The trail led downhill, and in the growing light, they saw they were at the end of a long valley. The mountains loomed darkly behind them, and on either side were low lines of rockbound hills.

"We must strike west towards the sea," Duirmuid said, steering Gwen up a slope.

Kilfannan glanced uneasily at the limestone pavements and boulders that littered the hillside. He sensed something sinister and unsettling in the subtle babbling of the streams that rushed out from between the rocks. It seemed to his restless eyes that there were ugly, mocking imps of Under-Earth hidden within the moss- and lichen-blasted boulders, and a lurking shadow seemed ever at their backs, waiting for an opportunity to do them harm. Realising that his overwrought imagination was becoming an extension of his consciousness, and that fearful suggestions were running rampant through his mind, he forced his thoughts into the now. He felt a slight resistance to his authority, but it soon faded. The evil visions melted away as though he himself had conjured up the shades, and the demons that haunted him were thought forms and had no real existence. It seemed to him that ever since he had gazed upon the Cathac, there had been a breach within his mind, and the sorcerous spells cast upon him by the Ghrian Sidhe had powered the portal to his consciousness for other evil dreams to find. He made up his mind that he would control his thoughts and not let them wander.

The ground became soft and springy, thick with gorse and ling, and as the path began to run downhill, they broke their horses into a canter. They had covered only a short distance when the Brax beeped out a soft warning and the company skittered to a halt. A few moments later they heard the hoarse cackle of a goblin behind a small hillock up ahead.

Duirmuid held up his hand in caution. "'Twould appear the goblins have received news of our coming," he whispered to the others. "But not knowing when, they are idling, and we have caught them unawares."

Slipping from Gwen's back and drawing his axe, Duirmuid said softly, "Cor-cannan, come with me! You're handy in a fight. Me guess is that the filthy creatures are hiding in the fen beyond the hill. No matter! We will take care of them." He then turned to the others and said, "Get out yees knives, and be prepared."

Duirmuid and Cor-cannan disappeared like ghosts into the gloom.

"Aine! Gather the horses together," Kilfannan said, slipping off Red Moon. "We will form a ring of guard around them."

Standing in a circle around the horses, the company drew their blades and waited. The time dragged by, and they heard and saw nothing of their comrades. Kilfannan waited tensely for the slightest sound to stir in the dead air. Suddenly he heard a muffled shriek followed quickly by another. Then an ominous, watchful silence fell. He turned his attention to the airwaves. Coming towards them from the southwest was the tramp of some very heavy creature and another, lighter, pair of feet. "A troll cometh with a goblin," Kilfannan whispered. "Only trolls have such a weight."

"The Brax doth not chime in warning, and the horses are not restive," Kilcannan said as the treading feet came nearer. "'Twould seem there is a mystery here." He did not have long to ponder on the reason, for Duirmuid appeared over the hilltop with Cor-cannan right behind him. The dwarf was carrying three dead goblins, which he threw on the ground.

Kilfannan grinned. "We thought you were done for! The footsteps coming towards us were so weighty we thought a troll was approaching."

"They were scouts," Duirmuid declared. He took a sharp intake of breath and exhaled forcefully. "I took this axe from one of their foul bodies. 'Tis a dwarf axe made of dolerite belonging to me kin." He tucked the axe in his belt. "A thousand goblin heads will roll in vengeance."

"What are we going to do with the bodies?" Fercle asked grimly. "We cannot leave them here, for they surely will be found. And the minute they are discovered, the whole filthy pack will be on our scent."

"We will just have to take them with us," Duirmuid said in answer. "Put rocks in their pockets and dump them in the nearest lake. Gwen and I will carry two; who will take the other?"

No one answered. At length Fercle broke the heavy silence. "I see the gentry are at a loss for words!" he joked, grinning at the sylphs. "Meself will take the foul thing. Duirmuid, load him up!"

In silence, the party climbed into their saddles and crossed the stream. They rode forward across a moor until Duirmuid called them to a halt. "Yonder lies the lake of Larne. 'Tis deep, and the goblins will sink and be eaten by the bottom-feeding fish."

The lake of Larne nestled in a vale between two lines of gentle hills, and the company trotted across a run of springy turf to the water's edge. Fercle and Duirmuid dismounted, and tugging the dead goblins off their mounts, they dragged the bodies across the rock-strewn shingle to the shore. Picking up rocks, they weighted down the goblins' pockets; and with a mighty heave, they tossed the corpses into the water.

"If all goes well, we will ride the sky road to Erin's Point before noon," Duirmuid said, washing his hands.

They started on again along a stony path, and they had gone only a mile or two when the Brax loudly chimed in warning.

"Goblins!" Kilcannan hissed. With every tendon tensed, the company moved forward, listening for any sound or movement in the bushes. The Brax chimed out another warning, but still no enemy could be seen.

Hoarse shouts suddenly split the listening air, and an arrow whined above their heads, and then another. Feeling a searing pain in his right hand, Kilfannan let out a cry. A black shaft had gone through the back of his hand, pinning him to his horse's neck. Red Moon whinnied in pain and then bolted back along the path. Hanging on to his horse's mane with his other hand, Kilfannan leant forward and whispered words of calming in Red Moon's ears. "'Tis all right," he said soothingly as his horse ran into a stand of scrubby trees.

Seeing Red Moon bolt, Kilcannan galloped madly after him. There was a trail of green blood on the path leading to a stand of alder trees. Riding into the woodland, he saw Kilfannan trying to calm his horse.

"Brother!" he cried, and slipping from Finifar's back, he ran to Kilfannan.

"A goblin shaft hath pinned my hand to Red Moon's neck," Kilfannan said grimly, "Holdest thou the reins whilst I remove it."

Once Kilcannan had secured his reins, Kilfannan pulled the arrow out. A sickening wave of pain shot through his wrist and fingers. Red Moon screamed and reared, and it took all Kilcannan's strength to steady him.

"Brother, we cannot tarry here," Kilcannan said anxiously. "We must rejoin the others. Goblin shafts are oft poisoned, and both thou and Red Moon are in need of healing." The Brax beeped another warning, and peering out of the trees, Kilcannan looked along the path to check for goblins. "Enemies are close, but the way ahead seems clear," he said to Kilfannan. "Methinks we should take a chance while peace prevails and make our way back to the others."

The Brax beeped again, louder this time. Kilcannan dismounted. "I will check the track." Drawing his bow, he crept out of the trees and, looking along the path, saw a dull flash in the bushes up ahead. There it was again – a slight movement and the glint of metal. Stringing an arrow, he took careful aim and waited. Seeing another stirring in the leaves, he let loose his shaft. A shriek rang out, followed by a thud, and then silence. "Wait here," he said to Kilfannan. "There was an assassin up a tree. I will check that he is dead."

Moving swiftly along the track, he saw a goblin lying on his face in the bushes. Poking him with the toe of his boot, he turned the goblin over. The arrow had penetrated his skull. Satisfied the scum was dead, he swiftly went back to Kilfannan.

"Goblin scum!" Kilcannan said angrily. "His bow was strung and an arrow fitted – destined for us, no doubt."

Leaving the woodland, the brothers rode along the greenway to the place where the goblins had attacked them. "There is no sign of our friends," Kilfannan said, fearing the worst.

"I will send a signal," Kilcannan said, and cupping his hands, he warbled sweet notes high into the air. There was no response. Kilcannan called again. At last, to their relief, they heard a crow call up ahead. Suddenly Cor-garran appeared out of the shrubbery. His hair was matted, and his cloak and breeches were tattered and covered in black blood.

"Well met!" Cor-garran cried out when he saw them.

"What hath happened, nephew?" Kilfannan asked anxiously, looking at his bloody and dishevelled clothes.

"After Red Moon bolted with thee and Kilcannan took pursuit, we hid amongst the brambles," Cor-garran answered. "All was quiet for a time. I chanced to look around and noticed Duirmuid was gone. 'Where is the dwarf? 'Tis not like him to wander off alone', I whispered to my brother. Suddenly we heard harsh cries up ahead, and we could hear the roar of Duirmuid's voice above the din. Throwing caution to the wind, we burst from the bushes and ran forward. There in a clearing was a ring of five goblins around Duirmuid, jabbing and thrusting with their blades. We joined in the fray and killed four of them. One got away. As soon as I could, I went after him. I was just about to give up the search when I heard thy call."

"What of Duirmuid and Cor-cannan?" Kilfannan asked.

"They returned to Fercle and Aine, who are waiting at the riverbank with the horses."

"Thou sayest a goblin got away. I killed one; I wonder if that were he," Kilcannan said. "He was hiding in the bushes." He pointed to the riverbank. "The goblin had an arrow fitted to his bow."

"The goblins that attacked Duirmuid, were they from Clare?" he asked Cor-garran.

"Nay. These were miners from the northern hills. Their skin was white and leprous."

"Damnation!" Kilcannan cried in alarm. "The goblin I killed was brown and wizened. That means the filth escaped and will alert the others to our whereabouts. We must leave as soon as possible, but first I need Fercle to doctor Red Moon."

Cor-garran led the way to a small clearing. The rest of the company were sitting with the horses under a willow tree at the water's edge. "Well met!" Fercle said as Kilfannan dismounted. "You are injured," he said in dismay, staring at Kilfannan's hand. "Pray, let me tend to your wound."

"First help Red Moon," said Kilfannan. "He hath an ugly lesion on his neck, and I fear the shaft was poisoned. I will wait for thee."

The wound in his hand was throbbing, and he sat down with the others on a great root of a weeping willow tree. Leaning back against the trunk, he breathed in the river's fragrant breath and tried for a moment to distance himself from pain and care.

"Brother," Kilcannan said. "Bring out the map, and let us take counsel together while we wait." Kilfannan took the map from inside his jerkin and gave it to Kilcannan. Spreading the map on his knees, he said, "The goblins know we were at Lake Carn, and they will guess we will follow O'Shallihan to the island. The nearest harbour to the isle is Erin's Point, and they will try to intercept us, for our trail is plain to see. We have to make a plan to avoid detection as long as 'tis possible. The coast runs flat aways south from Erin's Point, and maybe we could reach the port by travelling along the beach."

"We will consult the map as we draw nearer to the port, and see if there is another way," Kilfannan answered. "'Twill be a game of cat and mouse from here on out, for the enemy is before us, behind us, and on either side. But we have no choice but to persevere and take to the water, no matter what the odds."

"Kilfannan! Wash your hand clean in the swift waters of the river," Fercle said, taking Red Moon's bridle. "'Twill cleanse the wound and help to numb the pain."

Kilfannan plunged his injured palm into the crisp, clear water. The cold current chilled his hand, and it felt good, and he sat for a moment watching the rush of dead wood and twigs hurrying madly past him. Staring at the fern-fringed river, he noticed there was something strange about the water. Dark and oily ripples met his eyes, and one swirling spot didn't seem, to his mind, to belong to the rest of the river. The ripples were not in harmony with the flowing of the water, and the sinister greasy spot seemed to have a rhythm of its own.

"Meself hath doctored Red Moon," Fercle said, tearing strips from a small roll of cotton sheeting. "We are in luck, for there was no taint of poison in his flesh. Now 'tis your turn." Picking up Kilfannan's hand, Fercle examined the wound. "The shaft has gone clean through your palm." Taking a bird quill from his pouch, he spat a wad of chewed roots into the wound. "This will hurt a bit, but only for a moment," he said encouragingly as he gently guided the paste into the wound.

Kilfannan felt a burning sensation, but it soon passed. Shaking his hand, he flexed his fingers. "My hand feeleth as good as new. Many thanks to thee."

Fercle wound a bandage around Kilfannan's hand. "There! That's finished. Now on your feet, good sir; the horses are waiting. We cannot linger. Come on! Meself will give you a leg up on Red Moon." Getting to his feet, Kilfannan took a last glance at the river. The greasy pool was darker than before, and the oily film was spreading.

"Hold the reins," Fercle ordered as he grabbed Kilfannan's foot and lifted him upwards to the saddle.

"Meself and Aine will take the lead," Duirmuid said, fingering the axe blade in his belt.

Following Fercle through the scrubby thickets to the lane, Kilfannan felt a cold and clammy threat creeping down his spine – a malignancy that chilled him to the core. Looking back over his shoulder at the river, he saw the water twisting in torment, and out of the sooty ooze, the horned head of a sea serpent emerged from the swirling water. A seething miasma of menace welled from the titan lizard, distorting the sunlight into shade as it slid greasily onto the bank and began to snake towards them.

A sickening knot of revulsion tightened in his stomach. "A serpent!" he screamed, his voice strident and sputtering in shock. "Ride!"

He saw Aine look back at the river, and terror was in her eyes as they jumped off and thundered forward. The road ran along a broad swathe of grass parallel to the river, and after a distance, the road began to climb steeply. Topping the rise, they pulled up on a bleak crag that overlooked the sea.

"The serpent cometh after us," Kilfannan said, looking back in affright, "yet I do not see sign of its pursuit."

"Nay, the serpent will not follow us far upon the land," Aine replied, "but will return to the river and the sea." She glanced at him anxiously. "'Tis the same serpent emissary of me father that meself saw rise from the Lake of Carn."

"Manannan! He hath risen?"

Aine briefly met his eyes and then looked away. He knew she would not express in words the answer to the question they were both holding in their minds.

From the high point, Kilfannan looked out over the world's rim. A shiver ran through him as he beheld the dark, forbidding ocean. Far below, he could see the fishing port of Erin's Point; and on the horizon, the shape of an island cresting the water. "Brother," he said, pointing out to sea. "That must be the island of Inishark."

"Aye," Kilcannan answered thoughtfully. "Kilfannan! I have a plan that may throw the trackers off our trail." Calling to the others to join him, he dismounted and laid the map out on the ground.

"I will keep watch for goblins and birds that spy for the enemy," Cor-cannan said, riding to the top of the ridge, "whilst thou hatchest thy plan."

"Grad is aware that we will follow the thief to the island," Kilcannan said. "He knoweth not why we are in pursuit of the mortal, but he knoweth that we are. His mission is to kill us and destroy our house, and he will follow upon our trail like a hound. We have to find a way to lead him in the wrong direction, giving us time to hire a boat and get to the island. Knockers he hath with him, and their maggs. If't comes to conflict, we will be outmanoeuvred and outnumbered."

"Duirmuid," Kilfannan said, "my brother speaks the truth. We are in a desperate position. How much time dost thou thinkest it will take for Grad to catch up with us? For 'tis he that will lead the main assault against our house."

"Once Grad found out we had escaped from Binn Breac, he would have sent messages through the mines. By the time the alarm was raised, we were through the tunnel and on our way along the valley. Me guess is the filth will be on the sky road within the hour. Our tracks are plain to see, and the rabble will be upon our trail like nose dogs."

"Less than an hour," Cor-garran repeated. "But that giveth us no time at all. We cannot win in a battle against so many and being so near to the sea." He blanched. "We may meet other enemies."

"Kilcannan! What is your plan?" Fercle asked impatiently, peering over his shoulder at the map. "There are clouds building thunderheads on the ocean, and a storm is brewing. We must hurry on."

"The ridge we are upon travels south for many a mile." Kilcannan traced the spine of stone with his finger. "If we ride along it, we will leave little sign of our passing. The land below the ridge is full of brooks and pools, and it may be that we can leave the high ground and travel across the water meadows to gain the beach, and strike back north from there. For the coast that reaches to the sea is flat and lined with dunes."

Kilfannan shivered. To travel beside the sea with the serpents of Manannan hunting for them was madness, he knew. But what else could they do?

"'Tis a sound plan," Duirmuid said. "And if we ride fast upon the beach, 'tis likely we will get to Erin's Point before the trackers find any sign of our trail. With luck, the tide will be in our favour and wash away our tracks before evil seeks them. And perhaps while we are on the road, we can make a false trail to further lead Grad astray."

"Brother!" Kilcannan said in a low voice as they mounted up. "There is a way to get to the isle and leave no tracks at all. For we ride steeds shod with the flying shoes of Mercury. We can fly across the sea to the island, take the key from the thief, and return. What sayest thou?"

Looking out to sea at the stealthily moving storm, Kilfannan was suddenly assailed by evil visions. He saw lightning strike them as they rode their horses through the clouds, and huge tentacles grasped for them from the roiling sea. Fear thrilled through him as his imagination conjured up the evillest of deeds, and with an effort of mind he brought his thinking to the now. Before he could give an answer, he heard Cor-cannan cry, "A rider approacheth."

Kilfannan was joined by Kilcannan, and looking down the hill, they saw a horseman, his dark cloak billowing behind him, galloping up the slope towards them. They heard the sound of tiny bells tinkling with the song of falling water, and even though it was day, they could see starlight sheen shimmering in the rider's short, nighted, slicked-back hair. The rider was a handsome nobleman dressed in an indigo body suit girt with a sword belt, and a chain of silver leaves around his neck. With a soft word to his horse, he pulled up beside the company, for his steed knew no bit, spurs, or saddle, just a gentle voice and a coverlet of silver cloth that fluttered in the wind – a shining blanket daintily bedecked with ribbons and tiny shrilling bells. He slipped gracefully from his horse and stood before the company.

"'Tis me brother!" Aine cried, running forward to greet him. "Thou hast come at last."

"Heart of me heart, sister love," Kilfannan heard him say. "Meself hath found thee." He took her in his arms and kissed her deeply.

Kilfannan's heart fell. At a precipitous moment of their quest, Aine's brother had arrived for the mating. There was no place for petition, no stall for time, because once the hunger came upon her, all thoughts fled but the burning need to replicate her kind. He felt a stab of doubt pierce his heart; he had come to rely on her courage and good counsel, and for a moment he couldn't contemplate going on without her. Feeling a trifle resentful at the timing of this situation, he took the up-breath and tried to smother his disappointment.

"Meself is Nala, second born of Manannan," the incubus said, his voice rippling with the wild music of untamed rapids, waterfalls, and lulling rivers. Seductive beauty flowed from his indigo eyes, illuminating his antique yet youthful face, and a perfumed cloud of desire and sensation issued from his lissom body.

"Well met, sir. I am Kilfannan of the House of Kilfenoran, and this is my brother, Kilcannan."

Well met indeed!" Nala answered, giving a quick, respectful nod of his head to the brothers and the rest of the company.

Sensing a probe of strange, uncertain energy trying to gain access to his mind, Kilfannan saw Nala staring at the emerald on his forehead. As their eyes met, the incubus looked away and began whispering to Aine. Kilfannan noticed with disquiet that she shot a sudden worried look at him before whispering to her brother in reply.

The air fizzed with the perfume of the wood, and with the proud and regal carriage of High Faerie, Aine and Nala stood before Kilfannan. Mighty they were – warriors dressed in clinging mists of blue and orange that were ever changing into sparkling waterfalls, dark pools, the thrash of rain, and the roaring of the sea.

"I have come for Aine, the firstborn," Nala said, and the sound of his words was like lapping waves breaking on the beach of Kilfannan's mind. "'Twas a long ride from me sacred stones of Crann Conagh to me lady's woods to find her not at home. Following the perfume of the wood, I have tracked her hither. 'Twould seem there is a riddle here." He glanced at Aine in concern, and then, turning his eyes on Kilfannan, he said, "Pray tell meself why there is a price upon the heads of thine House of Kilfenoran and why me sister love hath joined thy company and journeys with thee into peril."

"The enemy of old hath risen and seeks to destroy the House of Air," Kilfannan answered. "His will runs like a dark river through Under-Earth, and the price upon our heads is the bounty he will pay for our destruction. The House of Air hath fallen into shadow, and the Green of leaf, meadow, and tree is in peril. We have embarked on a deadly quest and are a tiny beam of light still shining in a darkening world. That, sir, is why thy sister hast pledged her High Faerie self to the House of Air."

Nala's eyes grew grave as Kilfannan told the story of their flight and their quest for the key. The catkins blooming in his face suddenly withered, and in their place dark nightshades spread their poisonous berries. He stared at Kilfannan in incredulity and horror. The sylph's words had stung him in the heart, for had he not noticed that the brilliance of the Green had been blocked from the fullness of its sweet, invigorating message? Had he not noticed that some subtle counter influence had distorted it? He looked at Aine, and in her eyes he saw the same fear, the same poignant sense of loss that now burgeoned in his heart. He strode forth to his horse, took a ribbon from the silver coverlet, and gave it to Kilfannan. "Me liege," he said, his eyes shining with the ethereal exquisiteness of High Faerie, "many rumours have I heard on me road from Connaught, and 'tis said throughout the bars and taverns in Galway that knockers will give great reward for news of he who weareth a star emerald upon his brow." He stared at Kilfannan with concern. "Use the ribbon as a headband to cover up the emerald, for thine hope lieth in secrecy and concealment."

"The House of Air and the living Green are in thy debt," Kilfannan said, tying the ribbon into place. He turned to the company. "I think a stiffener is in order and a toast upon our lips." He took out his flask and, holding it in the air, said, "A toast to the water and the wind."

Making sure Cor-cannan was still on watch, Kilfannan called the company together. "We find ourselves in a predicament where danger presses on every side. Aine and Nala are leaving for the mating, and I wish for them to counsel us before they depart."

"Brother! Shall we take the wings of Mercury to the island?" Kilcannan asked. "There would be no tracks to follow or goblins to pursue us. What sayest thou?"

Remembering the terrible visions that had assailed him, Kilfannan replied, "The way to the island is long, and there is a storm driving in. Brother, at your first suggest, I saw terrible visions in my mind of our horses' deaths upon the water. Nay, my heart telleth me it could be a further tragedy in the making."

"Kilfannan speaks wisely," Aine said. "Foul things lurk within the sea and air. The serpents of me father are abroad, and there are other fell creatures he will call upon." She met Kilfannan's gaze, and he saw the turquoise light of prescience shining from her eyes. "We must beware the cloud of darkness that issues from the Giant's Cliffs."

"'Twould seem the evil that cripples souls and brings all to naught hath us all in its clutches," Nala said, putting his arm around Aine's shoulders.

"There may be a way," Kilfannan said thoughtfully. "Aine! Canst thou takest four of our horses with thee on thy way to thy sacred circle and keep them safe within the confines of thy power? The six of us will take the skies to Erin's Point on Finifar and Red Moon."

Aine nodded. "'Tis a grand idea," she said. "The goblins will follow our tracks, thinking it is yourselves they are pursuing. They cannot draw nigh the stone circle, for the dolmens are made of crystal and their light is poison to them. I trust that by the time they realise their mistake, you will be upon the water."

"Erin's Point is three miles as the crow flies," Nala said. "At the top of the steep hill leading to the port is an inn. 'Tis called the Blue Buoy. The landlord is a friend of mine. His name is Darkle. Mention me name, and he will shelter your horses in his stable. He will lock and bolt the doors. His temper is swift and strong, and no foul thing dare come against him."

"After the mating, meself will return to Erin's Point and stable Nemia at the Blue Buoy," Aine said. "If you have left and taken to the sea, meself will swim after you to the island."

Sensing the couple were impatient to leave, Kilfannan and the company bade them farewell.

Aine mounted her black mare and Nala his white stallion, and in a thunder of hooves they galloped down the hill with the four horses following close behind them.

"With our charges safely stabled at the Blue Buoy, we shall be free to find a boat, for 'tis easier to hide ourselves from spying eyes than 'tis to hide the horses," Kilfannan said to the others.

Duirmuid sighed. "'Tis hard to be parted from Gwen."

"I have perfect trust in Mistress Aine and her brother," the House of An Carn responded, mounting up behind Kilcannan. "Our horses will be safer with her than with ourselves."

Fercle got up behind Kilfannan, but Duirmuid hung back. "What aileth thee?" Kilfannan asked, looking anxiously at the threatening sky.

"'Tis vertigo," Duirmuid answered sheepishly. "Meself is at home under the mountains, not over them."

"Ride in front of me. I will make sure thou dost not fall."

A feeling of despair swept over Kilfannan as he glanced at the boiling clouds. The tempest was moving inland, born on devils' wings. He reckoned they had but an hour or two before it would engulf them and a storm would make it nigh on impossible to hire a boat to take them to the island.

"Brother! What is the word of wings the smith gave us?" Kilcannan asked. "It hath slipped my mind."

"A-num," Kilfannan sounded, and as the word vibrated in the air, with a graceful rush the horses rose into a bank of low clouds.

A bolt of lightning rent the clouds as they flew into the heaving sky. Kilfannan's visions of tragedy returned as thunder crashed around them. Ordering Red Moon to descend below the clouds, he saw the town of Erin's Point below them. At the top of the hill at the end of a line of tall houses, he saw a brightly painted inn with a paddock and meadow at the back. "'Tis the Blue Buoy below."

Sending mental images of the paddock to their horses, they slowly descended and landed gently on the grass. The company dismounted, and leaving the House of An Carn to stand guard, they climbed over the paddock rail and through the back door into the pub.

"Well met, gentlefolk," the landlord said as they entered. "Me name is Darkle. How can I be of service?"

"Nala sent us," Kilfannan said. "We have left two horses in the paddock, and we are in need of stabling for this night and will collect them on the morrow."

"Right you are, sir," Darkle said, disappearing into a room behind the bar. In an instant he was back. "Meself hath sent the groom to stable your charges. Any friend of Nala's is a friend of meself," he said cordially. "Drinks and stabling are on the house."

The brothers bowed. "The House of Air is in thy debt."

The company sat down at a table and were soon joined by the House of An Carn.

"The stables are sturdy; the door hath been barred, and the bolt shot," Cor-cannan said, sitting down with his brother at the table.

Kilcannan nodded. "I feel they will be as safe here as anywhere."

The landlord brought a tray of drinks to the table, two saucers of cream, and a plate of cheese. "Meself thought that you might like some refreshment," he said, smiling at the sylphs.

"Much appreciated," Kilfannan and Cor-garran said, whipping out their spoons.

"Likewise," Kilcannan said, grinning at Cor-cannan, who had a mouthful of cheese.

"And for yourselves," he said to Fercle and Duirmuid, "A glass of moonshine from me cellar to warm the cockles of your hearts. 'Tis going to be a rough and chilly night, and there is a storm blowing in. May I ask what your business is in town?"

"We have to go to Inishark this eve," Kilfannan answered. "We need to hire a boat and a skipper to take us there. Dost thou know of anyone with a boat for hire?"

The landlord thought for a moment. "Putting to sea in this weather will not be easy. But you could ask Buckle Rua, the landlord of the Jack O' Lantern. He's crazy enough to hire you a boat for a hefty fee, greedy as he is. The inn's down the high street a ways."

They finished their drinks and, saying goodnight to the landlord, went to the entrance. Kilfannan opened the door and peered cautiously into the grey and dismal street. In Faerie, the steep, narrow road to the harbour was empty, apart from a troop of elves arguing with one another outside an alehouse further down the road. There was no sign of goblins, and the Brax was quiet, and in that he found comfort.

Switching his gaze to the mortal world, he saw the road was quiet, and he was just about to beckon the others forward when he saw a battered old lorry drive slowly by. An ugly shiver ran through him, and feeling a threat, he dodged back behind the door.

"I fear there is a mortal spying for the enemy. I felt his heart as he drove past. It was black with the hate of Under-Earth. We must make our move quickly in case he doth return."

CHAPTER 17

TROUBLE AT THE DOCK

The sky began to darken as the clouds rolled in, and a cold rain blew in their faces as they made their way down the street to the harbour. Kilfannan sensed a touch of malignity on the airwaves and wondered if a storm spell had been laid against them. A fusillade of thunder rumbled in the distance, accompanied by a stabbing lightning far out on the sea.

They found the Jack O' Lantern halfway down the high street. The pub was painted red. Over the door was a sign trimmed in gold letters and edged in black. "Buckle Rua, landlord", and "Welcome" it read. Light filtered out from the thick glass in the deep-set windows.

The faerie bar was warm and homely. There were heavy black beams in the ceiling, and a great fireplace at one end of the room sent out the sweet smell of burning apple wood.

"Greetings!" a fear dearg said affably from behind the counter. "What can meself getteth for you good folk?"

"Six blackberry brandies, and one for yourself," Fercle replied, slapping a guinea on the counter.

"Dost thou know of any boat that could take us to Inishark tonight?" Kilfannan asked. "My friends and meself are looking for something on the island, and speed is of the essence."

"Meself hath a boat for hire. Her name is the *Poseidon*," he said, staring at their bows and quivers. "There's a storm coming in, and 'twould be best to wait 'til morning."

"We need to go to the island tonight," Kilfannan said urgently. "And with luck we will return in the morn."

The landlord was quiet for a moment, and then he said, "'Twill be fifty guineas to take the night tide. That will cover the cost if me boat should sink." He rubbed his hands together greedily and then looked enquiringly at Kilfannan.

Fifty guineas, Kilfannan thought, was a bit steep. He realised the landlord was trying to take advantage of their need to get to the island, but as this might be their only chance to catch up with the thief and steal the key, he had no choice but to pay the asking price. Taking out his purse, he said, "If the boat doth not sink and we return safely from our voyage, is a refund in order?"

"Meself will give you back thirty guineas for the safe return of me boat."

"Very well," Kilfannan answered. Taking out his purse of gold, he counted out fifty coins and put them on the bar.

The landlord picked up the coins and put them in his pocket. "The turning of the tide is around eleven," he said, consulting the tide clock hanging on the wall behind the counter. "That's a wait of an hour. Can I get you any repast?"

Kilfannan shook his head. The landlord was a skinflint, and no doubt a saucer of cream would cost a guinea!

"Skipper!" the innkeeper called through a door at the back of the bar. A fat fear dearg poked his head out.

"These good folk have hired the *Poseidon* for a trip to Inishark. Hasten to the dockside and make the boat ready for the trip."

The skipper looked flustered. "There is a thunderstorm moving in," he said doubtfully. "'Twould be best to wait until it passes."

"Our visitors have paid a heavy price, and we will do what is necessary to accommodate them."

"Meself will get to it right away," the skipper answered. "Meet me in the courtyard outside the back door at ten thirty," he said to the company, and with a nod of his head, he disappeared from view.

Looking for a dark corner they could sit in, Kilfannan glanced around the bar. In an alcove at the back of the room he saw a sign that read "The Horsebox – sitting room". "There's a private room yonder," he said to the others. "Let's see if it is empty." Picking up his drink, he slipped off his stool. Going over to the half-door, he peered over the top into the room. "'Tis empty," he called, beckoning them over.

The snug was rectangular. Soft lights gleamed upon the walls, and the floor was covered with fresh rushes. "Now meself would never think of drinking in a horsebox!" Fercle quipped as he sat down beside the company at the table.

"I've had many a drink in Finifar's box after a win at the racecourse," Kilcannan answered, raising his glass. "Slainte!"

Kilfannan's thoughts were on the sea journey. None of them knew what to expect, and therefore they could make no preparations for defence. "We are in a bind," he said anxiously once they were assembled at the table. "The storm that cometh, I fear, is a spell and an omen of ill portent." A fey light glowed from his eyes. "The tempest hath been called to prevent us getting to the island and to ensure our destruction, for we will be caught in a wedge between the goblins and the monsters in the sea."

"What can we do?" Cor-garran asked with shadow on his brow.

"Be ready to defend ourselves, come what may," Duirmuid growled, fingering the axe hanging from his belt.

"Not only will there be a physical assault, but a spell of fear will be cast against our minds," Kilcannan said, "for myself and Cor-cannan have been victims of the mind spell, and if we are in fear, 'twill only add power to the darkness of the enemy and weaken our resolve."

They sat in contemplative silence, and Kilfannan could feel the strain of their uncertain situation growing stronger every minute. At a quarter past ten, Kilcannan got restlessly up from the table. "'Twill soon be time to leave. I will check the road outside for enemies."

Leaving the snug, Kilcannan took a quick look around the bar and went out the front door. Across the road, a tall mortal was whispering to two knockers outside the entrance to an inn. Quickly dodging back inside, Kilcannan peered round the frame and saw the man get into a battered lorry and drive down the street towards the quayside. The knockers lingered on the pavement for a moment and then disappeared back into the inn.

"Knockers!" Kilcannan hissed through the doorway of the private room. "They are talking to a mortal outside the inn across the road. Let's get out of here and find the skipper before we are discovered."

The company left their unfinished drinks upon a table and went swiftly through the back door, where they saw the skipper in a mackintosh and rubber boots, standing in the yard.

"Meself was just coming to look for you. Come! 'Tis a short walk to the moorings." He led them round the back of the inn and down a narrow alleyway to the street. As they got to the junction, Kilfannan came to a cautious stop and peered guardedly from the corner of the alley at the road. In Faerie, the high street was deserted and the knockers were nowhere to be seen, but he knew they were there, hiding in the shadows.

Switching his vision to the mortal world, he saw two drunks standing at a corner, arguing over a pint of wine, and another mortal vomiting on the pavement. The sounds of an engine caught his ears, and he watched as the lorry he had seen earlier moved slowly past. The mortal was patrolling, driving back and forth along the high street to the quayside.

"Are you hiding from someone?" the skipper asked, perplexed.

"Nay," Kilfannan replied. "I just want to make sure we are not followed. Is there any other road that will take us to the harbour?"

Hoarse shouts broke out in the high street behind them.

"Goblins are abroad, and we have no wish to tangle with the

scum. Is there any other way to the harbour?" Kilfannan asked again.

The skipper frowned. "Well, yes, there is another road, but 'tis not direct."

"We will take it," Kilfannan said.

"All right, follow me."

Thunder boomed over their heads, and the rain came pelting down as the skipper led them through an alley to a road running parallel to the high street. As they started down the steep hill towards the harbour, Kilfannan heard the raucous shouting growing nearer, along with the sound of an engine, and the noise of rushing feet was echoing in the narrow streets around them. The sound of the engine drew nearer. "Hide!" Kilfannan said to the company. Halfway down the hill, a patrolling lorry drove slowly across the intersection. Kilfannan saw the driver look up the road towards them. Seeing the brake lights go on, he pulled the skipper into a dark doorway. The lorry speeded off, and Kilfannan knew the chase for them was on.

"What the deuce is going on?" the skipper cried anxiously. "Meself hath no quarrel with goblins or mortals. I don't want to get involved with any fight that you might be concerned with. I's only being paid to take you to the island, and that is risk enough in this foul weather. Methinks I should return to the inn and give the trip a miss."

There was the sound of shouts and rushing feet.

"There's no time for discussion," Kilfannan answered sharply. "We must get to the boat!" He grabbed the skipper by the arm and pulled him forward.

At the bottom of the hill, the company turned left along a narrow and ill-surfaced cobbled street that led to the waterfront, keeping close to the tall buildings and flitting from one dark doorway to the next.

Seeing the skipper quivering with terror, Kilfannan said, "'Tis too late for thou to return to the inn, and I am sorry that we have brought this evil on thee. Our only deliverance is to gain the safety of the boat and cast away." He turned his attention to the company. "Come! 'Tis but a few strides to the quayside."

They sprinted to a narrow opening near the dockside.

Kilfannan and Kilcannan looked cautiously around the side of the crumbling stone warehouse on the corner of the wharf.

"Can ye see anything?" Duirmuid muttered.

"The lorry that's been patrolling is parked by the sea wall, but the cab, 'tis empty," Kilfannan answered. "I see no sign of goblins." He looked along the quayside but could see no boat at mooring. Fear struck at his heart. "Where is the boat? I see no sign of any vessel," he said to the skipper.

"She's moored in the inlet around the corner of the headland. 'Tis not far."

"Brother!" Kilcannan whispered, pointing left to the decaying buildings that lined the wharf. "There is a sparking in the darkness."

Just a little ways along the quay, Kilfannan saw a tiny glow in the blackness and sensed the acrid smell of tobacco smoke in the water-laden air. "There is a mortal hiding in a doorway," he said to the others. "He watcheth for us and will give alarm the minute we appear."

"Is there any way around the headland that means we can avoid the quay?" Kilcannan asked the skipper.

"The way is slippery in the rain, and 'tis naught but rocks to climb. The tide will have turned by the time we reach the top. Our descent will be slow, and by the time we get to the boat, she will be sitting in the sand."

"We have to take the chance and make a rush for the boat," Kilcannan said. "Once the mortal seeth us, the hue and cry will be given. Knockers and their maggs are close behind, and they will surely find us. Draw thy blades and be ready."

"Meself is no fighter," the skipper said miserably. "Nor much of a sprinter either."

Looking into their anxious faces, Kilfannan said, "On count of four, we will make the dash."

On the count of four, Kilfannan grabbed the shivering skipper by the arm and sprinted forward across the quayside with the others. Following the sea wall, they were rounding the bend towards the inlet when Kilfannan looked behind.

Two grey streaks charged out of the street they had just left and made their way onto the quayside, followed by their maggs. He heard the mortal shouting, "The faerie scum are running to the inlet. After them!"

The wind began to blow with vengeance as the company sprinted forward, and in its fury Kilfannan heard a terrible, hungry shrieking that clutched with terror at his heart. How he wished this nightmare journey of peril and flight would end.

"There's the boat up ahead," the skipper wheezed.

A hundred yards away Kilfannan could see a small white cabin cruiser through the driving rain. The boat bobbed up and down in the deep water of high tide, straining on the rope that secured it to the dock.

Arrows whined past his head and fell clattering on the stony ground as Kilfannan and the skipper reached the dock and jumped onto the boat, followed by Fercle and Kilcannan. Looking anxiously back, Kilfannan saw Duirmuid help Cor-garran up from the ground where he had fallen, and he pulled him from the dock onto the deck.

As the company assembled on board the boat, a hail of stones and arrows assailed them. Waves crashed over the breakwater, and the boat heaved and tossed in the heavy swell.

"Get the moorings loose while I start the motor," the skipper shouted, scrambling down below. The engine roared to life, and a fitful yellow light lit up the cabin. As the skipper came back onto the deck, he shrieked and fell down. Fercle ran to him and, putting his arm around him, tried to pull him to his feet. The skipper's body was limp, and there was an ugly black shaft through his eye.

"His fire is extinguished," Fercle said. The goblins came surging across the dockside towards the lighted craft, brandishing their knives and hammers.

As Cor-garran gained the boat, a goblin leapt at him, wielding a hammer. Drawing his knife, Cor-garran sidestepped the attack and stabbed him in the throat. "Help me toss him overboard," he shouted to Duirmuid, who was rushing to his side.

"Meself will do it," Duirmuid shouted back. "Cast off! Cast off!" Cor-garran launched himself forward, grasping for the rope, but the craft listed to one side as a huge wave crashed against the breakwater, throwing him against the rail.

"Cast off!" Duirmuid shrieked again over the howling wind.

CHAPTER 18

MAELSTROM OF EVIL

Cor-garran struggled to his feet and slashed frantically at the rope with his knife. Arrows and stones from slingshots flew in the darkness, and a pack of goblins scurried forward. Fercle, Duirmuid, and Kilfannan were fighting furiously by the rail.

"Kill! Kill!" a knocker was screaming to a line of goblins armed with slingshots. A large stone sailed through the air, hitting Cor-garran in the throat and knocking him down. With a last effort of will he crawled forward and hacked at the rope until it frayed and broke.

The *Poseidon* rose and fell, and it then listed off the dock. In the heaving swell, Cor-garran lost his balance and fell backwards, grasping vainly for the guardrail.

"Brother!" Cor-cannan screamed, running to his aid. But it was too late; Cor-garran toppled off the boat and into the sea. Another hail of missiles crashed around them, barely missing Cor-cannan, who was standing in a state of shock, peering into the raging ocean. Seeing him motionless, Kilcannan grabbed him and pulled him down the steps into the cabin below.

"My brother hath been swept out to sea," Cor-cannan moaned, sobbing uncontrollably. His breath came in short gasps, and realising his nephew was labouring for air, Kilcannan took him in his arms and took the down-breath for him.

"We must trust to the stars that Cor-garran swims to safety," Kilcannan said once Cor-cannan had calmed and was breathing on his own.

In an instant the wind changed direction and the craft was swept out to sea, where it was tossed like a piece of driftwood in the heavy swell. The ship's wheel spun round like a top. Duirmuid grabbed it and tried to turn it to the west, but the wind snatched it from his grasp. Huddling together in the cold, cramped cabin, the company were banged from side to side by the listing vessel.

Remembering Prince Donne's warning to beware of evil in the water fuelled Kilfannan's mounting terror. Manannan's power was rising, and he could come upon them in the sea – and destroy them. He realised his hands were shaking and desperately tried to turn his mind to the music of the Green.

To their relief, the storm slowly abated. The clouds broke up, and a fitful watching moon shined eerily down on the dark and tossing sea.

Leaving the confined space of the cabin, the company ran swiftly up the stairs and onto the deck. Fercle grabbed the wheel and turned it westward, towards the island of Inishark.

"I fear 'tis but a lull before another storm. We must make haste," Duirmuid said, joining him on the wheel.

With a churning of the water, the boat surged forward on the tide, skimming through the waves into the yawning darkness.

"By the living stone, I hope we don't capsize," Duirmuid growled. "Meself can't swim."

"Meself is in the same plight," Fercle answered grimly.

Fercle left the wheel to Duirmuid and joined the rest of the company on the rail. "There's land ahead!" he whooped.

Through the ragged moonlight, far out in the yawning chasm of the sea, Kilfannan saw a small, bleak-looking island. "I trust 'tis Inishark! Ahoy!" He was apprehensive, for although the odds were good that O'Shallihan would be on the island, there was also a chance he would not be there. *What then?* he wondered. Knowing that thoughts were alive and their vibrations created reality, he turned his mind to a positive outcome for the quest. O'Shallihan would be on the island, and his intuition told him the mortal would be carrying the key upon his evil person.

He turned to his companions, who were beside him on the rail. "If we arrive safely at the island, we must have a plan to get the key away from the mortal. The thief hath goblin sight and will be instantly aware of us, and in his hatred of the Green, he may throw the key into the sea for evil water wights to find."

The sea began to swell and roll, showering them in suds of unclean froth and tossing the boat hither and thither like a straw. A bank of acid-yellow clouds that seemed to issue from the sea rushed towards the boat, sucking up the moonlight. The clouds were suddenly split asunder by a furious welter of red and indigo lightning flashes that streaked towards them like electric demon eels across the surface of the sea. "Draw thy bows and weapons and make ready," Kilfannan shrieked in alarm.

On a sudden stench-filled wind, they heard the whirring of wings and the sound of nightmarish screeching. "'Tis the hag-birds from the Giant's Cliffs," Kilfannan cried out as he glimpsed darting forms writhing in the fume.

Kilfannan saw the gnawing hate of legend screeching from the clouds and circling above the boat – the sagging-breasted, bony, half-bird, half-crone hags from the Giant's Cliffs. Ragged feathers and tattered filthy rags trailed out behind their stringy forms with tentacles of matted hair sticking out from their balding, crusty pates.

Overwhelmed with nausea and fear, the sylphs steadied their hands upon their bowstrings, waiting for the hags to get within range of their arrows.

Duirmuid stood beside the wheel, his axe clasped firmly in his hands, grimly watching the sky, while Fercle was standing by the steps to the cabin with his sword in hand, ready to hack and hew any sea hags that landed on the deck.

"Take aim and fire!" Kilfannan thundered as the screaming horde darted downwards in the demented bloodlust of the hunt.

The arrows flew thick and fast into the shrieking hags, but as they fell with crumpled feathers into the noisome sea, others took their place. Clawing and shrieking, they swamped the deck. With a mighty battle cry, Duirmuid swung his double-sided axe at their hideous faces.

Putting the bows across their shoulders, the sylphs drew their blades and began cutting, thrusting, and chopping at the malodorous horde of writhing, clawing harpies, their weapons glittering blackly in the fitful, lightning-storm-racked clouds. A hag-bird slammed into Kilfannan and, piercing his jerkin with her talons, jabbed at his eyes with her long, cruel beak. Repelled by the web armour, she was unable to keep a grip upon his chest and fell onto the floor. With a clean sweep of his blade, Kilfannan severed her skinny neck, and her head fell with a slippery thud onto the deck.

Wave after shrieking wave of hag-birds descended on the boat, and they were hard-pressed to defend themselves. Seeing the battle was going ill, Kilfannan shouted desperately, "Take thy bows and take aim. Fercle! Set fire to the arrows."

Fercle breathed a gust of flame around the arrows, and the shafts lit up with flame.

"Fire!" Kilfannan screamed over the drumming waves.

The flaming arrows lit up the gloom as they sped into the hellborn babble. The rags and feathers streaming behind the hags burst into flame as the creatures darted and wheeled around the deck. The flames spread from hag to hag, and the air was alive with dreadful shrieks as one by one the harpies fell like burning brands into the ocean.

The stinking wind dropped, the shrieking of the hag-birds ceased, and a deathly hush fell upon the sea.

Kilfannan looked around the deck at the smouldering corpses.

"Help me throw the hideous carcasses overboard," he said to the others.

When the deck was clear of filth, Kilfannan noticed that the water on the floor was suddenly evaporating, and in a few moments the wooden planks were dry. Bending down, he touched the wood with his fingers and immediately withdrew them. "There is more mischief about," he said worriedly to the company. "The floor is dry and cold, and the air is hot and stale, yet the sea and spray are wet." He gazed out over the undulating, supernatural sea. "Only a great evil linked to the black gulfs of Under-Earth can reverse the elements and turn wet into dry in the face of wet."

The clouds thinned out, and the moon's reflection shined on the sea with a sickly spectral glare. Kilfannan stood with his brother and Cor-cannan on the guardrail. As one in mind, they looked towards the dark shape of Inishark and saw a mass of craggy rocks sticking out of the sea like jagged teeth frothed by a flying spume of foam.

"Rocks ahead," Kilfannan said to Duirmuid. "We must take care not to run aground."

Around the jagged outcrop in the sea, an eddy was forming in the water.

"'Tis so!" Kilcannan voiced. "Duirmuid, turn the wheel away from the island."

The boat heaved and tossed, and Kilfannan sensed the sky was alive with malign directiveness, and he shuddered as the sea began to swell around them once again. As Fercle joined Duirmuid on the wheel, they valiantly strove to turn the boat against the ebbing tide that swept them towards the rocks. Waves broke over the bow, sweeping the deck from stem to stern and pouring down the stairs into the cabin. A savage wind whipped them off their feet and tried to snatch them upwards into heaving clouds.

Kilfannan looked desperately around the deck for rope that could secure them to the handrail, but there was none. He remembered seeing a coil of thin, strong rope in the cabin, and battling the wind, he fought his way towards the stairwell and went below into the darkness. The water on the floor was already around his ankles, and groping with his hands, he found the sodden rope. Struggling under the weight of wet hemp and scourged by the howling gale, he crawled to the guardrail, where the rest of the company were huddled with their hands firmly clenched upon the railing. Cutting the rope into lengths with his knife, he gave one to Kilcannan and the other to Cor-cannan. "'Tis an evil force that comes against us in the sea and in the air," he shouted "Tie thyselves to the handrail with a secure knot, but one that can swiftly be undone, for if the boat sinketh, we must make quick our escape."

Tying the ropes onto the guardrail and around their bodies, the sylphs clung together on the listing deck and peered into the boiling miasma of the sea. In a wilderness of foam, they were swept dizzyingly upwards on the cresting swell to the pinnacle of a mighty wave and down into the teeth of the hellborn sea. The plunging descent made Kilfannan feel sick and dizzy, and he tightened his hold upon the rail. In the heavy seas, the island had disappeared, and the craft began to list dangerously in the swell.

"I cannot hold the wheel," Duirmuid cried out as he and Fercle wrestled to control the boat.

The sea vibrated with thunderous sound as the craft was swept up once again. Panic clutched Kilfannan's throat as he saw a ghastly glowing ship with three large-masted sails appear on the horizon.

As the *Poseidon* was borne up again to the giddy pinnacle, Kilfannan saw the ship cutting through the tossing waves towards them with cyclonic speed, its huge, antiquated, and rotting hull rising above the greasy titan waves like the stern of a demonic galleon.

Standing at the helm of the glowing ship was a giant of a man in a long oilskin coat. His dark face was hidden by a large, flat black hat with a wide brim. Below that, his livid eyes shined with the quintessence of damnation, encompassing all the terror that evil had the power to mould. Kilfannan's heart lurched with dread, for it was Manannan at the helm, in human form. "'Tis Manannan," he screamed. The knowledge that Manannan was free stunned his mind and froze his heart, taking away all power of action or reflection.

The sylphs' mind numbed as the galleon bore down on them. *This is the end*, they thought, and in that hopeless moment they welcomed death, for naught could be bitterer than the slow death of the Green.

"Free thyselves from the guardrail and dive into the sea," Kilfannan shouted.

As Kilfannan's numbed fingers undid the knot that tied him to the rail, a crashing wave deluged the boat, followed by another. Losing his balance, he felt himself swept up in the swirling water and thrown into the sea.

As he struggled to surface, his motion was suddenly arrested. He tried to twist and turn, and move his arms and legs, but his body would not obey him. He was being drawn downwards into dark depths by a malign force that wound itself invisibly around him like a band of steel.

In the gloom, he was aware of dark, sinuous forms gliding through the water, and his heart froze with terror. Thrashing their fish tails towards him were the meresna, their green hair streaming out behind them, and triumphant malice glowing from their orange-and-black slit eyes. Cruel talons seized his feet, and he felt himself being dragged into a yawning grotto of foetid water, ooze, and weed at the bottom of the sea.

CHAPTER 19

THE LIE

The mating was over, and in the coupling Aine had given Nala, her brother, the mortal sperm she had collected, and had fertilised the eggs of the mortals he had fed upon. Using their own secretions, they had created four hybrid eggs – two incubi and two succubi – to perpetuate their race. Nala would hatch and raise their children. Aine was now free to aid the House of Air in their quest for the key. Her High Faerie nature was settled, harmonised, and fulfilled only in the explosive beauty of the life – the life that was Green, vibrant and sustaining. "Brother," she said, clinging to him, "we are one, and 'tis only the evil that came upon our mother that hath created the darkening of our light. I know in me heart that we share the same fear. This repeated mating and draining the life of mortals to sustain our life and the House of Water is an evil dream, for 'tis a struggle of one nature against another, and meself yearns for peace."

With a sweet kiss, Nala replied, "Love of me love, we know the time of destiny approaches. Manannan will rise and seek the firstborn of his corrupted seed. He will attempt to mate with thee and in his wickedness bring forth a travesty, a terrible parody, a twisted terror of who we once were." Tears welled from his indigo eyes in orange gushes. "Sister, lover, self," he said, "meself would rather perish than lose me High Faerie nature; for 'tis the only part of me that is sane." The willow flowers in his skin faded, and the scarlet hearts of love-lies-bleeding blossomed in their place.

Aine felt a tear trickle down her cheek as the fear of her faerie annihilation welled up from her soul, and she saw the same fear mirrored in her brother's eyes. "Manannan hath risen, and as he waxeth, our hunger groweth, for in the past, the secretions of a mortal lasted for a moon, but in these latter days, me hunger hath increased sixfold." She held him tighter. She wanted to meld, to share the grief she felt; but she knew he felt it too. "Brother, me will to resist the feed is failing, and meself fleeth in mind to Ahascragh – but of late to no avail, for desire overwhelms me. What are we to do?"

His fragrant breath of flowers was warm upon her cheek. "'Tis thyself, Aine, that our father desires. He wanteth to possess thee in every corner of thy being and drive out the last vestiges of thine High Faerie soul. As his firstborn, 'tis thou that must confront him."

Aine released him and stood back. "Meself is weak, and I have no weapons to fight the monster that is our father, for he is ripe with necromancy and hath the elements fog, storm, and thunder as his allies." She clutched his hand. "If we are being assailed by Manannan, our sister and brother will also be in peril. Hast thou heard word of Graine, the third born?"

"Our sister is safe within the Limarteen woodland, and Ta-ala, the fourth born, awaits her there for the mating. But dear one" – he touched her cheek gently with his fingers – "the threat is to ourselves, and 'twill be thyself he will come for at the start. If thou art consumed, thy rape and fall into his darkness will strengthen him, and together thou wilt hunt us one by one until we are all possessed by shadow."

Aine gave a deep sigh. She asked herself how she could succeed against the virulence of evil personified in her father. A cold thrill of consummate fear rippled through her mind and body, sending a stabbing tremor through her faerie soul.

Nala caressed her cheek. "All hope, me dearest, lieth within the centre of the energetic charge, the quiet space of the heart of life. For 'tis our only shelter against the raging battle of our minds – a sanctuary where fear entereth not, nor hope deceiveth."

"Yet," Aine answered, "the struggle for me mind is growing stronger. Who will win – me father or me faerie self? I do not know. But I must strive to act for love and take the consequences … whatever they may be. For 'tis meself that has to face him."

"Meself would gladly take the burden," Nala answered. "But it can only be wrought by thine hands alone; all I can do is stand beside thee in the heart." He kissed her deeply and with longing. "The destiny of our accursed kind awaits, and thou, sweet Aine, art the spiritual warrior in our midst." He handed her his talisman, a small silver hare. "'Tis time, me love."

Aine stiffened at the sight of the sexual charm he was offering her. "This can never be," she said in horrified surprise, "for we have been told from the beginning of our life that to exchange the charms of our sex would lead to the immediate disintegration of our being."

Nala looked at her with clear eyes, and in them she saw no trace of doubt. "All the beauty of creation is with thee," he said, "for the High Faerie light that shines from thee, even the shadow of our father cannot dim. In truth! All that we hold dear is threatened, and if the Green dies, our destruction is assured. Exchange the symbols, for are we not as one in heart?" Aine slowly nodded. "Then have no fear, for fear is the weapon of our father. Come, sister love, let us exchange the symbols of our gender and test the lie that we are separate. For we are High Faerie in our essence, and our unity would mean we would not have the need to feed upon hapless mortals. Meself is as tired of the hunt as thou art, me love. As the power of the curse grows and the power of the Green wanes, there is a decision to be made. All I can say is that this reality of lust versus love is not for me." Tears welled from his eyes. "Meself chooseth love."

Aine hesitated for a moment, and then, she took the symbol of the horned god from her necklace and handed it to Nala, taking his talisman as her own.

Their fingers touched; the symbols were exchanged. There was no cataclysm; no darkness of the nothing; all remained the same. Aine laughed at her foolishness; she had believed the lie her father had etched with fear into her being. Gazing into Nala's eyes, she breathed in the light perfume of the double-headed snowdrops that blossomed in his face. "'Tis time for me to leave and take up the quest," she said.

Nala nodded. "Meself will keep the horses safe until thou dost return." With a sweet kiss goodbye, she left him under the hawthorn boughs.

Dark cloud banks scudded overhead as she mounted Nemia and rode out through the stones. The air was thick with goblin stench, and she recognised that they had swallowed the bait and followed the horse tracks to Crann Conagh. She wondered uneasily how many were hidden in the rock-bound pasture below. Somehow she had to get clear of them, and that would be no easy task. Drawing her blade, she rode cautiously forward.

Up ahead she saw a stand of rocks, and as she drew near, Grad and the magg charged out from behind the boulders and, fanning out, formed a line three deep to block her passage. She made a hasty count of the foul issue. There were a hundred at least. She could not fight them; there were too many, and she needed to feed before she could shape-shift. She would have to try to bluff her way through.

Grad swaggered out from the line, planted his feet in front of her, and snarled, "Where ye be going, water witch?"

"Meself is returning to me sacred woods, and as thou canst see, meself is alone." Breathing out the fragrance of the wood, Aine waved her blade at him. "Make way."

Grad coughed and cursed as the perfume flooded him; his cyanic flesh quivered and turned purple, but he did not retreat. "You is going nowhere until you tells I where you is hiding the Kilfenoran scum," he hissed, baring his fangs and signalling to his magg to surround her.

She could feel Nemia's body quivering beneath her, and from

the corner of her eyes, she saw the horde slowly pressing in around her. The stench of their foul bodies caught in her throat, and an icy hand of fear clutched at her heart. She was going to have to fight her way out.

"Thou hast erred in thy judgement and hast followed a crooked track," she said scornfully, trying to keep panic from her voice. "Meself hath thrown dust in thine eyes, and thine arm is too short to reach the House of Air. Now make way before thou feelest me venomous serpent wrath."

She saw some of the goblins break the line and try to run, for their hides were scored and blackened by her venom from their last encounter.

"Shoot the deserting rats," Grad bawled to his archers.

"I's not going to let ye get away from me," he said evilly, his bestial face livid with anger. "I has a score to settle with ye on account of me knocker Aeguz." He spat a glob of mucus on the ground and clawed at the snot on his nose ring. "And when we's done with ye, we's going to eat your horse alive bit by juicy bit until there's nothing left, and then we'll gnaw the bones." He poked out his thick blue tongue, waggling it about in an obscene gesture. Then, pulling out his knife, he shouted, "Quick, lads! Let's hack up the witch and eat her before she changes into snake."

Fury rose in Aine's heart, and the fire of death shined from her eyes. She felt her brother's presence, and from the silver talisman around her neck she felt the unity of water – the surge, the power of the rising and falling tide. Faster and faster the waves beat against her temples until the tempest of the tide flowed through her. With a dreadful cry of torrent, she urged Nemia forward, and as the black marc jumped off, she made a desperate sweep of her blade. Grad's head fell with a thud as she clove it from his shoulders.

The magg stopped in their tracks as they saw their leader fall, and as Nemia trampled them underfoot, the rest took to their heels with yells and curses and fled back behind the rocks.

Aine thundered on. The shrieking wind blew stinging rain into her face as she rode to Erin's Point. Leaving her horse with Darkle at the Blue Buoy inn, she started down the high street to the harbour. Halfway down the hill, a dry, cold vibration shivered through her being, and sensing danger, she dodged into a dark doorway. Peering round the wall, she saw a grey form, darker than the sheeting rain, floating motionless above the junction where the quayside met the road; and on the wind, she could hear the foul voices of goblin rabble at the harbour. She felt the knocker's mind stare past her up the hill and wondered if he had sensed her presence.

The grey shape disappeared, and immediately concerned for the company, she wished she could morph into reptile form. With the thought came the sensation that her bones, muscles, and organs were readjusting themselves into snake form, and the awareness that she could transform without the need to feed brought a rush of hope to her heart. *It could only be the exchanging of talismans that allowed the transformation from one form to another.*

Inserting the hare charm into the skin beneath her heart, she took the form of a small lizard and let the rainwater take her to the quayside. With a gush, she landed on the stone and slithered into the shadows on a dock. Looking round, she saw goblins sheltering against the warehouse walls in the tumult of the storm, and two knockers were at the window of a vehicle, talking to a mortal. She saw one knocker point out to sea, and following his direction, she saw under tainted yellow clouds a small white craft being tossed skyward by the swell. Bolts of furious red and purple lightning strikes stabbed like stakes into the sea, and from the clouds a horde of dark, stringy figures swept towards the boat.

The knowledge that the harpies issued forth from the Giant's Cliffs only when the salmon made their run filled her with terror. Only her father had the power to call them forth at will, and with her increasing need to feed, she realised Manannan had risen from his underwater city of slime-ridden stone.

A shuddering fear picked at her soul. In his liberation, he would have released the Cathac from his rock-bound prison in the cliffs.

She shivered at the thought of the clamouring masses of hellspawn behind the gates to Pandemonia that waited impatiently in their hunger for ravening release.

Diving into the sea, she expanded her size. She began swimming towards the boat with vast wave-raising strokes.

A groan in the water field vibrated as she neared the boat, and she heard a throbbing warning of turmoil in the waves. Breaking the surface, she saw the craft again swept up to the pinnacle of the foaming sea and dropped like a stone into the belly of the trough. The groaning in the sea came again with renewed torment, and before her eyes appeared a terrible sight. In a miasma of seething hate, she saw the huge phosphorescent bulk of her father's grotesque galleon cutting through the sea between the company and the island.

In an instant, Manannan's lust-filled eyes were upon her, seeking for a holding place in her mind, and instinct screamed at her to dive and swim away. Doubt invaded her soul. She could not face his gnawing malice and hope to come away the victor. So great was the lusting hatred that engulfed her that her mind began to slip from oneness into separation.

A sea quake rumbled beneath her; the roiling clouds burst forth lurid flashes of sickly green lightning that dove into the water, morphing into shoals of tiny glowing snakes. Her heart froze; the snakes were the love vipers of Manannan. One strike into her flesh and her father would extinguish all that was beautiful in her life and possess her for eternity. The thought of his hideous flesh and what awaited numbed her mind with terror, and in that instant she felt another will trying to overtake her mind. For a heartbeat she felt the heat of lust shiver through her body. Her soul shrank back, and she screamed in agony of soul for her brother.

The sound of a mighty conch horn reverberated in the water, and looking around at the charging snakes, she saw them suddenly arrested and swallowed by the sound. Feeling Nala's strength surge through her, she clung to it as if it were a rock in shifting sands. *Stay in the heart*, she thought.

Another quake shook the sea floor, and the vibrations sent her spinning through streams of fire that belched from the seabed. She felt searing pain in her legs and face as the burning vomit of tortured stone rushed by her to the surface. Again she heard the sound of the horn reverberate through the water. Glittering blue flame shot around, cooling her skin and suffocating the fiery blasts with blankets of sea dust.

Realising that she had been succoured by an unknown ally quickened her heart, and gathering her will, she opened herself to the All. Enveloped in the power of High Faerie and clothed in the rushing waters of her being, Aine, daughter of Erin, rose from the sea; and standing upon the waves, she turned her eyes upon Manannan.

Imperishable love and the yearning to sacrifice self for the All shined from her eyes like a golden nimbus of flame, and as the High Faerie light blazed forth, she saw her father wince. Pulling his cloak across his face, he staggered backwards, and shape-shifting into reptile form, he stood upon the deck.

Flashes of violet lightning burst forth from the clouds, and the sea began to rise. From out of the depths, she saw an army of tall High Faerie knights clad in golden armour and mounted on glistening seahorses rise. The shining hosts stood in ranks beside her, their helms shining like suns in the hate-filled gloom. With outstretched hand, the captain raised aloft a banner of flickering, shooting stars, and in the centre of the star dance, she saw the golden head of a great lioness appear. Mighty was the power that flowed from her glowing amber eyes, and on her regal brow sat strength.

The captain blew three long blasts on a conch horn, and the knights put forth their golden lances. The lioness roared, and a shining wind went before them like a shimmering waterfall. Forward the faerie host advanced, and charging at the towering galleon, they battled against the dark miasma, trying to push the shadowy galleon into Under-Sea.

Aine realised that her High Faerie transformation had allowed them to ride forth from elder days, and even though they could not destroy her father, they could drive him back into the vibration of Under-Sea. She felt his uncertainty as he was poised to take the water, and for the first time, she saw the glint of fear in his reptilian eyes. Shape-shifting back into mortal form, she saw him raise his hands, and a great black net billowed out from between his fingers. Scads upon scads of netting rode the night sky, dropping like a binding rain upon the faerie host.

The sound of the horn rent the air, and from the sea, great glittering swordfish leapt into the sky, slashing at the netting that tried to bind the warriors and prevent them from advancing. Stabs of lightning struck at the fish as they sawed through the cord, and as the warriors became free of Manannan's snare, the lioness roared and a terrible cry of battle issued from the warriors' lips. The knights surged forward against the rotting hull, and Aine saw Manannan create a swirling smokescreen of charnel fog around the galleon. For a moment, there was a struggle of dark light against the bright, and with a dreadful scream of malice, Manannan and his demon ship vanished from the sea.

The wind dropped, the sea calmed, and the moonlight glowed between the scudding clouds. The host of High Faerie stood before Aine, and the captain raised his banner. The gentle eyes of the lioness were upon her, and she heard loud purring that comforted her soul. Meeting the lion gaze, she stood as one transported to a time of unity and love – a time before the Separation.

The captain furled his banner, triumphantly raised his sword, and led the faerie host back beneath the waves. Aine heard the ringing of his horn slowly fading into the bosom of the sea.

She was alone, and as a cool wind freshened around her, she looked desperately at the sea. There was no sign of the craft or any wreckage, and she could see no bodies floating in the surf. Realising the boat had sunk in the tumult, she shape-shifted into reptile form. As she dived into the sea to search for the company, she heard her brother's warning thought: *Beware! The Cathac cometh*. His words filled her with fresh terror, and breaking the surface, she looked out at the horizon. The heaving coils of a monstrous serpent were issuing from the water, eerily silhouetted against the moonlit sky.

For a moment she froze; the great evil that had split the worlds was free and searching for the House of Air. Forcing fear from her mind, and pulling together her resolve, she again dived into the water.

Printed in the United States
By Bookmasters